Tanner's fingers wrapped within the thick strands of Diana's lustrous hair. His mouth worked its magic first on her lips, then on the smooth column of her throat, then down to the sensitive tops of her supple breasts.

It wasn't decent, it wasn't right. He had to stop—but Diana just couldn't bring herself to issue the command.

"Do you want me to stop?" Tanner asked quietly. "I will if you want me to. Otherwise, I'll make love to you on this spot. Tell me what you want. Tell me!"

Tanner was doing something so wonderful that nothing mattered, nothing and no one. All she wanted was for the achingly pleasant sensation to continue, to increase, to erupt!

"I . . . want . . . you." She sounded breathless.

Diana arched to meet Tanner's sensual stroking. Indescribable splendor was about to happen, she just knew it!

Suddenly a harsh voice cut through the night. "Diana!"

Just at the moment when Diana would have experienced the ultimate pleasure beneath Tanner's hands, her feelings froze and she opened her eyes to Kingsley—her fiancé. . . .

# HEARTFIRE ROMANCES

## SWEET TEXAS NIGHTS (2610, $3.75)
by Vivian Vaughan

Meg Britton grew up on the railroads, working proudly at her father's side. Nothing was going to stop them from setting the rails clear to Silver Creek, Texas—certainly not some crazy prospector. As Meg set out to confront the old coot, she planned her strategy with cool precision. But soon she was speechless with shock. For instead of a harmless geezer, she found a boldly handsome stranger whose determination matched her own.

## CAPTIVE DESIRE (2612, $3.75)
by Jane Archer

Victoria Malone fancied herself a great adventuress, but being kidnapped was too much excitement for even Victoria! Especially when her arrogant kidnapper thought she was part of Red Duke's outlaw gang. Trying to convince the overbearing, handsome stranger that she had been an innocent bystander when the stagecoach was robbed, proved futile. But when he thought he could maker her confess by crushing her to his warm, broad chest, by caressing her with his strong, capable hands, Victoria was willing to admit to anything. . . .

## LAWLESS ECSTASY (2613, $3.75)
by Susan Sackett

Abra Beaumont could spot a thief a mile away. After all, her father was once one of the best. But he'd been on the right side of the law for years now, and she wasn't about to let a man like Dash Thorne lead him astray with some wild plan for stealing the Tear of Allah, the world's most fabulous ruby. Dash was just the sort of man she most distrusted—sophisticated, handsome, and altogether too sure of his considerable charm. Abra shivered at the devilish gleam in his blue eyes and swore he would need more than smooth kisses and skilled caresses to rob her of her virtue . . . and much more than sweet promises to steal her heart!

*Available wherever paperbacks are sold, or order direct from the Publisher. Send cover price plus 50¢ per copy for mailing and handling to Zebra Books, Dept. 2854, 475 Park Avenue South, New York, N.Y. 10016. Residents of New York, New Jersey and Pennsylvania must include sales tax. DO NOT SEND CASH.*

# SAVAGE DECEPTION
## Lynette Vinet

**ZEBRA BOOKS**
**KENSINGTON PUBLISHING CORP.**

ZEBRA BOOKS

are published by

Kensington Publishing Corp.
475 Park Avenue South
New York, NY 10016

First printing: December, 1989

Printed in the United States of America

# Author's Note

The American victory at Eutaw Springs and the subsequent British withdrawal of troops from Charlestown (Charleston, South Carolina) occurred in 1782. But for plot purposes, I've moved the date up one year. Please excuse my tampering with history.

# Chapter 1

*Briarhaven Plantation*
*South Carolina, 1773*

She felt him watching her again.

Diana Montaigne, however, pretended an indifference she didn't feel whenever the man's black-eyed gaze swept over her, more disturbing than a hurricane. She'd been aware of the man ever since she had arrived at Briarhaven some days ago. Much too aware of him, she silently chastised herself, for an engaged young lady. But she found it hard not to notice this particular man. As he stood shirtless in the summer heat, Diana took stock of his broad shoulders and chest, bronzed from endless hours in the sweltering sun. Hair, the color of a moonless night, hung in shaggy strands past his collarbone and emphasized his face, which was possessed of high cheekbones and sensual, well-formed lips that no doubt had enjoyed many a female's kiss in the past.

7

A strange shiver part excitement and part fear rushed through her when she imagined how it would feel to be kissed by such a man. How would his lips feel? Would they be hard and cold or soft and moist? It was an absurd and wicked thought, but one Diana couldn't block from her mind.

Not that she'd been kissed all that often by gentlemen. Except for her late father, her sister's husband's brotherly peck upon her cheek, and the indulgent and friendly kiss upon her forehead by her soon to be father-in-law, she had never been properly kissed. Her fiancé, Kingsley Sheridan, had lightly touched her hand with his lips, but she didn't count that as a real kiss. Anne, her married sister, had told her how wonderful a kiss could feel when the man doing the kissing was the man one loved. She'd told Diana that a melting warmth suffused one's body and one's stomach fluttered like thousands of butterfly wings. "Sounds like a stomach upset," Diana had wryly commented, not quite certain she would care to be kissed.

"Oh, you'll like it a great deal," Anne had promised with a wink, shortly after she and David had approved Kingsley's courting of Diana.

Diana, who loved and trusted Anne, the elder by three years, decided that if Anne liked being kissed then she would too. Since she and Anne liked the same things, she trusted Anne's judgment. In fact, Diana decided that she must like it. Kingsley was always so solicitous of her, and any man who sent such lovely flowers and notes proclaiming undying devotion deserved kissing. Still, she wasn't overly thrilled when she agreed to marry Kingsley, doing so only out of a sense of loyalty to Anne and David, who both approved wholeheartedly of Kingsley. Kingsley was heir to Briarhaven, a fertile rice plantation along the Santee River, and he was handsome, one of the most handsome young men in South Carolina, Anne reminded Diana whenever she vacillated in accepting his proposal.

Indeed, Kingsley was handsome. He had light brown hair and eyes, but Diana thought his eyes held little warmth, despite his beautiful protestations of love. However, it wasn't his looks or wealth that eventually swayed her. She agreed to marry him because she felt herself to be a burden on Anne and David, knowing she couldn't live with them in Charlestown forever. Diana's father had died when she was only fourteen, shortly after Anne and David had married. Since their mother had died four years earlier, it was left to Anne to take on the responsibility of providing a home for Diana, which she lovingly did. Now Diana was seventeen, and she felt it was time she left her sister's home. Especially now that Anne was pregnant, Diana didn't want to be underfoot any longer.

So here she sat in the open carriage with her parasol unfurled to block the bright, hot sun of a Santee River afternoon from her fair skin. Kingsley sat beside her, the perfect gentleman in his gray frock coat despite the scorching heat.

Soon he would claim her as his wife; so why did she stare in fascination at an ebony-haired man with a whip in his hand, a man clad only in brown breeches and knee-high boots, a man whose every movement caused the muscles in his back and upper arms to ripple like strong ocean currents? Standing on a bank that gently sloped into the short but dense thickets of fragrant rice fields, he appeared formidable and all powerful as he oversaw the slaves at their toil. Yet somehow she sensed he would never use the whip or be unreasonably cruel. Still, Diana shivered again as his gaze, black and knowing, met hers. A queer feeling clutched at her stomach and she wondered if he somehow had read her thoughts and knew that she had fantasized about kissing him. Her face burned with the knowledge.

Purposely turning her attention to Kingsley, she smiled at him. "Briarhaven appears to be efficiently run."

Kingsley nodded, accepting her compliment as his due. "Yes, Father will have it no other way. The slaves for the most part are well behaved. Sometimes we have a bit of trouble and a wayward one *should* be whipped to within an inch of his life, but our overseer doesn't believe in whipping." His mouth curled into a sneer, and he inclined his head in the direction of the bronzed giant on the bank. "Tanner is rather soft on them. I constantly advise Father that Tanner should be dismissed, but he won't hear of it."

Tanner. So that was his name. Diana thought it suited him.

"Your father must believe that this Tanner is doing a good job," Diana noted, aware when Tanner stopped looking at her. She felt vaguely disappointed as she brushed aside a dark brown curl that had escaped from the long braid hanging to her waist. Perspiration trickled between her breasts, demurely concealed by the high-necked bodice of the pink, calico gown she wore.

"It's not that," Kingsley said much too harshly. "Tanner lives near the river with his squaw mother and can't be let go because he . . ."

"He what?"

"Nothing, my dear. There's no need to concern your pretty head with plantation and family affairs."

"But I'm going to be part of your family in a week's time, Kingsley," Diana reminded him.

Kingsley smiled at her like an indulgent parent. "Yes, you are, and you should acquaint yourself with the house and the house slaves and prepare for our wedding. Now, when are Anne and David arriving from Charlestown?"

"Five days from now," Diana said, perfectly aware that he was turning the subject away from Tanner.

"Ah, very nice. They shall be here for our engagement ball."

"Why must we have an engagement ball so soon before our wedding? Aren't we going to celebrate our marriage with a ball?"

11

Kingsley took Diana's chin in his hand and stroked her flushed cheek with the tips of his fingers. The warmth she had thought lacking in his eyes was now there, but it wasn't a warmth she found comforting because something else had leaped into the brown depths of his gaze, something she couldn't fathom. "I've decided that the grand celebration before the wedding would be better. All of our guests will arrive early and stay for the ball and the wedding. After our wedding ceremony we shall be toasted, then we'll retire to our room and everyone will leave. With all of the festivities out of the way, I can concentrate fully on my beautiful bride."

His voice sounded husky and thick, a tone Kingsley had never used before now. To her surprise, his face inched closer, and before she realized what was happening he had positioned his mouth upon hers, seeming to draw the breath from her body. She felt the urge to pull away but thought better of it. Kingsley was going to be her husband. He had the right to kiss her. Wasn't this what she had wondered about for so long? Now that it was actually happening to her, she felt unprepared and rather ill. Her stomach didn't feel fluttery at all but quite upset, as if she had been on a ship for too long and was seasick. What was wrong with her? Anne had promised that she'd enjoy it.

Kingsley held her tightly against him with eyes closed, but hers were wide open and darting nervously from side to side until her gaze came to rest upon the dark visage of Tanner, the overseer. He was shaking his head, scowling at her as if she were committing some sort of injustice against him. Even at this distance she saw the veins in his neck jut out and his hand tighten convulsively on the whip, almost as if he'd have taken great delight in flailing her.

The pressure of Kingsley's mouth increased, but she had ceased to feel it. Once more, she was very much aware of this other man. For some insane reason she felt that she was being unfaithful to *him* by allowing Kingsley's kiss.

It seemed they stared at one another for ages. She didn't know how long this would have continued, or when Kingsley would have stopped kissing her, if it hadn't been for the high, terrified shriek that cut knifelike from across the rice field.

"What the devil?" Kingsley muttered irritably and broke away from her to glance in the direction of the sound.

It was a slave woman. She ran screaming through the short stubble of rice like the devil was behind her, arms outstretched in Tanner's direction. The other slaves quit working, their scythes held in midair, and they stared in mute fascination at her until one slave woman broke the spell and pointed in horror at the fleeing woman.

"Oh, Lordy, have mercy!" the pointing slave screamed to the others. "Tilly's dead for sure!"

"She gonna die!" another one hollered. "Ain't no help for her now."

"What are they talking about?" Diana asked

Kingsley in bafflement. She received an answer when the running woman came closer, hobbling now with the effort of her movements through the dense stubble. "Good God!" Diana jumped up in the carriage with Kingsley beside her. She couldn't believe her own eyes. If she thought a devil was chasing the woman, she was nearly right. The devil in this instance was a large cottonmouth moccasin with fangs embedded in the heel of the woman's foot. The snake's tail was wrapped around her ankle like a fat, shiny black bracelet, and it didn't seem likely to break its hold.

"Kingsley, help her. Do something," Diana pleaded.

"What should I do? Run over there and yank the blasted serpent from her foot? She's as good as dead now. And Tilly was an expensive slave at that."

Diana couldn't believe that at such a time Kingsley was bemoaning the cost of a slave. She felt such pity for the woman that she made a movement to leave the carriage, but Kingsley placed a restraining hand on her arm. "Tanner will handle this."

And Tanner did. No sooner had the woman fallen before his feet than he jumped from the bank, pulling a large knife from a sheath on his belt loop, totally unaware of the slaves who milled about and cried openly for the unfortunate Tilly. Diana watched him take the knife and grab the snake's tail, slowly unwinding it from Tilly's

14

leg until it was stretched out straight. Then he swiftly cut the body from the head.

"Six feet long if I ever saw one," Kingsley commented in awe.

Tilly's sobs were audible. "I'm gonna die, Mr. Tanner. I'm gonna die. That old snake devil got all his poison in me."

"No, you're not going to die." Diana heard Tanner's deep, rich voice for the first time. She was amazed at how calm he sounded as he worked the fangs, which dripped yellow with venom, from Tilly's heel. Finally he threw the head with fangs intact on the ground, next to the still writhing body.

"How is Tilly?" Kingsley shouted to Tanner.

Tanner stood up. All of the slaves, even Tilly, grew quiet in their awe of him.

"Tilly will be fine," he assured Kingsley, and took a few steps closer to the carriage. Sweat beaded his brow and his chest glistened like copper in the afternoon sun. "The poison didn't get into her body because she has a thick cushion of skin on her feet from not wearing shoes. She was lucky. At this time of year, the mice and rats creep into the fields to feast on the rice and the snakes follow to feed on the rodents. Guess Tilly stepped on the snake."

"Well, send her back to work. We need every slave now."

"Kingsley, how can you suggest Tilly return to work after such an ordeal?" Diana demanded, horrified by Kingsley's disregard for the woman's health.

"She's perfectly all right, Diana. Tanner said so."

"Still it wouldn't hurt to be kind." Diana flounced in her seat and shot Kingsley a look of pure disdain.

Kingsley heaved a conceding sigh. "Do whatever is best for Tilly, but don't baby her for too long. All the slaves will expect preferential treatment if they so much as stub a toe. You're much too soft on these people, Tanner."

"Yes, well, I think they work better when they're not abused."

"That's debatable."

Kingsley motioned for Jim, a house slave and their driver, to be off. When the carriage started forward, Diana cast what she thought was a secretive sidelong glance in Tanner's direction, somehow aching to get one last look at him, finding him unaccountably brave and handsome. Her eyes widened to find him grinning at her, almost as if he had expected her to sneak another peek. Certainly this Tanner fellow wasn't a gentleman.

"I don't like him," she blurted out to Kingsley. "He seems very crass to me."

Kingsley smiled pleasantly and took her hand. "An astute deduction, my dear. Let's not dwell on trash such as Tanner but on us." He leaned closer and whispered into her ear. "My kiss earlier quite swayed you, didn't it?"

Yes, the kiss. She had nearly forgotten

Kingsley's kiss, her first real kiss. It had swayed her, but not with ardor, just total disgust. Could her feelings about the kiss be colored by the way Tanner had looked at her, how he had made her feel guilty for kissing her own fiancé? Of course that was it. Kingsley was the man she wanted to marry, the man she loved. Kingsley's kiss hadn't disgusted her because Anne had told her that she'd like it. It wasn't Kingsley's fault she felt ill. That half-naked giant had unnerved her.

"It was . . . nice," was all she could think to tell him.

"Nice? Is that all you can say, Diana?" Kingsley puffed out his chest and appeared totally outraged. "I'll have you know that many young ladies have found my kisses to be more than nice."

She'd upset him and she hadn't meant to do that, believing that she was complimenting him. A pang of fear shot through her for this man who could change from a considerate individual into a contemptuous egoist within a matter of seconds. He hadn't acted like this when he courted her in Charlestown, and she very nearly told him that. But she didn't want his vanity hurt further. Perhaps Kingsley was insecure about her feelings for him because she hadn't accepted his marriage proposal immediately but had kept him waiting two months for her answer. He would soon be her husband and as a good wife she must do his bidding, whatever that meant. Anne had told her that a wife always put her husband's needs and feelings before her own—even at times when she didn't feel like performing her wifely duty.

Diana wasn't certain why a wife had to do that and assumed that the duty Anne mentioned so hesitantly and blushingly had something to do with seeing to her husband's physical comfort. Diana recalled David sitting on the sofa one evening, and how Anne had immediately brought him a footstool. He'd told her she was a dutiful wife. Diana had thought that David was quite capable of fetching his own footstool, but Anne apparently liked waiting on him and seeing his silly grin whenever she praised him as being the most handsome and intelligent man in the entire world.

Is this what Kingsley wanted of her?

She supposed it wouldn't hurt to lie a bit to him. Maybe he'd stop scowling at her and she wouldn't feel frightened any longer. "The kiss was wonderful," Diana assured him with a bright smile. "I've never been kissed before, you know, but I want to do my duty and be a good wife."

Kingsley laughed, his ugly mood vanishing like a morning mist as he pulled her closer against him. "I know, my darling. You're a complete innocent, undefiled in any way. I have a great many things to teach you, and believe me, there is more wonder to come, and pleasant duties await." He winked at her.

Diana didn't have the vaguest idea what Kingsley was talking about or why he snickered in her ear. If there was so much wonder in her future, why didn't she look forward to it?

"I don't know, Miss Diana." Old Hattie, a longtime house slave at Briarhaven who had always looked after the mistress of the house, shook her turban-clad head and surveyed her charge with a frown. "That dress is red."

"I know what color it is." Diana swished around the elegantly furnished bedroom, taking delight in the airy feel of the silk material against her flesh. She delighted in the off-the-shoulder bodice with a froth of creamy lace at the scooped neckline and elbow-length sleeves. She thought the vivid color quite set off her alabaster-smooth complexion, especially her bosom, which was pushed upward by the tight stays beneath. Her waist looked extremely small above the scarlet overskirt that gently billowed over the creamy flounced underskirt. Hattie had piled Diana's dark hair high upon her head, leaving a long ringlet to hang bewitchingly over her right shoulder. But it was her eyes, a deep sapphire blue with golden sparkles in the center, that made her breathtakingly lovely.

"Ain't proper for a young lady to wear red to her engagement ball. When I done dressed Master Kingsley's mother for hers, she done wore white. Why you got to be different, Miss Diana? Master Kingsley ain't gonna like you wearin' red like you is a fancy trollop. He's gonna blame me for this, child."

Diana, used to doing what she wanted within limits, didn't see the problem, but she did notice that Hattie was very worried. "Master Kingsley has no say over my clothes, Hattie, and if he's upset with me, he better not take it out on you. You answer to me, not him."

"Yes, Miss Diana," mumbled Hattie as a knock sounded on the door of Diana's bedroom and Hattie admitted Anne.

"Red! Oh, heavens, Diana," were the first words out of her sister's mouth. "I had no idea."

"There's nothing wrong with the color. Red suits me better than white."

Anne Richmond's gaze flickered over her. "But it's just that . . . couldn't you have worn pink? You'll be the talk of the countryside."

Diana thought she looked rather nice in the gown. She'd chosen it because she was tired of being treated like a young girl. Since she was going to be mistress of Briarhaven, she wanted her future neighbors to see her as an adult, not the little girl over whom Anne still felt she must fuss. A moment's qualm did distress her, but she dismissed it immediately. She was grown up now, as of this night.

"I trust Kingsley will give me his approval."

Anne shook her light brown head, but even in her disapproval Anne was pretty in a gown of lavender satin, designed to hide the early stages of her pregnancy. "Well, I suppose you've made up your mind," Anne conceded at length, and smiled back at Diana.

Locking their arms together, Diana and Anne left the bedroom and descended the wide staircase to the festivities below.

When Diana reached the bottom step she became aware that everyone was staring at her, their earlier conversation seemingly forgotten at the sight of Kingsley Sheridan's fiancée in the scarlet gown. She nearly turned to run upstairs, but Anne steadied her with a grip on her wrist, a subtle reminder that she made her own choice and must live with it.

Diana held her breath when Kingsley came forward. In a frock coat of beige and tan satin he was quite handsome, but she was more interested in his reaction. He raised a sandy eyebrow but she couldn't read his thoughts. Finally he held out his arm to her and smiled. Visibly relaxing, Diana allowed him to lead her into the candlelit ballroom and convinced herself that everything was going to be fine now. She'd passed the first hurdle in becoming the mistress at Briarhaven.

The evening passed quickly. With Kingsley and Harlan Sheridan beside her she met the people who would be her neighbors. At one point Harlan bent his silver head low and whispered kindly into her ear, "I believe you've quite captivated everyone, Diana. Kingsley is an extremely lucky young man. With you as mistress of Briarhaven and the future mother of my grandchildren, I predict there are wonderful times in store for us."

Diana hoped so. She smiled at Harlan, who

made an impressive figure in his blue satin attire. She danced with Kingsley and David before finding herself to be the sought after companion of the other gentlemen present. She had triumphed in her scarlet gown, but she wasn't happy.

Diana begged off from the next dance and sat next to Anne, away from the center of the dance floor. "You look like you've eaten too many blackberries," Anne commented, seeing Diana's solemn expression. "You should smile, dear. At least you can dance the night away while I must sit here like a fat toad on a lilly pad, forced to listen to matronly conversation that would bore a preacher. Tell me, is something wrong? You don't look like a girl who is soon to become the bride of a rich and handsome young planter. What more could you want, Diana?"

"I want . . ."

"What?"

"I don't know."

Anne laughed gently and rearranged the curl that hung over Diana's shoulder. "You're nervous, that's all. Once you're married you'll be fine."

Diana knew Anne was being kind and concerned about her. She and David truly believed that Kingsley Sheridan would make a wonderful husband. But Diana didn't think that Kingsley would be as tender and gentle with her as David was with Anne. She didn't know why she thought that—Kingsley had never given any indication that he might be unkind—but the thought persisted and filled her with dread.

Also, she didn't feel comfortable admitting to Anne that Kingsley had kissed her and that she'd felt nothing. She imagined that Anne's response would be to reassure her that in time she'd feel a great deal. But what was it she should feel? And if she felt anything, would it be what Anne felt for David?

Her mind whirled, and suddenly she wanted to go outside into the garden and breathe in the sweet smell of the yellow jessamine that grew in profusion around the rose-tinged pillars of the house. While Anne started conversing with a young woman who had recently become a mother, Diana sneaked away into the balmy night.

She supposed she should have sought out Kingsley for this late-night stroll, but he was nowhere to be found in the ballroom and she hated to admit that she didn't *want* his company. Meandering away from the house, she took a well-trod path beneath ancient oaks whose leaves glistened with moonshine, before stopping on the bluff. Below her, the misty river rolled gently past, bathed in silver silence. The clear, star-filled night was scented with the spicy fragrance of the sea breezes that blew up the Santee from the Atlantic. It seemed a paradise, something out of a long forgotten past, but it was real. And Diana didn't want it.

She wanted . . . what?

"I don't know," she whispered into the night, feeling an ache within her breast she couldn't name. "I want . . . I want . . ."

"Tell me what you want and I'll get it for you."

Diana swung around at the deep voice behind her. Her dismay deepened when the tall broad-shouldered figure came forward from the path, where he apparently had been watching her for some moments. It was Tanner, but a Tanner she barely recognized from the one who stood on the bank and oversaw the slaves.

This Tanner had smoothed his hair back from his face and wore it styled in a queue, emphasizing high cheekbones over tautly tanned flesh. A flurry of white lace on the front of his shirt dipped down into a V, clearly showing his muscled chest. Though the shirt appeared worn in spots, it was immaculately clean and neatly tucked into black breeches. With ebony knee boots shining from a fresh polish, he presented a far different image from the sweaty, half-naked man she'd seen five days ago. He didn't resemble the person whom she'd declared crass at all.

Yet once again, as she stared into those eyes of his, eyes so dark that she barely discerned the pupils, she started to shiver.

"Are you chilled?" he asked.

"A bit," she answered. "The night has grown suddenly cool." It was far from chilly, but Diana couldn't admit that having him stand so near to her caused goose flesh to rise on her skin.

"Perhaps a dance would warm you. May I have the honor?" Tanner bowed from the waist and extended his arms to her.

"Oh, I don't know. It doesn't seem proper somehow. And the music from the house doesn't carry this far."

"Then you aren't hearing the music I hear." A grin slashed his sensual lips and in an instant she found herself locked in his arms, moving with him across the bluff. "Listen, Diana. Don't you hear the mellow tune of the sea breezes as they ruffle the river's surface, or the steady chirp of the crickets in the grass? Certainly you must hear the soft song of the nightingale in that tree above you, and hear the rapid beat of my heart as I hold you like this, hear the swelling cadence of your own. If that isn't music, my darling, then you aren't listening."

"I hear it," she said in a breathless voice that couldn't be her own. But it was. Suddenly she clearly heard nature's orchestra, not realizing she followed Tanner's lead in a scarlet swirl of silk and cream lace. His bronzed, handsome face mesmerized her, and in that second she'd have given him her soul if he'd asked for it.

Suddenly he stopped. "Let me kiss you, Diana. I want to kiss you just once."

"Oh, Tanner, I don't know. I'm frightened . . ."

"Of me?"

She nodded, wanting him to kiss her, but something about the pantherlike way he moved, the easy grace with which he held her, and the haunting and hungry way he looked at her scared her. No man had ever stared at her with such a feral gleam in his eyes, as if he wanted to devour her in

25

one large bite. Diana feared a man such as this wouldn't be satisfied with only a kiss.

"You have nothing to fear from me, Diana," he whispered into her ear, "I want to love you." His mouth began a sensual exploration of her earlobe before moving wantonly across her ivory cheek to claim the ruby treasure of her lips.

"No . . . ," Diana moaned, feeling herself melt. But it was too late to protest. Tanner had already claimed her lips in a kiss that stilled her speech and thoughts, a kiss that broke her will to resist. And she didn't want to resist. Nothing in the entire world would have possessed her to fight Tanner's arms as they circled her waist or stopped the thrill that soared through her when her breasts pressed against his chest. She lifted her hand, splaying her fingers on his shirt, and felt the rapid thump of his heart beneath the hard wall of sinew and muscle.

His tongue, hot and searching, found hers. This act of primitive plunder caused her to moan against his mouth.

"Oh, Diana, Diana," he groaned. "I want you so much. I've wanted you from the first moment I saw you."

He pulled her onto the soft grass, and she unresistingly followed him. His hands moved from her waist to her bodice as he lowered her gown from her shoulders to reveal her chemise-clad breasts. With agile fingers, Tanner worked the tiny lacings loose before Diana was even aware. It was only when his mouth, warm and

26

moist, settled upon one of her nipples that she realized what he intended to do.

"Tanner, you mustn't . . . this is wrong. I can't . . ."

His lips left her breast, and he looked down at her with eyes that shone so darkly that she could see herself within their depths. "This is right for us, Diana. I know you want me as much as I want you. I've tried to resist you, but you've become my obsession."

"But Kingsley?"

"Do you feel this way when he kisses you or touches you?" he demanded. "Am I wrong to think that you want me? Tell me you don't want me to do this . . ." He kissed her with a hot hunger that burned right through her. "Or this." His hands cupped her breasts, taking her fullness into the calloused palms. "Or this." And then his lips settled upon her nipple to suckle and drive her wild with a feeling she couldn't name.

This was how she had thought to feel with Kingsley, but she had no idea it would be anything like this. This was what she wanted, this incredible ache within her that was part pain, part forbidden pleasure—such dark pleasure she thought she might die from it.

Her fingers wove into the thick strands of his hair. "Oh, Tanner, please . . ."

She wanted him to stop, yet not stop. All thought of Kingsley fled as Tanner's hand slid up her skirt to stroke the softness of her inner thighs. His fingers traced a path higher and higher on her silken flesh. Diana stared up at the moonlit sky, her eyes widening in mute surprise. He couldn't mean to touch her *there*. It wasn't decent, it wasn't right. But when his fingers found her velvet target, stroking and readying her for what was to come, it felt glorious.

"Do you want me to stop, Diana? I will if you want me to stop. But you must tell me, otherwise, I'll undress you here and make love to you. Tell me what you want. Tell me."

His breath fanned her naked breasts while he suckled each nipple in turn. His fingers worked their magic within the heated crevice of her body. She had no will, no power to stop him. She felt as if she were going to melt and dissolve into nothingness. Tanner was doing something to her, something so unbearably wonderful that nothing mattered, nothing and no one. At this moment all she wanted was for the achingly pleasant sensation between her legs to continue. The thought of Tanner undressing her here and loving her aroused her senses and only made the ache flare with something so undeniably exquisite that she couldn't deny him.

"Tell me," she heard his voice again. "Tell me what you want."

"I . . . want . . . you." She sounded breathless.

"I love you, Diana." Tanner kissed her again, his fingers not ending their assault upon her lower body but moving more deeply within her until she found herself panting with a strange and powerful wanting.

The sky above them seemed to glow with silver and gold, her whole being shimmered like moonbeams upon the river as her body writhed beneath Tanner's sensual stroking. Her breath began to come in tiny pants and she knew something was about to happen to her, something so unbearably wonderful that she found herself arching to meet it.

Her hands found the broadness of his shoulders, clutching him in preparation for the wonder of it all. She shut her eyes. "Oh, Tanner, oh, Tanner—"

"Diana!"

Through her desire-shrouded brain Diana recognized the owner of the voice that cut like a razor through the night. She stiffened, and a sick feeling of dread destroyed the ultimate pleasure she would have experienced beneath Tanner's hands.

Opening her eyes, she saw Kingsley looming over them.

# Chapter 2

Kingsley wrenched Tanner from her, but Tanner instantly sprang to his feet and knocked Kingsley to the ground with a sharp jab to the jaw. "You bastard!" Kingsley growled up at him. "I'll make you sorry for that."

"Go on," Tanner baited. "Get off your backside and do something about it. I've been waiting for years for the opportunity. Or are you too much of a coward to defend your honor? What about defending Diana's honor, if not your own?"

Diana watched intently, barely able to breathe. From the hate shining in Kingsley's eyes she could tell he longed to attack Tanner. Instead he cradled his bruised jaw in the palm of his hand while Tanner helped her to her feet.

At that moment David came charging down the path. He stopped short, his gaze flickering over the scene, taking in the sight of a blushing Diana as she rearranged her bodice into some semblance of order. Tousled hair fell in shadowy locks around her shoulders.

David shook his red-blonde head in dismay before looking at Tanner with condemnation in his eyes. He extended a hand to Kingsley. "Anne is worried about you, Diana," David told her. "Please return to the house."

"No, I want to know that Tanner will be all right," she insisted and twisted around to see the man whose hands were warm at her waist. A shock coursed through her as she discovered that Tanner wasn't even looking at her but at Kingsley. From the scowl on his finely made lips and the loathing on his face, it was evident to Diana that Tanner hated Kingsley.

"I'll be fine," she heard Tanner say in a clipped tone of voice. "Do as your brother-in-law said."

Kingsley grabbed Diana's arm and pulled her away from Tanner to stand beside him. Tanner made a movement to spring forward but apparently thought better of it. Instead he waited, his powerful legs thrust apart in a bold and defiant stance. The pressure of Kingsley's fingers dug more deeply into her flesh, a not-so-subtle reminder of who she belonged to.

Kingsley made a snorting sound. "I find Diana's regard for your welfare most touching, Tanner, considering that I discovered you attempting to have your way with her."

"That's not true!" Diana blurted out, but Kingsley tightened his grip around her, forcing her to silence.

"Ah, such an innocent she is. Don't you agree, David?" Kingsley ignored her and didn't let David reply before turning his attention again to Tanner. "I trust I arrived in time before any true damage could be done to her. I should hate for her to be initiated into the rites of love by such a bastard. And you are a bastard, aren't you, Tanner? You know you are."

"Kingsley, please don't go on . . ." Diana interrupted.

"But I will go on," Kingsley continued, his voice growing more menacing. He moved her forward and placed her directly between him and Tanner. "Now, my innocent love. I want you to look at Tanner and remember him well. Remember the face of the man who tried to have his way with you. Look at my father's bastard son, my half brother, who shall always be little better than one of the slaves, who will never be a Sheridan. Go on, Diana, look at him and be disgusted to realize that such a man ever touched you."

Suddenly she couldn't bear to look at Tanner. *Bastard son. Half brother.* Tanner was Harlan's bastard son. She should have seen the resemblance between Harlan and Tanner. But that wasn't why she couldn't look at him.

She guessed Tanner must be humiliated to be an overseer on his father's plantation, never to be acknowledged as Harlan's son. He was a proud man, a kind man, and she didn't want to see his pain. But when she lifted her eyes to his face she stared into two ebony hate-filled pools. A tight pain clutched at her heart. Was his hatred for her, too?

She almost spoke his name, but Kingsley spun

her about on the path to face in the direction of Briarhaven. "I'm taking Diana back to the house. I know she'll want to bathe and wash away the feel of your hands upon her. But, Tanner, I'm not finished with you. Not yet." Kingsley pulled at Diana, literally dragging her with him.

Tanner moved forward with ready fists. "You can't treat her like that!"

Suddenly David jumped in front of him and restrained him with a strong forearm. "I suggest you cool off, sir," David suggested. "Diana isn't your concern."

"But Kingsley might harm her."

"No. Kingsley loves Diana and would never hurt her. Besides, Anne and I are with her. I don't know what happened here tonight, or what almost happened. Either way I hope you act the gentleman and leave my sister-in-law alone. You have no claim upon her and no future with her."

"Oh, but my brother does because he'll be master of Briarhaven. Yet I run Briarhaven. Doesn't that count for something?"

"Yes," David reluctantly agreed and was relieved when Tanner backed away to lean against a tree trunk. "But my wife and I want Diana's future assured."

"Ah, so it comes down to money and position. It always does with people like you." Tanner tilted his head to glance up at the night sky. "I'd be willing to bet that if I went after Diana she'd run away with me."

"I doubt it, Mr. Sheridan. Diana is very young and impressionable but she isn't stupid. She knows perfectly well that she'd be unable to survive on love alone. She is gently bred," David reminded Tanner.

Gently bred. It was a term that made Tanner wince. In the opinion of David Richmond and those of his kind he was a barbarian, uncouth and dirty. No lady of quality would ever deign to glance in such a person's direction. At least that's what men like Richmond and Kingsley wanted to believe. They were wrong. If the truth be known, Tanner had made love to quite a few "gently bred" young ladies who'd visited Briarhaven in the past. Tanner smirked at the memories, knowing Richmond would be soundly shocked if he had any idea of the number of proper petticoated girls who had sneaked away from their rooms at night, all eager to lie in the arms of Harlan Sheridan's bastard son. But he wouldn't tell Richmond any of this, because none of it mattered.

All that mattered to Tanner was Diana.

"I'm in love with Diana," Tanner admitted.

David sighed. "I do wish you hadn't told me that, sir. Knowing such a thing makes you more of a danger to her future happiness. If you only wanted to despoil her because of your hatred for the Sheridans, I could dismiss you. But a serious admission of love is sad and frightening to me. For all concerned, it would be best for you to leave Briarhaven."

Tanner reared upward, black fury on his face. "I'm not going anywhere!"

David backed away, not saying anything. He gave Tanner a probing look before turning his back and returning to the house.

"I don't know why you keep saying that Tanner would hurt me," Diana protested to Anne. "He told me that he loved me . . . and . . . and I love him too, I think."

"Heavens, this is worse than I thought. Come sit beside me, Diana." Anne patted the spot next to her on the large, comfortable sofa in the library. Diana moved from the window, where she'd been watching for some sign of Tanner, but only David returned to stand solemnly beside Kingsley on the veranda.

Harp music and the sound of merry voices floated from the ballroom. Diana felt less than merry as she took her seat by her sister. The golden candlelight emphasized the worry in her blue eyes. "Nothing bad will happen to Tanner, will it?"

"I don't understand how you can care about the beastly man. Kingsley told me he tried to have his way with you. Anything done to him will be only what he deserves."

"Kingsley is lying!" Diana stormed. "Tanner never tried to do that to me." In fact she wasn't even certain what "having his way with her" meant. "Anne, don't you understand? I thought you of all people would. I liked Tanner touching me. I liked it. I've never felt that way before. . . ."

"Please," Anne interrupted and stood up. "I don't want to hear about it. How can you say

35

such a thing or even imagine you liked that disgusting man touching you? Diana, I'm shocked at you."

Never in her entire life had Anne said something like that to her or been so disapproving either. Diana felt a bit sick to her stomach. She'd always wanted to please Anne because she loved her so much, but she couldn't help the way she felt about Tanner.

Her eyes were wet with tears as she looked at Anne. "I wanted him to love me."

Suddenly Anne was holding her in her arms while Diana cried. She felt guilty about what had happened with Tanner because she'd caused such pain to Anne and David, and Kingsley too, she guessed. And to Tanner. But she couldn't forget how his kisses and touch had made her feel. Yet she remembered the hatred she'd seen on his face when she'd left and she couldn't forget that either. Somehow she'd ruined everything.

Anne broke away and held her at arm's length. "I want you to listen to me. What you felt for Tanner was natural, in a way. You're a healthy young woman, and I have to admit that Tanner is . . . a virile man. But he is a great deal older than you and he took advantage of your inexperience. You must believe that when you marry Kingsley, you shall feel those same feelings for him. Be grateful that Kingsley knows you weren't responsible. He loves you a great deal, Diana. You're quite lucky Kingsley understands and still wants to marry you."

"But what if I don't truly love Kingsley?"

"You do love him," Anne insisted. "Kingsley is a fine man and the man whom David and I have chosen for you. We'd never do anything to cause you unhappiness. Kingsley will make you happy, just give him the chance." At that second David and Kingsley entered the room. David beckoned to Anne who instantly rose and followed him into the hall. Kingsley quietly closed the large oak door and came to stand beside her.

He gently wiped away the tears that sparkled like diamonds upon her cheeks. "I hope these tears aren't for Tanner. They're wasted upon such an unworthy fellow."

"I'm very sorry for all that has happened," Diana began to apologize. "I never meant . . ."

Kingsley brought her to her feet and enveloped her in his possessive embrace. "I know, my darling. You're an innocent. Tanner is to blame for all of it."

"But that isn't wholly true. I danced with him and I let him kiss me, and everything. Certainly you can't hold him responsible for what happened."

"Stop it! I don't want to hear any more from you in defense of my father's loutish bastard. As far as I'm concerned, Tanner is totally to blame. You can't actually think he might have serious intentions where you're concerned, Diana."

She didn't like that. It sounded uncomplimentary, as if Tanner couldn't be interested in her as a woman. "Why not?" she asked, and stiffened in his arms.

Kingsley laughed a great booming laugh that

echoed in the quiet library. "You don't understand yet. I thought Anne would explain it all to you, but apparently she didn't. Tanner hates my father and me. Father took a fancy to an Indian girl years ago. He built her a cabin on the edge of the property near the swamp, because he was already married to my mother."

"Why didn't Harlan send the girl away?"

"You *are* an innocent." Kingsley tweaked her nose, causing Diana to grimace. "He didn't send her away because men, well, men have needs, needs that proper women know nothing about. Anyway, he couldn't very well send her away after she became pregnant. Father is an honorable man and felt he had to see to the child's welfare. But whenever my mother was indisposed or was pregnant, and she was pregnant a number of times, father sought out Naomi, who is Tanner's mother. He took a liking to Tanner, but then I was born. No one can say father didn't do well by Tanner."

"He didn't give Tanner his name, Kingsley."

"Why should he have?" Kingsley hissed. "I am the heir to Briarhaven, not some bastard my father happened to whelp with a squaw. I find your support of Tanner to be most distasteful and distressing. The man wanted to have his way with you, and damn, I think you might have liked it if he had, Diana!" He jerked her hard against him, hurting her with the pressure on her upper arms. "You've gotten it into your head that he might love you. Tanner can't love anybody. He wanted you to get back at me. He wanted to have you first and destroy my joy in taking your innocence.

Tanner hates me so much that he'd ruin you to hurt me. And then, Diana, what do you think Tanner would have done after he'd finished with you? What? Tell me."

He was nearly shaking her. "I don't know!"

"Let me tell you then, my dear. He'd have left you lying on the ground like a whore. You're too innocent to realize what he intended for you. Believe me when I tell you that he can only hate the Sheridans. You're going to be a Sheridan so he hates you. He hates you, Diana. Remember that."

She was shaking so badly that she had to sit down. Kingsley stood before her with clenched fists. Could what he have told her be true? Was she so inexperienced that she'd mistaken Tanner's words, his actions, for love? She'd felt so wonderful when he kissed her and touched her. How could he have meant to use her or have his way with her like Anne and Kingsley said? Nothing he'd done to her had hurt her. But then she remembered the hate on his face, and she knew now that Kingsley must be telling the truth. She was going to be a Sheridan, and if Tanner hated his family so much, then Tanner might seek to harm them through her. And she'd been such an easy prey, so very easy that she felt ill to imagine Tanner chuckling over her body's betrayal in his arms.

"I don't feel very well," she told Kingsley. "I want to retire." Kingsley took her hand and led her upstairs. He kissed her on the cheek before leaving her at her door.

"Tanner's going to pay for this, Father. I swear he will."

Harlan Sheridan watched as his son grabbed for a whip, the long black tail coiling on the floor like a menacing swamp viper. The older man held up his hands to prevent Kingsley from storming out the library door. "Don't act hastily," Harlan advised. "Tanner is a fine overseer. I don't relish him lying abed for days during harvest time. We need all the slaves now, and especially Tanner. You know they don't listen to anyone but him."

"That's because you're weak, old man!" Kingsley hissed from between his teeth. He threw out the whip and grinned at the high, whining sound it made. "But I bet they'll listen to me."

Harlan was tempted to berate his son for this pitiful display of manhood. Sometimes he wondered from whom Kingsley had inherited such a mean streak. Celeste, his dear wife and Kingsley's mother, had been such a gentle, doelike person. She could never have harmed a soul. And he, well, he didn't like violence of any kind. Perhaps that was why he was so pleased with Tanner. Tanner had the ability to make the slaves work with little complaining because all of them stood in awe of him. They worked hard to please Tanner, not Harlan Sheridan, and certainly not Kingsley. In many ways Tanner was master of Briarhaven. Now, however, Kingsley planned to punish Tanner for forcing his attentions upon Diana.

Most certainly, Harlan agreed that Tanner should be punished. He should have known better than to lay a hand upon Kingsley's fiancée. The thought never crossed Harlan's mind that Diana might have welcomed Tanner's touch. But no matter what had transpired between Tanner and Diana, Tanner didn't deserve to be whipped.

"I'm certain I can decide on another course of punishment," Harlan assured his son. "You just forget the whole thing. Your wedding is two days away, and you can't waste your time on disciplining an overseer."

Kingsley reared back on his boot heels. "Oh, can't I? You'd like that, Father. I know what sort of punishment you'd dream up for Tanner, something short and brief like a severe dressing down, followed by a friendly pat on the back. I know you think Tanner is worth his weight in gold. I wonder sometimes if you regret not legally claiming your bastard so he can own and run Briarhaven one day. Certainly you've never had any confidence that I could do the job."

"That isn't true, Kingsley." But it was, and Harlan knew Kingsley didn't believe him. "You're my heir."

"Then stop giving preferential treatment to Tanner. *I'm* your legitimate son, not that squaw's bastard."

"But Tanner is an efficient overseer. I don't want him harmed physically and I don't want him run off." Harlan sat in the chair behind his large, satinwood desk. He suddenly felt very tired arguing with Kingsley, who was not one to let an issue

41

die.

Leaning forward, the palms of both hands bracing the edge of the desk, Kingsley impaled his father with a look of pure disdain. "In that case, I believe that Diana and I shall have to reside in Charlestown. You can keep Briarhaven and your beloved Tanner. I won't live where I am not master in my own home."

"You don't mean that, son."

"I do. Try stopping me from punishing Tanner and see if I don't mean to leave. You may not care that your bastard son, an overseer who is little better than a slave, pawed your future daughter-in-law. But I warrant that our guests might not look so kindly upon the situation. Some of them have young, pretty daughters and wives," Kingsley reminded Harlan, "and there's nothing a man hates more than to have one of his women fondled by a slave, or in Tanner's case, a half-breed. Many of the men recall the difficult times some years ago when the Cherokees rose up and butchered some of the people around here." Kingsley smirked, seeing the troubled frown on his father's face. "And some men might not be too forgiving of Tanner for touching Diana. After all, he is part Cherokee and they might enjoy taking some of their vengeance out on him."

"You'd actually like your brother to hang, wouldn't you?"

Kingsley shrugged. "Tanner means more to you than he does to me. Now, Father, what is it to be?"

Harlan was defeated and he knew it. He'd

wanted to protect Tanner in the best way he could. From the day the boy was born he'd looked after him and Naomi. He'd provided them with shelter and food, training Tanner for the job of overseer. He'd even had the boy tutored with Kingsley, much to Celeste's chagrin. The boy had never disappointed him, though Harlan guessed he had disappointed the boy many times. But Tanner had never asked him for anything. Now, however, Tanner was a grown man and he wanted Kingsley's fiancée. Diana was something Tanner could never have, and he should be able to see that. Yet lust had very little to do with the eyes, as Harlan well knew.

Truly, he didn't want Tanner harmed by the hatred of the neighbors, a hatred he knew Kingsley could incite to his advantage. That would only result in Tanner's death. There was but one alternative.

"Get that ugly smirk off of your face," Harlan demanded. "I give you my permission to punish Tanner, but I warn you that if Tanner is maimed or killed, I shall find a way to make your life a hell."

"My life is already a hell because of Tanner." Kingsley went to the door, clutching the whip in his hand. "After tonight, I can start living."

Harlan involuntarily jumped when Kingsley slammed the door. He felt like a coward, but he'd had to choose between his two sons. For the first time since his dear Celeste's death, he laid his head upon his desk and cried.

For the rest of Tanner's life he'd remember the shriek of the whip hissing through the air. As he lay on his stomach on the tiny cot in his room, and the hot summer breeze wafted over him, he thought he had died and gone to hell. His flesh burned and stung, bringing tears to his eyes. But he hadn't cried and wouldn't do so now, though he knew Kingsley had wanted him to cry out. Why else would Kingsley have personally lashed him after ordering two strong male slaves to tie him to a tree by the slave quarters? Tanner could still hear Kingsley's raised voice, "Cry out, you bastard! Beg me for mercy!"

What a spectacle he'd been. Trussed up and whipped for Kingsley Sheridan's amusement. Then, when he'd been near to fainting from the pain, Tanner had heard Kingsley laugh. "Here's your great overseer!" Kingsley had shouted to the gathered slaves. "Now you all know who is master of Briarhaven."

"I'm mas . . . ter," Tanner slurred aloud, vaguely aware that his mother was there to smooth ointment onto the ugly red welts on his back until he cried out with pain.

"Forgive me, Mariah," Naomi sobbed, referring to him by his Indian name. "I don't mean to hurt you."

After that he remembered nothing.

Would Tanner send a message to her? Would she see him again before she married Kingsley tomorrow? Diana wanted to see him and ask him if what Kingsley had told her was true. Had he only wanted her to ease his hatred of Kingsley?

Lying in her bed, she didn't know what to think. Her memory of Tanner and the moment they'd shared almost convinced her that Kingsley was wrong. Tanner must have felt something special for her, he must love her. He had told her he loved her. But why hadn't he come to her?

"Oh, Tanner, if you don't come before the wedding tomorrow I shall know that you don't love me," she whispered into the dark night, a sob welling in her throat. "And I shall hate you for the rest of my life."

"She hates you, Tanner. Diana hates you with all her heart. She was disgusted by your touch. She said you tried to rape her and hopes never to lay eyes upon you again, so when you're able to travel, you will leave Briarhaven." Kingsley stood above Tanner, more than a bit startled when Tanner, whom Kingsley thought was unable to move, lifted his head off the pillow to cast him a malevolent grin.

"I don't recall her complaining too much. She liked what I did to her. Maybe, Kingsley, you should wonder about your innocent fiancée's virtue. Did I take it, or did someone else before me?"

"You arrogant whelp!" Kingsley raised his whip and would have struck Tanner had not Harlan entered the room at that moment.

"Touch him again and I'll send you packing!" Harlan's usually calm voice boomed. "Now get out of here, Kingsley, and prepare for your wedding. You've wasted enough time and energy here."

"I'm finished here anyway." Striding to the door, Kingsley laughed. "Such a touching picture of father and son that my heart bleeds. But remember, dear brother, I'm marrying Diana. Think about her in my bed tonight and all of the nights when you're far away from Briarhaven." Seeing Tanner wince, Kingsley chuckled anew and went out into the bright sunshine of his wedding day.

Harlan sat on a small bench beside Tanner's bed. "I apologize for my son."

"Yes, you should apologize for him. He is a clod and an arrogant fool who shall make Diana's life a hell, but she's not my concern any longer. I'm leaving Briarhaven today."

To Harlan's surprise, Tanner slowly began to sit up. Harlan reached out to help him, but Tanner withdrew and practically growled at him. "I don't need your help!"

"I see that you don't," Harlan admitted with a hint of a smile. "You never did."

"And that amuses you?"

"I don't find it amusing, but I do respect you. You're able to stand on your own two feet and take life's punches, whereas Kingsley is weak like me. He would never have survived what you have."

"I doubt I'll survive it now." Tanner rose on

unsteady feet, grimacing with the hot pain that flowed across his back. "I'm leaving Briarhaven today. Please look after my mother for me."

For a second Harlan appeared disappointed, then he said, "I promise you that Naomi will be well cared for. Where are you going, Tanner?"

"Away. I don't know where and I don't care."

"Under the circumstances, this is the best thing for everybody. Do you need any money?"

"Nothing from you, sir."

Standing up, Harlan peered sadly at his older son. "You've never called me Father, always sir or Master Harlan, but never Father. I should like to hear you say it just once, Tanner."

Tanner swung around to face him, oblivious of the wracking pain caused by such a violent movement. "And I wanted you to call me Son, but you never did. Not even when I was a child and sick with fever, almost dying, did you call me anything but Tanner or boy. I've been nothing to you but a piece of handiwork, spawned on a cold winter's night on an ignorant Indian girl who was so besotted with you and your great wealth that she abandoned her people for you. I'm a disgrace to you, but you're such an 'honorable' bastard that you can't admit it. Tell me I'm wrong. Prove to me I'm wrong. Call me Son so I can call you Father."

Harlan's mouth dried up. He opened it to speak, but long years of denying Tanner's claim to the Sheridan name had forced him to behave in a certain fashion. For twenty-six years he'd pictured himself as the benevolent but distant

47

father figure who was assured of his bastard son's affections. Now he realized that Tanner's respect- fulness toward him didn't come from love but from a wound more angry and deep than the ones Kingsley had inflicted. Worst of all, he'd allowed Kingsley to hurt him. Harlan felt that he should be able to say to Tanner, "Yes, you are my son," but he couldn't do it. Not now, not after all of these years, not after what he had let Kingsley do to Tanner. He felt Tanner would be unable to forgive him, and he couldn't bear the brunt of Tanner's hate. What if he acknowledged him as his son and Tanner wouldn't call him Father?

Clearing his throat, Harlan moved to the door- way. "I have to dress for the wedding. My thoughts and good will go with you."

Then he was gone, and Tanner was left stand- ing in the middle of the tiny room until his mother reappeared. "Did you say your farewells to your father, Mariah?"

"I said farewell to Master Harlan, Mother," he snapped, his face ashen.

"You're unwell, Tanner," Naomi gently chided and placed a thin hand on his arm. "Rest. You can't leave today."

Tanner felt awful, worse than he'd ever felt in his entire life, but he was going away today and no one was going to stop him. Looking at his frail mother, he saw she resembled a tiny doll with large, black eyes. Delicate high cheekbones stood out starkly on a face that was much too thin and lined with years of worry. He gently touched the raven black braid, neatly plaited, that lay across her shoulder, then hugged her. "I must go. You see how things are."

"Yes," Naomi admitted. "You must leave and put this woman out of your mind."

"I can't forget her, Mother. She is somehow a part of me, like the earth that craves the warmth of the sun by day and the coolness of the moon at night. But she lied about me to Kingsley—and Harlan. I will make her pay for that lie."

"Don't let vengeance eat away at you, Mariah. Go into the world and make your way, make a new life and forget Briarhaven and this woman."

Tanner grinned despite the pain of his back and the sharper one in his soul. "I won't forget, Mother. One day I will return like Mariah, the wind, and like a windstorm I will sweep up everything within my path . . . Briarhaven and Diana. Especially Diana."

Tanner took a fine black stallion from his father's stables. After all, the old man *did* owe him something. He'd already told his mother goodbye and was a bit surprised to discover that his back didn't hurt so much. Perhaps leaving Briarhaven relieved some of the pain.

He'd tied a small sack onto the saddle, a sack filled with a heavy overcoat and his only other change of clothes. Now he wore a thin shirt and brown breeches and boots, his stomach recently filled with Naomi's freshly baked biscuits and sweet potatoes. He was more than ready to leave.

As he sauntered along the dirt road that led

from his cabin to Briarhaven, he spotted Jarla, a slave girl who was four months along with child. He reined in when he saw her, seeing a haunting pain in the girl's eyes. She was barely fourteen and already knew more about life than he cared to imagine.

"You really is leavin', suh?" she asked him. At his nod, she sighed. "I wish you weren't goin'. Now Master Kingsley gonna be real hard on us."

"I'm sorry, but I must go."

"You leavin' 'cause of Master Kingsley's woman?"

"No."

Jarla grinned and dug her bare toes into the soft earth beneath her feet. "Yeah, you is, but I'm glad Master Kingsley's gettin' married to her. Now I don't have to worry any 'bout him botherin' me agin." She placed her hands on her swollen abdomen. "Now he can have his way with her and git her a baby." Waving to Tanner, Jarla streaked away like a black comet.

Tanner felt suddenly ill to realize anew that Diana was going to marry Kingsley that afternoon. Had the wedding taken place yet? He didn't want to think about the conniving vixen or about the lie she'd told, having already decided that Diana was like most "gently bred" ladies. They wanted to frolic in the hay with someone beneath them, but then cried rape when they were caught. However, as much as he thought he hated her, he couldn't help veering off of the road when he came in sight of the house. He found a place, thick with verdant foliage, and spied upon the wedding ceremony.

All of the guests were assembled on the lawn. He saw his father and the Richmonds smiling as the reverend stood beneath the rose-covered trellis and married Kingsley to Diana. Tanner's heart stuck in his throat. He had not expected to find Diana so beautiful. In a gown of white satin with embroidered pink rosebuds, Diana took away his breath. Her lovely face was turned toward him, but she didn't see him as she gazed up at Kingsley and recited her vows. In the afternoon stillness, Tanner clearly heard her words. "To love and to cherish till death do we part . . ."

It was too much for him. Spurring the black stallion into a vicious gait, he rushed away from the touching scene and found himself on the road that ran either to Charlestown or up the coast. The choice was his.

He wanted to flee like the wind for whom he was named, but he had already decided that one day he'd return, and when he did, Briarhaven would be his. And Diana would belong to him. Tanner turned eastward, living only for the hour he could claim the deceitful Diana as his own.

# Chapter 3

She was married now and frightened of what was to come.

Hattie had long since left her alone in the bedroom after helping her change from her wedding gown into a white lace nightrail. "Don't you fret, child," Hattie had told her reassuringly as she brushed Diana's long dark hair. "You ain't got no cause to be scared. Master Kingsley loves you. He'll be gentle with you or old Hattie will take a hairbrush to his rear like I done when he was a little boy."

Diana was so frightened that not even that image could elicit a smile from her. What made her more fearful was the absence of Anne and David, who had left for Charlestown shortly after the ceremony. In fact, the house was empty now except for Hattie, Harlan having accompanied the Richmonds to give the newlyweds some time alone.

Night had fallen, and a single candle provided

the only light in the room except for a sudden streak of lightning. Thunder rumbled from the direction of the Atlantic, and Diana knew it wouldn't be long before the Santee area was deluged with a summer storm. She shivered at the eeriness of it all, her fear made worse by the weather.

What was Kingsley going to do to her that she needed to be scented with rosewater and dressed in a sheer nightgown to please him? What if she didn't please him? Her large blue eyes caught the candle's glow and widened with the terror of her own thoughts. Grasping the elaborately carved post of the bed like a frightened child who dreads the monsters of the dark, she trained her gaze on the door.

"But he's my husband, not some bogey man," she reminded herself. "I must do my duty by him and make Anne and David proud of me." Yet her palms perspired and she jumped every time lightning flashed in the heavens or thunder rolled. She wanted Kingsley to hurry up and come to her, yet she wanted him never to come. In her mind she heard Anne's parting words to her. "Do your duty by your husband, Diana. Let him have his way with you without complaint, and you shall find great happiness and pleasure."

She'd follow Anne's advice, that's what she'd do, and somehow she'd manage to push down the butterflies in her stomach. Suddenly she remembered what Anne had told her about that fluttering feeling when you loved someone. Maybe she did love Kingsley, Diana thought. She felt that sensation, but she didn't find it pleasant.

Unbidden came the memory of Tanner's touch, something she had found to be more than pleasant. If that happened with Kingsley when he claimed her as his wife then she would like it very much. However, thinking about Tanner upset her. He hadn't tried to see her or send a message to her. She learned from Hattie that he had left Briarhaven. Evidently he had very little feeling for her to leave like that. How very wrong she'd been to believe that he loved her! Perhaps she was wrong then to be afraid of what Kingsley would do to her. After all, she'd been such a poor judge of Tanner's intentions.

A creaking noise outside the door alerted her to Kingsley's approach. The breath seemed to wane in her lungs when she saw Kingsley silhouetted in the doorway. He wore a long green robe, open at the neckline to reveal a hairy, well-formed chest. She couldn't help but compare him mentally to Tanner, whose chest she remembered as being smooth and strong. Kingsley smiled at her, apparently pleased at the image she presented in the white gown with her dark hair spilling around her shoulders. Closing the door, he locked it from the inside and placed the key in the robe's pocket.

Diana's heart knocked against her ribcage. "Why did you lock the door, Kingsley?"

"To keep everyone out, especially Hattie. If you require anything, I'll call for her, but I don't want the old biddie interrupting us. I want you all to myself, Diana."

Of course, they were newly married and being

locked away wasn't unusual, but Diana grew uneasy with no way out.

"Hattie brought us some wine," she said, pointing to a crystal decanter and glasses on the small Chippendale table beside the bed. "Shall I pour some for you?"

"No, I had some downstairs."

A nervous smile appeared on her face. "What can I do for you, Kingsley?" she asked in all innocence.

Kingsley came closer to her and pulled the gown from her shoulders to bare her breasts to him. "A great deal, my love, a great deal."

It was over. Diana lay on her back, no longer afraid of the vicious thunderstorm that raged through the night. A numbness of soul consumed her; she felt dead inside.

Kingsley had had his way with her. The spot between her legs burned like fire and blood stained the inside of her thighs. She doubted she'd ever be able to get out of bed again or to walk normally.

The last two hours were a horrible nightmare from which she couldn't awaken. But Kingsley slept undisturbed beside her, his nude body atop the sheets. Even in sleep his hand was curled in the depths of her hair, preventing her from leaving him. She wanted to die in an attempt to erase the humiliation she'd suffered this night, to forget the crude words he'd whispered into her ear, to never feel the pain of his penetration again.

He'd been cruel from the very start, ripping her gown from her and pushing her onto the bed. She remembered staring in wide-eyed fright as he removed his robe. She had never seen an aroused man before and was totally innocent of how a man was even made. "I'm going to have my way now, Diana. Finally you're going to be mine. I had wanted to be tender with you, but you need to be punished for enjoying Tanner's hands upon you." He'd forced her to look at him, and she'd never forget how he'd scowled at her, almost as if she were vermin. "And you did enjoy his touch, didn't you? Well, didn't you?" He shouted at her over and over until she screamed that she had.

"If only you'd waited for me, my love. For all I know I may have married used goods."

"I'm not used," she proclaimed.

He laughed. "I hope not, but after tonight you will belong only to me. Yet I'll never forget how I came upon you and Tanner. For as long as I live I shall see you writhing on the ground beneath my brother and hear your moans while he suckled your beautiful breasts. Why did you allow such a bastard to feast upon your body while you let me kiss you only once? You're going to pay for all those months you kept me waiting, sniffing around you like a cur after a bitch's scent. You're my wife now and you'll do as I order, do exactly as I want without complaint. No one will help you if you go whining to them, not your sister or David, not my father. I'm your master now."

With that he parted her legs. She had no idea of what he intended to do. Anne had told her to do her duty, that Kingsley would guide her, but this was so foreign and appalling. What was more unexpected was when Kingsley rose up on his knees and grabbed that huge, awesome thing in his hand. She was unsure what he intended to do with it until she felt its hardness nudging at her. "No, Kingsley, you can't," she gasped when understanding dawned. But he did.

She screamed and tried to push him away, to somehow escape, but Kingsley held her pinned to the bed. He plunged into her with such force that she arched her back and clawed at him, frantic to be free and escape this torturous pain. Instead of releasing her, he plundered her more deeply, not heeding her cries. Luckily for Diana, Kingsley hadn't been with a woman for weeks. Though it seemed like hours had passed, it was only moments before he shuddered and filled her with a sticky warmth.

"You're mine," he crowed in triumph. "Mine. All mine." To prove that point, he took her once more before wrapping his arms possessively about her and falling asleep with his mouth at her breast.

Tears streamed down her cheeks. Anne had lied to her. There was no pleasure in letting Kingsley have his way with her. How did women bear this beastly horror over and over for years? She cried for her poor dear mother, who must have endured this same pain and humiliation at the hands of her husband. How could Diana's father, whom Diana remembered as compassionate and kind, have done this to her mother if he loved her?

Were all men brutes? Was David? Anne loved David, and he loved her, but Diana had no idea how her sister could tolerate or stand the pain. She always looked so well and happy, but Anne wanted children and so had her mother. Evidently women put up with quite a bit to conceive.

Kingsley had mentioned that he wanted an heir for Briarhaven. Maybe if she became pregnant right away, he'd leave her alone. She prayed it would be so, because she didn't believe she'd ever love Kingsley enough not to care what he did to her body.

Diana wiped away unexpected tears. A sob welled within her throat as she realized that Tanner wanted to have his way with her, too. Like a silly, stupid fool she had believed he loved her. He'd lulled her with something so blindingly wonderful that she'd have given her body to him freely. And then, after the glorious feel of his touch upon her, he'd have done the same hurtful and humiliating act to her in order to gain his vengeance upon Kingsley. She knew then that Tanner had lied to her when he told her he loved her, otherwise he would never have wanted to hurt her in such a way.

Glancing at Kingsley, she felt utter remorse for having married him. She'd have been better off to have married a stranger than a man whom she thought she might come to love. The outcome would have been the same. She knew now that she hated Kingsley and always would, but she was his wife and must do her duty by him, despicable though it was.

But she hated Tanner more for not coming for her and stopping the marriage, knowing she'd have run away with him if he'd asked her. But, again, nothing would have been different. Tanner would have taken his pleasure with her just as Kingsley had done. He'd have hurt and humiliated her after firing her flesh with his hands and his lips, something which Kingsley hadn't done but which she viewed as somehow even more deceitful and treacherous. She would have expected something glorious, only to be left with bitter pain and heartache.

For this betrayal she could never forgive him. At that moment she hated Tanner more than Kingsley.

Wiping away the last of her tears, she clung to the hatred in her soul as a means of escaping the ugliness of the marriage she'd made. She would hate Tanner forever and never cry again.

# Chapter 4

*December, 1780*

Hattie finished kneading the dough on the planked table and put the loaf into the oven. "Gonna be a sorry Christmas 'round here," she muttered to Diana as Diana walked out of the pantry. "Those redcoats eatin' up most all the food we got and sleepin' in our beds. When you suppose this war gonna be over?"

Diana placed two jars of jelly preserves on the table. "I hope soon, Hattie, but I trust you haven't said anything out of the way to Captain Farnsworth or insinuated how you feel. We're very lucky that the British chose Briarhaven as their headquarters. You know what damage has been done to the other houses along the Santee, what with the burnings by some patriots against Tories and the British burning out the patriots. As long as Farnsworth is here, we're safe."

Hattie clucked her tongue and slyly said, "And

we both know that no patriots are gonna burn us out either."

"Hush," Diana scolded lowly and spooned the jelly onto a Sevres china plate. "You never know who might be listening."

And that was true. Ever since Captain Farnsworth and twenty-five of his men had commandeered Briarhaven two months ago, she never knew whose ears might be pressed against the door. The war for independence had at last come to South Carolina upon the capture of Charlestown earlier that year. It had spread to the Santee area with the capitulation of two towns, Camden and Georgetown, by the rebels. Nothing had been the same for the Santee River residents since.

The British raided livestock and looted most of the plantations and farms for miles around. To make matters worse, groups of men called "outliers," who were neither Tory or patriot but thieves and ruffians, paid midnight calls upon those homes that hadn't been torched or looted by the British. Many of the Sheridan's neighbors were barely surviving, their slaves having run away to follow after the British conquerors. Briarhaven, too, had lost most of its slaves, but some, like Hattie and her son Ezra, remained.

Diana hid her hatred of the British behind a sweet smile that she constantly bestowed upon Captain Samuel Farnsworth and his men. She'd seen the damage they'd done to plantations with her own eyes and had heard the horror stories of women and children, after being looted and stripped of their clothing, turned out into the night to watch their homes burn to the ground. But Diana pretended to be a loyal British subject, as did Harlan, never admitting that Kingsley had joined a South Carolina regiment.

Farnsworth didn't have to know that her husband had fought and died for independence, or that her brother-in-law had been a lieutenant in that same regiment until Charlestown fell to the British. She'd told him she was a widow; that was all he needed to know about her.

Despite the fact that she dressed in widow's weeds, Diana could tell that Farnsworth was smitten with her. Under any other circumstances, she might have found the man attractive. With his curly blonde hair, muscular build, and elegant manners, Farnsworth was enough to make any woman swoon. But Diana wasn't any woman. She hated seeing that glimmer of lust in the man's eyes whenever he looked at her, and she dreaded the day he might decide to paw her. So far he hadn't, and she decided she was fortunate that Farnsworth at least acted like a gentleman. He could have thrown her and Harlan out of the house. But he'd seen that Harlan was now in poor health, having suffered a heart attack shortly after news of Kingsley's death. Farnsworth had given orders to his officers, who slept in the guest bedrooms, and the soldiers, who stayed in the barn, not to steal anything from Briarhaven or to disturb the occupants. An odd turn of events, Diana thought, given what she'd seen of the British handiwork in the area.

But for all of Captain Farnsworth's kindnesses,

Diana didn't feel one bit guilty about the secret she kept from him, a secret that, if discovered, could very well result in her swinging from the end of a rope. Both Hattie and Harlan knew her secret. Though Harlan didn't approve because he feared she'd fall into danger, Diana sensed he was pleased that in her own small way she was helping to defeat the British.

Once the freshly baked bread was taken from the oven, Diana sliced it into generous portions and arranged them on the plate around the jelly. She then took out a large silver tray from the cupboard and put the plate, along with a warm teapot and five cups, onto the shiny surface. As she picked up the tray she heard Hattie say, "Miss Diana, I can carry that into the parlor."

"No," Diana told her with a shake of her head. "You have too much to do around here already, what with cooking for Captain Farnsworth's men. I'll take it into Harlan and the captain. Besides," she said with a mischievous twinkle in her blue eyes, "one never knows what interesting tidbit of information one might accidentally overhear during teatime."

Hattie grinned, immediately understanding.

Entering the parlor, Diana discovered that Harlan, who sat on the divan with a blanket thrown over his legs, was playing whist with Farnsworth and two of the British officers. Upon seeing Diana, the soldiers rose to their feet and Farnsworth took the tray from her, placing it on the sideboard.

"Ah, that bread smells delicious," a junior

officer known as Smythe complimented her. "We could smell it in here."

"Help yourselves, gentlemen." Diana waited until the three soldiers had taken their bread and tea before serving Harlan. She couldn't help but notice that Harlan didn't look well. The lines by his eyes, lines that had once been thin, were now deeply carved into his pasty white skin, and he shook when he took the cup from her. But his smile at her was genuine and belied his ill health. Diana hated to see that Harlan wasn't getting any stronger. If there was only something she could do for him to make him well again she would, because she literally owed him her life.

"Join us, Mrs. Sheridan," Samuel Farnsworth insisted as he gallantly poured her a cup of tea. "It isn't everyday we get such luxuries as tea, now that that renegade Francis Marion is plaguing the area. The supply wagon was lucky to get through without being attacked by his rebel band."

Diana took a seat near Harlan and sipped her tea, a look of total innocence on her face. "This Marion, isn't he the one called the Swamp Fox?"

"Yes," an officer named McCall spoke up. "He's a wily creature and aptly named."

"Well, he can't be entirely wily, gentlemen, if a supply wagon made it through," Diana noted, and caught a warning glance from Harlan. "Perhaps he isn't as smart as he is believed to be."

Farnsworth guffawed and took a piece of bread. "He shouldn't be underestimated. He's quick and knows the swamp. Somehow he constantly manages to elude capture. And as for the supply wagons, from now on they'll be well protected."

McCall nodded. "That Swamp Fox won't get anymore of the supplies from Charlestown. Why, just tomorrow there's one due through here—"

"That's enough, McCall! Farnsworth ordered. "Go see to your men. You too," he said, speaking to Smythe.

McCall, his cheeks red with embarrassment, followed after Smythe and left the parlor. Farnsworth smiled apologetically at Diana and Harlan. "Sometimes the men forget themselves."

Harlan nodded. "Your men are quite young, as are you, Captain. What do you plan to do after the war?"

Samuel Farnsworth looked directly at Diana, his gaze raking over Diana's face and form. "Perhaps I'll marry, if I can find a woman who'll have me."

Diana grew uncomfortable at Farnsworth's perusal and jumped up to fuss over Harlan. "I think it's time you went to bed now," she remarked. "Naomi is upstairs and will help settle you for the night."

Rising from the sofa, Harlan laughed when Samuel rushed forward to take him by the elbow. "I remember a time when I could stay up until dawn. Now I have to retire before the sun even sets."

Diana watched as Samuel led Harlan up the stairs to his room. She found herself thinking that Samuel Farnsworth was a considerate man, though he was British. He too wanted more from her than friendship. But she had vowed never to be touched again by any man; just the thought of a man's touch made her skin crawl.

She returned to the kitchen, carrying the tray, and found that Hattie was gone. Little Jackie sat on a wooden bench, apparently waiting for her. When he saw Diana, he stood up and flashed her a beguiling smile. "I done been waitin' and waitin' for the longest time," he admitted. "My Granny Hattie said if I was a good boy that maybe you'd give me a piece of that fresh bread. Can I have some, Miz Diana? Please? I been a real good boy today."

"Certainly you can," Diana told him and handed the seven-year-old boy one of the pieces the soldiers hadn't eaten. She watched as he scooped a large spoonful of jelly onto it and then devoured it in no time. When she offered him another, the child greedily wolfed that one down, too.

Jackie licked his fingers and smiled again at her. "Thank you so much, Miz Diana. You real kind to me."

At that moment Diana felt like the biggest fraud. Evidently the child had never noticed that she resented him. But Jackie wasn't the reason for how she felt. Neither was Jarla, his mother. It was Kingsley who had caused her to feel this way about an innocent little boy, and she was pleased that Jackie had no idea that sometimes just his presence could rattle her. Suddenly she realized that she didn't feel that way any longer, not since Kingsley had left Briarhaven. So she smiled a rich, warm smile at Jackie, placed her arm around his slight shoulders, and gazed down at the child, whose eyes were light brown with a touch of green in them. Like Kingsley's.

"Anytime you want something from the kitchen, you don't have to ask. Just come in and take it."

"You mean that? I don't have to ask my papa or mama?"

"No, I'll tell Ezra and Jarla that you're welcome."

"Thank you, ma'am. 'Cause sometime I get real hungry."

Don't we all, Diana thought, and watched Jackie rush outside. For the first time she understood why Hattie proudly claimed Jackie as her grandson. It wasn't just because Ezra had married Jarla. He was such a dear little boy.

Diana sat down by the table and drank the tea she hadn't finished in the parlor. At the same time she kept an eye on the large black kettle over the hearth. It was filled with boiling rice, part of the evening meal for the soldiers.

A wry smile hovered around her lips. If anyone had told her one year ago that she'd be helping to cook for British soldiers on a plantation that was usually filled with over a hundred slaves, she'd have laughed at them. But the soldiers were a reality and Briarhaven no longer had a large number of slaves. Now she found herself helping Hattie cook and clean and wash British soldiers' dirty clothes. What a change from Briarhaven's pampered mistress, who had been showered with jewels and clothes by what the world termed "an indulgent husband."

Diana nearly choked on her tea at the memory of Kingsley and his gifts to her, his insistence that his wife be the best dressed woman in the county so he could appear well-to-do and influential, an adoring husband, in people's eyes. No one except Hattie, and later Harlan, would have guessed at the source of the black and blue marks those elaborate gowns hid.

A shiver slid up Diana's spine despite the flickering flames in the hearth. "I still hate him," she mumbled aloud, though Kingsley had been dead for nearly a year and couldn't harm her any longer. Except for two scars on her back, courtesy of Kingsley's riding crop, her flesh was unmarred. Still, she felt vulnerable and sometimes imagined that her body throbbed with pain.

The beatings had begun after they'd been married almost two years, around the time Kingsley decided that she must be barren. Previous to this, she'd done her duty by him without complaint until one night he came to her drunk and filled with rage, blaming her for the lack of an heir. She remembered rising up on the bed, screaming at him that the fault might lie with him. It was then he'd slapped her across the face, shouting that he could father a child. Wasn't Jarla and her brat proof of that?

But the years passed and finally Diana conceived. Her joy was boundless. She'd have the child she wanted, a child Kingsley wanted, but best of all, perhaps now he'd leave her alone.

Now she wouldn't have to listen when he sneeringly reminded her about Jackie, a slave girl's child, living proof of her failure. She was going to have a baby, wouldn't be forced to endure Kingsley in her bed or the stinging slaps when he was displeased with her. However, her dreams shattered on a summer afternoon early in her pregnancy when she miscarried.

Kingsley blamed her for losing the child, for making him look less than a man in front of his friends, who all had children. Every time he came to her bed his abuse grew, until the night arrived when he nearly killed her. In her mind's eye, Diana could still picture the riding crop as he raised it above her to strike her sensitive flesh. She still felt the cold wooden floor beneath her knees as she fell, trying to flee from him.

The crop kept rising and falling, never ceasing its relentless assault. She thought Kingsley was going to kill her that night, and he would have if not for Harlan. Her father-in-law was suddenly there, and for a man who was past sixty and hadn't been in the best of health he was surprisingly strong. He grabbed Kingsley by the scruff of the neck and threw him across the room. Kingsley landed on his backside, apparently dazed by Harlan's surprise attack. Diana found herself in Hattie's arms, her body bleeding and aching unbearably, but she'd never forget the utter disgust she'd seen on Harlan's face when he told Kingsley to leave Briarhaven and never return—that as far as he was concerned, he had no son.

Kingsley had whined he'd never touch her

again, that he had no place to go, and it was at this moment that Diana realized who was the true master of Briarhaven. The next day Kingsley sneaked away. With him went all of her jewelry, even some of the pieces that had belonged to her mother. However much Diana missed her mother's garnet ring and earbobs, she knew that anything was worth not having to endure Kingsley another moment.

It wasn't until word came of Kingsley's heroic death in defense of his country that Diana and Harlan learned he'd joined the militia. "At least he wasn't a coward at the end," Harlan had said upon hearing the news. Days later Harlan suffered chest pains and was put to bed by the physician, who privately told Diana that Harlan's heart was weak and he needed constant attention. Diana had decided to care for him, but Naomi appeared one afternoon and declared that she'd tend to Harlan. She explained that she owed him for taking care of her and her son all of those years ago, but Diana thought Naomi loved Harlan and that Harlan loved her. And so life slipped into a predictable and comfortable pattern until the British commandeered Briarhaven, forcing Diana to open her ears for any scrap of useful information about their activities in the area.

"Diana Sheridan, dutiful patriot," she mumbled under her breath and quelled the urge to laugh. She began washing the dishes. When she had finished and was drying her hands on her apron she turned to find Samuel Farnsworth staring worriedly at her. In his hand he held what looked to be a letter.

"I'm sorry to disturb you," he said, "but I just received a missive from General Lord Rawdon in Charlestown about your sister, Mrs. Richmond. It seems she has been taken quite ill and wishes to see you."

"Anne is sick? Does Lord Rawdon say what is wrong with her?" Diana was so upset at this news that she barely realized how odd it must seem to Farnsworth that word of Anne's illness would come from Lord Rawdon himself.

Samuel shook his head and tapped the paper with a well-manicured fingernail. "Lord Rawdon requests that you leave as soon as possible under my protection. I admit I find this most puzzling, because your sister is married to David Richmond, a lieutenant in the South Carolina militia. And if I'm not mistaken, Rawdon pardoned him and his men when we captured Charlestown, under condition that they not join a rebel band and fight against us."

Goodness but Farnsworth had a good memory for names, Diana decided, a bit on her guard. If Farnsworth knew that, then surely Lord Rawdon, who was in charge of the British forces in Charlestown, must remember David's name, too. What was happening here? Anne must be dreadfully ill for Lord Rawdon to send a message to the relative of a known rebel.

"You're quite correct," Diana admitted. "David was pardoned. Does the fact that my sister's husband fought for the opposite side bother you?"

"No, not if he has remained loyal to us. But, you see, I wonder sometimes if you have a guardian angel in the guise of Lord Rawdon."

Diana lifted an eyebrow. "I don't understand what you mean. I've never met Lord Rawdon."

A half smile of amusement and bafflement turned up the corners of his mouth. "In that case, my dear, then I can't explain why Briarhaven was chosen as my headquarters. Originally, the plantation five miles down the Santee was to be my choice, but at the last moment Rawdon commanded that we quarter here. In fact, when I protested he was most adamant about the whole thing. Very strange, but be that as it may, I suggest you pack what you'll need for our trip. We'll leave at dawn if that's all right with you."

"Yes, that's fine. Thank you, Captain."

He took her hand in his and kissed it. She couldn't help but flinch at the intimate contact of his lips against her skin. Instantly she pulled away. He stiffened, and she knew that she had offended him. "I had hoped that by now you'd welcome my attentions, Diana, but I sense that you don't return my feelings. Am I wrong to hope for something more than your friendship?"

Licking her lips, she observed him with all seriousness. "Captain, you are a kind man and a most handsome one, but I suggest you'd do well to look elsewhere for warmth. I have none left to give."

"I understand that you've been a widow for a short while, but I know you're not cold. Your feelings are buried under layers of ice. If only

72

you'd give me the chance to prove how much I care for you." He started to pull her into his arms, but Diana pushed him away and was more than a bit surprised when he didn't protest.

"Stop it, sir. I have nothing left to give!" She meant that with her whole heart. Kingsley had robbed her of her jewels and her feelings. "I dislike being pawed."

He considered her for a long moment. "I think it will take the right man to change your mind about that, and I'd like to be that man. However, I'm under orders not to touch you."

"I . . . don't understand."

"Neither do I, but that was part of my orders upon arriving here. Rawdon clearly expressed to me that you and your father-in-law, your slaves, and your household goods, were not to be molested or disturbed in any way. Believe me when I tell you that if not for that order, I'd have found a way to bring you to my bed." Farnsworth grinned at her. "Now tell me that you have no guardian angel." Bowing deeply, he left the kitchen, leaving her a bit shaken by his actions and his words. A guardian angel. What a ridiculous notion.

Still, it very nearly explained why Briarhaven and not Sinclair House, which was a more strategic location because of its nearness to the Atlantic, had been singled out as a headquarters. And Rawdon's letter about Anne—well, that was more than mind-boggling. Fear clutched at Diana to think that her sister had to be so desperately ill that perhaps David couldn't care for Anne and their three children. But even so, would Rawdon send for her out of the goodness of his heart, simply to please a known rebel like David Richmond?

None of it made any sense. Especially not Farnsworth's remarks that she and everyone at Briarhaven not be molested. Who would have dared to give such absurd orders? Before now the British had never cared who they hurt or what houses they looted and burned. Farnsworth must be mistaken, she decided, yet she welcomed such a mistake.

However, she couldn't stand here all day mulling over all of this, not when Anne needed her. She had to pack, but first she must tell Harlan of her plans and then wait until after midnight. Then the house would be quiet and the officers asleep. She'd be able to sneak into the underground tunnel and tell her informant about the supply wagon that was due to come through on the morrow. She smiled to realize how glad the Swamp Fox would be of such news.


"All clear, Miss Diana. I don't see a soul." Hattie turned from the doorway and grasped Diana's hand. "You be careful, child."

"I will," Diana promised and smiled encouragingly at Hattie as she'd done on many previous occasions. She left her room, clad in a black shirt and breeches that had belonged to Kingsley, Hattie having cut down the garments to fit Diana's petite frame. To protect herself from the bitter chill, Diana had thrown on an ebony colored cloak and hidden her dark tresses beneath the hood.

Nearing Farnsworth's room, Diana stopped and listened, but hearing only the man's snores she made her way to the back stairway. She took a lighted candle from the wall sconce and continued down the stairs, but it seemed that each of her booted footfalls on the wooden steps matched the beating of her heart. Every familiar creak sounded a thousand times louder to her own ears, and at any minute she expected Farnsworth or one of his men to appear behind her and drag her back. But no hands reached out to clutch her. It was only when she'd tugged open the door that led to the wine cellar and had firmly closed it behind her that she allowed herself the satisfaction of drawing breath again.

Without dallying, Diana hurried past the wooden shelves that had once held bottles of fine wines and liquors. She halted when she reached the last shelf. A gray stone wall, decorated with a grapelike motif, blocked her way, but not for long. Pressing her palm into the center of one of the clusters, she watched as a section of the wall gave way and opened for her. Diana squeezed into the opening, and once on the opposite side, she pulled the panel into place.

The candle flickered and sputtered as Diana rushed through the dark, damp tunnel. The tunnel had been built over one hundred years earlier by a Sheridan ancestor who had been a pirate. Harlan, who had shown her the tunnel shortly after she had married Kingsley, had told her that his great uncle had been quite a notorious character, marrying well and pretending to be quite proper in all respects. But love for the sea and zeal for plunder were in his blood, and he'd built the tunnel as a means of transporting his booty into the house. Harlan had laughed when he recounted how, at a lavish ball given by this same uncle at Briarhaven, the scoundrel had plied British authorities who were eager to prove he was a pirate with drink and food, all the while delighting in the fact that beneath the floor boards upon which they danced was the contraband that would have proven their case.

At the moment Diana understood the heady sense of elation that Sheridan ancestor must have felt. She'd been frightened when Clay Sinclair, a neighbor and good friend, had stealthily approached her about spying on Farnsworth. Now, however, the lurking sense of danger stained her usually pale cheeks with a becoming rosy flush, and she realized that she truly enjoyed these nights when she slipped into the tunnel, more than eager for the adventure. Who would believe that the prim and proper widow Sheridan, a woman who pretended to be a Tory, was in reality a spy for the American cause? Diana barely believed it herself.

She reached the end of the tunnel. Setting the candle in a holder on the wall, she turned a large handle on the stone door in front of her. The creaking sound seemed quite loud in the quiet night, but Diana didn't worry. She knew none of the soldiers would be so far from the house on such a cold night as this, and especially that no one would venture onto this part of the property.

Leaving ajar the stone door on the largest tomb in the Sheridan family cemetery and stepping outside, Diana took a deep breath, only to have it hang like a specter in the clear, frosty night air. Above her, a full moon illumined the white granite headstones. The ornate sepulcher stood on a marble slab, but it wasn't a tomb at all, having always been the entranceway into the tunnel. Since Kingsley was gone, no one save Harlan, Hattie, and herself knew that it didn't house the remains of deceased Sheridans.

The smell of pine from the nearby swamp wafted on the air, mingling with other wildwood fragrances, as Diana rushed about five hundred feet into the swamp. She felt grateful that the moon was full and lighted her way, confident that the soldiers weren't nearby. Only seconds after she'd stopped beneath a large pine tree Clay Sinclair appeared like a sudden mist.

"I've been watching for you," he whispered, a shy grin on his face. "I didn't know if you'd have anything to tell me, what with Christmas only a few days away."

"There's a supply wagon coming through tomorrow," Diana related and told him what had happened since she'd last seen him. "I won't be able to come for awhile, Clay," she managed to apologize, feeling like a traitor. "Anne is ill. Captain Farnsworth is escorting me to Charlestown in the morning."

Clay nodded his understanding, a shaggy strand of blond hair hung across his forehead. "I'll tell Colonel Marion to give orders not to interfere with the escort party. He'll be glad to learn about the supply wagon. We're running pretty low on things now."

Diana knew it must be quite hard for Marion and his men as they fought and lived in the wilderness. On such nights as this when the cold winds blew in from the Atlantic, she slept in a bed with a roof over her head while Clay and other patriots were lucky to have a warm blanket for protection from the elements. She felt guilty and it must have shown, for Clay grinned again at her.

"My mother and sisters loved the gowns you gave them after our house burned. They're real grateful."

"I bet if they knew the clothes were mine, Clay, they'd burn them rather than wear anything a loyalist owned."

"Now, don't be so touchy. I couldn't tell them where the gowns came from. I know you're a patriot and so does Colonel Marion. After this war is won, everyone else will know it, too. Sometimes people just have to do things they don't like to get the job done. Just be grateful that Briarhaven is still intact."

Diana was grateful, more than grateful, and that was the trouble. Whereas her neighbors, the Sinclairs, were without a home now, she still had hers. She couldn't help but feel doubly guilty when she recalled Farnsworth telling her that the

Sinclair house had been chosen to be his head-quarters but that Rawdon had insisted he use Briarhaven instead. If things had been different, the Sinclair ladies might have been forced to give her their hand-me-downs.

"Are your mother and sisters well?" she asked Clay.

Clay nodded. "Colonel Marion found a safe place for them to live. They're doing fine."

She started to tell Clay farewell when he startled her by pulling her against his broad chest and kissing her full on the lips. The kiss was brief, and when Diana's initial shock lessened she saw that Clay was blushing like a schoolboy, which was exactly what Diana had considered him to be until now. But she suddenly realized that Clay was eighteen and no longer resembled the scrawny lad she remembered, having grown into a muscular and rugged looking young man from his time in the swamps. It was apparent from the way he looked at her that he didn't consider himself anything *but* a man.

"I've been wanting to do that for a long time, Diana. I'm sorry if I've startled you, but I'm not sorry I kissed you. I love you and want to marry you when the war's over. I know I'm a little younger than you, but I'd make you a good husband, better than that bastard Kingsley. I swear I would."

Such an honest admission touched her. Clay Sinclair was a gentle and decent person, and she genuinely liked him and didn't want to hurt him. Yet she couldn't help reddening at the realization that somehow Clay had learned about Kingsley's abuse of her. Evidently one of the servants at Briarhaven had spread the word. She wondered how many other people had known. She felt suddenly stripped of her pride.

"I can't marry you," she said more harshly than she intended.

Clay's face seemed to fall, and she realized how she must sound to him, how she hurt him.

"It isn't that I don't care for you," she amended gently, holding his fingers, stiff with cold. "I'm very fond of you, but I won't marry—ever again. I appreciate that you care about me, but please find someone more deserving of your affection."

She thought he was about to deny what she said, but he placed her hand to his mouth and kissed it. "If you ever need me for anything, Diana, all you have to do is ask."

"That means a great deal to me."

He flashed her a smile and turned away. She watched for a few seconds, and then Clay vanished into the misty swamp.

## Chapter 5

When Diana reached Charlestown nearly three days later, she found that the beautiful city she remembered from her childhood had changed during the British occupation. Many of the grand and gracious homes stood empty and in need of repair from the American and British shellings; homeless people, mostly loyalists who'd come to Charlestown for protection, lived in squalor outside the city limits in a section called Rawdontown. The marketplace, which Diana recalled as picturesque and filled with fragrant smelling fruits and fresh meats, was now inhabited by ravenous buzzards who perched on the rooftops. With a sense of sick dismay, she watched as the creatures flopped beneath the hooves of passing horses to fight other buzzards and stray mongrels, even a person or two, when the market man appeared and threw scraps of meat and fish into the street.

"This is appalling," she spoke aloud and looked

at Samuel Farnsworth who rode alongside her. "Is everyone starving? General Lord Rawdon should do something about this."

Farnsworth clucked his tongue in disgust, apparently stung by her less-than-kind comment about his superior, a comment that also heaped blame upon himself. "Heavens, Diana, riffraff isn't Rawdon's concern, and certainly not mine," he made a point of reminding her. "Our people are well fed and clothed, no one who is one of us goes hungry. We have a large number of soldiers to feed to win this war. Certainly Rawdon is sorry, I'm sorry about many things, but as in all wars, some people must do without."

He sounded so callous to Diana's ears, but she couldn't deny the truth of what Farnsworth said. She just hoped that Anne and the children hadn't come to such a fate.

When she arrived at Anne's house on Orange Street a smile broke over Diana's face. As Farnsworth helped her dismount he held her against him for a moment longer than Diana thought was necessary. "Should I go inside with you?" he asked in a husky, suggestive voice that caused her to cringe. He'd been such a solicitous companion during their journey, never mentioning anything about what had transpired between them in the kitchen, not giving a hint that he felt anything more than friendship for her. Why did he have to go and spoil all of it now by making her feel uncomfortable?

"Thank you, but I'd like to be alone with my sister. I have no idea what might be wrong with her, and she could be contagious, you know." That should cool his lust, she decided.

It did.

Captain Farnsworth cleared his throat and released her, waiting until after she'd knocked on Anne's door and was admitted into the house by Ruthie, an old family servant, before departing.

"Whatever are you doing here, Diana?" Anne inquired minutes later when Diana entered the darkened bedroom.

Diana found Anne huddled in the large bed, a blanket wrapped around her. She looked at Diana like she'd materialized in thin air. The drapes were pulled shut and the room was unbearably cold. No fire roared cheerily in the fireplace, either here or in the parlor where Diana had greeted the children when she came inside.

"I thought you'd be more pleased to see me than that." Diana kissed Anne on the forehead and would have removed her own cloak but for the chill in the room. "It's no wonder that you're ill, Anne. The house is freezing and the childrens' noses are running. I've gotten here just in time. Wait until I see David. I'll take him to task for not bringing in firewood. Where is he anyway?"

Anne stared at her dazedly. "David's in prison. He . . . he . . . was arrested for trying to join his regiment."

"What! When did this happen, why did he do that? He knew the conditions of his pardon. Oh, Anne, how awful!"

Diana sat on the bed beside her sister, who started to cry. "I told him . . . not to . . . go,"

Anne choked on her tears, "but David has a stubborn streak. He assured us he'd be all right, but . . . but," Anne gulped convulsively, "he might be hanged."

Holding her sister against her as she wept, Diana felt numb with the cold and her own utter disbelief. David Richmond, a man who was kind and gentle but also determined, was going to hang. Diana shivered with the sickening dread that clutched at her stomach. She doubted that Anne and the children would be able to survive without David.

"Perhaps there's something we can do. Have you talked to Lord Rawdon?" Diana became calm, realizing that if she gave way to her own hysteria, Anne's dilemma would be worse.

Anne wiped her eyes with the back of her fists. "I can't even get into see the bloody swine."

Anne never used strong language, but in this instance Diana agreed with her and mentally cursed the British general in even stronger terms.

"Your showing up now is a kindness, a miracle from God, Diana. I need help with the children since I'm unable to care for them now. All I seem able to do is weep."

"You're ill and under a great strain."

"Why ever would you think I'm ill?"

"Because of the letter from Lo . . ."

Diana broke off, seeing Anne's baffled look. She was baffled herself. Now that she'd seen Anne she could tell that Anne wasn't sick at all, sick at heart, maybe, but certainly not sick physically. But the letter from Rawdon had said Anne was ill and needed her, yet Anne stated she'd never been able to see Rawdon.

"Have you contacted Lord Rawdon by message?" Diana asked.

"Humph! If only I could. Nothing and no one gets past his people except for the chosen few." Diana saw that Anne's face was flushed, her spirit seeming to return because of Diana's presence.

So Anne hadn't written or seen Rawdon. Then who sent the note to Briarhaven?

Diana opened the drapes to allow the mid-morning sunshine into the room and told Anne to rest, that she'd have Ruthie send up some warm tea so they could talk. Anne smiled gratefully, but the second Diana left the room Diana heard her start to cry again. Downstairs, she spoke with her nephew, who was named after his father and resembled him, and the two younger girls, Jane and Prudence. They were more than happy to see her, and as they ate some cold mutton and drank their tea with her, Diana listened and laughed with them, but she couldn't forget that Rawdon, or someone who forged the general's name, had commanded her to come to Charlestown. A sense of alarm swept over her as she wondered who it might be.

"Ain't got no more firewood except for the little in the stove," Ruthie told her later. "Ain't got no money either now that Mr. Richmond is in prison. Miss Anne is brave, but she can't make it without the mister. I don't what will happen to her and the children."

Ruthie's voice quivered and Diana hugged her. Ruthie had been with the family since before the Montaigne sisters were born and considered herself to be more than a servant, almost like their mother. "You shall all come to Briarhaven if David . . . if the unspeakable happens." Diana couldn't even say the word *hang*. How did Anne manage to live with the horror of not knowing how David was, of wondering if he'd soon be executed? For all of Anne's tears, Diana admired her sister for not falling completely apart as she feared she herself might do in a similar situation. "I have some money," Diana assured Ruthie. "We'll get some firewood and food. In fact, I'll do that this afternoon."

Checking upon Anne and finding her asleep an hour later, Diana decided that now would be the perfect time to run her errands. She'd told Ruthie that she had money, which was true, but she hadn't told her how little money there was. Diana doubted she'd be able to afford much in the way of food. She might even have to resort to fighting off the vultures at the market for the pickings, and as far as firewood, she hoped she could talk Anne into burning some of the furniture if she couldn't afford the wood. The children needed the extra warmth.

A blustery wind whipped the tendrils of Diana's hair about her face. The sun's rays slanted downward but barely warmed Diana as she pulled her black cloak closer against her body and stepped out of the front door. A handsomely rigged ebony carriage halted before her, pulled by two chestnut mares who snorted in the frosty air and seemed oblivious to the small, bespectacled driver who glanced down at Diana.

The man, who wore a dark walking cape and a tricorn hat, jumped from his seat and bowed low to her, startling her when he spoke to her. "I have a message for you, Mrs. Sheridan."

He handed her a folded piece of parchment and waited patiently while she read it.

If you hope to save David Richmond, please enter the carriage. Don't mention to anyone that you are leaving. The choice is yours.

Diana blinked. "Are you certain this message is for me?"

"Yes, ma'am, if you're Diana Sheridan of Briarhaven plantation."

"Who is it from?"

"I'm not at liberty to say anything, ma'am, just to escort you to your destination."

"And where is that?"

"If you come with me, I shall show you."

She didn't know what to do. Who had written this note? Was it from the same person who'd engineered for her to be here in the first place? And if so, how could she possibly help David? For all she knew she might meet with a horrible fate if she entered the carriage. If she did go, Anne would be frantic with worry, but she wondered if she could help David somehow. She had to find out. "I need to tell my sister that I'm leaving."

"If you do that, ma'am, I won't be here when you return. I have my orders," the man told her without the trace of an apology in his tone.

Diana grew more confused with each passing second. Apparently the man saw her indecision and he said, "I assure you that you shall be safe. If you wish, I can come back later and leave a note for your sister not to worry, but *only* if you come with me now. I'm obliged to tell you that time is running out for your brother-in-law."

Something in the man's thin face and tone of voice alarmed her. Had David's fate been decided already? She hated thinking about what might befall Anne and the children without him. She had to discover what this was all about, to see if she could help them — even at the expense of her own safety.

Without saying another word, Diana nodded and the man threw open the carriage door for her. In seconds the carriage was heading away from Orange Street to an uncertain future.


A cold wind blew off the Ashley River as the carriage halted before a buff-colored town house on Church Street. Diana was more than puzzled when the man attempted to help her out of the vehicle.

Her gaze took in the high brick walls and the large fan-lighted doorway that she knew led into the piazza of the house. "There must be some mistake. This is the Sheridan townhouse," she told him. The house had belonged to the Sheridans for a number of years but had been confiscated when the British invaded Charlestown.

"No mistake, ma'am," her driver told her and went to the front doorway to pound upon the massive brass knocker. Soon a black serving woman with a crisply starched apron tied around her gingham dress answered and solemnly admitted Diana into the main house, which consisted of a central hallway flanked by two rooms on each side.

Leading her up a flight of stairs to the parlor, the woman motioned for Diana to be seated in a Queen Anne style chair whose rosy background complemented the rose and green drapes on the floor-to-ceiling windows.

What am I doing here? Diana asked herself when she was alone. She glanced around the sumptuously decorated room that had changed very little since the last time she'd been here. Harlan no longer owned the house, but someone knew her well enough to bring her to it. Someone knew how much she wanted to help David and Anne. But who? She didn't like any of this intrigue. In fact, she didn't care for the frightened feelings within her, and when the woman returned with a warm cup of tea and wouldn't answer any of Diana's questions, Diana rose to her feet and pulled her cloak about her.

"I don't intend to be kept in the dark a moment longer. Please tell whoever is responsible for this . . . mystery . . . that I shall be at my sister's home. Good day." Diana had barely reached the doorway when the bespectacled driver appeared and blocked her way. "I wish to leave," she told him.

"As you like, ma'am, but if I take you back to Mrs. Richmond's any hope of freeing her husband is gone. You'll be responsible for his death, and I don't think you'd care to have that on your conscience. Not if by waiting here in the first place you could help him. Have we been unkind to you?" he asked and peered at her intently. "If so, I do apologize."

No one had been unkind to her, no one had harmed her. It was all of this mystery, this waiting here in a house that had once belonged to the Sheridans that caused her uneasiness. But she realized he meant what he said about David. If she left without first learning what all of this was about she'd never forgive herself if anything did happen to him.

"I'll stay," she told him.

"Very well, ma'am." He looked pleased. "My name is Curtis and the serving woman is Cammie. You must be quite hungry by now, so supper is waiting for you in the dining room."

"Thank you, Curtis. Have you left a note for my sister?"

"I shall do that immediately," he promised. "And I'll deliver a hot meal for all of them."

"And firewood, please. I'd be most grateful and I'll pay you back very soon."

"Don't worry about cost, ma'am. Everything has been taken care of."

With that, he bowed and headed downstairs,

leaving her to ponder how and who had taken care of everything.

After Diana had finished her meal of freshly cooked fish in a thick cream sauce and a salad of winter vegetables, she found herself still waiting for an explanation. The large clock in the parlor chimed ten when Cammie appeared to tell her that her bed had been warmed and was ready for her.

Diana started to protest, but she realized the futility of it and followed Cammie into the master bedroom. Diana remembered this as Harlan's room, but the green drapes that once graced the french doors leading onto the upstairs piazza were now cream colored with tiny flecks of rust. The counterpane on the large rice bed matched the drapes. Diana immediately saw that the furnishings had been rearranged, the bed now standing against the wall with a pair of french doors on either side. A mahogany chest of drawers and a dressing table graced the opposite wall, and to the right of that were twin wardrobes. On the left side of the room before the fireplace was an overstuffed chair that had been Harlan's favorite but was now covered in a vibrant shade of rust instead of drab olive. A doorway trimmed in alabaster white led into a small room that Diana recalled as a dressing room, but upon closer inspection she saw that it had been turned into a bathing room, complete with a porcelain inlaid tub and privy chamber.

Clearly whoever inhabited the townhouse now had made remarkable improvements.

Cammie opened the wardrobe door and withdrew a white nightrail with lace at the neckline and the edges of the long sleeves. She placed it on the bed along with a matching robe. Diana watched in confusion as the woman gestured to the silk, satin, and velvet gowns that hung in the wardrobe, then opened a lingerie drawer at the bottom to reveal pairs of silk stockings and lacy garters. "Matching slippers are lined up beneath the gowns, Mrs. Sheridan. I hope all meets with your approval."

"Everything is quite lovely," Diana told the dusky colored woman, not certain what she was supposed to say. What difference could any of this make to her? Cammie waited expectantly. "Is something wrong?"

"I shall help you undress, Mrs. Sheridan. A warm bath awaits you after your long journey today." Diana had no idea she was expected to bathe, but she gratefully allowed Cammie to undo the hooks on the back of her black gown and then stepped into the steaming tub of water.

After she'd finished bathing and was wrapped in a towel, Cammie entered with the nightrail. "I can't wear your mistress's clothes," Diana protested.

Cammie laughed softly and held out the gown to Diana, who reluctantly took it. "The gown is for your use, Mrs. Sheridan, as are the clothes in the wardrobe. I thought you understood that. Evidently Curtis didn't mention this to you."

There were many things Curtis hadn't mentioned, but Diana was so tired that the absurdity of the situation didn't faze her any longer. She had no idea whose clothes and room this was, but she delighted in the feel of the soft material, which hugged her body as it fell into place. It had been a long while since she'd worn anything so fine and delicate. Her own nightgown at home had become quite ragged, but it was all she had. For the time being, Diana luxuriated in the softness of the nightrail and the sweet lavender-scented sheets. It seemed that her head had no sooner touched the pillow than she was asleep.

Sometime during the night she wakened, certain that someone had touched her cheek. Swiftly sitting up, Diana glanced around the room to find that the fire in the grate had burned low and suffused the room in a golden glow, but she saw no one. Yet even after she'd convinced herself that she must be dreaming and had once more drifted off to sleep, she could still feel the warmth of invisible fingers against her skin.

"But this scarlet gown is quite pretty and much warmer than your black dress, Mrs. Sheridan. Please wear this one. The master will be most upset if you don't."

Diana's eyes blazed with controlled fury as Cammie laid the velvet gown on the bed. "I'm quite happy with my own clothes and have no intention of wearing anything else. Your master, whoever he may be, has no say over my apparel. He coerced me into coming here, but I won't wear those!" Diana gestured furiously toward the glittering and beautiful dresses in the open wardrobe. "Just do the hooks on the back of my dress and let's be done with all of this nonsense, Cammie! I'm eager to speak to your master and be on my way."

"Yes, ma'am." Cammie reluctantly began to fasten the back of Diana's gown.

Diana could barely restrain her rage or her curiosity. Impudent man, she silently fumed, having learned from Cammie that the master was waiting for her in the downstairs parlor. How dare this stranger think that he could spirit her away to his home, feed her and provide lodging and clothes for her and tell her what to wear. Who did this person believe he was to keep his identity a secret, to treat her as if she had no choice concerning her own comings and goings? And she didn't have a choice at all, she realized. Not when David's and Anne's futures rested on her acquiescence to this unseen person.

She'd stayed the night as he'd wished, but she'd be damned if she'd wear any of the clothes in the wardrobe simply because he demanded it. If her widow's weeds weren't good enough for her to wear to discuss David's plight then this dictatorial stranger would have to back down. Diana felt almost as if this master of whom Cammie spoke with such awe was attempting to master *her*. Well, she wouldn't allow anyone to control her. Kingsley had nearly killed her with his sadistic mastery. Never again would she give anything of herself to another human being—and she refused to be at a man's mercy.

Still the gowns in the wardrobe seemed to beckon to her. It had been a long time since she'd worn pretty clothes, and her black gown was becoming quite shabby. But she didn't want to draw attention to her natural beauty so she chose to pull her dark hair in a severe knot at the base of her neck. In her widow's weeds Diana felt comfortable and more likely not to attract a man's attentions. Of course Farnsworth and Clay Sinclair seemed more than taken with her, but she decided that the war prevented them from seeking out eligible and willing women. Once the conflict was over, Diana reassured herself, both men would forget her.

Catching sight of herself in the dresser mirror, Diana only shrugged at her plain but tidy appearance, realizing that it wouldn't be difficult for a man to forget her. She'd grown used to doing without the rouges and pretty clothes to enhance her appearance, to attract eligible men. She thought herself long past the age of girlish preening, but when Cammie finished doing the hooks, Diana's gaze wandered to the gown on the bed. For an instant she imagined herself in the scarlet creation, envisioning how beautiful she'd look, especially with her hair rearranged in long curls down her back—the way she'd worn it the night of her engagement ball—the night that Tanner had . . .

"Cammie, tell your master I shall be down in a few minutes!" she declared harshly, pushing the intrusive image of Tanner Sheridan from her mind.

"Yes, ma'am," Cammie curtsied to her as if she were a duchess and hurriedly left the room.

Diana breathed deeply, seeing the rosy splotches on her cheeks. She touched her face, wondering what was happening to her. Even after all these years, that memory could still undo her. Tanner's face as he gazed down at her. Tanner's arms around her waist when they danced. Tanner's laugh. Tanner's kiss. Tanner's hands.

"Stop!" she demanded and attempted to compose herself. Was she going suddenly insane? Why in the name of heaven was she thinking about Tanner at this moment? David's predicament should be uppermost in her thoughts now, that and the man who waited downstairs, a man who conceivably might be able to help him—not Tanner Sheridan. Never Tanner.

Moments later, after Diana had composed herself, she walked down the flight of stairs to the parlor that adjoined a larger room that had been used as a ballroom whenever Harlan stayed at the townhouse. But now the double doors to the ballroom were closed. The breezy overcast morning barely penetrated through the sheer hangings on the windows, but she heard the rustling sound of the palmettos in the garden outside as the plants brushed against the house.

A man's broad back was to her. He was looking out of the window, and Diana thought he hadn't heard her enter the room, thus allowing her a second to take in the elegant cut of his black velvet jacket and trousers, the way the expensive leather black boots fit snugly around his calves. His hair wasn't arranged in the fashionable queue of the times but was cut short, the silky strands so dark that they blended with his attire.

She started to clear her throat but his deep voice stalled her. "I know you're here," he said.

"Then would you please be so kind as to turn around. It's quite rude for you to ignore me if you know I'm standing here, sir."

Cammie's entrance to light a candelabrum on the piano brought Diana's attention to her, but after Cammie left the man still hadn't faced her.

"I understand that you wish to speak to me about my brother-in-law," Diana began with an edgy note in her voice.

"Yes."

"Well, sir, please tell me what it is you have to say, otherwise, you've wasted my time and yours. I do have other duties and responsibilities more important than . . ."

"More important than Richmond's life?" He stiffened.

"More important than playing games with you! Good day to you. I'm leaving."

Diana grabbed her skirt in her hands and swung around, but she barely moved before the man was by her side, his hand gripping her upper arm. The very nerve of the man to touch her like that caused her to grimace and glance up at him, ready to berate him for the deed. But the black eyes that raked across her face impaled her, and Diana felt unable to move, hardly able to breathe.

"Games are what you're best at, if I recall,

Diana. Tell me, why didn't you wear the scarlet gown? Is it because your guilty conscience won't let you?"

Shaking her head in mute disbelief, Diana couldn't speak his name aloud. It had been so long since she'd seen him, but suddenly it seemed like the many yesterdays that separated them melted away.

Her heart thumped out his name. Tanner. Tanner. Tanner.

# Chapter 6

"Sit down, Diana, before you collapse." Tanner led her to the sofa, where he placed her like a fragile doll on a shelf. Sitting side by side, they looked at one another for long moments before Diana finally felt the breath reach her throat and she was able to speak.

Her eyes condemned him. "You should have come to me directly instead of going through all of this intrigue."

"Would you have come if I had?"

"No!" she blurted out and then reddened at the vehemence projected behind her answer. He'd believe she cared about him if she wasn't careful. And she didn't care about Tanner Sheridan. In fact she hated him.

Tanner stared at her until she grew uncomfortable and squirmed in her seat. His sudden smile, so bright in his tanned, handsome face, nearly undid the last vestiges of any composure she'd managed to maintain. She was unwillingly reminded of how handsome she'd found him that night by the river, but if possible Tanner had grown more handsome and stronger with the years. The hold he still had on her arm was proof of that strength, and the warm fingers wrapped around her arm caused her to shiver with a sensation she recalled from that long ago night.

"Let my arm go," she demanded.

His smile collapsed to be replaced by a mocking frown. "Excuse me, Mrs. Sheridan. I forgot myself." Tanner stood up and went to the sideboard to pour himself a brandy out of a large crystal decanter. "Would you care for one?" he offered gallantly. At a quick shake of her head, he leaned against the sideboard and perused her thoroughly, from the top of her severely coiffed hair to the bottoms of her well-worn shoes. "You look awful, Diana."

Her mouth fell open in mute surprise, and she had to force herself to close it. His comment stunned her. Though she knew it was true, she hated to think she looked so terrible that someone would have the gracelessness to tell her so. She'd lost weight the last months and was reduced to dressing like a beggar. Her widow's weeds were worn not because she had loved Kingsley but because the gown was the best she owned. Shifting in her seat, she grew all too self-conscious of her thinness, especially in her chest, which had once been full-breasted. Now her gown hung on her like an ill-measured drape.

"Never let it be said that you don't know how to compliment a lady," Diana said dryly.

"The gowns in the wardrobe are for your use," he told her. "I expect you to wear them and get rid of that ugly thing you've got on. It's little better than a rag."

"I will not!" she insisted, and decided that no matter how he insulted her she'd stand her ground. Tanner Sheridan wouldn't dictate to her. Who did he think he was? He wasn't Briarhaven's overseer any longer, and she wasn't a slave. "I'm in mourning for your brother, or probably you don't care. Still, I don't see what I wear or how I look has anything to do with this meeting. I thought I was brought here to talk about David. Or am I mistaken in that?" she asked suspiciously.

"No, you're not mistaken." Tanner took a seat in a chair covered in a rose print and stretched out his long legs until the toes of his highly polished boots were almost in contact with the hem of her gown. "David Richmond is going to hang within two days' time. That's why I was unable to speak to you last night. I was with Lord Rawdon, trying to arrange for his release."

"And did you?" Diana now knew that Tanner had written the note, and if he had been with Rawdon, then he must be one of the very few people who had any influence with the man. Her hopes rose. Maybe Tanner was the answer to Anne's prayers.

"Yes and no. Yes, I can arrange for Richmond's release. Today, in fact. But I won't unless you can promise me that I'll be repaid."

"Money? You want money?" Diana was incredulous. Tanner wanted payment to release David from prison when he had all of this? She gazed around the room then shot blue fire in his direction. "I don't have any money and neither does Anne! You're an awful man, a horrible person. . . ."

"I didn't say money, but I do want payment. I've learned never to do anything unless there's something to be gained from it, otherwise, the consequences might be too much to bear." Watching her, his frown deepened until he shook himself and rose to refresh his drink. "You must realize by now, Diana, that I didn't go to all of this trouble to get you here just so I could tell you that I can arrange Richmond's release."

A shiver of apprehension slid down her back. "What do you want then?"

A nonchalant smile appeared on his face. "I promise that Richmond and his family will be taken to safety away from Charlestown this very afternoon, but only if you agree to one condition."

"What condition?"

Tanner smirked and swirled the liquid in his glass without taking his gaze from her. "You'll probably balk when I tell you, but I think that once you see the value of the situation, you'll believe it's for the best. Richmond will be released today, and your sister and her children taken to safety, only if you agree to marry me."

The blood drained from Diana's face. She felt cold, horribly cold. Tanner couldn't mean to force her to marry him as a way of saving David.

It was blackmail, she knew that. But why would Tanner insist she marry him to help David? He didn't love her, had never loved her even when he spoke the words that night on the bluff. He'd lied to her to gain his vengeance on Kingsley and Harlan. Was he lying now? But why? Apparently he owned the Sheridan townhouse and must be a very wealthy man, so what could he hope to gain from marrying her, a nearly penniless widow, when he appeared to have so very much? Then the answer came to her in a flash. Tanner wanted something of hers; he wanted Briarhaven.

Heat shot back into her body with the force of an arrow. Her cheeks grew warm and her eyes gleamed like sapphires in the sunshine. Her anger rose to think of how truly despicable he was to blackmail her like this.

Diana stood up and clasped her trembling hands in front of her. "I won't marry you."

"Why not?"

"I don't believe anything you've told me. I doubt you can free David at all. I know what you want, Tanner, and I'm not going to let you have it."

Tanner placed his drink on the sideboard and came to stand in front of her. She felt dwarfed by his height, the broadness of his physique, and the very strength contained within his body. But she refused to be intimidated by him and stared up at him in defiance even when he was so close to her she could smell the brandy on his breath.

"I doubt you know what I want at all." His soft whisper fanned a wispy tendril at her ear that had escaped the knot. A shiver slipped through her when he suddenly touched her hair and gently coaxed the stray lock into place. She couldn't deny that his fingers felt warm upon her earlobe or deny that a sudden longing swept through her. Tanner's face was so near, his sensuous and mesmerizing lips were scant inches from her own. Her eyes were unwillingly trained upon his mouth, unable to draw back as an invisible force seemed to be pulling her toward him, and once again she was waiting for something as she had on that long ago night. Waiting. Waiting . . .

"He wanted to have his way with you!" Kingsley's voice from the misty past of her wedding night harshly intruded into her thoughts. "Tanner hates all of the Sheridans; he hates you, too—"

"No!" came Diana's protest. At first she had no idea she'd spoken aloud until she realized that Tanner had drawn himself up sharply and was watching her with a mixture of anger and something that hinted strongly of repulsion. She knew then that he didn't desire her for herself, that he'd meant his earlier comment about her appearance. He really did want Briarhaven and would go to any lengths to claim it, even by marrying a woman he clearly didn't desire.

He still must hate his family, and her, to use her so shabbily to achieve his goal. A lump formed in her throat, but she swallowed it down, vowing not to cry like a silly goose in front of Tanner.

"You're lying about David. I don't believe he's

going to be hanged at all. What you want is Briarhaven, and I won't allow you to have it or to hurt your father again."

"Or besmirch my dead brother's memory either," he put in and sneered.

Diana flinched, saying nothing. In fact there was nothing but awful things to say about Kingsley, so she refrained from even mentioning him. "Then you admit you do want Briarhaven."

"I admit nothing, but this says a great deal." Tanner took a piece of paper from his jacket pocket and handed it to her. Diana glanced at it, seeing three names upon it. David's name was second. "That list is the execution schedule, Diana. The first fellow is going to be hanged tomorrow, and Richmond the following day. You can say anything you like to me. You can refuse my marriage proposal, but Richmond will die if you don't agree."

"Your marriage proposal is blackmail and you know it! I don't know whether to believe you." Her eyes implored him, but Tanner's face was inscrutable, expressing no emotions. The choice of saving David was up to her. Her head swam with the implications. If she refused, David could die. She still wasn't at all certain that Tanner wielded enough power to free David, but the very fact that he'd arranged for her safe passage to Charlestown and was evidently in close communication with Rawdon dispelled some of her doubts. But marriage to Tanner was something else again.

Would he demand his husbandly rights? Would

he hurt her like Kingsley had done? But of course he would. A wife must endure her husband's animal lust, and somehow she knew that Tanner would be more ferocious and possessive in bed than Kingsley. Yet hadn't Tanner asked only that she *agree* to marry him? Once she gave him her word and David had been freed, then she would have done what was asked of her. Somehow she'd hedge on marrying him—that was all she need do. Tanner only wanted her word, and when the Richmond family was safe she'd break it.

"I agree to marry you," Diana told him.

Tanner quirked an eyebrow, but he smiled and took the paper from her, replacing it in his pocket. "Such a ready acceptance makes my head spin. But you've done a wise thing, my dear. Now I suggest you fetch your cloak and let's progress to the next stage of our relationship, because time is of the essence in this case."

"What . . . do you mean?"

"Why our wedding, of course, Diana. Curtis has brought round the carriage for our ride to St. Phillip's where the minister is waiting to perform the ceremony this morning. I knew you'd agree so I made the necessary arrangements in advance."

"But . . . but . . . you said only that I agree to marry you."

"And so you have, my love, but if you want Richmond and his family safe, then you will marry me today."

"That wasn't what we agreed upon!" she stated hotly, standing with arms akimbo. "I want some proof that David and my sister and the children are safe."

"I promise you shall have it soon enough, but do hurry, Diana." He glanced at his pocket watch. "Not many hours are left until the execution; even as you stand here dawdling and arguing about semantics the scaffold is being readied for your brother-in-law."

Tanner's threat was obvious. Diana knew she was beaten for the moment and sent Tanner a baleful look. Once she was in the carriage for the ride to the church she didn't so much as look in Tanner's direction, but she was aware of his large frame filling the small confines of the carriage, acutely aware of his masculine scent, which seemed to curl her very toes. He in turn watched her like a large hawk with its prey, unnerving her to such an extent that she trembled. However, it was not until he took her arm to lead her into the reverend's study and a not unpleasant jolt of attraction surged through her that she finally focused fully upon him.

"I shall always hate you for this," she confessed.

"I know that."

And that was all Tanner said to her until he repeated his vows.

Diana stood on the piazza of the townhouse that overlooked the crashing waves of the Atlantic. The purplish haze of dusk descended like a gossamer counterpane, and overhead a thin sliver of a moon broke through a cloud. Soon it would be dark and still she waited, as she'd waited in the cold since the minute she'd arrived from the church earlier that day. She felt unable to wait inside, felt that the warmth of the townhouse wasn't truly hers to enjoy, not until she knew with no uncertainty that David was free and reunited with Anne and the children.

A flash of gold on the third finger of her left hand caught her attention. Tanner's ring to her, a tangible reminder that she was his wife now, binding her to him forever and always. She wanted to cry.

The gentle creak of the french door behind her announced Tanner's presence on the piazza. He held a riding crop in his hand, a clear indication that the reason she hadn't seen him the last few hours was that he'd taken a ride. The wind ruffled the ebony strands of his hair and caused him to appear much younger than he was. "Supper is waiting," he informed her.

"I can't eat until I see them."

"You must be the most stubborn woman I've ever known. I told you earlier that Curtis was helping Anne pack before David was released. Cammie told me you've been out here all afternoon when you could have been inside, warm and with a full stomach. And by the way, you need some fattening up. Why can't you be sensible?" He tapped the riding crop against the palm of his hand and Diana flinched, reminded of Kingsley and his assault upon her.

"I'm not a slave or a servant and not under your or any other man's dominion. I won't have you dictate to me!"

"I fail to see where common sense should be regarded as dictatorial."

Diana turned and looked at him, not missing a feature on his face. Tanner had changed a great deal over the past seven years, and not just physically. Something in his bearing and attitude was different. He was no longer the simple man she remembered. His speech was greatly improved, and though he'd appeared confident at Briarhaven when he oversaw the slaves, he now reeked of self-assurance. She saw that his clothes were expensive, fashioned in the latest style, not foppish looking but extremely manly. She couldn't remember meeting a more handsome man, and she knew that any other woman would have willingly melted if he'd smiled at her. But the smiles he'd bestowed upon Diana that day contained little warmth. The hard, angled lines that made up his face never softened, and his eyes never once expressed any tenderness for her.

But why, she asked herself, did she need to experience tenderness from Tanner? The man had tried to use her years ago and now finally he'd succeeded. Still, Tanner intrigued her more at this moment than he had at Briarhaven.

"Are you deciding if you like what you see?" he asked, half sitting on the white balustrade.

Diana flushed, aware that she must have been examining him too closely. She fingered the tassel on her cloak. "I was thinking about how much you've changed. You must admit that you're quite different now."

Tanner inclined his head. "Maybe."

"Well, you are. Tell me, how did you become so wealthy?"

"What makes you think I'm wealthy?"

"Your clothes and the townhouse, of course. A poor man couldn't afford such things. But what interests me is how you made your money and how you are close enough to Lord Rawdon that you can arrange David's release from the hangman's noose—that is, if you can do what you said," she reminded him.

For a split second, Tanner looked quite uncomfortable. He glanced down at the garden and then shrugged when he turned his attention back to her. "Since leaving Briarhaven, I've not been idle, Diana. I've worked hard and made a number of investments that have paid off handsomely."

"What sort of work and investments?"

"You are a curious kitten, but what I've done isn't your concern. Just know that I have plenty of funds to keep you in the grand style to which Kingsley allowed you to become accustomed."

Goodness! Tanner made it seem as if she were a fortune huntress who'd married him for his wealth. How dare he imply such a horrible thing when he damned well knew why she agreed to marry him. "Your money isn't my . . ."

"There's Curtis," Tanner broke into her sentence and pointed as a plain dark carriage stopped on the opposite side of the street, allowing them a clear vantage point from their elevated position.

In the fading twilight, Diana watched while

Curtis went to the door and opened it. He spoke to the occupants, and when David and Anne emerged, followed by the three children, something tugged at Diana's heartstrings. They looked rather confused, but all of them were safe.

"I must speak to them," she told Tanner, and turned to run through the french doors. Tanner stalled her with a strong hand on her waist.

"Our agreement was that you see they're safe, not that you speak to them."

"But I have to talk with Anne—"

"No."

"Tanner, please!"

"No."

Before Diana could say anything else, Tanner whistled and Curtis ushered the Richmonds into the carriage and then they were off. The steady clip-clopping of the horses' hooves over the cobblestones was a clear indication that her family was gone. She had no one now. No one but Tanner.

Tears burned her eyes and abject misery shrouded her features when she shrugged off his hold of her. "You're a cruel man, Tanner Sheridan. Anne must wonder about me."

"Anne knows you're safe." His voice sounded as controlled as he looked. Not a flicker of an eyelash betrayed the fact that he might feel remorse for not allowing her to bid her sister farewell. "Curtis is transporting them to safety tonight. You need not worry about them any longer. I promise you that no harm shall befall them."

What could she say to that? Tanner had kept his word and had David released from prison, there was no reason not to trust him further. Yet she was alone now, very much alone and at Tanner's mercy. Frustration and anger warred within her, her eyes shooting sparks of fire. "I intend to hold you to that promise, Tanner."

"I have no intention of breaking it."

"Good. I hope you don't since I've lived up to our agreement by marrying you." Diana struggled with the need to berate him but gave up, knowing it wouldn't do any good. "I'm suddenly very tired. Tell Cammie I won't be eating, that I'd appreciate some help in undressing for bed."

Diana swished through the doorway that opened into the bedroom from the piazza. She thought she had closed the doors, but when she began to take off her cloak she found that Tanner was standing inside the room, shutting the door quietly behind him.

"I told you to get Cammie for me."

"Cammie's gone for the evening. I dismissed her."

She was more alone than she thought. "Then I shall undress myself. Good night, Tanner."

Shrugging off her cloak, Diana turned away from him. Her cold fingers began to fiddle clumsily with the hooks on the back of her gown, but she stopped when she sensed that Tanner was still in the room and watching her.

"I'd appreciate some privacy," she told him archly.

"Fine, Diana, but are you prepared to sleep in

your dress? It's plain to see that Hattie still helps you disrobe."

His comment made her feel helpless and useless. "Certainly Hattie helps me to undress. These hooks are quite difficult to manage on one's own, but I'll manage. . . ."

"Here, let me see." Tanner strode forward and threw the riding crop on the bed. He reached out to touch her but Diana pushed his hands away.

"Don't you dare touch me!"

"I was going to help you unfasten your gown."

"I can do it myself," she insisted. "I wish you a good night, just leave me alone."

Tanner drew himself up to his full height of six feet, standing stiffly before her. "This is my room. I have no wish to leave it, and may I remind you that we are married, so you'd better stop being so modest with me. I can assure you that as my wife there will be many instances when I will see you without clothes. So you might as well get out of that hideous garment and come to bed."

Diana watched in dread and embarrassment as Tanner took off his jacket and proceeded to unbutton his shirt. He couldn't mean to demand his husbandly rights tonight. No, not tonight. Not ever as far as she was concerned. She'd married him so the bounder would help her family, and in turn he would claim Briarhaven through her. Well, she'd done everything he wanted, but she'd never be a true wife to him. She'd rather die first than live through such humiliation and pain again.

113

"What are you waiting for?" he asked when he saw that she didn't move.

"I won't . . . let you touch me."

Tanner stood there with his shirt unbuttoned, startled into inactivity by her words. The taut skin on his hard, muscled chest gleamed a deep umber in the candlelight. Diana didn't miss the way his ebony gaze raked over her like hot coals burning her very flesh. "You're my wife," he reminded her. "I have the right."

Diana shook her head. "You forget our bargain. I promised to marry you, nothing was said about . . . this part." Her eyes settled on the bed and then on him. "I'll fight you if you try and force me. I give you my word on that." He made a movement toward her, but Diana backed away. "I *will* fight you, Tanner."

She had no idea how she appeared to him at that moment. With her dark dress shrouding her figure and the way she clutched at the neckline of the ugly creation, she looked small and frightened. And repulsed, an inner voice nagged him. Tanner felt hope die within him at that second. All of his plans, all of the finagling to free Richmond and help Diana's family had been for nothing. She wouldn't come to him on her own and he wouldn't force her. What would be the sense in taking a woman who didn't want him, a woman who loathed him? And Diana should loathe him. He hated himself for the things he'd done in the past, things he couldn't think about without dying a little inside at the memories—some things he could never tell her. But he wanted her regardless of the lie she'd told about him seven years ago. He'd never admit to her just how much he still wanted her and was unable to tell her how much her rejection of him stung.

"You've bested me," Tanner said with a hint of smile. "You're quite correct about the bargain we struck. Nothing was said about your performing a wife's duty. I took that aspect of the marriage for granted. I'm sorry, Diana."

Did she hear Tanner correctly? Was he going to give up so easily without an argument? Though she should have felt relief when he retreated to a seat in the large chair by the fireplace, she couldn't deny she felt slighted. Evidently Tanner didn't desire her at all, and she'd been correct in her original assessment that he wanted Briarhaven and not her. God, how humiliating all of this is! she thought to herself, and was at a loss as to what to do now.

"I need to undress," she stated inanely.

"Go ahead."

"But the hooks, and you're sitting here . . ."

"Come here this instant, you silly wench!" His command caused her to jump, and for whatever reason, whether fear or something else, she found herself waiting in front of him before he turned her roughly around and pulled her down on his lap. "Don't even think of wriggling away until I get these damned hooks undone," he demanded, his hot breath wafting across her naked back, which wasn't concealed by the thin chemise she wore. When he'd finished with the dress he surprised her by holding her head in place and pulling the pins from the knot at her neckline. Her heavy dark tresses fell into the palms of his hands. A tiny surge of shock coursed through her as his fingers stroked and settled the silken curls into place at her waistline.

"Diana." His voice sounded thick and husky. "You may get up now."

Standing up, she nearly stumbled toward the bed, very much aware of how the warmth of Tanner's body still clung to her backside. She faced him, all too conscious that her cheeks were flushed from the intimate way he'd attended her. "I can manage on my own," she said stiffly, believing that Tanner would be on his way. She needed time to think about all that had happened to her today, to drive away the feel of his fingers on her flesh, in her hair. But Tanner only lifted an eyebrow.

"I'm quite content here and won't leave my own room so you can ready for bed, if that's what you're implying, my sweet."

"Well, you can't stay here and watch me undress. It isn't proper."

"We're married, Diana, remember."

"But our bargain . . ."

"Our bargain was that you agree to marry me, and I told you that you bested me and I won't demand my husbandly rights. However," his black eyes danced with amber sparks of devilment, "I don't think our bargain would be broken if I watch you undress, do you?"

"I won't!"

Tanner considered her and indolently tapped

the crop upon his knee. "I think you'll do as I say, Diana. Curtis isn't too far away for me to stop him from his destination."

His threat was clear, and it caused Diana to shudder. "You're blackmailing me again."

"Call it whatever you like, but you will step out of that horrid gown you're so valiantly clutching to your breasts, and I'll watch while you do so. It was no small feat for me to convince Rawdon to release your sister's husband. Rawdon wasn't receptive to the idea at all, but I convinced him." Tanner leaned forward, the strength of his massive shoulders not to be denied, and the clenching of his jaw an indication that he'd brook no further outbursts of temper from her. "I'm eager to see what I bought in exchange for obtaining Richmond's freedom."

God, he was a merciless cad, and the words to deny him nearly slipped past her lips. But he leaned back and tapped the crop in the palm of his hand, almost if he were waiting for her to refuse. Diana stared hypnotically at the beastly thing, so thin and seemingly harmless, but so very damaging when applied to tender flesh. Even now, after more than a year, the faint scars on her back seared like pinpoints of fire. She'd never be able to survive another such attack as the one by Kingsley. A quivering coward, that's what she was, unable to tear her gaze from the fearsome, black instrument.

She didn't look at the man who held the crop as she pulled off her dress, allowing it to fall in a dark puddle around her feet. Her white chemise hugged what little curves she possessed, the material so thin from constant wear that it was nearly transparent, but it was a buffer of security between herself and Tanner's lecherous intentions. Until he ordered her to remove it . . .

She trembled like a frightened doe before Tanner. She, Diana Sheridan, the silly twit who bravely passed information to the Swamp Fox about the British, was letting this man rule her and force her to undress before him because she feared a riding crop. But she was afraid, more afraid than she'd ever been of being captured on her nightly sojourns into the swamps. She'd always been a bit scared of Tanner's strength, the power over the slaves that forced them to obey him and not Kingsley. At that moment she was little better than a slave ordered by the master to strip for him. And she stripped down to nothing because he held the crop.

"Look at me, Diana!"

Hearing his raised voice, she jumped and did as she was bid, knowing the crop's position every second.

"I assure you I won't bite you, so stop being so nervous and skittish."

"Can I dress?" she asked in a breathy voice, eager to cover herself now that she'd done what he wanted.

"I haven't looked my full yet."

Stifling a groan, Diana wasn't able to halt the consuming blush that colored her body in rose-petal splotches when he gestured her to come closer. The crop dangled along the side of the chair. Tanner seemed to have forgotten it; she hoped he had, because his frank appraisal of her body was about all she could handle at that moment.

"You're much too thin," he noted, "but with Cammie's good cooking, you'll soon fill out." He leaned back in the chair, perusing her as thoroughly as an artist deciding on his subject, missing nothing.

Let him look, Diana decided. He couldn't touch her intimately, he'd promised her that. That knowledge made her a bit smug. But seconds later she realized she'd underestimated Tanner— again. As the crop rose toward her fear paralyzed her to such a degree that she was unable to move or speak, certain he would beat her. The memory of her on her knees before Kingsley flashed through her mind, her own pitiful begging words resounded in her ears. She must fight this time, she must win, but she steeled herself for the assault.

Expecting wracking pain, Diana was more than startled to find the crop lazily slithering up her calf, past her thigh, stopping at her waist to hover in the slight indentation. She willed herself neither to look at Tanner or to move, even when the tip began a slow ascent to the rounded mounds of her breasts, circling them with a lover's touch and gently lapping at the rosebud nipples like a velvet tongue.

Something deep, dark, and wicked stirred within her, and she helplessly lifted her eyes to find an equal amount of darkness and wickedness reflected on Tanner's face.

"You promised . . . not to . . . touch me," she whispered.

Tanner smiled, and a strange feeling clutched at her, bringing an ache to her lower body that she hadn't felt since the night he tried to have his way with her. "I'm not touching you. The crop is," he contended.

Still, it was as if he had touched her and filled her with this fire and wanton longing for something she'd never known. This was wrong, *wrong!* her mind screamed at her. Why wasn't she frightened of the damned crop any longer? Why did she suddenly, almost pervertedly, crave the sensual movement of the blasted tip across her body? The very instrument of her torture was now causing a melting feeling in the center of her womanhood, and all because Tanner wielded it. She'd never experienced this sensation when Kingsley had touched her. Why with Tanner? Why did she suddenly wish he'd use his fingers? Why did she see Tanner as naked as she, the two of them falling to the rug before the fireplace, their bodies entwined?

"Stop it!" Diana demanded of him and of her own daydreams, fearing he'd hurt her again. "You've looked your fill for one night and I've done my duty by you. I'm getting ready for bed."

How authoritative she sounded! How far from the way she felt! But she slipped hurriedly into the nightgown that Cammie must have left on the bed earlier that evening and dove beneath the bed covers to pull the quilts up to her neck.

120

"Madam, your modesty overwhelms me."

He was making sport of her, but she didn't care. Let him say whatever he chose. Words hurt far less than a physical beating or her own body's betrayal by the very object she'd come to abhor.

"Thank you, sir," she mocked his tone of voice. "At least I take no delight in perversion."

She saw him lift an eyebrow before bending over her. His arms locked on either side of her. "Perverse, am I? Well, my darling wife, I'm not the one who turned to a mass of quivering flesh at the touch of a riding crop. In the future you'd do well to curb your perverse responses, otherwise a man might believe you're used to such odd pleasuring."

"I detest you! Get out of my room."

"Our room, dearest," he reminded her.

Clutching the quilt tightly about her, Diana sensed he was leaving when he stood up and straightened the snow white cravat at his neck and dusted off a speck of dust on the black velvet jacket with a casual flick of his hand. He shot her a smile that might have melted her heart once long ago, if she'd been able to trust him.

"I'm going out for a while, but I'll return later, never fear. Since you seem so fond of it, I'll leave the riding crop with you. Perhaps you can put it to good use." Tanner winked at her and laughed at the venomous look she threw his way when he placed the crop on the bed beside her.

Hot anger boiled through her, but she wasn't allowed the chance to say anything, for at that moment he abruptly vacated the room. His deep, booming laugh echoed from downstairs, but the slamming of the front door sounded less than amusing.

"I tell you, lads, she couldn't get enough of me. Every minute she had her hands on me and in a place I daren't mention, either."

"Aw, Captain Farnsworth," the tavern keeper skeptically commented. "I remember the lady's father and seeing the two of them on the street together, too. A more respectable girl I'd never seen."

"I assure you she isn't that way any longer, is she, Smythe?" Farnsworth nudged the man sitting next to him, causing ale to spill onto the sleeve of Smythe's uniform. "Tell Mr. Dinwoody what I said is true."

Smythe hid his scowl and wiped the stain away, but he lowered his head and mumbled into his cup. "What the captain says is true."

Farnsworth grinned, his complacency all too apparent to Tanner, who sat across the taproom from him.

Motioning to the serving girl, Tanner had her refill his own cup. He'd arrived at the pink-colored tavern on Chalmers Street two hours ago. Smoke and the smell of spirits permeated the room, as did the loud guffaws coming from Farnsworth's table. Whoever the woman was that Farnsworth bragged about must be a hot-blooded wench, and Tanner was envious. He'd had his share of women over the years, but the last few months he hadn't touched one, somehow unable to imagine being with any woman other than Diana.

"What a simpleton I am," he muttered and quaffed the ale in one gulp.

His attention was diverted once more to Farnsworth. The man stood up and suddenly spied Tanner sitting at a corner table. Drunkenly swaggering over to him, Farnsworth held out his hand, which Tanner summarily shook.

"Goodness, Mariah, it's been ages since I last saw you. New York, wasn't it? Two years ago?"

Tanner nodded and motioned for him to sit down. "I'd appreciate it if you wouldn't refer to me by that name," Tanner informed him none too pleasantly. "I'm not Mariah any longer. I gave up my . . . work . . . a few months ago."

"Certainly, man. I understand." Farnsworth lowered his voice. "What shall I call you? I never did know your true name? In your sort of work, well, I can understand your reason for anonymity."

What was it about Farnsworth's impeccable manners and good breeding that constantly irritated him? Even in New York, where he'd report to Farnsworth if General Clinton wasn't available, he found the man aggravating and false. Then again, perhaps he wasn't the one to judge whether Farnsworth was false or not. Over the last seven years he'd played many people for fools and been less than honest. In fact, he'd been a traitor to his own people. A British spy—a man who willingly had turned in many a patriot for gold and now was reaping the rewards of that deviousness by buying the Sheridan townhouse, claiming Briarhaven, and forcing Diana to marry him. God, he was richer than he'd ever dreamed of being, but he felt poorer than the lowliest beggar.

Now he was retired from the spy game, and game it was, too. He had loved outmaneuvering his opponents in a match that was risky and deadly but always exciting. Rawdon knew about him and so did Farnsworth. Tanner could trust Rawdon to keep silent about his past. He wasn't certain about Farnsworth.

"I hope you do and that you understand the implications," Tanner stated in a doleful tone that caused Farnsworth's ears to perk up and a serious look to shadow his face. "My name is Tanner Sheridan. As far as I'm concerned, Mariah is dead."

Farnsworth nodded a bit too quickly, but he grew pensive. "You can't be a relative of the Sheridans at Briarhaven plantation."

"Not as far as I'm concerned."

Farnsworth didn't catch the hidden meaning in Tanner's words but went heedlessly on. "I commandeered Briarhaven for my headquarters months ago. In fact I recently escorted Diana Sheridan to her sister's home. Funny about that, however, because Mrs. Sheridan seems to have disappeared along with her sister."

"Really?"

Farnsworth smirked and nudged Tanner with an elbow. "I'd like to find Mrs. Sheridan. Diana.

I was telling the boys about her. A lusty widow, and a finer piece of womanhood you won't find in all of South Carolina."

Tanner saw red at that second, growing suddenly and sickeningly aware that the woman Farnsworth had bragged about to his men was Diana. His Diana had lain with his man, had allowed him to touch her, to make love to her. He couldn't believe it, but then again what could Tanner expect? Diana had been widowed for nearly a year when Farnsworth arrived, just ripe for the plucking. But she hadn't wanted Tanner Sheridan's touch. In fact, she'd been revolted by him. He'd waited years to accumulate the money to impress her, to arrive in triumph, and God only knew the horrible deeds that soiled his hands. But he'd done it for her, no matter the lie she'd told his father. He still wanted her. And this mincing, prancing bastard who smiled like an imbecile and mouthed off about what an insatiable wanton was Diana Sheridan had had her.

Life wasn't fair!

With powerful hands, Tanner clamped Farnsworth around the collar and lifted him bodily from the chair. The man's feet dangled precariously above the floor and his face turned the same shade as his uniform from his wind being suddenly cut off.

"Nooooo," was all Farnsworth could utter.

"Ever mention Diana Sheridan to any of your friends again and I'll seek you out and kill you. Understand?" Tanner shook Farnsworth like a rag doll, so overcome with jealousy that his strength was far superior to the other man's.

Farnsworth tried to nod but choked. Tanner dropped him into the chair, but Farnsworth tottered and fell onto the stone floor, gasping for breath.

The men who'd been with Farnsworth earlier crowded around at the commotion. All stood dumbly by as Tanner pushed his way to the door. Turning he issued a warning. "And none of you better bandy her name about again or you'll deal with me. No man speaks about my wife in such a manner and lives." Then, like the black wind for which he was named, he disappeared.

Diana was asleep when Tanner returned to the townhouse. With her dark hair spilling across the snowy white pillow and the pristine gown with ruffles at her neck, he found it difficult to believe she'd slept with Farnsworth. She looked like an angel in his bed. Yet he knew better than anyone that looks could be deceiving. He'd played enough roles as spy to know that.

Tiredness assailed him, and he undressed by the candle's glow. Just as he started to slip into bed beside her, he stiffened at the long black object he spotted beneath the chest of drawers. Peering at it, he discovered it was the riding crop, not the serpent he'd originally thought.

How had it gotten under the chest? It was almost as if it were deliberately hidden. His gaze riveted upon Diana, and he knew that she'd placed it there. But why?

He pushed it back where he'd found it, entirely out of sight and then climbed into bed. He settled beside her, aching to hold this wanton witch who'd filled his dreams the last seven years but resisting the urge. Instead he watched her while she slept, familiarizing himself with her profile, the rise and fall of her breathing, counting how many times she sighed or changed position.

He wanted to learn everything about her, his obsession.

# Chapter 7

Diana snuggled deeper into the warmth of Tanner's body, totally unaware that sometime during the night she'd sought him. It wasn't until her lips brushed against skin that she opened her eyes to find herself wantonly pressed against his naked chest.

"Oh!" she gave a startled moan, her horror at the situation deepening when she tried to sit up but found that her gown had risen nearly to her waist and that her bare legs were entwined with his. What was more humiliating was her discovery that Tanner was awake and smiling in amusement.

"Sleep well?" he asked.

"I should have known you wouldn't keep your promise to me," she accused. She pushed away to untangle her legs and pull down the nightrail in one motion. Then she leaped from the bed.

"And what promise might that be, Diana? I don't recall breaking any promises."

"You know very well that you said you

wouldn't touch me. You gave me your word like a gentleman, but I shouldn't have believed you. You've never acted gentlemanly with me."

Reclining on his elbow, Tanner wasn't the least bit self-conscious that most of his torso was bared to her gaze, the blanket bunched into a ball beside him from Diana's frantic scrambling. He didn't mind at all if Diana saw him naked, but apparently it meant a great deal to her that she'd been in his arms with her legs wrapped intimately around him. Dammit! he cursed himself, the wench didn't seem the least aroused by any of it, only angry. If anyone should be angry, it should be he. Because of Diana's unexpected nearness he'd been unable to fall asleep. Though he hid his frustration behind a smile, he was grouchy as hell.

"I assure you that you found me. I never touched you, you wrapped yourself around me like a little monkey."

"I would never . . . never think . . . never do anything like that," she said, but then she remembered that one of her legs had been on top of his. Diana's long hair spilled in dark waves around her shoulders and down her back. The sun streaming through the thin curtains on the french doors highlighted the deep auburn, creating an aureole effect. She had no inkling of how beautiful she appeared at that moment, nor did she have any idea that the sun shone through her gown, revealing her body's outline to Tanner, and she certainly had no idea of the physical effect she had on him. "I was sleeping and can't be held accountable," she finished lamely.

Tanner's jaw tensed. He remembered how seven years ago she'd lied to his father and brother that he'd tried to rape her. She was still the same lying creature she was then, not able to take the responsibility for her own actions. "No, you've never wanted to be held accountable for anything."

"Just what does that mean?"

"Nothing, Diana, nothing at all." Tanner slid out of bed, magnificent in his nudity and not the least bit embarrassed by it or by the erection caused from Diana's closeness of minutes ago.

Diana stared at him in spite of herself, unable to believe that any man could resemble a statue of Adonis she'd seen in a museum when she was a child. But Tanner was more ruggedly handsome and thus more appealing to her than the smoothly muscled and perfectly chiseled stone features. In fact, she found Tanner's nose to be slightly crooked and one eye a tad smaller than the other. She thought it was absurd to be thinking about Tanner's facial features when so much more of him was clearly exposed. So much more that wasn't made of stone.

Gulping, her gaze settled on the part of him that sprang hard and erect from the dark bush on his lower torso. She'd thought Kingsley was well endowed, having never known any men with whom she could compare, but now she knew that Kingsley was far from Tanner's equal. She couldn't stop staring at him, and she wondered what it would be like if Tanner did what Kingsley had done to her.

"Diana, stop taking inventory!"

"What?" Tanner's voice startled her and she jumped. She realized then how intently she'd been looking at him and flushed with the knowledge.

"If you wish a sample, I'll be happy to oblige." Tanner went to the wardrobe and waited. "Just say the word, my love, and I'm yours."

"Doesn't your conceit have any bounds? I have no such inclination as far as you're concerned."

"Liar!"

Diana flushed. "I'm not lying." At that moment, she was telling the truth. Tanner's physical endowments frightened her, bringing back all the pain of her marriage to Kingsley. If Kingsley had hurt her each time he claimed her body, then Tanner could very well kill her.

Something dark settled around his face. "Perhaps you find other men to your liking. But I remind you that I'm your husband, and I won't tolerate a wanton wife."

Diana had no idea what this veiled comment had to do with her. She only knew that Tanner had a way of pricking at her calm and composed surface and exposing emotions she didn't want to deal with. In fact, she didn't know how to deal with emotions any longer. Since she'd married Kingsley she had closed herself off from happiness and pleasure, having no idea that marriage could offer her both. In her mind she associated marriage with pain, and a husband with the source of the pain.

"I don't care what you do at all," was the shrewish retort she hurled at him. Bending down, she scooped up her black gown from the floor and started to walk to the bathing room.

Tanner stood before her and grabbed her wrist. "What are you doing?"

"Getting dressed, do you mind?"

"Not in that rag, you're not."

Silver and gold sparkles crystalized and flared within the depths of her sapphire eyes. "I shall wear whatever I choose, Tanner. I'm in mourning for my dead husband."

"I'm your husband now!"

Before Diana could utter another sound, Tanner wrenched the gown from her grasp and before her startled eyes rent it in two.

"You've ruined my dress," she stormed at him. "I haven't anything to wear now."

Flinging open the wardrobe doors, Tanner pointed to the row of gowns, more dazzling in their varied colors than gemstones. "Wear one of these."

"I'd rather wear a sack than something you've provided for me."

Diana flinched when he moved dangerously close to her, like a panther who has sought his prey and is now ready for the kill. "Wear the damned bedsheet for all I care." His voice sounded like a tiger's low growl. "But you're never going to wear black again to honor my brother, because if you do I'll tear the dress from your very back."

Tanner stalked away from her and in one movement he lunged for a pair of breeches, a shirt, and his boots before leaving her alone. The slamming of the bedroom door only increased her ire at him, and though she knew she should be frightened by his display of temper and displeasure, she wasn't. With Kingsley, in a like situation, she'd have buckled at the knees. However this was Tanner, and by all accounts she should be trembling and quaking with fear. She knew he was quite capable of tearing the gown from her body, and would probably do it, too, if he had the mind.

Yet suddenly Tanner didn't scare her. She remembered his gentleness with Briarhaven's slaves and achingly recalled how he'd tenderly held her in his arms when he'd claimed her for a dance on the bluff all those years ago. The same ebony pair of eyes that had gleamed with tenderness then had also glinted with black anger. Diana felt he mistrusted her, disliked her, and didn't desire her at all. How wrong she had been! Maybe he did marry her to seek his revenge upon the Sheridans by claiming Briarhaven, but no matter how he felt about her, a man's body didn't lie.

The excited shiver slipping up her spine at the memory of that was nearly her undoing. *Tanner wanted her.*

"I won't think about him at all," she decided and set her mouth in a thin little line. Tanner's physical attributes or sexual prowess weren't her concern. She married him to save David and to help Anne and the children, that was all. Nothing intimate would ever happen between her and Tanner.

Men were animals anyway, eager for any available woman. Something told Diana that many women had probably availed themselves of her new husband over the years, but that wasn't her concern. The small jab of jealousy she felt meant absolutely nothing. She'd never be Tanner's wife in the truest sense of the word, not that part of her didn't find him attractive. She did, and she might as well admit it to herself. Kingsley had been attractive too, but what he'd done to her had sickened her. She had had enough of the pain and the disgust to last her a lifetime. No, Tanner would never have her, and he'd do well to convince his body of that fact.

Glancing down at the black dress still on the floor, Diana felt a perverted sense of relief gush through her. She wouldn't have to pretend to mourn Kingsley any longer. For the first time in a year, Kingsley was truly dead to her and Tanner's very destruction of the gown had done it. She didn't have to play the proper widow for him or anyone else.

The opened wardrobe beckoned to her with its finery. Deciding that she couldn't wear a bedsheet, Diana availed herself of the clothes Tanner had provided for her.

Diana ate a hearty breakfast for the first time since the British occupation, having cream and sugar for her tea, and bacon with a delicious omelet prepared by Cammie. Tanner was already gone, and Diana squelched the bit of disappointment she felt. His very presence overpowered the rooms of the house, and she missed his hugeness, the baritone voice that seemed to fill every niche. But there was no need to care whether Tanner was home or not, she convinced herself, and allowed her tongue to linger on the sweet taste of her tea. Their marriage was a simple arrangement.

"You look very pretty," Cammie said, complimenting Diana's choice of an emerald green gown. A red bow pulled up Diana's dark tresses, which fell in curly ringlets past her shoulders. "Mr. Tanner has excellent taste in clothes."

"Did he really choose these gowns for me or were they for other women?" Diana didn't know why she asked this question. Cammie stopped clearing the table and looked puzzled.

"What do you mean, Mrs. Sheridan?"

"I mean Tanner—Mr. Sheridan—must surely have many lady friends, women he has brought here, and the gowns may have been used by them." There, she'd said it! Now she'd learn the truth and shout triumphantly at Tanner that she knew he hadn't bought any of the clothes expressly for her. She needn't feel this urge to be beholden to him or to soften her feelings for him or even miss him when he wasn't there.

"Oh, no, ma'am. Mr. Tanner made a list of colors and fabrics that would suit your complexion and hair. He even had a gown made to match your eyes. Didn't you see it?"

"Yes, I saw it." Diana recalled the sapphire blue gown in the wardrobe. It was velvet with small slivers of crystals entwined with gold braid.

Cammie smiled and picked up Diana's plate. "I

remember he said that your eyes had more gold than silver speckles in them, but when you laughed the silver ones up and multiplied, causing your whole face to glow like the sun on a warm afternoon or the moon on a cloudless night. That Mr. Tanner can be real poetic when he takes a mind to it."

Diana couldn't think of anything else to say at that point. Cammie's comment had put her in her place. She felt utterly wretched for misjudging him, for believing that he was foisting off another woman's clothes upon her. But what else could she believe? All men had other women besides their wives. Kingsley had had Jarla, throwing up the slave girl's fertility in her face so often that she'd come to believe she was less than a woman. And he'd gone into Charlestown on numerous occasions, always letting her know that he'd spent the night at some sort of a brothel, going so far as to taunt her with what the whores had done to him, then forcing her to do the same to him.

Just thinking about some of the horrible things she'd been forced to do to Kingsley caused her stomach to feel queasy. "Act like my whore, Diana." She could hear his voice in her ear still, almost imagine she felt his breath upon her neck, his fingers on her shoulder.

"Diana?"

"Oh!" She twisted around in shock to realize that someone was whispering in her ear and fingers were on her bare shoulder. Expecting to see a ghostly apparition of Kingsley, she saw a very healthy looking Tanner. "You startled me!"

she accused.

"It seems I'm always frightening you. I've never seen anyone jump the way you do." Tanner sat in the chair nearest to her. "What are you thinking about so hard?"

She had no idea how pale and distraught she appeared from her humiliating memories. "I was thinking about Kingsley," she said sadly.

Tanner examined his well-manicured nails. "Yes, of course."

"Have you eaten?" she asked, needing to change the subject. "Cammie fixed a most appetizing breakfast."

"I ate before I saw General Lord Rawdon. I'm glad you liked the food."

Diana raised an eyebrow. Rawdon again. "I was quite happy to taste tea with real sugar and to have pork. At Briarhaven, we've been living on what we stored over a year ago, but all of the animals were slaughtered by Farnsworth and his men and eaten. Sometimes a British supply wagon does get through and Captain Farnsworth shares his rations with us."

"I'm certain you repaid him for his kindnesses to you."

The remark went over Diana's head. "Oh, yes, Harlan and I made certain Farnsworth and his officers were welcome." She tried to hide the blush that stole across her face when she recalled how Farnsworth and his men *were* repaid. She wondered what Tanner would say if he knew their small kindnesses had resulted in her relaying information about British activities to the Swamp

Fox. After all, it seemed Tanner was quite chummy with Lord Rawdon. Only someone well connected could obtain the release of a condemned man, purchase a piece of confiscated property, and have food that other people would kill for, not to mention the expensive and elaborate gowns in the wardrobe. "Captain Farnsworth has been most accommodating."

Tanner scowled blackly, picked up the silver teapot on the table, and filled a cup, foregoing the sugar and cream, and took a large sip. Diana could tell something was bothering him, but since Tanner didn't see the need to tell her what it might be, she ignored his dark look.

"Would you care to know how your father fares?"

Holding the small china cup in his huge hand, he hesitated for the fraction of a second before placing it on the matching saucer. "I doubt he cares how *I* am."

Diana shrugged a milky white shoulder. "He may care more than you believe, but Harlan hasn't been well. His heart is weak."

Did the bronze of Tanner's complexion pale a shade? She thought it did, but when he spoke he sounded quite uncaring. "My father is a basically weak man."

"You're being very unfair to him. Harlan is a strong-willed individual. I don't know why you persist in . . ."

Tanner held up a warning hand. "Let's not argue about my father, Diana. It will only lead to what happened between you and me that night on

138

the bluff. I doubt you want to remember any of that again."

This time she blushed furiously. If only he knew how many times she went over that night, how often she had wanted to feel that same way again. But she saw that Tanner didn't seem the least bit disturbed by the memory or anxious to speak about how he'd ruined her life with his touch, his melting kisses, and the lie of loving her. Well, she too could be nonchalant about the whole disgraceful episode. Shaking her head, she gave a lilting laugh. "I was so young and silly then—so inexperienced." Where had that come from?

His eyes darkened to the color of pitch, but a tiny flame of amber leaped into them. Tanner bent forward until he was so close that the top of his dark head touched hers. She caught the unmistakable masculine scent of him, enveloping her in such a torrent of warring emotions that she grew dizzy and warm. His lips were but inches from hers, and her eyes traced the contours of his sensual mouth. Was he going to kiss her? Did she want him to kiss her? Dear God, she nearly choked on her breath. She did!

"Perhaps I shall benefit from your experience," she heard him say. "I suspected you were a whore at heart."

Tanner rose quickly to his feet, nearly pushing over the Queen Anne styled chair in his haste to leave the room. Diana felt as if the wind had been knocked from her body. It took a few seconds for her to regain her breath and her tongue. She screamed at his departing back. "I detest you, Tanner Sheridan! I'll hate you for ever and always!"

He stopped in the doorway and turned around. When he did so, his gaze seemed to strip her of her gown. Out of nowhere she realized that she'd dressed to please him and that he hadn't said a word about how she looked. "That's quite a long time to hate someone, my dear, but I've had a head start on you." Spinning on his heels, he left. The door slamming behind him told her that he had gone.

"I wish you'd stop slamming the door whenever you take your leave!" she shouted at the air. "I wish just once you'd stay and finish a fight and not run away."

But Tanner hadn't heard her. Diana sank into her chair and refused to believe that the dampness on her cheeks was tears.

# Chapter 8

Diana stood on the dock that ran the distance from the bay to the offices and warehouses on Vendue Range. She had no idea why she'd come here and now was sorry that she had. She sniffed from the combination of the cold and her sorrow when she saw the condition of the building that had once been her father's brokerage house. Broken panes of glass hung in jagged shards at the windows, and the oaken front door had been kicked in. No doubt vandals had done their dirty work inside, probably destroying the dark paneling in the room that had served as her father's office.

Her father had supplied slaves to the nearby plantations, and it was because of his work that her family had come into contact with the Sheridans, who were always in need of good slaves. She recalled standing on the street with her father beneath one of the wide sheds, waiting for the slaves to take their turns on the auction block, raptly listening to her father's soft, well-modulated tones as he explained why a certain slave would fetch a huge price and another wouldn't. At the time, Diana hadn't thought too much about how those poor people must feel, how traumatic it must be for them to be spirited away from their homes and families along the Madagascar coast and transported thousands of miles to South Carolina, and to lose their freedom in the process.

Well, she possessed some inkling about how they felt now.

She wasn't a slave, but she had lost her newfound independence by being forced to wed Tanner. No longer could she come and go as she liked without reporting to him. And the arrogant man had the nerve to prohibit her from strolling by herself. "Too dangerous to be out alone, Diana," he had cautioned whenever she mentioned leaving the house. So Curtis was enlisted to bring the carriage around and take her wherever she wanted to go. Diana guessed Curtis always told him where that was.

The cold wind stung her eyes and she returned to the carriage. "Where to, ma'am?" Curtis inquired kindly.

Diana wasn't certain. She didn't know too many people in Charlestown any longer, and she hesitated going back to the townhouse. Tanner was gone so often. Not that she cared, but the time seemed to drag without someone to talk to or fight with. Suddenly she remembered Marisa Delaune, her young cousin who she hadn't seen since before Kingsley joined the army. Marisa's mother, Frances, was Diana's mother's only sister. She'd been remiss in visiting them, but with all of the commotion concerning David and Anne and Tanner, she hadn't given the Delaunes a thought. She gave Curtis her aunt's address and smiled to think what an enjoyable afternoon she'd pass with her aunt and cousin.

Marisa was more lovely and sweet than Diana remembered, immediately embracing her when a servant announced her presence. "It's been much too long since we've seen one another," Marisa gushed. "You've been secluded on that plantation and I've been here in town with mama. You must join us for dinner. Please say you will, Diana."

Diana laughed. "I'd love to stay, but I notice that you have guests." Strains of animated conversation drifted from the parlor into the foyer where they stood.

Marisa wrinkled her nose in distaste. "Lady Gabriella Fox is staying with us over the holidays while her husband is fighting for the British. You remember her, don't you?"

Clutching her muff, Diana nodded. How could she forget Gabriella Fox? The woman's insatiable carnal appetite had been thrown up to her by Kingsley more than once. Gabriella, it had been rumored, would have married Kingsley except that he'd decided he wanted Diana as his wife. Marrying a wealthy man shortly after Kingsley married Diana hadn't stopped her from seeking out Kingsley every time she and Fox attended a ball at Briarhaven. Whenever Gabriella was in residence, Kingsley never bothered Diana. Diana had decided this was fine with her, but each time Kingsley returned to her bed, he'd tell her what he and Gabriella had done and what a ninny she'd married. Then he would comment on the lush fullness of Gabriella's breasts, her voluptuous body and perfect tongue, which knew how to drive a man to ecstasy.

Diana hated Gabriella Fox, not for those stolen minutes with Kingsley but for the hours afterward when she had to emulate Gabriella's performance.

"I'll visit with you and Aunt Frances another time," Diana said.

"Indeed not! I won't have you leaving because of that—that—trollop. You're family, and besides, all of the guests are acquaintances . . ." Marisa's voice dripped with sarcasm, ". . . of Gabriella's and will soon depart. They were invited just for tea. Come into the parlor and greet mother, Diana. She'll be thrilled to see you again."

Following her dark-haired cousin, Diana saw that Marisa, who was five years younger than she, had grown into a beautiful young woman.

They entered the parlor and Diana immediately saw her aunt sitting on the divan. Laughing and talking at once, the two embraced, oblivious of the men who gathered round a sloe-eyed Gabriella. "It's been so long," Frances told Diana as she patted her niece's hand maternally. "What are you doing in Charlestown, dear? Do you plan to stay for awhile?"

Diana hesitated, not certain whether she should

tell Frances and Marisa about her marriage. She decided not to say anything for the present. There were too many people in the room. Instead she gave a slight smile. "I don't know how long my stay shall be." This was true. Tanner might send her packing to Briarhaven if he decided he wasn't pleased with his new wife. Oh, she hoped so!

Diana wore a lilac day dress, trimmed in green at the tight-fitting waist and long sleeves. She felt dowdy and plain when Gabriella, who wore a stunning gold silk gown, excused herself from a British officer and walked over to where Diana sat. The vibrant gold matched her hair, and her ruby red lips formed into a parody of a smile before dutifully pecking Diana's cheek.

"Diana, darling, how nice to see you've reentered the world of the living for the moment and left Briarhaven. But such a little homebody as yourself must be incredibly lost here in Charlestown. Your little heart must flutter from sheer anguish to be so far from the cows and pigs."

Diana pasted an equally false smile on her own face. "I assure you, Gabriella, dear, that I can handle it."

Gabriella opened her Chinese fan, her movements hasty and stiff. She slyly narrowed her eyes. "If I recall, you had a difficult time in handling, let's say, the hard part of something."

*What a horrible, uncouth woman,* Diana thought, struck by Gabriella's audaciousness. A sick feeling clutched at Diana's stomach at she grasped the true meaning behind Gabriella's words. Frances and Marisa both wore puzzled

145

expressions, but Diana knew that Kingsley must have confided to his erstwhile lover about her lack of response in bed. She swallowed her dismay, not bothering to give Gabriella the satisfaction of a response.

Gabriella fluttered her fan, a gleam of triumph in her eyes. "Oh, by the way, Diana, I must congratulate you on your marriage. Everyone is talking about the suddenness of it."

"Marriage?" Frances and her daughter repeated at once.

"Yes," Diana admitted, not able to hide the flush from her face. "I was married last week to Tanner Sheridan."

"I always say it's best to keep things in the family," Gabriella continued with a wicked grin. "And, Diana, I shall be certain to tell Tanner when I meet him for an intimate, late-night supper tonight that I saw you today—and that you look well. Adieu, dear." With that, Gabriella swept away to join the enclave of her fawning admirers.

"Diana, you should have told us about your marriage," Frances whispered. "Aren't you happy about it?"

"Certainly, I'm happy." It was a lie, but there was no reason to distress her family. She attempted to smile but failed, feeling wretchedly chilled to know that Tanner was acquainted with Gabriella Fox.

"But the awful thing that Gabriella said about a late-night supper with your husband . . ." Marisa broke off at the chastising look Frances threw her way.

"I don't believe a word of it," protested Diana. "Gabriella's lying and wants to upset me." And she had.

"More brandy, darling?"

Tanner looked up from where he lounged on the elaborately carved settee in General Lord Rawdon's private chambers. Gabriella stood over him, holding a crystal decanter filled with brandy and smiling enticingly. Her voluptuous, pale flesh beneath a pink bit of fluff and lace was enticing too, and left very little to Tanner's fertile imagination. His loins fired at Gabriella's blatant sensuality. It had been months since he'd been with a woman, the last time having been in New York when he'd walked out on a beguiling female spy named Annabelle who'd turned out to be conniving and heartless. But the half-clad beauty before him wasn't particularly heartless or conniving, or for the most part, anything special. She was beautiful and eager for him, a potent aphrodisiac for a man who was married to a woman who couldn't bear the sight of him.

Holding out his empty glass to her, Tanner watched Gabriella refill it. She placed the decanter on a small round table beside him, her movement causing the heady scent of her perfume to waft over him as she sat down next to him. Pressing close, she artfully arranged herself in a pose that Tanner guessed was meant to arouse him with the view of her lovely exposed thigh. Shrugging, she allowed the gown to fall from her shoulders and reveal the milky white swell of her breasts. Tanner smiled at the contrivance but he didn't mind. He liked the fact that a beautiful woman wanted to seduce him.

Gabriella batted her long, golden-tinged lashes at him and whispered huskily, "Do you have everything you need?"

"Yes." His answer was abrupt even to his own ears. He did not care for the sudden image he had of a dark-haired temptress in Gabriella's place and he tried to drive it away.

Gabriella didn't seem to notice as she planted warm kisses on the part of his chest revealed by his open shirt. "You're certain that Rawdon won't return tonight, Tanner?"

"He's in Camden, so no one will bother us."

"How accomodating of him." Gabriella made a purring sound and swirled her tongue in lazy circles on the taut expanse of bronzed flesh. Pushing aside Tanner's linen shirt, her hands trailed wantonly in the wake of her tongue. "You're so handsome and strong, Tanner," she whispered hotly against him. "I want you, ache for you. Do you remember how it was between us years ago, that spring night I attended the ball at Briarhaven?"

Tanner closed his eyes and moaned. He really didn't remember too well. Apparently it was during a ball or some festive ocassion when Gabriella had snuck away from the main house to join him in a tryst, one of the many ladies who sought out Harlan Sheridan's bastard son for pleasure. He grunted his response because at the moment it felt wonderful to be touched and kissed, to feel a woman's soft body against him, to ignite beneath fiery fingers. He was in a rapturous void, growing harder and larger as Gabriella's practiced hands opened his breeches to stroke the hot length of him. Grabbing a thick handful of Gabriella's hair, he imagined the curls were brown . . . and did the unforgivable by moaning aloud another woman's name.

The stroking stilled, the hands instantly departed, and a high-pitched cry reverberated in the room. "You called me your wife's name!" Gabriella instantly rose from the settee and Tanner opened his eyes, his desire waning. The woman who stood so angrily before him certainly wasn't brown-haired and blue-eyed. "How dare you insult me like this," she ended on a high note.

"Did I? Forgive me." Tanner sheepishly sat up and began to button his shirt, suddenly weary and wanting to go home. To what he wasn't certain, for no doubt a cold reception awaited him there, but this late supper was a dreadful mistake. He didn't really like Gabriella, finding her to be too conceited and much too sexually aggressive. Sometimes he liked the woman to take the lead, but this night he'd wanted a more leisurely lovemaking session. This clearly wasn't what Gabriella had in mind, but he was expert enough to know that he would eventually have taken control and slowed the pace, allowing both of them to enjoy each other's body. No matter now, he'd spoiled everything by calling Diana's name. He felt unnerved to know that he couldn't put Diana's face and form from his mind when another woman pleasured him. What *was* happening to him?

Gabriella paced, the gown swirling around her. "I've never been so insulted in my life. And to think I gave up an evening with a British major. Well, no more bedazzled married men for me." She twisted around and faced him. "What do you see in such a mousy woman? I never understood why Kingsley married her or how he endured bedding such a frigid bitch all of those years. He told me she hated lovemaking and acted like she was doing him a favor by opening her legs for him. All she ever did was lie there like a martyr, thrown to the lions."

Tanner finished pulling on his boots, his discomfiture vanishing. "Kingsley told you that about Diana?"

"I certainly didn't make it up. 'Detested the entire act' were his very words. Really, I'm at a loss . . ."

"Don't fret over it, Gabriella," Tanner snapped as he grabbed his jacket. "Why don't you send for your major? It's a pity to waste such lavish accomodations."

"I'll do that!" she shouted, and he had no doubts that she would.


The clock in the foyer chimed twelve times. Diana had been in the tub for over an hour, not aware that the time had passed so quickly. She'd arrived home earlier after spending a nice time with Frances and Marisa catching up on family gossip. When the three of them sat down to dinner, Diana's happy mood fled. Gabriella appeared to wish them a festive holiday. The smiling harpy told Diana she'd be passing a wonderful time with Tanner and that Diana shouldn't wait up for his return home.

"Disgusting tart!" Diana muttered and venomously plopped her washrag into the cool tub water in an attempt to drive the sordid image of Tanner and Gabriella from her mind. What must they be doing at that moment? she wondered, and detested herself for even thinking about them, for caring what Tanner did and with whom he did it. She didn't care, didn't care at all, she reminded herself. She was Tanner's wife in name only, nothing else. She must stop thinking about Tanner and Gabriella, so she started to hum a silly tune her father had taught her years ago.

At last the water grew chilly and her flesh started to pucker. The candle had burned down to a nub. Diana hesitated ringing for Cammie, whom she had dismissed for the night. She could very well tend to herself, and she'd wished to take a leisurely bath without interruption from anyone, especially Tanner. Tonight was perfect for a long soak because the bounder wouldn't be home at all. Gabriella had made that fact so perfectly clear that Diana grimaced as she reached for the towel and stepped out of the tub to dry off.

When she'd finished she reached for the thin gossamer nightrail that Cammie had placed in the bathing room. Diana had seen her when she brought the creamy colored creation into the room and nearly told her to bring one of the calico nightrails, which modestly covered all of her except for her head, hands, and feet. That was the sort of gown she usually slept in when Tanner shared the bed with her. She didn't want the conceited man to see any extra bit of flesh and get the wrong idea.

But since Tanner wasn't going to be home that night she hadn't said anything. This was one night when it didn't matter if she wore the nightrail. For days it's sheer beauty had beckoned to her from the wardrobe and she'd ached to wear it. Now was her chance.

The gown flowed over her body in shimmering and undulating folds of silk and lace, as transparent as butterfly wings. Diana tied the white bow that rested beneath her breasts, astonished to find that it was the only tie on the gown and that it did very little to stop the front of the gown from parting and revealing her naked body. But a sense of daring filled her, and she silently chastised herself for being silly. No one was there to see her. She was free to wear whatever she liked without fear of Tanner's dark gaze.

Though there wasn't a mirror in the bathing room to examine her reflection, a giggle of approval escaped her. Diana pirouetted, her long dark hair cascading like a velvet waterfall around her shoulders. But when she turned to face the doorway the delighted excitement in her eyes died and her rosy flushed cheeks grew instantly pale.

It was Tanner . . . leaning against the door of the bathing room, dressed in only his boots and breeches. His shirt was gone, and the powerful muscles on his chest resembled golden mounds in the dying candlelight. His thumbs were hitched in the belt loops of his pants. He appeared tall and strong, a massive presence filling the small bathing room. But it was the raw desire she saw in the black pits of his eyes that caused her to falter and clutch at the top of the gown.

"I didn't hear you come in," she mumbled, feeling the heat return to pinken her face.

"Not with all of the humming you were doing."

"Forgive me if I bothered you."

"I wasn't bothered, Diana. Must you always take offense or become defensive with everything I say or do?"

"I hadn't realized I did that. I'm sorry. I shall not try to be so touchy in the future." She sounded cold to her own ears. Very proper, very prim.

Tanner sighed. "There you go again, and don't dare tell me you're sorry."

"Well, if I've disturbed you I am. This is your house, after all." Diana made a move forward but Tanner blocked her passage into the bedroom. She waited, her head barely reaching his shoulders. Her eyes skimmed the planes of his broad chest, fixing on the taut nipples at mouth level. She couldn't stop staring at him, finding him to be the most perfectly handsome man. Her fingers burned to touch him and to discover if he was flesh and blood like other mortals. He looked so much like a statue most of the time.

They stood that way for what seemed like minutes, even if it was only seconds. She could feel his eyes upon her, feel the odd sensation rising in her chest and threatening to strangle her. As he touched her chin and lifted her face to peer into her eyes she let out a tense sigh. "This is your house, too," he reminded her softly, "and I have to tell you that the gown suits you, Diana. You look beautiful. I'm pleased you're availing yourself of the clothes in the wardrobe now."

"Gown?" she repeated, as if in a hypnotic spell.

"Your nightrail. I'm glad you decided to wear it. It shows off your attributes. Dare I hope you wore it to please me?"

*Anything to please you,* her mind seemed to say. But suddenly his words sliced through her brain with the speed of a knife and the spell was broken. The gown! Instantly she pushed past him. Within less than a heartbeat she'd jumped into the bed and had pulled the quilt up to her neck.

Tanner was looking at her with his brows arched over those black eyes, which held little reflection. "What the hell is wrong with you?"

"I'm not decently dressed, you bounder! If you were a gentleman you'd realize that."

"I'm grateful that I'm not. There's no cause to hide yourself away. Why don't you want me to see you? We are married."

*I don't want you to see me because you make me feel strange sensations, things I don't understand.* "Ha!" she cried aloud. "Our marriage is a

154

sham and you well know it."

"It doesn't have to be," he said in such a husky, suggestive voice that her toes curled beneath the covers. "I'm willing to live up to my marital duty if you are."

A primitive sort of yearning coursed through her as she imagined Tanner possessing her body, but possession meant pain to her and she'd never be hurt again by any man, especially Tanner. "How noble of you. Yet I fail to see what living up to that will avail you since you have already snared Briarhaven." It was a shrewish remark and one she hadn't meant to utter but she needed some ammunition. After all, he'd just left Gabriella's bed, and now he intended to plant himself in hers. She wouldn't allow him to use her body for his own gratification. She smiled a bit triumphantly at him to let him know she wasn't a fool, but his reaction surprised her.

Tanner grew very still as he stood beside the bed. Nothing in his face expressed any emotion. At that moment he *did* resemble a museum statue, something made of stone, something so impenetrable that Diana's heart constricted. His gaze never wavered from her face, but for just a fraction of a second she saw a sliver of pain surface within those dark depths. "I could have possessed Briarhaven long ago, Diana. I didn't have to marry you to get it." His large hand circled the bed post and squeezed. "In fact, Briarhaven was saved only because Rawdon knew it was mine. I gather you don't think it odd that Farnsworth came to set up his headquarters there, but I assure you that Briarhaven wasn't his first choice. No, Briarhaven was already mine because I asked Rawdon to make it a present to me. You see, if not for me, you and Harlan would have been cast out on the road and the place set ablaze. But it belonged to me then, as it does now. I didn't need to marry you to possess it."

He said all of this tonelessly and this was more terrifying to her than if he'd declared her an ingrate, an insufferable and silly woman. But she was shocked by his admission, never before having realized the obvious. Tanner had been instrumental in saving Briarhaven and seeing to it that she and Harlan had a roof over their heads, something to call their own, but it wasn't theirs, not really. Briarhaven belonged to Tanner. She could only guess at the amount of influence he must have with Rawdon to arrange David's release, but how much more influence must he have commanded in order for Rawdon to give him a vast plantation that had been designated for destruction.

Who was Tanner Sheridan that he could command such respect from a British general?

"Why did you marry me then?" she asked, refusing to humble herself by declaring herself grateful. "Evidently you coerced me into marriage when you knew all along that Rawdon would grant David's release. Why did you want me? Why? I know very well that you haven't been alone the last hours. When I visited my aunt today I met your paramour and she made it very clear that you wouldn't be home tonight. So I don't understand why you wanted me, why you think you might want me . . . now."

Tanner came closer and bent near to her. Her fingers clutched the bed covers tightly, not knowing what he intended to do. His breath fanned her face and a bronzed finger snaked out and stroked her cheek. "I want what you gave to my bother. I want you rutting beneath me, Diana Sheridan, to know that I own you, now and forever. I'd think you'd understand that."

His words knocked the wind out of her. That strange sensation was back again, turning her legs to jelly though she hated the thought of what he'd just said. *Rutting*. How horrible! He couldn't mean that, could he? What about love? But then again, Kingsley had never loved her, and rutting was just what he'd done. Even so, a naughty shiver of something like excitement caused her to tremble, unwillingly surprising her.

"Ladies don't . . . do that. I never will. Not with you."

"With me you will, Diana. I guarantee you will."

She shook her head in defiant denial, but Tanner ignored her and began to undress. Hurriedly she blew out the candle, and when he settled himself beside her in the large bed, she sensed he was smiling.

# Chapter 9

"Frigid bitch! You're worthless to me in bed and out. You can't even give me a son."

Kingsley loomed over her, a maniacal gleam in his eyes. In his clenched fist he held the riding crop. She lifted a terrified gaze to him, begging him not to hurt her, but she couldn't hear her own words. Instead she felt the blinding pain shoot across her back. A blood-curdling shriek cut through the air. It was her own scream, she knew, knew too that she must escape Kingsley, her tormentor, but her legs, frozen and paralyzed, wouldn't move. *This is a dream!* her mind shouted, but she couldn't wake herself. He was above her, shaking her and hurting her. She knew this time he was going to kill her. . . .

"Diana, wake up!"

It was Tanner's cry that finally wrenched her out of the nightmare and returned her to the reality of a misty dawn. Soft streaks of violet-blue light were creeping into the bedroom when

Diana opened her eyes. From a distance she heard church bells, but Tanner's breathing sounded ragged to her own ears and she whimpered softly from the night terror that still plagued her.

"Are you all right?" she heard him ask in the purple darkness and realized that he was bending over her, his hands holding her arms above her head on the pillow. "You were thrashing about, wild and screaming. I thought you were going to hurt yourself. As it is you gave me quite a wallop on the chin."

"Oh!" Diana gave a great shuddering sigh. "I didn't mean to hurt you. Forgive me, Tanner, it's just that I was dreaming, trying to run, to get away. . . ." Her voice drifted off, and she was aware suddenly that she must sound weak to a man who was always as controlled as Tanner. She doubted he ever had nightmares or that there was any situation with which he couldn't deal. At the moment she felt like a frightened kitten, a weakling who couldn't stop trembling from fear. *But Kingsley's dead,* she reminded herself. *He can't hurt me again.* Yet her body didn't seem to know that and shivers taunted her. "I'm fine now," she lied.

Doubt speckled Tanner's response. "I don't think you are. I tried to wake you but you kept hitting me and shouting 'put it away.' What were you dreaming about, Diana? What are you afraid of?"

"I'm not afraid of anything or anyone," she insisted. "You're making something out of noth-

159

ing. It was just a stupid nightmare and I'm awake now. Your taking control of my life doesn't give you the right to probe into my dreams. I am allowed some privacy, even in sleep."

"God, but you're the most infuriating woman I've ever known! You're lying to me and you know it, but you're too damned proud to share your fears with me. At this very moment you're trembling, yet you pretend you're not. Diana, don't you understand that I want to know everything about you, that I want to know all of you — intimately? But you insist on treating our marriage like some sort of stupid mistake when you know in your heart you want me. Admit to your feelings, be honest with yourself for once. Is your body trembling solely because of a nightmare or because you realize that I'm lying atop you, naked and starved with desire? Do you know that your gown is open and nothing separates us?"

A strangled moan rose in the base of her throat as the realization of the situation struck home with lightning speed. Somehow during her thrashing about the tie on her gown had loosened and the gown was entirely open, and when Tanner had tried to waken her, apparently he'd positioned his hard, muscled body near to her. Now he was entirely on top of her, and for the very first time she felt the hugeness of his manhood nestled against the velvet nub of her femininity. He felt wonderful, awesomely strong, and every vein in her body seemed to suddenly ooze with liquid heat. But she fought this deceptive sensation, knowing it would bring pain, only pain.

"Get off me," she hissed. "I don't want you touching me or saying such filthy things to me. I hate you, I'll always hate you and you know that. Leave me alone."

Diana expected him to release his hands, but he didn't. Instead of saying anything further, he surprised her by gently kissing her. "Stop it. Stop!" she insisted, but Tanner was more insistent.

"Kiss me back, Diana," he whispered, his face hidden in the depths of the violet shadows. "I want you to kiss me back."

"No!" She turned her head away from his searching mouth, but Tanner managed to find her lips.

"I know you think I'm trash, not good enough to bed you, but you want me and I want you, so don't deny your body's cravings. You can hate me all you want later, but for now, Diana, give in to love."

Before she could reply, Tanner's mouth captured hers fully and completely in a kiss that set her pulse pounding and her head swimming. She squirmed, however, because this feeling was foreign to her and she wished to be free of the golden warmth that flowed through her, free to hate Tanner as she'd vowed to do all of those years ago. This treacherous man had broken her heart, promised her something she couldn't name only to destroy her love with his need for revenge. And what better vengeance than to have Kingsley's wife writhing beneath him. Even if Kingsley was dead, Tanner's perverted sense of revenge would still be assuaged.

She wanted to fight him and herself, but the second his mouth left hers to find the peak of one of her nipples Diana's eyes widened. Tanner's lips seductively suckled the nipple, and she was shocked not by the fact that Tanner would do that, because Kingsley had done that very thing to her, but because this time she didn't feel a sense of violation. Somehow Tanner had the right to suckle her, to lave her breasts, to increase the heat of her body, which now felt unbearably warm, no longer cold and shivering from fear but hot and trembling from something that frightened her in a different way. It was this difference that upset her greatly. She'd never felt anything like this before, and she was more afraid than she'd ever been in her life, because for the first time her body wasn't her own.

"Tanner, stop . . . you must stop." Was that her voice? It sounded thick and husky.

His tongue continued its search and he said nothing. Strangely, Diana didn't want him to speak or to stop what he was doing, because nothing felt more wonderful than this man who taunted her breasts so expertly. Nothing seemed more natural than for his tongue to leave them and follow a downward path, moving lower and lower, still lower, until Diana gasped as his warm breath flowed over the intimate part of her and stirred up a heat wave within. "Oh, Tanner," she murmured, not certain what she was going to say, not certain what she *could* say as he brushed aside a diaphanous piece of gown from her thigh. Without realizing it, she arched upward, somehow inviting Tanner's full possession of her body. It was an invitation Tanner couldn't refuse.

As if in a trance, she heard him softly say, "Part your legs for me, sweetheart." And she did, lost in a slumbrous, hypnotic world, waiting . . . waiting. Then he filled her with a deep plunge that took her breath away and she realized what she'd invited. Dear God, she was letting him have his way with her, blindly allowing this man who was now her husband to hurt her. The nightmare from which she'd awakened was becoming real again. Pain, pain awaited her, she knew it. Once more Tanner had lulled her into acquiesence with the promise of something glorious. She couldn't bear for that feeling to be destroyed again. Not ever.

Diana strained against him, realizing how pitifully weak she was with this man atop her. "Tanner, no, no," she murmured, fearful of what would come after he finished with her. She must think her way through this, put a mental distance between herself and Tanner as she had done with Kingsley, since it seemed Tanner was determined to have his way with her. Would he beat her like Kingsley had? Would he never free her hands? Or did he hold her so tightly because he feared she might retaliate? And when he finished having his way with her, would the pain be unbearable? These questions swirled around in Diana's head, but then they somehow faded, for even though Tanner was invading her body, he wasn't hurting her. No, he wasn't hurting her at all. In fact, a tiny shard of something darkly pleasurable prickled within her and began to slowly build. She wasn't certain if she cared for this or not, and at that moment she felt destined never to know, for Tanner plunged into her one last time and groaned her name over and over like a litany.

Diana stiffened beneath the limp weight of his body. Her mouth went dry with fear. He was finished with her.

He lay atop her panting, his warm breath sounding ragged in her ear. She felt his heart beating against her breast, then he kissed her again and released her hands. The sunlight that now streamed into the room perfectly illuminated his powerful and superbly built body as he suddenly rose from the bed. Diana tensed, barely aware that the front of her body was naked for him to see clearly in the morning light. All she cared about was that he was going toward the dresser and stooping down beside it. The crop! He'd found the crop!

"Don't hurt me!" she cried and made a move toward the head of the bed, putting her hands up in an attempt to ward him off. "Please, I'll do anything you want, anything, I'll pretend to enjoy whatever it is you do to me, but don't hit me with . . . that thing."

Tanner straightened and looked so baffled that

if Diana hadn't been so frightened she'd have laughed aloud in relief. In his hand wasn't the crop at all but the blanket.

"Why would I want to hit you with a blanket?" he asked.

"All I was doing was picking it up off the floor. You kicked it off during your nightmare." He laid the blanket over her and sat on the bed, his dark eyes not leaving her face. When he joined her beneath the covers, he took her into his arms. "You're tense," he noted. "Relax against me. I won't hurt you. I promise. Is that why you didn't climax?"

"Climax? Whatever are you talking about?"

A slight blush appeared beneath the layer of Tanner's bronze-colored cheeks. "You know, when I made love to you. But then again, I think I better apologize, for the fault is with me. I wanted you so badly, I've wanted you for so long, that I couldn't control myself. I'm sorry, Diana, if you didn't find any pleasure. I promise you that you will the next time, and the time after that and the time after that." Tanner started nibbling on her ear and raining kisses down her throat.

"Tanner, stop," she begged and gazed up at him with troubled blue eyes. "There won't be a next time."

He arched a brow. "Really?"

"Don't patronize me," she snapped. "You know full well why I married you. What happened between us this morning was unplanned. Evidently you needed a woman and so you took advantage of me."

"Stop playing the outraged and virtuous lady, Diana. You wanted me too, and allowed me to make love to you."

She shook her head. "I didn't. I mean I did but I didn't really want to. You seduced me into wanting you like you did that night by the river, and I went along with it because I was unstrung by the nightmare and can't be held accountable for what happened."

This time it was Tanner who stiffened. "Ah, I see. You're not accountable for wanting me. Quite a lame excuse. I suppose you use that one with all your paramours."

Tanner must be mad! What was he talking about? "I don't have any paramours."

He fiddled with a piece of lace on the nightdress. "Tell me about Captain Farnsworth. I heard that you and he struck up quite a friendship."

"We're reluctant acquaintances."

Tanner laughed a deep, rich laugh. "That's a unique way of putting it." His laughter died. "Was Farnsworth able to satisfy you?"

"He's been quite generous with sharing his rations and keeping his men in line, but then you already know that since you're the one who has Rawdon's ear. Yes, our relationship has been quite satisfactory." After a few moments of scrutiny by Tanner, Diana blurted out, "Why are you looking at me as if I'm a simpleton?"

Sighing, Tanner shook his head. "Either I'm the simpleton or you're the most conniving baggage I've ever come across. Sometimes, Diana, I'd almost believe you were untouched, a pure and innocent virgin."

"I'm no virgin, as you well know!" she stated huffily and tried to pull away from him. Tanner, however, wouldn't allow her to leave the circle of his arms and pulled her closer against him. She inhaled the manly scent of him and felt a bit dizzy because her hands were pressed intimately against his strong chest. Finally she was touching him and imagining she felt something stir within her, but again, the mind did play tricks upon a person sometimes.

"We're man and wife now," she heard him say, and he flashed her a smile that caused her silly heart to pound. "And you know what that entails."

A ragged sigh split Diana's lips. "Complete submission. Yes, I know very well what being a wife means, Tanner. I was Kingsley's wife, and even with you my lot hasn't changed. I suppose it's a woman's destiny to be submissive to her husband, to be humiliated."

"Is that what you think I've done to you?"

Diana shrugged her shoulders. "At least you haven't hurt me physically."

Tanner grew very quiet, his eyes sliding toward the dresser and then back again to fix on her face. "So that's why you hid the riding crop. You were afraid I'd beat you with it. Is that how you came to get those two thin scars on your back? I saw them last night when I was watching you dry off," he explained. "Kingsley beat you with the crop."

She nodded and turned her face away from him. Now her humiliation was complete. Tanner would know she hadn't been a dutiful wife, a wife whom a man could be proud of, a wife who gave her husband fine sons.

"Never turn away from me," she heard him say, as he gently cupped her chin in his hand and made her look at him. "You can't hide anything from me. I want to know all about you, even the unpleasant times. My touching you must be quite a chore for you, because I'm certain your other lovers were gentlemen. . . ."

"I wish you'd stop saying such horrible things, Tanner. I don't know why you think I've had lovers. You're the second man who has had his way with me. Kingsley was the first."

Something suddenly seemed to make sense to Tanner and he smiled. "That's an odd choice of words. 'Have my way with you.' Why do you say that?"

"Because a man always has his way with a woman. Men enjoy such activities, for what reason I can't fathom. Pleasure, I suppose. But for a woman it's sheer torture."

"Is it? I had no idea. All of the women I've ever been with have seemed to like what I did to them. I think you did too, Diana. Or," he amended, "you might have if you'd allowed yourself to enjoy my touch and not fight what you were feeling."

"I didn't feel anything!" she retorted hotly, hating for Tanner to know that once again his

168

touch and kisses had started a simmering sensation within her. "And I will not be made to suffer for it. No matter what, I'll fight you if you try to hurt me. I won't . . ." her voice cracked and she had to swallow deeply to control herself. "I won't be beaten again. Ever again!"

"Shh, quiet," he comforted, and held her tenderly in his arms. "I promise I won't harm you. I could never hurt you, Diana. Do you believe that I would hit you with a riding crop like Kingsley or beat you for your lack of response in bed? Do you think I'm that heartless a man?"

Lying like that in his arms she had no doubt that Tanner would never hurt her the way that Kingsley had done. He reminded her of the gentle Tanner she'd seen that day when the slave woman had been bitten by the snake. This was the Tanner she liked a great deal. "I don't believe you're a bad person," she confessed. "Deep down, you're very kind."

Tanner grinned. "Thank you, I think. But we have a problem here, Diana. A problem we must solve."

"Oh?"

"Most definitely. Here I am holding you, and you have very little on, and mind you, I've just 'had my way with you,' as you so succintly put it, and . . ."

"Do you know that you have a wonderful vocabulary?" she interrupted. "You're quite well spoken."

"Again, thank you, but my speech isn't the subject of our conversation at the present time.

*You* are, or, I should say, your lack of response when I make love to you is."

Diana groaned, flailing about, ready to flee. "Not that again, please. You remind me of Kingsley now."

He stopped her from moving by holding her tightly and peering into her luminous blue eyes. "I am not Kingsley, nor will I ever be like him, Diana. You must realize one thing. No matter what has happened between us, we're attracted to each other and we're married. I want you to feel what I feel when I make love to you."

"You mean when we rut," she shot back.

Tanner looked embarrassed. "I'm sorry about saying that last night. I didn't mean to sound so crass. Believe me, you're the last woman in the world I want to rut with."

"Ha! Thank you so much for that."

"I don't mean to insult you, either. I want to make love to you, woman, not just spill myself within you. The biggest joy in my life right now would be for you to find pleasure with your own body, with mine. There's more to mating than the act, a great deal more, and I'm going to tutor you."

Disbelief clouded her features. "There is nothing more, Tanner. Not for me. I don't know about other women, but I'm frigid, cold, just like Kingsley said."

"Kingsley was wrong," he insisted. "And he was a damn poor teacher, too." A half cocky smile turned up the corners of his mouth. "I'd wager that within a week I'll have you so well instructed that you'll beg for me to make love to you, that you'll experience the greatest pleasure when I do."

Tanner was mad! He must be to even think of such an outlandish and preposterous wager. But she was intrigued by it all the same and wondered if that tiny sliver of excitement she'd felt earlier was an indication of what might happen if she gave into Tanner's tutelage. Oh, it couldn't be anything at all, she found herself reasoning. Tanner only wanted to prove the same old point to himself and to her—that he could master her by having his way with her. A perfect act of revenge against the Sheridans.

She was tempted to turn down his offer, but instead she found herself saying, "What will I gain if I don't respond to you?"

Tanner thought for a second. "Briarhaven, of course," he decided. "If you don't respond to me, don't beg me to make love to you by the end of the week, then I lose and you can go merrily on your way to Briarhaven. The house will be yours, I'll turn it over to you with instructions that Farnsworth and his men retreat and that you and Harlan are left alone. You'll never see me again. Of course, if your response is so passionate and intense that you lose control, then I win Briarhaven *and* you, and for the rest of your life you'll come to my bed and promise to enjoy yourself. Is that fair to you?"

Diana disentangled herself from his arms and sat up to gaze at him. Tanner was a strange sort of man. He was so handsome he could set her heart to pounding, but it wasn't his handsomeness that intrigued her. There was something else, an indefinable quality of elusiveness, of being unable to adequately read his thoughts or to guess his next move. He always seemed to keep a part of himself hidden from view, yet when he claimed her she'd glimpsed a tiny fraction of deep emotion. She wondered what it must be like to feel the way he had earlier, but then he was a man, and this sort of thing seemed to come easily for men. Never for her. And she knew she'd never feel anything like that.

It was this assumption that forced her to agree to Tanner's bet. He was so assured of success that he didn't think he might fail at all. She, however, was certain of his failure. The chance to win Briarhaven from him, to have the man out of her life for good, was too strong for her to refuse. Holding out her hand to him, she said, "I agree to your terms."

His eyes narrowed speculatively. "You understand, of course, that I'll know if you're holding back, Diana. I've been with enough women to know what games they play."

"I never play games," she declared.

"If you say so."

She didn't care for the sound of that, it was almost as if he were accusing her of something she'd done, and she had no idea what it might be. But she wouldn't dwell on Tanner's sensibilities now. Briarhaven was within her reach.

Starting to get up, she gasped when Tanner yanked her toward him. "Where are you going?"

he asked.

"Why, its getting late and Cammie will be serving breakfast downstairs soon. It is Christmas day, you know, and I've church services to attend."

"Christmas has never been important to me," he remarked. "I was raised a savage, as you well remember, and my mother never believed in Christian ways. Stay in bed with me and I'll start your lesson."

"What lesson?"

"Lesson one — kissing."

Diana was horrified. "You want me to stay in bed with you on Christmas Day to learn how . . . how to kiss!"

"Why not?" A lecherous grin appeared on his face at the same moment he pulled her into his arms. "You're a woefully bad kisser, sweetheart, but I promise you that if you learn quickly I'll escort you to church myself."

"Oh, Tanner, you're insane, you're uncouth, you're . . ."

"A savage, but we made a wager and you're going to live up to it. Or do you welsh on your bets?"

"I'm not a welsher," she said stiffly. "I'll stay for my first lesson."

"Ah, a Christian martyr thrown to the savage beast. Here, come lie next to me." Tanner patted the place she'd recently vacated and she lay down, pulling the transparent gown around her. His hands tangled with hers and he forced her to remove them from the gown. With sensuous fingers he parted the material, allowing himself a long, lustful look at her breasts, the delicious expanse of silken skin from her waist to the tempting dark thatched mound, and downward, past her ivory thighs to the tips of her toenails. "You're an exquisitely beautiful woman, Diana."

"Don't look at me like that or say such things."

"Why not?"

"You frighten me."

"Don't be afraid of me. I want only to love you."

It was an odd thing for Tanner to say, she thought, since he'd wanted her from the first only to humiliate his family. But what difference does any of it make now? she grudgingly asked herself. Why was he so intent on proving a point if there was no one to know but her? If he wanted to love her as he said, why then make a game out of it? *Because he needs to know he can break you down, you foolish ninny!* her mind answered.

"You can skip the pretty words, Tanner. I'm immune to them."

"Ah, I see, so then we can get down to brass tacks, so to speak, and forget the hearts and flowers."

"Exactly."

"If you insist." With a grin lurking on his handsome face, Tanner positioned himself on his elbows and leaned over her. Cupping her face within the depth of his two hands, his eyes turned a smoky shade of black. "I want you to relax."

"I . . . I can't," she admitted and blushed. "Not when my gown is undone and you can see . . . all of me."

"Forget that, not that you aren't a fetching sight, Diana, but I promise not to touch you anywhere else during this first lesson. Kissing is an art, and no matter who you decide to fall into bed with next I think you should be adequately tutored. I'm certain the gent, whoever he may be, will thank me." He looked less than pleased at the thought but continued in a velvety voice. "A woman should be slowly initiated into lovemaking, and I happen to believe that in bed a woman is only as good as her teacher. When I'm finished with you, you shall be very, very good."

"Goodness," her voice caught in her throat. "You are an arrogant, conceited fellow."

Tanner grinned broadly. "That's part of my devastating charm, sweetheart. Now close your eyes and forget who I am. Go on, close them," he whispered and Diana reluctantly followed suit. "Listen to my voice while I instruct you and don't say anything. Do as I say and I promise that kissing will come naturally to you, so naturally that soon I won't have to talk at all, and all you'll have to do is feel my kisses and enjoy them."

"I won't . . ."

"Quiet, Diana." He lulled her with his voice and ordered her to breathe deeply, which she did though she thought it was silly, but after a few deep breaths she found she didn't feel as tense. She wasn't certain why she was even involved in this stupid exercise, expecting this time like all of the times Kingsley had kissed her to end in the same disappointing and frustrating way. Yet something compelled her to obey him and to wait in fascinated wonder.

She was barely aware of Tanner's lips when they first touched hers with surprising gentleness. They moved warmly against her dewy soft mouth, moist yet firm in their possession. His breath mixed with hers, and she discovered that she very nearly stopped breathing when his tongue temptingly teased her mouth to open for him. A feeble protest died in her throat as his tongue sought and found hers. She made an attempt to draw it away, but Tanner, like an ever-stalking hunter, snared his elusive prey in a sensual trap that threatened to destroy Diana's control. She'd thought to remain unaffected and to easily claim Briarhaven with her frigidity. But something unforeseen was happening to her. With each tantalizing flick of his tongue against hers, Tanner drew her into a maelstrom of heat and fire. Diana was gradually sucked into a golden whirlpool of feelings so intense that she was at a loss to explain them. What was happening to her? What was the strange sultriness that stirred within her and built slowly like a tropical storm? Why did she suddenly feel as if not blood but liquid gold now ran through her veins, threatening to scorch the very essence of her?

Kingsley had kissed her like this, she remembered his loathsome and demanding invasions of her mouth. But those kisses were nothing in comparison to this one. Never had she expected to be kissed in such a fashion and to actually find that she didn't want it to end. Tanner's lips and tongue fully possessed hers and enveloped hers like a lover's caress. Each sweep of tongue against tongue was a primitive dance, igniting something deep and dormant within Diana. It seemed that waves of intense heat gyrated through her, causing her no longer to think but to feel and respond, to finally surrender to whatever it was that caused such melting warmth.

She didn't realize that though Tanner's hands still cupped her face, her arms were no longer resting demurely by her sides. They were clasped around his neck in an attempt to bring his face closer to her. Also, she hadn't yet realized that her naked breasts were wantonly pressed against Tanner's broad chest and that she was writhing beneath him, or that tiny mewling sounds of pleasure emanated from her own throat.

It wasn't until Tanner finally broke the mind-drugging kiss to replace it with a lingering one on her lips that she grew aware of her surroundings and the position in which she found herself.

"Why did you stop?" she blurted out in a breathy voice that surprised even herself.

Tanner shook his head and groaned. "You are an innocent, Diana, if you have to ask. I'm a mortal man who has reached his limits with you. I want you again, and I'd have you, too, but I promised you that all I'd do was kiss you and I won't go further."

Diana watched in a daze as he rose from the bed to stand. The dawn's light gilded his magnificent body in a transparent gold hue. Tanner looked large and masculine as he stood there, extremely masculine, she decided, as her eyes found that part of him that indicated his desire for her. She wanted to glance away but didn't, somehow deriving some sort of strange satisfaction from looking at the object that had claimed her earlier and wanted to claim her again. A ragged sigh rushed through her lips as she unwillingly imagined that, but she adopted an indifferent air.

"I have absolutely no wish for you to go further," she said and pulled the diaphanous robe around her and sat up. With dark hair all atumble around her shoulders, Diana smiled. "Your kiss affected me not at all."

Tanner bent over and suggestively rubbed his forefinger against her cheek. "If you say so, my sweet." He straighted and flashed her a winning smile. "Now get dressed and let's attend services on this Christmas morning bright with promise."

Diana watched as Tanner began dressing. He whistled and grinned smugly to himself. The infuriating grin was still on his face two hours later when they entered the church. Diana sensed that he didn't believe her, not one bit.

# Chapter 10

"Deceitful devil," Diana groused as she finished packing the rest of Anne's gowns into a trunk. Cammie, who was nearby and occupied with the childrens' belongings, heard her.

"Did you say something, ma'am?"

"Just talking to myself," was Diana's curt reply, knowing it wouldn't do any good to repeat what she had said because she'd been complaining aloud about Tanner and Cammie was loyal to him. In fact it seemed that the whole world was loyal to her husband. Curtis and Cammie doted on his every whim and word. Even Ruthie, whom Diana assumed would be harder to win over with the Sheridan charm, had fallen for his dark, masculine handsomeness. And though Tanner might hate admitting that he was Harlan Sheridan's son, he couldn't deny the resemblance to his father.

Yet Diana's irritability had very little to do

with the servants, much more to do with Tanner himself. Granted, he'd been more than pleased to send Ruthie on to wherever it was he'd spirited David, Anne, and the children, and Ruthie had been more than eager to join them. Diana didn't mind packing extra things for her family or closing up the Richmond house. She did mind that Tanner didn't trust her enough to tell her where the Richmonds were. She missed her sister and the children but had to remain content with the knowledge that they were safe. She couldn't help but feel that Tanner held the trump card in the deck by keeping her in the dark and in her place.

However, she could deal with that. What she couldn't deal with was Tanner's hobnobbing with the British. Since Christmas Day, she and Tanner had attended a number of parties hosted by Tories and attended by British officers. Captain Farnsworth had been at one such gathering, and had explained to her that he would soon leave for Briarhaven and that he hoped to see her safely returned. He congratulated her and Tanner on their marriage, making a grand show of it by offering a long-winded toast to the newlyweds, but Diana sensed he wasn't as pleased as he pretended and that the polite smile on his face was there only for Tanner's benefit. For some odd reason it seemed that Farnsworth didn't wish to offend Tanner Sheridan, and he wasn't the only one. Diana had noticed a number of British officers hovering around her husband, speaking intimately to him, acting like obsequious fools. At one point Tanner had drawn away from them by saying with a blunt edge to his voice, "I'm retired now," and seeing that she was watching him, he'd taken her arm, and they bade their hosts farewell and departed.

But what was he retired from? This thought haunted Diana day and night. Once she'd gathered the nerve to ask him and been told again that he'd had business contacts with the British, but still she had no idea what sort of business it was, and he didn't volunteer the information — which was one reason why she decided he was a deceitful devil.

The other had to do with her nightly bedtime instructions. Even now as she stood to catch sight of herself in Anne's bedroom mirror, Diana saw that she was blushing. Over the last four days they had progressed from her kissing lessons, in which, according to Tanner, she was beginning to excel, to fondling. The memory of the way his large warm hands had cupped and massaged her breasts before kissing and teasing them with his lips was still vivid. She actually shivered with a sudden tremor to recall how it felt when he'd leisurely suckled the taut nipples, filling his mouth with what he termed her sweetness. His velvety voice ordered her to lie still and relax, to concentrate only on the feel of his hands and his mouth, to enjoy herself.

She'd later told him that she had felt nothing, again aware that he didn't really believe her. In fact something had stirred within her, but it was something she couldn't name and she was a bit more than sorry when he told her that the lesson was over for the night. Lying there in the huge bed with Tanner asleep beside her, she knew that only three days were left until their bet officially ended. Three more days—New Year's Eve—and she could claim Briarhaven as her own and be free of Tanner Sheridan forever. Yet for some odd reason it was becoming more difficult to lie dispassionately beneath Tanner's touches and kisses. He hadn't made any effort to have his way with her again, and she knew he was waiting until she wanted him in that way. But she'd never want Tanner or any man like that, and she couldn't explain why she felt so odd, almost frustrated, when Tanner finally gave up and fell asleep.

"It's only three more days," she said to her reflection, "and then I'll never have to see him." But that thought felt a bit discomforting and she was glad to hear Curtis's voice and know that he'd arrived to take the trunks. Going to tell him that the trunks were in the two upstairs bedrooms, she saw that Curtis was already heading past her on the stairs and that Tanner stood nonchalantly by the bottom step, one elbow propped on the banister.

His gaze swept possessively over her figure. She was dressed in a pale blue velvet gown with long sleeves and white lace at the square neckline. Like a ninny of a schoolgirl, Diana felt high spots of color stain her cheeks.

"I've always liked the way you blush," he told her and took her hand in his when she reached the first step.

Her lips were level with his, and a sudden urge to kiss him gripped her but she resisted, knowing that Tanner always managed to snare her in a sensual trap—only to destroy her.

"A gentleman wouldn't comment on such a thing."

A short laugh escaped from his perfectly formed lips and he slowly shook his head. "You already know I'm not a gentleman, so I can ask you straight out about what naughty thoughts are hovering in the back of your mind, because I know that some are. Admit to me that you're beginning to feel something when I kiss and touch you. You're thinking about what I did to you last night, just as I am."

"I was not!"

"Liar."

"Cammie and I have finished with the packing," Diana muttered stiffly, eager to stop this conversation. She started to move past him, but Tanner stopped her with a slight tug on her fingers.

"The best is yet to come, Diana. I promise you."

A thrill of something darkly pleasurable swept through her at the thought. But she'd been married for years to Kingsley and nothing remotely pleasant had happened to her in bed.

Whatever it was that Tanner wanted her to feel wasn't about to occur for her, and suddenly she felt less than a woman in his eyes. Surely, if this pleasure that Tanner told her about, this delight he'd given to many women over the years, didn't happen to her, then she was just like Kingsley had said. Cold. Frigid. But nothing wonderful would happen to her beneath Tanner's hands. Nothing had happened so far, had it?

She must retain some dignity if all of this tutorship came to naught. Tanner had wounded her years ago by leaving her to Kingsley's abuse, and she could wield cutting remarks that would hurt him almost as deeply as she had been hurt. "Perhaps you've overestimated your prowess in the bedroom," she said. "I remember you told me that a woman is only as good in bed as the man who teaches her, and to be truthful I'm not very good, am I?"

This time it was Tanner's face that filled with what she assumed at first was a blush, but she quickly realized that it was red with rage. "You'd be damned good if you'd forget for a moment who I am, forget that I'm a bastard by birth. Try thinking of me as one of your fancy suitors from years back, or pretend I'm Farnsworth, the proper gentleman. Right now I wonder if your heart is made of ice or stone. Ice can melt but stone can't." He looked deeply into her eyes. Never before had she seen his eyes so hard and black. "I ought to forget the whole idea, Diana. It might be utterly hopeless."

"Does this mean our bet is off?"

"Hell no! You're a challenge to me now." He gripped her by the upper arms and brought her against him. "I want you to mewl like a contented kitten when I touch you, to know that you want me. But more important, I want you to experience passion for yourself, to feel your womanhood blossom beneath my hands. Otherwise, you're only going through the motions and are half a woman. I want more for you than that. I want you to experience desire."

Sudden tears of tenderness sprang to her eyes for Tanner. He truly wanted her to be a whole woman, but she doubted she'd ever experience this indefinable something he claimed existed. This thought prompted tears of impending defeat to mingle with the other ones until she could barely speak. Why did he have to reenter her life and churn up emotions she'd thought she'd buried years ago? She hated losing control.

Tanner wiped away her tears somewhat clumsily with the pads of his thumbs. "Don't cry. It will happen for you, Diana, I swear it will."

"I'd like to go home now," she told him, unable to say anything else. For some odd reason she hoped Tanner was right, but if he was then she'd lose Briarhaven and the chance to be free of him. She didn't relish being at any man's mercy, especially this man's. There was a great possibility that if she won the wager she'd never see him again and could go back to the same dull life she'd led up until a few weeks ago. This was what she wanted, why she willed herself not to enjoy Tanner's lovemaking, but the dull aching pain that wrapped around her heart like iron fingers at such a thought surprised her.

The carriage ride home was silent and took longer than Diana had anticipated because Tanner had business on the outskirts of Charlestown. She had no idea where they were headed until the small, squalid settlement known as Rawdontown came into view. When they stopped, she looked at Tanner in perplexity. "What are we doing here?"

"Helping out a few friends. Come along." Holding out his hand to her, Diana automatically took it and stepped from the carriage to find herself surrounded by dozens of dirty and ill-kempt people who seemed to materialize out of their primitive lean-tos like foxes out of their lairs. Dressed in her elegant and very warm sable cloak, Diana felt terribly out of place. She was all too aware of the envious looks thrown her way by women warmed by shawls that had seen better days.

Children of all ages ran hither and yon, shouting in excitement. A few pulled on Tanner's coat tails. "What you got for us today, suh?" a little boy of about five asked as he wiped his runny nose with the back of a dirty hand.

Tanner stooped down and smiled warmly at the lad and ruffled his sandy hair. "Andy, my boy, you've grown since last month. Your coat no longer fits you."

Diana saw that the child wore a coat that was two sizes too small and was riddled with gaping holes. But it seemed that Andy was one of the luckier children to have any coat at all. Most of the boys and girls didn't even have that.

Andy grinned. "I know. My mudder says I'm gonna be big like my papa." The child's smile died. "He was killed by those bad patriots, you know."

"I know," was Tanner's solemn reply. Motioning to Curtis, who immediately began pulling down the trunks that Diana had spent packing all afternoon at her sister's house, Tanner helped drag them from the top of the carriage to the ground.

"What are you doing with those trunks?" Diana asked as he placed one on the ground and began opening it.

"Distributing goods to the needy," he replied without looking up at her.

He couldn't mean to give these people her family's clothes. It was inconceivable that he'd do this, not when her sister, David, and the children might have need of them. She told him so and wasn't prepared for the disdainful curve of his lips or the condemnation in his eyes. "Your family is well cared for, Diana. They're warm and clothed, fed three times a day. I doubt if they'd mind sharing their goods with those less fortunate."

"But these people are Tories," Diana whispered, horrified to even consider giving aid to those whom she secretly fought against. It was treasonous.

Tanner stood up and considered her for a long moment, oblivious to the excited people who waited with eager hands. "I had no idea you were such a staunch little patriot, but if that's the way you feel then so be it. We'll close the trunks and haul them back home where they'll sit in the attic, doing little good for anyone. You do surprise me, however. I would have thought you'd be quite willing to help your fellow man in times of trouble, whether he be Tory or rebel. But the decision is yours, Diana. I'll abide by whatever you decide, and I do apologize for taking liberties with your family's possessions. That was wrong of me. I should have asked you first."

Tanner *should* have asked her permission, but that wasn't the point. He wanted her to decide what to do with the clothes. From what she'd packed, Diana knew that Anne had warm and serviceable gowns, that David had perhaps as many as four topcoats and woolen undergarments, plus shirts and pants. The childrens' apparel was so abundant that they filled three trunks and would easily clothe all of the dirty urchins here. But these people were Tories, driven from their homes by the very enemy she spied for. How could she ever explain any of this to Tanner without giving away her secret? But how could she not distribute the clothes to people who were needy and cold? No matter what side they were on, they were still South Carolinians, the same as she. Just ordinary people. Wouldn't she hope someone did the same for her family?

Her decision was expressed in the sweet smile she sent in little Andy's direction as she began rummaging through one of the children's trunks. Tanner joined in helping her, and before the hour was out, all of the clothes were gone.

"Mr. Sheridan is a fine man." Mike Candy expressed his sentiments by stroking the brown topcoat that had belonged to David Richmond and was now warming Mike's burly frame. He sat in his lean-to with another man who drank from a cracked bowl containing an unappetizing, watery gruel. "You should have come out and gotten something from his pretty wife. Did you happen to see her?"

"I saw her," the man blurted out and threw aside the bowl, causing the contents to splash on Mike's new garment.

"Hey, you ain't got no cause to act so mean, Mr. King. You seem to forget that I was the one who nursed you back to health last year. I took you in and I've gotten only rudeness and nastiness for my trouble. I may not be as grand a fellow as you think you are but I got my pride." Mike sniffed haughtily and dabbed at the stain with a dirty rag. "If you don't like it here, well you can just leave."

"I'd do it, too, if I could," the man snapped. "But my leg hasn't mended properly yet."

Mike stroked his chin in thought and craftily observed, "Yea, mighty funny about that leg. Always seemed odd to me that a British soldier would be wounded by his own men. I mean that musket ball I dug out of you was English made, but you don't strike me like a Brit."

"Shut up, Candy. I'm tired and want to get some sleep. I'm sorry for being unkind to you, for staining your coat."

This sudden turn of face from a man who could be mean one moment and civil the next appeased Mike Candy. Candy had no real desire to know anything about this uncommunicative stranger whom he'd helped last year and taken in. He wanted to live his life with as little discord as possible because he was tired of wars, sick of fighting. "That's all right, son. Get your rest, you need it to make you strong again. Maybe next time Mr. Sheridan and his wife come you'll be hearty enough to hobble out and get something."

For the first time since Mike had met this Mr. King, the man threw back his head and laughed. He clutched at his frayed jacket and lay back on the pallet, covering himself with a ragged blanket. "Oh, I'll come out and get something, Mike Candy, I promise you I will. The high and mighty Tanner Sheridan and his pretty wife owe me, and I intend to collect."

Mike didn't say anything else to the man, who every so often would grunt in his sleep. If the truth be known, Mr. King frightened Mike a bit. Sometimes he'd have nightmares and would call out a lady's name, followed by foul curses that even made an experienced old sea captain like Mike Candy blush. Mike never asked Mr. King about his dreams, but he felt sorry for the lady and wondered what she might have done to cause Mr. King to hate her so much.

But she had a pretty sounding name, a name that reminded Mike Candy of happier times before the war, for he'd once had a sweetheart with that same name—Diana.

Diana hugged her arms close against her thin wrapper to ward off the chill in the drafty hallway. She wished she'd worn slippers to pad downstairs in search of a book, but in the bedroom the fireplace had provided more than adequate warmth, causing her to be unaware of how cold the rest of the house could be on a dark December night.

Entering the small study at the back of the house, she saw a blazing fire in the hearth and smelled the sweet scent of burning pine logs as she neared the bookshelves. She thought it odd that Cammie would keep a fire burning down here when Tanner had gone out earlier—no doubt to visit Gabriella Fox, Diana decided dismally and reached for a book.

"Can't sleep?"

Tanner's voice startled her and she whipped around to discover that he was sitting in a large cushioned chair near the fireplace. An empty wine glass stood on the end table.

"I didn't see you there. I thought you'd gone." She gave a relieved giggle to find him home.

He shook his head. "I've been here all evening."

He'd been home all the time! He hadn't gone to see Gabriella Fox. "Do you often sit down here by yourself in the dark?"

"Yes, the dark can be quite comforting."

Diana drew nearer to him. "I wanted something to read."

"I see that."

She suddenly felt quite ill at ease as she stood before him dressed in her thin white wrapper with lacy inserts at the breasts. She wore nothing underneath because she'd recently stepped out of the tub and didn't believe Tanner was home. After all, he'd have to be made of stern stuff to want to stay with a woman whom he couldn't inflame with his lovemaking skills, not when Gabriella or any other woman would melt willingly in his arms.

"Well, I'll go upstairs now." She wouldn't ask him if he'd join her, she was frightened he'd refuse.

"Diana, wait."

Half turning, she clutched the book in her

arms, stupidly attempting to cover her breasts, which seemed to strain toward the sound of his voice. "I want to thank you for helping today. Many people are grateful to you," she heard him say.

"I really didn't have much choice," she admitted. "But you were right to want to help them."

Tanner's gaze skimmed over her thin attire. "You're shivering. Are you cold?"

"Just a bit, but once I'm upstairs I'm certain I'll warm up."

"Why wait so long? Sit beside me. I've plenty of room in this chair."

Diana saw that the chair was quite large, even filled with Tanner's broad frame. In the flickering firelight he looked so handsome as he sat there with an earnest appeal on his face that the will to refuse him never reached her lips. She found herself magnetically drawn to him, barely aware that she'd stepped across the floor until she found herself huddled against him with his arm around her waist.

His right hand reached out and gently brushed aside the wispy tendrils of her hair from her neck. "You have the most beautiful hair," Tanner praised. "I remember when you first came to Briarhaven how I'd watch you, how when the sunlight touched your hair the strands would gleam red-gold until the color was no longer dark brown but a burnished copper. That day when you were with Kingsley in the carriage on the river bank and he kissed you, your hair was that same unusual color. I wanted to be the one kissing you, touching your hair. It was at that moment I decided to take you away from him."

Her heart jumped in her chest as his fingers stroked through the thick tresses to slide sensuously past her neckline and hover at the base of her collarbone. "I was very young then," she muttered thickly.

"And so pretty that I couldn't think straight when I looked at you. Of course, you're no longer pretty."

"I'm not?"

Tanner's features relaxed into a teasing grin. "You're beautiful now."

This time her heart seemed to slam into her ribcage with such force that she heaved a deep, shuddering sigh. How could he think she was beautiful, even passably comely, when she was still so thin? She'd gained a few pounds since marrying Tanner, but not enough to tempt a man who was able to have any woman he wanted. At least that's what Diana thought.

His index finger traced the shape of her mouth. "You don't believe you are beautiful, do you, Diana?"

"Not really." *Not beautiful enough for a man like you.*

"Believe that you are."

Whenever he looked at her with those black eyes, eyes that at this moment danced with amber fire, she could imagine that she was. It seemed that that fire singed her soul, melting it within her. She knew he was going to kiss her, in fact she was already opening for him like a rosebud in the sun, welcoming the consuming heat. The book plopped to the floor as her arms voluntarily wrapped around his neck and pulled him closer to her.

Their mouths met first in a gentle kiss that tasted like sweet wine. Tanner's lips tasted hers, moving across them with feather-light strokes. Diana moaned under his tender assault, vaguely aware that she was the one who began to deepen the kiss. She expected an immediate response, but Tanner surprised her by not participating. Accustomed to Tanner's instant arousal, she now realized she was going to have to work for it. This was probably part of his lesson for her, she decided, but she also knew she was up to the challenge.

With the skills he'd taught her and her own inborn sensuality, Diana proceeded to tease and taunt his tongue with hers until Tanner moaned and ended the resistance. "You're like wildfire, love," he whispered against her mouth. "Your heat is scorching me alive."

And it was. Never had Diana felt so warm, so filled with fire. The flames grew higher as Tanner opened her robe and cupped her breast with his hand. She found herself writhing beneath his touch, tiny whimpering sounds issuing from her mouth. When his head bent low to suckle each of her nipples, something liquid and hot began to flow through her body. "Oh, that feels wonderful," she gasped and arched toward him.

"There's more, Diana," Tanner promised and with that he positioned her until she was lying across him, her head cushioned in the crook of his arm. In a daze, she allowed him to help her shrug out of the robe until nothing covered her but golden firelight. He bent low to feast upon her breasts, gently nudged her quivering thighs apart until his fingers found the tender nub between them.

*Pain!* Diana's brain screamed, remembering those times when Kingsley had touched her there, hurting her and humiliating her. She balked and tried to close her legs, but Tanner's hand steadied her, refusing to be moved from her velvet warmth. "I'm not hurting you, Diana. I won't hurt you," she heard him say. "Soon you're going to feel great pleasure. Lie still and feel it happen. Enjoy what I'm doing to you, sweetheart. Feel my fingers moving across the silken folds of your womanhood. See, I'm touching you now and it doesn't hurt, does it?"

Diana could barely speak. She felt that her breath had stopped in her throat, that if she sighed she'd miss something incredibly wonderful. Tanner's voice lulled her, hypnotized her with his words before his mouth continued to suckle her breasts. His fingers stroked her, causing moist heat to gather within her. With her gaze trained on the ceiling, she saw shadows dance to a rhythmic, pulsating beat. Suddenly she found herself among the shadows as her body started to move with abandon, wanting to rid itself of the scorching heat that suddenly claimed her but just as eager to be inundated by the flames.

Something was going to happen. She knew it, but she didn't know what, and she was somehow frightened of it. It was when she felt Tanner's finger slide inside her that the fear intensified, for the stirrings of pleasure were so great. "Tanner, please, no . . ."

"Feel it happen, sweet, feel the heat and don't fight it," he told her and his mouth found hers, stilling anything further she might say.

With each thrust of his tongue in her mouth, his finger followed suit until Diana imagined her body was so hot that it would soon explode. Instead of fighting the sensation, she suddenly discovered that by gyrating her hips she could ride his finger and deepen the strange, churning pleasure that left her wet with wanting.

She had no idea what was going to happen to her. She felt exactly as she had that night with Tanner on the bluff. The stars and the moon had been out that night, covering the heavens with millions of pinpoints of light. Suddenly it seemed that all of those lights gathered into a firey ball and centered within the deepest part of her femininity. Nothing prepared Diana for the light that flashed before her eyes as her body arched upward to seek the heavens. Her body exploded with a force that caused her to cry her pleasure into Tanner's mouth and left her trembling and panting, not quite certain she was still alive.

Moments later she found herself wrapped in Tanner's arms. Her head rested upon his chest, and he stroked her hair while he murmured endearments. She couldn't look at him, more embarrassed than she'd ever been in her entire life. She'd lost control of herself, but in a strange way, she'd found herself, too. Finally he tilted her chin so she'd be forced to gaze into his eyes. He was smiling at her.

"You don't have to look so pleased," she said softly.

"Ah, but I do. It isn't everyday that I see a woman get her first taste of sexual pleasure."

"How many women have you seen?"

Tanner blushed and admitted with some hesitation, "You're the first for me, Diana. All of the women I've known have been very experienced and knew what to expect."

"Is what happened to me supposed to happen every time?"

"It depends, but if so, then consider yourself to be very lucky." Tanner intimately kissed her earlobe. "I consider myself to be lucky, too. You're definitely not a piece of stone."

Diana shifted her position and her backside made contact with something hard inside Tanner's trousers. She stiffened. God! he wanted her, but more than that, she wanted him. In fact, she could feel that heat gathering inside of her again, craving release. Suddenly she felt violated and more vulnerable than she ever had with Kingsley. Tanner had turned her into a wanton with only his hands and his lips. What might happen to her if he loved her fully and she experienced that same pleasant, mind-drugging explosion? She'd never be able to leave him and would once more be at a man's mercy. Her freedom would be taken away from her and she'd be a slave to something so powerful and potent that it might destroy her. And she refused to be destroyed by Tanner.

Sitting up, she reached for her robe and began pulling it on. "So now you know that I'm flesh and blood, one of your many mewling women, taken in by your 'special talents.' But you still haven't won the wager. I didn't beg you to make love to me, nor shall I."

"But you did respond to me," he reminded her in a somewhat puzzled tone of voice, standing to tower over her.

Her hand tightened around the silken sash at her waist. "Yes, but . . ."

"But nothing!" Tanner practically growled at her, and any gentleness he'd shown to her earlier had fled. He grabbed her by the wrists and pulled her against him. "You're the most infuriating woman I've ever had the misfortune to know. A few minutes ago I would have bet that you were truly made from something other than stone, but now I think you're heartless." His face was filled with such pain that Diana felt guilty.

"I thought that if I were tender with you, gentle, you would respond to me, and you did. You had no idea how you looked, how utterly beautiful you were when you climaxed. Your pleasure was my joy because I could do that for you, but now — now you're back to the cold and self-controlled Diana. The Diana who can't see beyond her own mistaken notion of what and who I am. No, you didn't beg me to make love to you, but you would have in time, and you'd have lost Briarhaven and your precious freedom in the process."

Tanner thrust her away from him, total disgust registering in his eyes. "So you've got both of them. You can have Briarhaven and your freedom; I don't want either one of you." He grabbed his heavy topcoat and started for the door. "And don't bother to ask me where I'm going, because I know my whereabouts don't matter to you. But I'll tell you that I'm going to find someone who'll appreciate my 'special talents,' as you so delicately put it, because, lady, it's apparent that you don't."

He was gone before she could summon the words to call him back, but she knew it wouldn't have done any good. She'd lost Tanner before she'd even truly had him, but she'd won Briarhaven and her freedom. Strangely, she found no consolation in the knowledge.

Instead of going upstairs, Diana sat in the chair until the feel of Tanner's body heat had dissipated. The fire still roared in the fireplace,

200

but a chill settled over her like an autumn frost. Despite her resolve not to cry, Diana felt tears start to trickle down her cheeks, and within seconds it seemed that a dam had broken loose inside her. She'd won, but it was plain now to her that she had indeed lost something of great value.

# Chapter 11

Diana waited in the dressmaker's salon while Marisa whirled about in a daring gown of amber and green flounces before coming to stand before Diana for her opinion. "What do you think of it?" Marisa asked. "Do you think I should have the bodice raised? It really is a trifle too low." Marisa fidgeted with the neckline and waited expectantly for her cousin to answer.

"Did you say something?" Diana focused on the pretty young woman, suddenly aware that Marisa had spoken. "I'm sorry, I wasn't paying attention."

Marisa sighed and bent down to pat Diana's hand, which rested on the chair arm. "No wonder. All you've done the last two days is mope about. If mother and I hadn't arrived for a visit, you'd still be sitting in that house all by yourself. We'd never have known about what happened between you and . . . your husband.

At least not right away," Marisa amended and blushed. "But Gabriella Fox has such a big mouth that all of Charlestown must be aware that Tanner has left the townhouse by now."

Diana grimaced, knowing that her marriage was the talk of Tory circles. With Gabriella still residing at Diana's aunt's home, Diana surmised that Aunt Frances and Marisa must be privy to a great deal more about Tanner Sheridan and Gabriella than they were letting on. Diana silently thanked them for not saying very much. She didn't believe she could bear knowing for certain that Tanner had taken up with Gabriella again, though she was almost positive he had. She wanted to bite her tongue rather than inquire about Tanner, but she found herself uttering the words before she could stop herself. "I imagine he spends a great deal of time with her."

"Not at our house, I assure you, Diana. Mother would never allow such goings on under her roof. And besides, Gabriella is married, as is Tanner. You're his wife and our closest relative. We'd never dream of letting him visit her there. She's our guest only because her husband was so very friendly with Papa. Anyway, Gabriella mentioned she received a letter from Mr. Fox. He's coming home most anyday and they'll retire to their plantation. Gabriella seemed almost pleased at the news. Apparently she's growing bored with the men of Charlestown and must be ready to turn her attention to him.

Poor devil," Marisa muttered but did the unladylike by swearing under her breath. "I'm sorry, Diana, if I've said too much or spoken out of turn. Really, Mother and I are quite upset over all of this and to learn you're so unhappy."

"But I'm not unhappy," Diana protested and smiled disingenuously. "My marriage was doomed from the start. Now, tell me if you plan to wear that dress at the party on New Year's Eve. You look beautiful in it."

A becoming smile lit up Marisa's face and she pirouetted. "I do look rather grown up, don't I?"

"Yes, and soon you'll be marrying, no doubt."

"Gracious no, Diana!" Marisa lowered her voice. "There's hardly a patriot left in Charlestown and I refuse to even consider a Tory for a husband, or one of those redcoats Gabriella is always inviting to the house. I'm an American," she proudly pronounced, "and I shall marry only an American. But no one can tell when that will be or if I'll ever meet the man of my dreams."

An image of Marisa with Clay Sinclair stirred within Diana's brain, and she instantly concluded that they'd be perfect for one another. "You must come visit me at Briarhaven very soon, Marisa. I have a feeling that the man of your dreams might soon become a reality."

"And what about the man of your dreams?" Marisa countered. "Do you believe Tanner will show up for his own party?"

Diana made an attempt at smoothing out the wrinkles of her gray satin day gown, then absently played with the drawstring on her reticule. "Tanner arranged this party weeks ago. Cammie and the servants are doing everything, and I suppose all I have to do is dress and go downstairs." She took her cousin's hands in hers. "I'm pleased that you and Aunt Frances will be there at my invitation. At least there will be two friendly faces among a sea of gossip mongers."

Marisa smiled weakly, and Diana knew she hadn't answered her question about Tanner showing up. It would be just like him not to come to his own party, to make her humiliation complete. She could almost imagine what everyone would say, but she couldn't hide in her room all night. She refused to allow anyone to believe she was a weakling or to think that Tanner's leaving her had totally undone her. To a great extent it had, but no one needed to know that. Let them say what they wanted. She didn't have to apologize to anyone for anything. But why did she need to see Tanner just once more before leaving for Briarhaven on New Year's Day? She felt she must say something to him; there was so much left unsettled and unsaid between them.

"Which gown are you planning to wear?" Marisa asked Diana.

She hadn't thought about a gown before now, but a naughty smile turned up the edges of her lips. "I have the perfect one in mind," she told her cousin. "If anyone comes to the party expecting to find me prostrate with grief over my husband's desertion, they'll be quite surprised."

"How long shall you avail yourself of my hospitality, Tanner?"

Tanner glanced at the young man who spoke to him and threw his napkin onto the table with barely a hint of disgust in the gesture. The tasty meal of quail and sweet potatoes was left uneaten, but he gestured to the servant hovering nearby to refill the wine cup. "I don't know," Tanner answered General Lord Rawdon in all seriousness. "I do appreciate the use of your quarters and realize that I'm putting you out. I apologize for any problems my presence might be causing you."

Rawdon shook his head, his youngish appearance belying a skilled leader, and leaned back in his chair. "Stay as long as you like" he offered, "but I wonder if you wouldn't rather be at home with your wife. I haven't met the lady, but my informants have praised her beauty and her virtue, and from what I've learned she doesn't seem to be shrewish. So why are you really here?"

Tanner looked sheepish. "Diana scares the hell out of me."

"What? I can't believe that the great Mariah, a man whose very name has caused brave men to cower with fear, is afraid of a mere woman." Rawdon didn't hide his pleasure or stifle his hearty laugh. "Tell me what power this wench wields over you that you run from your home like a whipped dog with your tail between your legs."

Tanner abruptly rose from his chair and looked out the window at the clear, star-filled sky. If any other man but Rawdon had made such an insulting comment to him, Tanner would have already wrestled him to the floor. But Tanner liked Rawdon and they respected one another, and he knew that the general didn't mean to laugh at him. After all, the situation *was* a bit laughable and ironic. Mariah could inspire fear in brave men while Tanner Sheridan quaked in his boots before a woman. He wondered what was wrong with him, why he constantly felt the need to run, but he realized he already knew. No matter what lies Diana had told about him years ago, he loved her. Yet he already suspected, as he had at Briarhaven, that his love was doomed. He was beneath her, so inferior to her that no matter his power and his wealth now, he couldn't make her love him.

When Tanner turned back to Rawdon, the flickering golden lights of the candelabrum on the table emphasized the pain in his eyes. "Perhaps by loving a heartless woman I'm being repaid for some of the horrible things I've done. I'd rather be whipped to within an inch of my life than suffer this . . . torment of soul."

"Good God. I had no idea that you felt this strongly about Diana Sheridan. I knew you wanted certain things done as a way of seeking some sort of vengeance upon her, but it seems the tables have turned. We've known one another for quite some time, Tanner, and I've never known you to fall in love before."

"There's a first time for everything, my friend, and a last." Tanner shrugged and wiped an imaginary stain from his frock coat, which was dark blue and made of the finest velvet. "The problem is that Diana is the only woman I've ever loved or will love. And she hates the very ground I tread upon."

"There are other women in the world," observed Rawdon. "Gabriella Fox is quite smitten with you."

"Gabriella is a whore."

"Yes, well . . ."

"And as far as other women, they don't exist for me. They aren't Diana."

"The great Mariah, brought low by a woman. I don't believe it." Rawdon twisted the wine cup between his hands. "Then I assume you won't attend the party at your house this evening."

Tanner's eyes glittered like black pearls. "Never assume anything about me, old friend."


It seemed that every Tory in Charlestown was at the party. Diana wandered among the elegantly dressed women and men, mingling with the British redcoats and gritting her teeth the whole time, exchanging pleasantries. She couldn't wait for this farce of a party to end. The only person she cared about was Marisa. They stayed near each other, both feeling horribly out of place in this sea of British loyalists and hoping that no one would discern their rebel sentiments. Wearing the scarlet gown Tanner had bought for her, Diana appeared the proper Tory, and with the huge smile pasted on her face, she didn't resemble a discarded wife in the least. Over the years she'd had enough practice with Kingsley to play her part well.

She downed a glass of champagne and mumbled to Marisa, "If ever I get the chance to see Tanner Sheridan again, I will tell him what an awful man he is not to show up for a party he planned in the first place. I swear I think he wants to humiliate me."

"Oh, I doubt it. Maybe he believes you don't care about him and feels there's no reason to come. . . ." Marisa's voice drifted away at the same instant her gaze moved to the parlor doorway. "Prepare yourself for a shock," she advised Diana. "Your husband has just arrived with Gabriella Fox."

Diana heard the hush fall across the room as Marisa finished speaking. Suddenly she found herself the center of attention as Tanner came toward her with his painted harpy hanging on his arm. *Miserable man!* she silently groused, but a gnawing pain settled in her heart to think that Tanner would humiliate her by flaunting the woman just like Kingsley had done with Jarla or one of his tarts. Diana couldn't help but be struck by the notion that Gabriella belonged here at the party more than she herself did. Tanner owned the townhouse and had the right to bring anyone he wished to his own party.

Acting the charming hostess, she smiled pleasantly and hid her hurt, but she couldn't quell the blush that rose to her cheeks at the memory of her body's response beneath Tanner's hands only nights ago. She prayed he'd think the spots of color on her cheeks were from too much champagne and laughter, and not because of him.

Diana held out her hand to Tanner like a queen to a noble knight, but she wasn't prepared for the jolting shock when their fingers touched. "How glad I am that you showed up for your own party. And Gabriella too. How divine."

"I'm sorry we're late," Tanner apologized and his dark gaze swept appraisingly over Diana. "You look beautiful," he whispered near Diana's ear.

She couldn't find the words to acknowledge that compliment. She ached to tell him that he was devilishly handsome in his elegant frock coat. No man in the room was as handsome as Tanner.

Tanner turned his attention to Marisa and

Gabriella sidled up to Diana. "The weather has turned unbearably cold, Diana dear. I do hope you're making proper use of the warming pan at nights. Those sheets can get horribly chilled when one sleeps alone. I, on the other hand, wouldn't know about that as I never sleep alone. My bed is quite warm."

"Oh, I had no idea that Jasper has been keeping you company at night."

"Jasper?"

"Yes, Aunt France's basset hound, but then again, Gabriella, darling, I would expect you're used to lying with dogs. Of course, I did think old Jasper had better taste. Now excuse me, dear, I have guests." Diana moved through the throng of people, very much aware that Gabriella's gaze bored through her back.

For the next hour, Diana watched while Gabriella openly flirted with Tanner. She was very aware that he seemed more than taken with the immoral creature, not batting an eyelash in Diana's direction. She felt slighted and angry. Tanner was her husband, *her husband,* and he didn't care enough about her even to speak further to her. By the time she'd consumed three more glasses of champagne, Diana had convinced herself that she didn't care at all about Tanner *or* Gabriella. In fact, she began flirting outrageously with a Captain Cummings, pretending she found his boring stories about battles to be pure heroics of the highest order, when in fact she didn't hear one word he uttered.

At one point Marisa touched her arm and drew her aside. "You've had too much to drink, Diana, and you're making a spectacle of yourself to get Tanner's attention."

"I am not. For the first time in months, I'm enjoying myself. And anyway, Tanner's attention isn't worth beans. He hates me, absolutely detests me." She grew quiet a second and her voice broke. "I can't blame him for ignoring me. I've treated him horribly."

"Then tell him so. What are you afraid of?"

Diana clutched at Marisa's wrist and a sob bubbled up in her throat. "I'm afraid I might love him . . . and that's . . . the worst thing that can happen . . . to me. There's so much you don't know about us."

"For heaven's sake," Marisa grumbled, "tell him how you feel and get it over with. I'm sick to death of the way you two keep eyeing each other. If you don't admit how you feel about him, then some woman, be it Gabriella or someone else, will take him away from you." Her tone softened and she kissed Diana's cheek. "I have to leave now. Mother is ill and home alone, but please think about what I've said."

After Marisa left, Diana couldn't stop thinking about her cousin's advice, but she lacked the courage to do anything about it, fearing that Marisa was wrong. She hadn't noticed that Tanner had been watching her. In fact, she didn't see him or Gabriella at all now, and she wondered fleetingly if they had departed. It was just as well if they had, she decided. She couldn't bear seeing Gabriella holding Tanner and knowing that people were gossiping about her marital situation. Oh, why wouldn't everyone just leave?

Taking another glass of champagne, Diana began to sip it delicately when she suddenly realized the room felt stuffy and warm. She wandered onto the piazza, glad of the cold wind on her face as it seemed to vanish her unpleasant mood. She thought she was alone until a slight noise in the shadows near a large potted palm caught her attention. Two figures were locked in an embrace, or rather, a woman held tightly onto a man's broad shoulders, but his hands were barely touching her waist. Diana emitted a tiny gasp of dismay when she suddenly recognized the two as Tanner and Gabriella.

She knew she should turn in a huff and go back inside, but she couldn't stop staring at them. Gabriella was pushing her voluptuous body against Tanner's. The lower half of her was blatantly rubbing against his manhood, leaving no doubt as to what she wanted. Diana's face flamed with the knowledge because she herself knew what it was that Gabriella craved. But she wouldn't think about it, couldn't think about what it was Gabriella wanted, because if she did she'd go insane remembering the feel of Tanner's hands upon her own body, how it felt when his practiced fingers slid inside her. As much as she hated standing here and being witness to this outrageous display of carnal lust, Diana couldn't move toward the doorway. She stood mesmerized by the two of them.

"Tanner, Tanner, please take me with you tonight. I hate sleeping alone." Gabriella's husky plea was quite audible to Diana's ears. "You know I can please you, and you know exactly what I like. Let's go now."

Shameless hussy! Gabriella was trying to seduce Tanner in his own home with his wife not twenty feet away. But neither of them knew that she was listening, and suddenly she didn't want to hear Tanner's reply. In a flash she'd made up her mind what she intended to do, and if he didn't like it then he could take his whore and leave!

Diana was vaguely aware that she now stood next to them. It was Tanner who saw her first, and he nonchalantly broke away from Gabriella, though the loathesome woman still clung to him.

"Heavens, for such a cold night you both are on fire," Diana declared, her eyes blazing hotly. "Especially you, Gabriella. I believe the time has come to cool you off." Lifting her champagne glass, Diana hurled the contents at Gabriella, staining the expensive gold satin gown the woman wore. Diana turned deaf ears to Gabriella's screech and threw down the glass at Tanner's feet. "I won't be made to look the fool any longer," she raged at him. "I'm your wife, and as your wife, I shall be treated with respect. Otherwise . . ." and here Diana faltered, realizing that she'd lost control but also realizing for the first time that she must be in love with her husband to act this way. Her world seemed to shatter into shards of glass like the broken crystal. Her glare died to be replaced by tears of anguish. When she noticed his stunned expression and lack of reply, she thought she'd lost him.

"I'm sorry." Diana choked on the words as she finally admitted to herself that her love for this man had come too late. "Forgive me, please. . . ." And with that, she found herself running down the length of the piazza, through the maze of blurred bodies and faces, and then up the stairs to her room, where she gulped back tears that threatened to strangle her.

"Ma'am, can I help you?" Cammie asked worriedly when she came out of the bathing room with one of Diana's nightrails over her arm.

All Diana could do was to shake her head and brokenly tell Cammie to leave her alone. She lay across her bed and staunchly refused to cry, but soon she found herself wiping away the tears she had never thought to shed again over Tanner Sheridan. But when at last the tears had given way to huge, gulping sobs she found a kerchief pressed into her hand. Thinking Cammie was the one who stood beside the bed, Diana lifted her head and opened her eyes to thank her for the kindness. A ragged sob caught in her throat when she realized it was Tanner standing over her.

"I'm sorry you saw what you did," he said, and Diana thought that his voice cracked a bit. He stood with his hands in his pockets and for the first time that Diana could recall, Tanner appeared less than confident.

Hurriedly Diana wiped her eyes and sat up. How distressing it was to her that he should see her cry. She knew she looked wretched whenever she cried. Probably Gabriella always looked lovely. No wonder Tanner didn't want her when Gabriella was available.

"I'll apologize to Gabriella in the morning," Diana began. "You won't be bothered with me for much longer. I'm leaving for Briarhaven tomorrow." She glanced up at Tanner, and her heart constricted when she realized that this was the last night she'd spend under this roof, in this bed, as his wife. "I won't hold you to . . . our wager. Briarhaven is yours. Harlan and I will leave. . . ."

"Diana, stop it!"

His voice boomed loudly in her ears, and she jumped from the sound of it, then jumped again as he fell atop her on the bed. Tanner's weight was crushing her, but strangely she didn't mind when his lips claimed hers in a kiss filled with so much mastery and passion that her head spun. "Admit you love me," he whispered after breaking the kiss. "Tell me you want me

. . . forever."

His lips were raining kisses upon her neck and shoulders, and Diana couldn't think clearly. Something pleasant and aching began to build within her, and she knew what was to follow if she gave into the sensations. And God only knew how much she wanted to give into them!

"Where's Gabriella?" she asked breathlessly. "Why are you here when she's the one you love?"

Tanner ceased the delightful assault of her senses and stared in bafflement. "I don't love Gabriella. I love you, Diana. I've always loved you." Grabbing a handful of her dark hair, he buried his fingers within the thick strands. "You're mine. Never, ever, will I release you, because no matter what you may have said or done in the past, no matter how hard you deny it, you love me too, and you want me." His breath was warm and soft against her lips. "Say you want me, say it."

A shiver of desire so raw and intense ripped through Diana at that moment that nothing could have stopped her from saying the words, "I . . . want . . . you. I . . . love . . . you." And those last three words she meant with all of her heart.

Tanner's eyes filled with sparkling fire, and he pressed her close against him. "You said you loved me," he whispered hoarsely. "I can't believe you said it. Do you mean it?"

His sudden insecurity touched Diana in a way

that made her love him all the more. Tenderly she stroked his cheek and gazed up at him with pure love shining in her own eyes. "I've loved you each and every hour of every day since we met. I'll never stop loving you, Tanner Sheridan, and from this moment on you'll never be rid of me. I promise you that."

Taking her hand, he pressed her fingers to his lips. "I'm going to hold you to that promise, Diana Sheridan."

Her name sounded wonderful when he said it, almost as if she heard it for the first time, and in an odd way it was. Now she knew she loved him and belonged to him and had a right to the name. She smiled beguilingly and pulled his head down, burying her hands within the thickness of his hair. "Make love to me," she urged in a husky voice. "I want you, I need you."

"You'll forfeit all now," he warned good-naturedly, but the teasing light in his eyes died to be replaced by one of hot desire when her hand left his hair to trail wantonly down his thigh and settle on the bulging spot within his trousers.

"I'm a gracious loser," was her soft reply.

To prove the point, Diana's hands began unbuttoning his frock coat. With a smile of disbelief still hovering on his lips, Tanner's eyes began to darken to an intense shade of black, broken only by amber lights that flared within the centers. Diana shivered from the dark pleasure that roiled inside of her, recognizing his desire. Daringly, she offered further assistance by removing the rest of his clothes. It seemed that her very fingers ached to touch him, and when he stood by the bedside, naked and unabashedly aroused, she didn't feel the least bit shy or hesitant. She was on her knees on the bed, leaning against him when she placed her hands on his chest to gently skim across the bronzed surface. He felt strong like steel, but also smoothly supple beneath her questing movements, and strangely vulnerable, too, when she placed her palm on his pounding heart.

*Tanner was human,* she found herself thinking; *he could be hurt.* She'd hurt him often in the past — perhaps without knowing it. She didn't want to hurt him any more, because now she had done the impossible by admitting to herself and to him that she loved him.

"I've always loved you," she said in an aching whisper. "I hope I'm not too late to tell . . ."

His mouth swooped down and captured hers in a kiss that stopped her very words and thoughts but left no doubt that he wanted her, no matter how long it had taken for her to tell him. Warm and hungry lips trailed from her mouth to her neck, gently sucking before moving downward to the valley of her scarlet-clad breasts and flicking his tongue within the lush indentation.

"As much as I like this dress, Diana, it has to go. May I remove it?"

God, she loved this man! Diana stifled a

sound that was half giggle, half moan. "Do you have to ask?"

"I don't want to hurt you or do anything that might upset you. I'm not like Kingsley."

"No, you're the man I love. You needn't ask me anything right now, Tanner. I know you won't hurt me. I trust you."

With that, he said nothing else.

When the last of her clothes lay in a scarlet and white heap on the floor beside the bed, Tanner blew out the candle and joined her beneath the quilts. But when the heat and intensity of their bodies and burning kisses became too great, Tanner threw off the covers.

He gazed down at her face, clear and silver-hued from the full moon's luminous light outside the window. "I believe I've taught you too well," he noted and grinned. "How to kiss, that is. My whole body's aflame. I've never felt like this before." The last sentence was filled with awe.

"Tanner, I love the way you talk, but sometimes you talk too much." Diana met his lips and arched toward him in one motion and for once Tanner seemed more than delighted to be quiet and to allow his body to speak for him.

Diana thought he had wonderful hands, hands that could move caressingly across her body and then fill with a fire, a fierce urgency to pleasure her. She couldn't stop touching him, touching him in places that caused him to moan in ecstasy. She wanted to know all of him, to

220

give to him that same wonderful pleasure he'd given to her a few nights ago. Her palm wrapped around that part of him that was simultaneously hard and velvety smooth, and he guided her in the motions. Strange as it was, she wasn't repulsed as she'd been with Kingsley. In fact, she enjoyed hearing Tanner's moans. But suddenly he stilled her hand and pushed her onto the mattress, his warm, wonderful hands coaxing her thighs apart.

He held her thus while he kissed her mouth and then laved attention upon her breasts. Tanner had wonderful lips, too, she decided, as he loved each of her breasts in turn—loved them so well that she felt herself trembling and aching to close her legs, but his hands held them apart.

Lower his mouth trailed, skirting across her stomach and navel to her abdomen, then lower still. No, not there! He couldn't mean to place his mouth there. Kingsley had done that very same thing to her and had hurt her. Tanner had promised he wouldn't hurt her, but her body hadn't forgotten those long ago hours of pain when she was Kingsley's wife.

She tried to close her thighs, but he held them open, not looking at her, seemingly not aware of her fear.

"Tanner, don't. No, no." But it was too late. His mouth found her and explored her, tentatively at first, but growing bolder when Diana started to relax. His hands became gentle, no longer unyielding on her legs. In her mind she imagined that Tanner was speaking to her, assuring her he wouldn't hurt her, urging her to enjoy . . . enjoy. But it was so sinful to give into this, so darkly wicked . . . so heart-stoppingly wonderful.

Something fluid and hot started churning within the very center of her femininity. Now Diana recognized the sensation for what it was. She knew she wouldn't be able to stop it and didn't want to. This was what she'd craved from the moment Tanner had kissed her on the bluff all those years ago. This was what she'd ached for since he'd left her three nights ago. It was going to happen again. Her body was controlling her and she didn't care.

She made tiny mewing sounds and gyrated her hips, more than eager to accommodate his lusty feasting. Rearing upward to give him better access, she gave a groan of disappointment when he suddenly stopped. But her dismay was short-lived. Tanner lifted himself onto his knees, and with such deliberate slowness that Diana thought she was going to die from wanting, he slid his length inside of her.

Then, as if they were of one mind, they began to move together, almost in dancelike tempo. Their bodies fit perfectly well, so well that they seemed fused with each rise and fall of every thrust and arch. The churning within Diana grew into a fire so intense and heated that she felt destined never to know peace again, but she didn't care. All she could concentrate on was how Tanner looked.

His eyes were so black and yet golden, his face so handsome and manly, yet beautiful, his kisses so breathtaking that she felt weak, yet strong. She felt as light as the moonbeams on the ceiling, and her whole body glowed with Tanner's possession. It was impossible not to, because she knew that at any moment she would explode.

When Tanner thrust into her with a powerful urgency that tapped her very center, Diana was the one who couldn't be quiet. "Tanner, Tanner, Tanner. It's . . . going to happen . . . again." Total disbelief on her part.

"Let it, love. Let it." He pulled her toward him and ground his pelvis into hers, but it was his fire-filled kiss that finally pushed her over the edge.

Never did Diana expect to feel anything so intense. It was so vibrant that she thought she had died and been born again in one instantaneous flash of pleasure. Her whole body experienced the ecstasy in undulating waves that reached into every cell and nerve. She had closed her eyes at the very beginning, but now she opened them in wonder because Tanner started to moan and spill himself into her, and the fire was still fresh and raging within her. She instinctively arched against him and circled her hips, drawing the very essence of him into her, and the subsequent explosion of her own body caused her to cry out against his mouth.

Tanner held her close for long moments afterward. Diana was too numb to say anything. Instead she started to cry.

"What is it? Have I hurt you? Good God, Diana, tell me what I've done." Tanner bent over her, a worried expression on his face when he didn't get any response except tears.

Diana stroked his cheek in an attempt to wipe away his worried look and finally composed herself. "It's just that . . . I've never . . . known what to feel . . . never experienced anything except with you." She gulped back a tiny sob. "I don't know if I can stand it, Tanner. It feels so wonderful that I think I might die from it. Am I being silly? I know I'm not like your other women, I'm not really experienced. . . ."

"I'm glad you aren't like any other woman I've ever known, otherwise, I wouldn't love you so much." He kissed her with tender solemnity. "And as far as experience, well, my bewitching vixen, I'll give you as much as you can handle."

He began laughing, and Diana realized he was teasing her, but she wasn't teasing when she pushed against him and forced him to lie flat on the bed while she wantonly rested atop him. "Promise me that," she said.

"Taunting tease, I'd promise you my soul if you asked for it."

"Hmmm, I might just take you up on that, but for now," Diana's tongue began licking at his lips, "I'd rather something else."

The teasing light left Tanner's eyes, darkening

to that ebony black that always made her shiver with anticipation. The proof of his desire nudged at the juncture between her thighs, growing with each bold movement of her body. When he positioned her atop him, Tanner more than adequately lived up to his promise.

# Chapter 12

In the full light of day, Tanner and Diana finally got up and began to eat the hearty breakfast left for them outside of the door by Cammie. The house had long been quiet, the party ending, Diana learned, shortly after she'd rushed into her room last night. Tanner had immediately ordered everyone out—even Gabriella, who left in a snit on the arm of a British officer.

Tanner lounged on the bed while he ate, naked and without so much as a sheet to cover him. It never ceased to amaze Diana how comfortable he was with his own body. She, however, wore a robe. She told him she was chilly, but in reality she still felt shy in front of him.

Diana sat next to him and ran her fingers along the broad planes of his back. "What are these scars from?" she asked, concern in her eyes. "Were you whipped at one time?"

His muscles stiffened beneath her fingers for an instant before relaxing. "Yes, a very long time ago, a time best left forgotten."

Her lips silently planted tiny kisses along the whip lines before saying, "I know how much it must have hurt. I remember . . . the crop."

Tanner instantly gathered her to him and stroked her hair. "Kingsley is dead, Diana. You must forget him and what he did to you."

"I have forgotten him, for the most part." She hesitated a moment. "Still, sometimes I dream about him and he seems very real, very menacing. Lately I have this strange feeling that he's more alive than ever—and I get so frightened."

"Kingsley won't hurt you again. He is dead, sweetheart. Nothing will hurt you now that you're my wife."

Diana wrapped her arms around his neck and inhaled his musky scent. She smiled up at him. "I want to return to Briarhaven, our home."

Tanner's hold tightened around her waist. "Ah, Diana, I do, too, but my father . . ."

"It's time you made peace with one another. Harlan is an old and sickly man. This would be the perfect way to begin the new year. Please forgive him. You're all he has."

Tanner nodded. "I know that, but I'm not Kingsley, and he better not expect me to be."

"He doesn't, and I'm glad you aren't Kingsley, so very glad." Their lips met and a fierce yearning once more filled them. Both couldn't help

227

but wonder if their lovemaking would always be filled with fire.

"Here's a bit of potato soup for you, Mr. King. I know it ain't the best but it's all I could come up with. In fact, I was mighty lucky to have found a decent potato, what with all the hungry folks around here." Mike Candy offered the cracked bowl to the invalid man, who lifted himself off his pallet and rested on an elbow while he drank the soup. "There now," Candy commented affably. "You'll be feeling as good as new soon." He made a gesture to touch King's forehead, but King instantly drew back.

"My fever's broken," King snapped. "I don't need you to play nursemaid."

"You sure as hell did the other day when you were so sick," Candy reminded him. "You know, Mr. King, you're an ornery fellow, but I let you stay here because I know you don't have a home to go to."

"I do have a home!" King shot back. "I have a home that would put the best house in Charlestown to shame."

"Then why don't you go there?"

King frowned and retreated into a stony silence that always managed to unnerve Mike Candy. Candy looked out the door of the hovel and pointed to the road that led away from Charlestown. "Well look there. It's Mr. Tanner Sheridan's coach. I recognize it from the last time he was here."

"Let me see. Help me up!" King demanded, and with Candy's assistance he made it to the door.

"He has his wife with him," Candy commented, a smile in his voice. "She sure is a pretty lady. Wonder where they're going?"

"They're going home." Mr. King's voice cracked. Candy looked at him, ready to ask him how he knew that, but there was a hideous black rage festering within King's eyes. Instead, Candy led him back to the pallet. "I feel sick," King admitted, and Candy saw that the man was shivering and extremely pale. Candy felt his forehead and found it warm to the touch.

"Better rest, Mr. King," was Candy's advice.

"No rest for me," King mumbled and lay back. "No rest until I get the jewels and rid myself of that half-breed and claim Diana. Diana. *Mine, always mine.*"

The hatred in King's voice caused Candy to grimace and shake his head sadly. King constantly spoke in his delirium about the half-breed and this woman called Diana. And Candy, gentle soul that he was, felt extremely sorry that Mr. King was so unhappy. But he was sorrier still for this woman named Diana. Apparently King was obsessed with her, and from what Candy could ascertain, he might be dangerous, too.

"Poor lady," Candy muttered. "For your sake Mr. King better not get well enough to claim you."

Farnsworth and his men were still at Briarhaven.

Upon their arrival, Tanner escorted Diana to her bedroom and was instantly summoned away by Captain Farnsworth. Diana tried not to think about Tanner, the man she loved, in conversation with the British officer. Yet Tanner had mentioned during their trip that he knew the British would still be quartered at Briarhaven and that their stay was a good thing for all concerned.

"Why?" Diana had asked, growing a bit peeved that Tanner could think in such a way but without admitting how much she hated the thought of it.

"Because," he had explained, "supply wagons will come through to feed the troops and all of us at Briarhaven will be fed. The Santee area is starving, Diana, and these patriots running through the woods and stealing from the wagons won't do any of us any good."

"I know that!" Diana colored at the vehemence of her own statement. She hoped Tanner had no way of ascertaining how much she cared about the situation along the Santee River. But then, he wouldn't know or surmise that she was one of the Swamp Fox's informants—one of the very people who passed information about British supply wagons and any other news she overheard that the rebels might find useful in their fight for independence.

She recalled the appraising way Tanner had watched her, with one dark eyebrow cocked in thought. To pull him away from whatever he might be thinking, Diana placed her gloved hand in his and cuddled up to him before kissing him. For the rest of the trip, everything was fine.

But now Diana paced her room while Hattie unpacked the trunks she'd brought from Charlestown. "Lord, Miss Diana." Hattie's awe-filled words could scarcely be heard in the bed-room when she opened the small jewelry box filled with jewels. "I thought you done brought some pretty gowns home, but Mr. Tanner must be powerful rich to afford these."

"He is, I suppose."

"Hmm hmm. Just how did you and Mr. Tanner meet up again and get married so quick?"

"Don't ask questions, Hattie, but I have some questions for you." Diana stopped pacing. "Have you heard anything about the Swamp Fox or Clay Sinclair?"

Hattie shook her head. "No, ma'am."

"There hasn't been any activity of any sort while I was away?"

"No, all been quiet."

"Too quiet, I think," Diana mused and grinned. "Maybe it's time to stir things up a bit."

Tanner shook Farnsworth's outstretched hand and settled himself into the comfortable chair in his father's library. Farnsworth leaned back in the chair behind the desk, a proprietary air about him. "Your bride is fine, I take it."

"Diana is very well, thank you," Tanner commented.

Farnsworth smiled sheepishly. "I must apologize for what I said about her in the tavern that night. I had too much to drink. None of it was true."

"I know that."

Farnsworth scowled. "You don't have to be so quick to agree, but your bride's virtue isn't the matter at hand here."

"What is?"

"You, Tanner Sheridan, and I may call you that since that is your name. I am curious about why you told me you weren't related to the Sheridans of Briarhaven when I asked you."

"I said I wasn't related to them as far as I was concerned. I didn't deny that Sheridan blood runs through my veins. Why the interest, Farnsworth?"

"How blunt you are." Farnsworth fiddled with his quill pen. "Evidently you don't want your wife or anyone else to know about Mariah."

"How astute you *are*," Tanner complimented, but he didn't smile. "Now, what do you want?"

"A spy, my man, a good spy, and you're the

best."

"I've retired. I told you that."

"I'm certain you can come out of retirement to appease me. Before I left for Charlestown, I was very distressed about the rebel situation in this area. The Swamp Fox and his men were running rampant, and it seemed that somehow information about our activities was being relayed. My men have walked into a number of traps on occasion, and supply wagons have been commandeered. Needless to say, General Lord Rawdon is less than pleased."

"I'm sorry to hear that."

"I don't wish to be replaced, Sheridan."

"How is activity now?" Tanner pressed.

"Quiet."

"Then you don't need me."

Farnsworth leaned forward, a determined eagerness on his face. "I need to know that if the situation arises, you'll discover who the informant is and bring him to me . . . only to me. I'd take great delight in hanging the rebel cur. He's made me look like an absolute fool in Rawdon's eyes. I won't tolerate that. I won't! Now, you must promise me you'll do this for me if I have need of you."

Folding his arms across his chest, Tanner shot Farnsworth a penetrating look. "In other words, you're saying that if I don't spy for you if the occasion arises, then you'll tell my wife that I was a spy. So, go on. She's a loyalist."

"Ah, my good man, she may be a loyalist but

she's still a woman, and now a wife. Wives can be very jealous, and I remember an assignment in New York that concerned a beautiful spy, and let's say that your relationship with this woman wasn't all business."

"So?"

"So, Tanner, I can make your life in the bedroom miserable for you. It's plain you love your wife. I do recall seeing her at one such affair in Charlestown and her reaction to Gabriella Fox. Clearly she disliked the woman because you were sleeping with her." Farnsworth threw down the quill in a triumphant gesture, extending a hand. "Have we reached a compromise?"

Tanner didn't believe Diana would understand about Mariah. Reluctantly he shook Farnsworth's hand.

Diana was pleased that Farnsworth didn't join the family for dinner that evening. For the first time in a long while the dining room glowed with light, and Diana could almost imagine that the British weren't encamped on the grounds and in nearby bedrooms.

Harlan sat at the head of the table, the soft candlelight caused his unusually pale complexion to glow, and Diana realized that it wasn't only from the candle. He hadn't taken his eyes from Tanner. Their initial meeting had been strained, neither one of them too inclined to be the first to embrace. Instead they had shaken hands and Tanner had inquired about his father's health.

Harlan had declared himself to be well, but Diana knew he wasn't. As he lifted his wine glass to his lips his hand shook, and she noticed he ate very little. But no matter the true state of his physical condition, it was clear that at this moment Harlan was happy.

"I can't believe that the two of you are married," Harlan noted, and smiled warmly at both Tanner and Diana. "This is the best news I could have received. Maybe you'll make me a grandfather soon."

Diana laughed and glanced at Tanner who sat in stony silence. "We're working on it."

"Good, good," Harlan seemed more than satisfied at her remark.

Diana could tell that Harlan wanted Tanner to say something, but neither spoke directly to the other, and the slight strain that had been evident earlier was now intensifying. Harlan directed all of his conversation to Diana, but Tanner couldn't seem to get up the nerve to speak directly to his own father. She had hoped the two men would put aside their differences, but now she realized that that hope was a vain one.

"Where is Naomi?" Diana asked Harlan.

"In the kitchen. She didn't wish to join us at the table."

"Did you ask her if she'd like to eat with us?" were the first words out of Tanner's mouth since sitting down.

Harlan blanched at the disdain behind the question, but he answered defensively, "Of

235

course I asked her. Your mother is a very stubborn woman, Tanner. She said she doesn't feel comfortable eating in such grand style. Usually we eat in my room and then she reads to me before bedtime. I would have liked very much for her to join us in celebrating your homecoming."

For a second, Tanner appeared guilty but he said nothing else. And that was how the meal progressed until Harlan excused himself at Naomi's appearance and went upstairs to ready himself for bed.

Diana stood up, intent upon saying something to Tanner, but she didn't get the chance. "I don't want to be chastised like a child, Diana. So, just forget whatever it was you wanted to say."

"Harlan is your father. He's an old man, a very ill man, or didn't you notice," she reminded him anyway.

"I noticed."

"He may not have much time left. You might have to make the first move."

For a second Tanner's eyes filled with tears and he said hoarsely, "I can't. I thought I could, but too much happened between us. Anyway, why should I be the one to offer my hand to him first? He's as much to blame, perhaps more." He took a cheroot out of his coat pocket and stayed seated at the dining room table, his black look defying her to say anything further.

Diana knew when she was head to head with defeat. Going upstairs, she met Naomi coming out of Harlan's room.

"Is Harlan settled for the night?" Diana asked. She was rewarded with a brisk nod of Naomi's head and an even blacker look than the one Tanner had bestowed upon her in the dining room. Naomi attempted to move past Diana, but Diana stopped her with a hand on the woman's arm. "What's wrong, Naomi?"

At first Diana thought Naomi wasn't going to respond, but she turned in a fury, her gray streaked braid whipping around and bouncing upon her shawl-clad shoulder. "Such a strange question from you! You're what is wrong, Diana Sheridan, wife of my son. Why did you marry Tanner? Why can't you leave him alone to live in peace? You'll bring pain to him, pain and loneliness. Once before you hurt him, now you shall destroy him."

Diana didn't know what Naomi was talking about. She never hurt Tanner; he had hurt her. "You're not making any sense . . ."

"Silly girl! I cannot speak to one so shallow as you. Leave me be, leave my son alone."

"I . . . I love Tanner."

Noami laughed shrilly. "If you love him like you loved your first husband then my son is indeed doomed." She left Diana standing in the hallway with her heart in her throat and a dreadful feeling in her soul. Never had Diana realized the extent of Naomi's dislike for her.

But why did her mother-in-law think she had hurt Tanner, why did Naomi believe she would destroy Tanner when she had been the one hurt all of those years ago?

Diana was so intent upon what Naomi had told her that she barely realized she was nearing Farnsworth's room until she heard his voice and that of one of his officers. The door stood slightly ajar, and Diana immediately halted, her ears alert for any information.

"Another supply wagon is due to come through two days from now," she heard Farnsworth say. "And Smythe, make certain that the Swamp Fox, doesn't get to it first."

"I will, sir," Smythe assured his superior. "Marion and his men have been rather quiet. I see no reason to assume that they have information about the wagon."

"Humph! You take too much for granted. That's why you won't rise in the ranks. Never assume anything."

"I'll take care of it. Don't worry."

Diana heard Farnsworth sigh. "I hope so, Smythe. I do hate to call in Mariah."

"I thought you said Mariah was ready if needed."

"He is, but he's not too keen on the idea."

"I see, but we won't need him."

"I hope not, Smythe."

Assuming the conversation was at an end, Diana hurriedly turned and ran quietly to the stairs to give the impression that she was just coming up. Smythe saw her on the landing and smiled. "Good evening to you, Mrs. Sheridan."

"Good evening," she cheerily returned and made her way to her room. Hattie glanced up at Diana's entrance and finished turning down the bed. Diana grinned. "I'm going to need you for a lookout, Hattie."

Hattie's mouth dropped. "You will? You got somethin' to tell . . ."

"Yes."

"But what about Mr. Tanner? Ain't he gonna sleep in here with you?"

Diana's excitement waned a bit. She'd forgotten that Tanner would share her bed, and though she felt anticipation at the fact, she couldn't help but be somewhat dismayed. How was she going to sneak away into the tunnel? Tanner was a light sleeper and was aware of her every movement. "I'll manage to get away somehow," Diana decided. "I only hope that Clay is waiting for me when I do."

However, her plan to leave later that night wasn't put into effect. Tanner did join her in bed, and when he expertly kissed and touched her, arousing her unbearably and taking her to rapture's heights throughout the night, she forgot all about Clay and the supply wagon. It was only when she drifted off to sleep near dawn that she remembered.

One month later, Farnsworth's operation was in shambles. Two supply wagons had been captured by the Swamp Fox and two of his best men had been killed in a surprise attack some five miles away. He didn't have a clue as to how confidential information was being leaked to Marion. Was the man a spirit, could he become invisible and sit in on secret meetings at Briarhaven? There was no way Farnsworth could figure out how information was being passed.

At first he thought someone in the house was spying and was determined to discover who it was. His men had been posted at all the doorways leading outside. He knew that if someone was spying then that person would be captured. But no one left the house. So how, how in the name of heaven, was confidential strategy being relayed to Marion?

"I have no other alternative," Farnsworth said to Smythe one morning. "I have to call in Mariah."

"I'm surprised you've waited so long," Smythe remarked.

"Believe me, I am too. But I didn't want the blasted man to think I'd failed. You know whose ear he has, and I don't relish looking like a perfect fool."

"Well, if anyone can discover who's passing information to Marion, then Mariah can. He's one of the best-trained spies we have."

"He is. By this time next week, with Mariah's

help, I intend to have Marion's little ragtag band as my prisoners, and I'll take great delight in discovering who has been passing information and even greater delight in learning how it left Briarhaven in the first place."

Her ear pressed against the library door, Diana turned hurriedly away when she saw the front door opening. Tanner entered, looking fit and trim in brown trousers and boots with a dark brown jacket thrown over his broad frame.

He smiled at her, and instantly Diana felt herself color and grow heated, not only from the fact that he might realize she'd been eavesdropping but from their passion-drenched nights. The fact of the matter was that Tanner didn't come to bed until quite late. He often spent a great deal of time downstairs with Farnsworth and his men, playing cards. Not once had she complained about the card games, because they allowed her the opportunity to sneak away into the tunnel and find Clay in the swamps whenever she had information, but she felt very guilty deceiving Tanner.

If Tanner suspected that she'd been listening at the library door, he didn't say anything. Instead he pulled her into his arms and kissed her. "How's my girl this morning?" he asked her.

Diana snuggled willingly against him. "Lonely without you. You woke early and left me." She forced her mouth into a mock pout.

"Then I suppose I'll have to remedy that."

"Now?"

"Now," he whispered huskily into her ear and suggestively nibbled on the lobe.

"Tanner Sheridan, you're a shocking man and I love you for that."

Laughing, they began to ascend the stairway, but Farnsworth's voice halted them. "What is it?" Tanner asked in a growl.

"I need to speak with you, please, about your losses at cards."

"Let it wait until later."

"I can't. Remember we discussed that I might need your resources." Farnsworth returned to the library.

Tanner cursed under his breath. "I'll join you upstairs as soon as I can," he promised Diana.

"I'll be waiting." Diana watched as her husband joined Farnsworth and Smythe in the library. She decided that she was gong to have to speak to Tanner about his losses. She hated gambling. His departure, however, lent her adequate time to think about what she'd overheard.

Once again Farnsworth had mentioned a person named Mariah. Evidently he was a spy, soon to be engaged to discover Marion's informant. She must warn Clay Sinclair about this Mariah. She didn't consider her own safety since she had the security of the tunnel and could come and go at will. Clay had only the swamp and palmettos for cover and was always vulnerable to capture.

And if this Mariah person was as good a spy

as Farnsworth had said he was, then Clay must be warned soon.

Tanner rose above Diana and slid effortlessly inside of her. She met his first thrust and moved with him, feeling the warm and utterly devouring sensation writhing within her. He held her tightly, taking the breath from her but driving her wild with wanting. It seemed that she never got enough of Tanner's lovemaking; her body could flame with the fire of his kiss and not be quenched until they both lay panting and satiated in each other's embrace, only to be roused to desire again when he touched her.

What was this spell Tanner had woven over her? She couldn't put a name to it, knowing only that she loved him more and more every day.

The moment of fulfillment drained both of them.

Slowly they returned from their private paradise, filled with awe at their bodies' responses. Tanner took her face between his large hands and whispered, "You're a temptress who has stolen my heart."

"Oh, I hope not," she disagreed. I'd rather you gave me your heart. I hate the thought of stealing it. It sounds as if I'm a thief who came in the night."

"You are, Diana. You took me unawares. I was determined not to love you, but I couldn't help myself because I've always loved you."

"Will you love me forever?"

"Forever."

That answer always appeased Diana. Sometimes she worried Tanner would stop loving her. They were so different in so many ways that she knew he wouldn't understand about her connection to the Swamp Fox. But he'd never discover that fact, because tonight would be the last time she'd go and find Clay—at least for the time being. She had to warn him about this spy named Mariah.

Afternoon sunshine spilled across the bed and covered their bodies in a golden counterpane. For the first time, Diana felt that their problems were behind them. Now they could concentrate on each other, no longer filled with past hurts. And maybe, just maybe, she might conceive a child.

A beguiling smile tipped the corners of her mouth. "What do you think about our chances of making a baby?" she asked.

Tanner didn't smile. "But you said you'd lost a child. Are you sure you want to risk that again?"

"Oh, Tanner. I want your baby."

Possessively he covered her body with his. "Anything you want, anything at all."

He came into her willing body and brought her to ecstasy again.

\* \* \*

"Where's Mr. Tanner?" Diana asked Hattie from the doorway of her bedroom later that night.

"He's done downstairs, playin' cards with Captain Farnsworth and his officers."

"Good, that will give me time to leave and warn Clay."

"What you warnin' him 'bout, Miss Diana?" Hattie raised an eyebrow in suspicion.

"Nothing, really. Don't worry about it." Diana threw on her black cape, intent upon not worrying Hattie further. Jarla had recently died in childbirth, the baby not surviving either. Ezra, Hattie's son, was having a hard time coming to terms with his wife's death and was unable to adequately care for Jackie. Thus Jackie's care fell to Hattie, and with the old woman's other responsibilities, Diana didn't want to frighten her about a spy in the area.

Diana had to warn Clay this one last time. She prayed she wasn't too late. The grim possibility existed that by now Clay could have been captured—or killed. She wouldn't dwell on the image of Clay Sinclair being hanged or lying dead in the swamps. She couldn't. Time was all-important now.

Hattie clutched at Diana's arm. Her dark eyes welled with tears. "You be careful. I get so scared with you runnin' 'round the swamps at night. If Mr. Tanner would ever find you gone, I don't know what I'd say to him."

"I suppose you'd have to make up some ex-

245

cuse, but I promise that tonight will be the last time for a while."

"Did you know that there are soldiers guardin' every door to the outside?"

Diana hadn't known that. Farnsworth had never placed guards on the entranceways before now. Did he suspect that the news being relayed to Colonel Marion was coming from inside the house? A shiver of apprehension slid down her spine. This *would* be the last time.

"I'll be all right," Diana assured her. "Now go check the hallways for me."

Dutifully, Hattie did as Diana requested, and soon she motioned Diana forward from the bedroom. Diana made her way to the backstairs and then to the cellar, where she let herself into the secret tunnel. With a torch lighting her way, she meandered along the damp corridor to the tomb's doorway. She soon found herself outside beneath a moonless sky as she stealthily padded into the murky swamp.

Peering into the darkness for some sign of Clay, she almost gave up hope of seeing him that night. But his low imitation, like that of a nightingale, drew her attention to a nearby cypress tree. "I've been waiting for you," Clay explained when she drew near to him.

"I have news." Diana hurriedly began telling him about the spy named Mariah. She'd never felt apprehensive about her nightly visits before now, but she did tonight. The sooner she returned home, the better off she'd be. "Until

Mariah is gone from the area, this is the last time we'll meet. I can't take the chance of my husband discovering I'm gone. I don't know what I'd tell him, because Farnsworth's men are guarding the doors and I don't know how I can explain my absence."

"What about your husband?" Clay asked with a hint of jealousy in his voice. "You told me the last time we met that he was sympathetic to the British. Do you think he trusts you?"

"Tanner doesn't have a reason to mistrust me. He may wonder about my sentiments, but I've been more than circumspect in my actions and my words."

"Don't take chances, Diana. Just know that Colonel Marion is pleased with the information you've brought him all of these times. He also knows the risks you've been taking. So do I. If ever you have a reason to contact me in the future, leave a piece of ribbon on the branch of a nearby tree. I'll find it and will be on the lookout for you."

Diana smiled and hugged Clay around the neck. "Take care of yourself."

Clay assured her that he would, and as silently as he'd approached her, he left.

A ragged sigh of relief rushed through Diana's teeth. It was over for now. The danger of imparting information had grown too great. But the real reason she was relieved had to do with Tanner. She didn't have to lie to him any longer about what she was doing. Not that she'd lied in the first place, but she'd never mentioned her secret life, which was almost the same thing as being untruthful.

Now to return home and be with her husband. Diana's body quivered with the sense of anticipation at their lovemaking. It seemed that it just got better with every time. Now she felt truly like a woman, Tanner's woman. She almost giggled with joy.

Her mind was so filled with images of Tanner that she barely heard the sound of a horse's hooves coming toward her when she left the swamp. The inky blackness of the night enfolded her, but suddenly, almost as if it were destined to happen, a sliver of a moonbeam emerged from behind a black cloud and cast a silvery glow upon her. It was then she heard the soft grunt of the animal and lifted her head. What she saw almost stopped her heart.

A large powerful horse reared upward, its dark-clad rider silhouetted against the moonlight. She stifled a gasp but wasn't certain she'd been spotted, even though she was out in the open with no trees for cover. Glancing to her right, she saw that the cemetery was within one hundred feet of her, but fleeing to it was impossible since the black horseman blocked her path. Instead Diana stood stock still, barely breathing, her heart beating so hard that she knew the man must be able to hear it. But apparently he didn't, and he didn't see her either, at least not until the horse either sensed or smelled her presence. Her worst nightmare suddenly became reality when the horse turned toward her, causing the rider's gaze to settle upon her.

"Surrender yourself!" came the man's booming voice.

It was this harsh command that spurred Diana to finally move.

Her legs turned of their own accord, headed for the swamp. Clay must be nearby, he had to be! Somehow she knew that the rider pursuing her was the spy called Mariah, and she knew that if she didn't find Clay she'd soon be at Farnsworth's mercy. Her mind quickly played out scenes of Tanner looking on as she was led away to prison or the gallows. She saw herself swinging by the neck, and she doubted her husband wielded enough power to free another condemned person—even his own wife.

She must make it into the swamps and to Clay.

By some miracle she outran the horse and rider, rushing headlong into the swamp and passing the spot where she and Clay had stood only minutes earlier. She splashed into the knee-high water, pushing deeper into the palmetto darkness. How far did she have to go? Where was Clay? she wondered. The skirt of her gown billowed around her like a balloon and she hung onto tree roots and overhanging limbs to keep her balance when her legs grew heavy as the soft bottom sucked at her feet.

Diana made an aborted attempt to call for

Clay, but her vocal cords were paralyzed with fear, her lungs threatening to burst. Instead, sobs of frustration rose in her throat and choked her. A primal darkness enshrouded her figure, preventing her from seeing anything at all, and this gave her hope that Mariah would be blinded too.

But her hope was short-lived. She heard the splash behind her and felt the warm breath of the horse on her neck. Instantly, as if she'd been plucked from the bowels of hell by a deity who was even more hellish, she found herself lifted from the water by a strong arm to be unceremoniously positioned across the back of the horse with her head drooping downward. The cold steel of a pistol dug into her backside.

"Scream and you're dead," the man named Mariah growled.

She couldn't speak, much less scream. Instead she nodded that she understood, horribly aware that tears streamed down her cheeks. Silly twit, she silently groused, hating herself for her weakness, her fear. What sort of a patriot was she when she could be reduced to a quivering idiot? Her life was over, she knew that. With each step the horse took out of the swamp, her time on earth diminished.

Please let me be brave at the end, she prayed. But it wasn't so much her fear of death that frightened her but the idea that she'd never again lie in Tanner's arms. Never again would he take her to paradise, never would she feel the absolute awe of the climactic moment when their souls soared to the heavens. All of the wonders that Tanner had taught her about her own body had been for nothing.

This man was going to kill her.

# Chapter 13

Mariah reined in the horse outside of the swamp, dumping a soaking wet and shivering Diana onto the grass. The hood of her cloak covered most of her head, preventing her from glancing up at her assailant, but she didn't need to see him. She knew he was powerfully built and strong from the way he'd picked her up and then dropped her onto the ground. But she instantly decided that she wasn't going to be at his mercy or swing from the hangman's noose, not if she could help it.

Apparently he thought she was much too weak to run because after he'd gotten off of the horse he stood on the other side of the animal, fiddling with the pistol. Now was her chance of escape. The white of the Sheridan headstones loomed in the distance. If she could make it to the cemetery, if she could somehow outrun him . . .

Which was exactly what she tried to do. With lightning speed, she jumped from the ground and bolted in that direction. But with even more speed, Mariah easily grabbed her by the waist and tackled her to the ground.

He fell atop her, his voice sounding ragged in her ear. "Now, lad, what did you want to do that for? You'll only make things harder on yourself."

Lad? Diana's head shot up. How could he think she was a boy? Then she realized that her wet skirt hugged her legs, causing her to appear to be wearing breeches. But whether he thought her to be a woman or not, she wouldn't let this man win without a fight.

When he turned her over on the grass, she lashed out at him. Her nails raked the side of his face, and she knew she drew blood by the sticky warmth sliding down her fingers. She'd have done more damage, but he was much stronger than she. His two hands pinned her arms above her head and his lower body leaned on top of hers, quelling her urge to kick out.

"God, you are a wildcat, son. Now tell me how you're getting information from Farnsworth and passing it to the Swamp Fox."

Mariah didn't waste any time. Diana didn't either. She lifted her head, allowing her hood to fall away and spat at him, hitting him directly in the face. "I won't tell you anything. I won't. You'll get nothing out of me, you bounder."

Suddenly she felt the man's body tense, fearful that she'd gone too far, that now she was truly doomed. Then his hold slackened upon her and his hand touched her face so she'd be forced to finally look at him.

"Diana."

Diana looked at him, really looked. The incredulity written on his face matched what she felt. "Oh, no!" was all she could think to cry. She didn't know whether to be glad or more afraid, because the man staring back at her was Tanner.

"How did you get out of the house?" he asked her, his shock abating as he pulled her into a sitting position. "Farnsworth has every door and window guarded. But more important, what in hell are you doing out here?"

"I can ask the same of you," she retorted.

Tanner shook his head. "God, I don't think I want to know."

"Then don't ask, Mariah!" she shot back.

He expelled a deep breath. "So you know about me."

"I know enough."

"I can assume that you're the one who's been spying and passing information to the Swamp Fox."

"You may assume nothing." She sounded haughty, and she was quite unprepared when Tanner shook her by the shoulders.

"This is serious," he reminded her. "I've been sent to do a job and I have succeeded. Now, I find that my quarry is my own wife. What am I going to do with you?"

She really didn't know either. In fact she realized she knew very little about Tanner and his past. So Tanner was the great Mariah, a British spy. No wonder he was so very wealthy. There was no doubt he'd earned his money through nefarious deeds. No telling how many patriots he'd turned in to the British. Diana's teeth chattered from the sudden chill that flooded her with the realization of who her husband really was. He wasn't merely a Tory sympathizer, he was a British spy. He was one of them, the enemy!

"I suppose you'll hand me over to Farnsworth. How much did he offer you for my capture? I do hope I'll fetch you a good price, because I'm the only one you'll be paid for. I'll never tell anything about anyone else. You can torture me, you can force me at the point of a rapier, but . . ."

"Be quiet!" Tanner rasped. "I have to think." He took a clean kerchief out of his coat pocket and dabbed at the blood on his face. A wave of compassion flooded Diana and she very nearly reached out to help him, but then she stopped herself. He was her love, her enemy. If their situation had seemed impossible before, she knew it was hopeless now. Tanner was a trained spy, and trained spies were able to harden their hearts to situations and people. He'd have to turn her in, otherwise he'd be committing treason against the Crown. He didn't have another alternative.

Finally, when she thought his sullen silence would drive her mad, she stood up. Tanner followed suit. "Afraid I'm going to run away?"

she taunted.

"That's what I want you to do."

Her mouth fell open. "What?"

"I don't know how you left the house," he said. "I don't want to know, so don't ever tell me. Just return the same way. I'm going to leave before you do. I'll tell Farnsworth I didn't see anyone. Do you understand?"

"Yes."

Tanner grabbed her arm before she could move. "You better be waiting in our room for me. We have to talk."

She nodded and he let her go. After he'd mounted the horse and headed back to Briarhaven, she ran to the cemetery and wasted no time in opening the tomb. She practically flew through the tunnel and made it up the back stairs and into the bedroom minutes before she heard Tanner speaking to Farnsworth in the hallway.

Hattie had helped her out of her wet clothes and had just pulled Diana's nightgown over her head when Tanner entered. The blistering look he shot at Hattie caused her to leave the room without a backward glance. Diana, however, stood in the center of the room, prepared to take the great brunt of his rage. But she was angry, too.

"That black scowl doesn't frighten me, you traitor. Hattie may scurry away like a timid mouse but I won't."

The only indication that she'd hit home with him was the slight tensing of his jaw. She expected him to grab her by the arms again and shake her. Instead, he calmly sat in a chair by the fireplace, his long legs extending near hers.

"Consider yourself lucky, Diana, that I was the spy Farnsworth engaged. Anyone else, believe me, and you'd either be dead right now or in a worse situation."

"What could be worse than death?"

"Remember Kingsley and all the nasty things he did to you and made you do to him? Remember how he beat you into submission? If Farnsworth knew you were the one passing information all of Kingsley's perversions would be child's play in comparison to what would be happening to you right now. Believe me, you'd consider death a mercy."

She felt that the breath had been knocked from her body. She'd never considered any of that. "Have you ever, I mean, have you ever done such horrible things to . . . a woman?"

"No, but I know men who have."

She felt supremely glad to know this. At least Tanner wasn't that much of a monster. "What will you do with me now?"

"You tell me."

Diana didn't care for the tone of that. Tanner was making it sound as if she had done something wrong. Stiffening her back, she stood ramrod straight, not aware of how the action caused her breasts to strain against the front of her nightgown. "I've committed no crime. You, however, are a traitor to your own people, to your family. Harlan is a patriot, and never forget that your brother, horrid as he was, died bravely in defense of the rebel cause. Perhaps you should tell me what I should do with you. Maybe I should turn you into Marion as a spy."

"You won't do that."

"Why not?"

"Because you love me," he said levelly.

A sob shook her. "Yes . . . I do love you, but I no longer like you, Tanner, or trust you. You can't trust me either."

Considering her for a long moment, he said, "We've reached an impasse with but one thing to do. I'll send you away."


Tanner and Diana bade a fond farewell to Harlan, who was much aggrieved at their departure. Naomi stood stoically by, her cold eyes slicing through Diana. Farnsworth, however, wasn't the least bit upset by their leaving. He slapped Tanner on the back as they stood on the porch. "Have a happy honeymoon trip, and don't return too soon. And you, Mrs. Sheridan, take care of your condition. I'm certain the sea air will greatly improve it."

"Thank you so much, Captain Farnsworth, for caring." Diana extended her hand to the man to kiss at the same time she daintily coughed into a kerchief. Farnsworth pretended he didn't see it, but he looked ready enough to bolt all the same.

"Go now, Sheridan! The sloop is ready." Then he abruptly headed inside.

Tanner helped settle Diana into the carriage for the drive to the dock, where a sloop waited for their journey to a British frigate at the mouth of the river. A soldier guided the sloop away from the shoreline as little Jackie came running, waving his small arms. "Bye, Miss Diana, Mr. Tanner. I'm gonna miss you."

They waved farewell and soon were on board the frigate and ensconced in a small room.

"Why that silly Farnsworth," Diana groused. "He actually believed the lie you told him. And such a horrible lie it was, too. The very idea that I have a touch of consumption."

Tanner's dark eyes danced with devilment, and he stood so close to her that for an instant Diana thought he might kiss her. Instead, he threw himself into a straight-backed chair. "He believed it, didn't he? That's all that matters. Farnsworth detests illness. He's frightened he'll catch something and die. I had to give him a good reason why you should leave Briarhaven, and consumption was the best I could do."

"You're impossible. I think you enjoy lying."

His eyes darkened to the color of onyx and were just as hard. "You're very adept at it yourself."

"There you go again." She sighed her exasperation. "You're always insinuating that I'm dishonest. I wish you'd tell me what it is I've supposedly done."

Tanner thrust his hands into his jacket pockets and stood up. "I'm going on deck. We should spot Oak Island soon."

He left her and Diana flounced into the chair he had vacated, irritably tossing her reticule onto a nearby table. What in the name of heaven had she done to earn his distrust? Granted, she'd spied on Farnsworth and caused Tanner a great deal of upset. But she had as much right to her political opinions as he did. And he was saving her life by spiriting her away from Briarhaven with the lame excuse of consumption. Probably she wouldn't be able to return until the war was over, because Farnsworth would expect her to be quite ill. Tanner knew all of this, she also knew that he still loved her though he hadn't made love to her since that night four days past, before he found her in the swamps.

Tanner admitted to her that he told Farnsworth he had found the spy and had killed him during a fight and buried the body in the swamp, something Farnsworth didn't dispute. Diana knew Tanner was taking her away from Briarhaven because he couldn't trust her. He might love her, but he didn't trust her not to pass on more information to her nameless informant. Even if she got on her knees and swore never to spy again, he wouldn't have believed her. So it always came down to trust between them.

She hadn't forgiven him for leaving her all of those years ago, and for some reason he wanted her to admit to something—what she didn't know—but the thought persisted that it was somehow related to what had happened before

260

her marriage to Kingsley.

"I'll go crazy if I keep dwelling on Tanner and what he wants," she grumbled aloud. But she couldn't help herself. No matter what had happened between them seven years ago, she still loved him and always would.

Oak Island was a windswept paradise off the South Carolina shoreline. A soft breeze rustled the skirt of Diana's cream-colored skirt and fluttered the lace on the collar of her long jacket. She breathed deeply of the fresh sea air upon stepping onto the dock, which ran for about fifty feet across the glistening sand, ending in a thatch of grass, emerald green, and thick scrub.

How beautiful was this enchanting island, whose live oak trees were silhouetted against the golden sunset like black obelisks. Diana couldn't help but be appreciative of the natural beauty surrounding her. When she and Tanner reached the end of the dock, she became aware of the white house in the distance. A small creek, interlaced with patches of green marshland and fringed with a mixture of oleander and oak trees, lazily meandered beside the two story cottage.

"What a lovely place!" Diana gushed. "Who does it belong to?"

"Us," was his terse reply, and he took her hand to lead her across the verdant lawn to the front porch, whose banisters cast long thin shadows on the grass.

Diana had no time to be surprised, but then nothing Tanner did should surprise her any longer. However, she did get a delightful shock when Anne suddenly burst through the front door, followed by the children. The four of them bounded down the front steps, the children giggling, the two women crying and embracing.

"I never thought to see you again!" Anne squealed and sent a chastising glance in Tanner's direction.

"Oh, Anne, I've been so lonely, so worried about all of you. Tanner told me that all of you were well. How is David? How are you? I had no idea you were here."

Diana knew she was gushing, but she couldn't contain herself. It wasn't until after she was inside the cozy, well-furnished house sipping tea in the parlor and eating freshly baked cookies served by Ruthie that she missed Tanner. She swore he had followed them inside, but she'd been so engrossed in catching up on what had happened to her family that she hadn't realized he had not come inside at all.

"Where's Tanner?" she asked.

"I haven't seen him since his arrival." Anne sounded curt and cold. Her voice became a hiss. "How could you have married him, Diana? The man spirited you away from the house. I thought something awful had happened to you until that Curtis person came for us."

"Anne . . ." David's tone warned her to be

quiet.

"It's true, and you know it, David."

"He saved my life," David reminded her.

"Hah! Who said so?"

"David's right," interjected Diana, growing a bit miffed with Anne's attitude toward Tanner. "If Tanner hadn't intervened, David would be dead now. I'd think you'd be more than grateful to my husband. He didn't have to help David, and he didn't have to bring the lot of you here. You're living in grand style now. If you were in Charlestown, you might be starving, if not dead." Diana took a deep breath. "I need to find my husband."

David gently patted her shoulder. "I intend to thank him personally for all he's done."

A grateful smile lit up Diana's face and she went out onto the porch. She had upset Anne, she knew that, but it was time Anne learned that she couldn't expect her to feel about things the same way she had. If Diana had known that seven years ago, she'd never have encouraged Kingsley merely because Anne had approved of him.

A gentle twilight bathed the island in lavender and blue hues. The ocean surf could be heard above the sorrowful cry of the seagulls overhead. Suddenly Diana felt bereft, felt that a part of herself was missing. She ached to find Tanner.

Leaving the porch, she walked along the creek, which she had learned was called Oleander Creek, and crested the top of a large sand dune. The beach stretched below her and she spotted Tanner, sitting some yards away on the sand. He'd removed his jacket, and though Diana found the evening to be quite chilly, Tanner didn't seem to mind the cool breeze whipping through his dark hair and ruffling the white lace on his shirtfront. He gazed out at the endless stretch of purple, swelling sea, oblivious to everything.

She wore only her cotton gown, having forgotten to reach for a shawl or coat when she left the house. Folding her arms about herself, she stood beside him. "Don't you want to come inside?" she asked.

Tanner barely glanced at her and threw a shell into the swelling surf. "Maybe later."

Suddenly she felt ill at ease. How strange that was, she found herself thinking, after all of the nights she'd spent naked and panting in Tanner's arms. Now something had changed between them. Certainly her secret life had something to do with it, but then again he was Mariah, a trusted and trained British spy, a close friend of General Lord Rawdon. Her escapades in the swamp were nothing in comparison to what Tanner must have accomplished on his missions, the people he must have hurt. Diana didn't want to think about any of it, but she couldn't stop her thoughts. Perhaps it wasn't so much that he had changed but that she now knew the truth about him and saw him in a different light. Maybe now that the mystery about him was unfolding, he sensed a difference in her attitude.

"Anne's prepared a room for us. She had to move the girls and put them in the attic bedroom, but they don't mind. You know how children love an adventure, a change."

"No, not really," Tanner admitted. "I wasn't allowed to be a child."

"Why not?"

"Because I spent all of my life preparing to take my rightful calling as Briarhaven's overseer. I was even tutored with Kingsley, much to the displeasure of Kingsley's mother. I wasn't allowed to cry; my mother told me that. She told me that I had to be strong and accept my place, not to let anyone know how much I hated them. When lessons were over, I was dismissed by Kinglsey's governess, a hateful old hag who hated me as much as I detested her. I can't count the number of times she cracked me across the knuckles with her wooden ruler. God, it hurt, but I didn't cry."

"Tanner, why are you telling me this?" Diana's voice was a whisper. She could see he was in pain, and though she wanted to hear about his childhood, she didn't want to know about his suffering. It made him more human to her, more human at a time when she wanted to put a distance between them.

Glancing up at her, his eyes expressed his inner torment. "Maybe because I want to hurt you, or have you feel sorry for me. I don't know."

Dropping to her knees, Diana wanted to

touch him, but nothing intimate had passed between them in days and she hesitated to do so. Instead she licked her lips and smiled sadly. "I wish I had known you then. There's so much about you that I don't know."

"Be glad of that, Diana," he said harshly, causing her to flinch. "If you had known me then you'd have treated me the same way you did when you first came to Briarhaven. You thought I was beneath contempt and you were right. What could I have given you if you'd left with me? Nothing, absolutely nothing. Your family would have disowned you. I can imagine Anne's reaction. She'd probably have suffered some sort of a fit. As it is, she can't abide me."

"Anne doesn't know you, Tanner. You must be patient with her. David is quite grateful to you, however."

Tanner sighed and pushed a stray curl from Diana's face. "Are you grateful to me, Diana?"

"Yes, of course."

"Is that all you are, grateful?"

She knew he wanted her to tell him that she loved him and had forgiven him, but the man she had come to love so desperately in Charlestown didn't seem to be the same man sitting on the beach. In her mind, she'd built up an image of a noble but scarred man, but since learning the truth about his past, about his dual identity, she thought of him as mercenary rather than noble. Though she cared about him and worried about him, even craved for him to kiss her and make love to her, he was her enemy. He was

Mariah.

"Your silence speaks more eloquently than any words," Tanner mumbled when she didn't respond. Standing up, he dusted the sand from his pants and handed her his jacket. "Put this on and go back to the house."

"You're not coming with me?" Diana slipped into the too-large sleeves.

"Not at the moment." He placed a light kiss upon her forehead. "Good night, Diana."

"Tanner . . ."

He turned and started walking down the deserted, wind-tossed beach with his hands thrust into his pockets. Should she run after him? she asked herself, and knew she should. That would be the appropriate response for a wife, but she didn't, because the man who had just walked away from her was a stranger.

# Chapter 14

The coolness of winter gave way to spring and then to a warm summer, filled with lazy days sitting on the porch and overseeing the children as they frolicked on the lawn, or hours spent on the beach where Diana and Anne watched David teach the youngsters how to swim.

Diana was constantly amazed at the energy the children possessed. She was even more in awe of her sister who kept up with them. "Is this what I have to look forward to when I have children?" Diana laughingly asked Anne on a hot June afternoon.

Anne toweled Jane's hair and then waved the little girl away to join David and the others in the water again. "Yes. You'll be nagged to death to wipe drops of water out of eyes, to dry hair, just so the scamps can get wet again and return for another drying. You shall have no peace and quiet, no time even to bathe yourself, but you'll find that when the children aren't bothering you you can't concentrate because you know that the moment you start something one of them will call you." A satisfied smile ringed Anne's mouth. "I'm quite happy, however."

"I know that. You don't have to tell me." Diana grew quiet and adjusted her position on the sand, rearranging the skirt of her pink and white striped dress. A caressing breeze stirred the wisps of hair she'd pulled back from her face in a matching bow. "I suppose I'll never have children now."

Diana colored, realizing she'd said too much about her personal situation with Tanner. They had slept in the same bed for the last four months, and in all that time they hadn't touched. If by chance their hands accidentally met or their thighs brushed in the darkness, they quickly drew away. Diana was miserable. Tanner was miserable. They barely spoke. Their marriage was over.

Anne stood up and motioned to Diana. "Follow me," she mysteriously said. Diana found herself walking down the beach with her sister in silence until Anne halted some distance away in a place Diana had seen before. She recognized it as the spot where Tanner spent a great deal of his time . . . alone.

"I apologize to you," Anne began, "for the awful things I've thought about your husband. We had a talk one day, Tanner and I, and I realized how much he loves you. And he does

269

love you, Diana. That's why he doesn't join us for supper too often, why he keeps to himself so much. I know it's because he doesn't believe he's good enough to associate with us, that he isn't good enough to be your husband. The few times I've seen him with the children convinces me he'll be a fine father one day. Little David thinks he's so wonderful, and the girls agree that their Uncle Tanner is the most handsome man in the world." Anne's eyes misted and she gulped back a sob.

"Maybe I shouldn't be telling you any of this, but I've misjudged him. No matter what he's done, and I really don't want to know what that might be, he saved David's life and offered us the safety of Oak Island. Now I think you should go to him and tell him you love him. Put the war and the strife behind you both. Diana, on Oak Island there is no war. You can be Tanner's wife and he can be a husband to you. Isn't this what you want?"

"Oh, yes, Anne, yes it is," Diana admitted, her voice quivering with emotion.

"Then go to him," Anne urged through teary eyes. "I promise that you won't be disturbed, even if I have to tie those hellions of mine to a tree."

Diana laughed, unable to picture her gentle sister rounding up the children and tying them to anything. Hugging each other, they parted.

This part of the island was in a secluded covelike area, surrounded by lush palmettos that blew gently and made a hushing sound. An ancient spring bubbled up from the earth to fall and trickle silently between the rocks into a shimmering, clear pool. It was in this pool that Diana saw Tanner.

His bronzed back was turned to her and suddenly he disappeared beneath the water, only to surface at the other end. Sparkling droplets of water, resembling diamonds, dripped from his powerful torso. With his dark hair slicked back from his face, he looked so young, so carefree. This was a Tanner she had never seen. In fact, she never remembered Tanner being carefree or playing during the entire time she'd known him. Most of the time he was so serious, and during the last months he'd been less than happy. Sometimes she wondered why he stayed at Oak Island, why he didn't just leave. She knew, however, and felt unaccountably ashamed of herself on account of it.

"He stays because of me," she murmured, not able to take her eyes off of him when he again dived beneath the water and swam across the pond, his powerful arms slicing through the water with ease.

Anne was right, she knew. On Oak Island there was no war, no reason not to be together. The politics that divided them didn't exist here. For once, they could simply be husband and wife—Tanner and Diana Sheridan. No ghosts from the past would haunt them; the future didn't matter. She wanted him so badly that she ached. All of those nights, lying next to him, hearing him breathe, knowing he was but scant inches away. . . . Well, no more torture for her. Not any longer. She must make the first move.

Resolutely, Diana undressed. The summer wind moved lazily over her, heating her already warm flesh. She wanted him, wanted him, wanted him. Without the slightest bit of shyness, Diana came forward from the royal palmettos that hid her from view and entered the pool like a queen with her head held high. But she felt less than queenly, almost humble, when Tanner heard the gentle splash of water and turned his head to see her. Instead of waiting for him to come to her, she moved toward him like a graceful water nymph. Will he want me? she asked herself. Fear clutched at her. She knew she'd die if Tanner rejected her. But she had to take the chance. She needed him so very much.

She stopped before him, unaware of how beautiful she looked at that moment. The afternoon light spread a golden hue across her face and naked breasts, and her hair, pulled back by the pink ribbon, caught the sun's fire and dazzled Tanner with its brilliance. Diana didn't know any of this, but she did know she had to touch him. She placed her palms on the wet hardness of his chest. She'd have spoken first, but Tanner only gazed at her with wonder in his eyes and said, "Diana, are you sure?"

Her hands slipped up the slick wall before her and wrapped around his neck. "Yes." And this was all the answer he seemed to need, because with that one word she turned herself over to him once again, body and soul.

He took her right there in the water, their need so great that preliminaries were unnecessary. Their bodies burned with wanting; primitive fires licked at the cores of both their beings. Their mutual passion, so long denied, flowed hotly over them like an unchecked volcano. It wound within them and through them, causing such a fierce, sweet plunder of their senses that nothing and no one could have prevented their joining.

He lifted her from her feet and entered the moist warmth of her body in one motion. Instantly she responded. Her legs wrapped around his waist, her body arched to meet his wild, sweet thrusts. "Oh, Tanner," she cried, ecstasy claiming her in a sudden and fierce climax as Tanner shuddered, pulling her buttocks closer as he filled her.

Afterward, both stared into each other's eyes for long moments, not fully conscious of anything save one thing—they loved one another.

"I've missed you," he admitted, endearing himself to Diana further with this honest admission. "I'd begun to think I'd have to enter a monastery."

Diana laughed and kissed him full on the lips. "What a dreadful waste that would be, besides breaking many ladies' hearts, I'm certain."

"Would your heart be broken?"

The playfulness disappeared from her blue eyes and they glazed over with renewed desire.

"Mine most of all."

"Perhaps I should prove to you that I'm not ready for a monk's life," he suggested, and that's exactly what he did.

Over the next two months, Diana and Tanner were closer than they'd ever been. Much of their time was spent alone in their own secluded cove, the rest with Anne, David and the children, cavorting on the beach. Nights they spent in their own bed, either flushed with passion or asleep in each other's arms. The war had ceased to exist for them, utterly and completely. They trusted one another, and finally Tanner explained about his past as Mariah, leaving out none of the highlights. She realized he didn't tell her all of the details because she suspected some of the things he'd done in the name of the Crown were probably wicked and dark, things better left unsaid.

He even told her about a woman named Annabelle, whom he'd come to care about at one time and thought he loved until he realized what a heartless conniver she was. "But I know now that my life was with you," he told Diana and kissed her tenderly. "I can't imagine not being your husband. I wanted to marry you from the moment I first saw you."

"I loved you, too," Diana admitted and leaned against his naked chest. Moonlight cast soft streaks of light upon the bed, encasing their forms in silver. "That night on the bluff I knew I loved you. I told Anne so, but she wasn't very happy about it. In fact, I believe she may have cried. But I hoped and prayed you'd come for me . . . but you didn't. Kingsley told me you wouldn't."

"And you believed him."

Diana shook her head. "At first I didn't. It wasn't until he told me about you and your wanting to have your way with me that I began to doubt. Just a tiny bit, mind you, but I did doubt you. I'm sorry."

"What happened then?" Tanner's voice sounded oddly strained.

"I don't understand what you mean."

"What did you tell Harlan and Kingsley about when I kissed you?"

"I didn't tell Harlan anything. I did try to tell Kingsley that I was responsible for what happened. I told him I wanted you to kiss me, but he said I was too innocent to know what I was talking about."

Tanner took a deep breath and hugged her tightly. "And then?"

Diana glanced up at him, seeing that his eyes were hooded. "I waited for you to come for me. I thought you would, and I'd have gladly gone, but you didn't . . . and I married Kingsley." Her voice started to quiver. "You know, Tanner, I hated you for my marriage and decided that Kingsley had been right about your wanting to avenge yourself against him because of me. Now I know he was wrong. Kingsley lied to me and I was silly enough to believe him."

Tanner shook his head in a gesture of regret. "We were both silly, both of us believed a lie."

"What lie did you believe?"

"It isn't important any longer, but I have a great deal to make up to you."

"No, you don't," Diana insisted, not caring for the contrite kiss he placed upon her lips. She didn't understand all of these questions, or why Tanner felt he'd wronged her. They were truly in love now; the past was gone. Still, she felt the need to unburden herself about her dual identity, now that he'd told her all about Mariah and his retirement from spying. "I should apologize to you for sneaking through the secret tunnel to meet Clay Sinclair and pass on information about Farnsworth. I could have put you in great danger, and Harlan and Hattie, too."

Tanner had been nibbling at her ear while she spoke, but now he stopped, apparently interested. "There's a tunnel beneath Briarhaven?" Diana yawned and explained that the entrance was in the wine cellar. "And Clay Sinclair, is he related to the Sinclair family who lived five miles from Briarhaven?"

"Hmm, hmm," Diana mumbled, growing sleepy and burrowing within the crook of Tanner's arm.

"Sinclair was your informant."

"Hmm, hmm."

Tanner was silent for a few minutes. Diana was nearly asleep when she heard him speak again, his voice sounding far away, "If you needed to get in touch with Clay Sinclair again, how would you do it?"

She very nearly didn't answer him as sleep began to overtake her, but he asked the question once more. "Put . . . a . . . rib . . . bon . . . on tree limb . . ." In seconds she was sound asleep.

But Tanner wasn't. He lay with Diana in his arms until nearly dawn. He kissed her mouth, and even while she slept he felt her respond. He knew he could easily wake her and arouse her to passion. However, he didn't. Instead he watched her while she slept and memorized her face.

Getting up, he hurriedly dressed and packed a few belongings before he went to the desk in the parlor and scribbled a note of farewell. He went outside and plucked a rose from the garden beside the house, a rose that was as pink and lovely as Diana's lips. Returning inside, he placed the rose and the note beside Diana's beautiful face on the pillow. "It's better like this, my love," he whispered to her sleeping form. "Maybe one day you'll forgive me."

Then he left.


Diana lay in bed, her hand clasping the note and the rose. She was too stunned to move. Not even Anne's insistent knock on the door could rouse her.

"Diana! Diana! Answer me," Anne cried.

"Go away!" came Diana's half sob.

"I'm coming in," Anne said, which is exactly what she did. She stood by the side of Diana's bed, looking down at her younger sister with pity in her eyes. "You can't stay in bed forever. Some time or other you'll have to get up."

"What difference does it make if I get up or not? I've lost my husband, Anne. Don't you understand? Tanner's left me. Left me," Diana reiterated.

"He'll be back. I'm certain of it. He loves you. Most probably he has business to attend to at Briarhaven. Tanner saw David before he left this morning, and he told him he'd try to return soon. For the life of me I don't understand why you're taking on so, Diana."

Anne wouldn't understand, and Diana couldn't tell her sister that the man she suddenly and so hotly defended was a British spy, and not only a former spy, as Tanner had led her to believe, but a very active one. God, she wanted to die! Because of her stupidity and her own need to unburden herself she'd revealed too much. She'd told Tanner about the tunnel, about Clay Sinclair, even about the ribbon on the tree branch.

Diana groaned and faced the wall, ignoring Anne. Getting no further response to her prodding, Anne finally left Diana alone.

Tears fell from Diana's eyes onto the pillow. What a fool she'd been to imagine for a moment that she could trust Tanner Sheridan. And what an even better spy he was. No wonder countless patriots had spilled information to him. He could seem so trustworthy, especially when he led one to believe that he was actually being honest, revealing his own dark secrets.

What appalled her more than her own foolish heart was that Clay, the Swamp Fox, and his rebels were now in danger because of her unthinking tongue. No doubt Tanner would rush to Farnsworth with his news and collect a large sum of money for the information and the rebels' subsequent capture. And all because she had fallen in love with a man whose low birth and mercenary heart prevented him from loving. And he hadn't loved her, didn't love her, could never love her. Otherwise, Tanner wouldn't hurt her like this.

"You are a bastard, Tanner Sheridan," she whispered, choking on her tears. "I never want to see you again, never. You'll never see your own child. I'll make certain that when my baby is born, you know nothing about her."

Somehow Diana knew that the child she carried beneath her heart, the child she had so desperately ached to give to Tanner Sheridan, was a girl.

"Why didn't Diana return with you?" inquired Harlan of Tanner. The old man pulled the lap robe around his legs. "I miss her."

Tanner hedged. "The island is quite pleasant now. Besides, I don't think her being here is a good idea anyway." Sipping his brandy, Tanner surveyed his father. "Why didn't you tell me about what she'd been doing for the patriots?"

Harlan shot a glance at the bedroom door in confirmation that it was tightly closed and grinned at Tanner. "Old men like to have some secrets. Farnsworth treats me like an imbecile. My body may be going, but my mind is quite active. Those redcoats are a bunch of pansies. The girl sneaked away from the house right under their very noses and passed information to the Swamp Fox. She really kept things hopping around here." Harlan leaned back against the pillows, a congratulating smile on his face. "Diana's quite a woman."

Tanner's own face hardened. "Why didn't you talk her out of it, old man? She could have been captured or killed."

"Well, she wasn't."

"Stubborn old coot. Don't you care about her?"

"I love Diana like my own daughter," Harlan insisted, much affronted by this personal attack against him.

"Yes, I know how you love your children. I've been a recipient of your own special fatherly love in the past, and it's a wonder Diana is still alive at all."

Harlan's trembling hands held onto the lap robe. "I . . . did my best."

"Liar."

"Get out," Harlan ordered, his voice breaking. "I'm an old, sick man. I don't need this. . . ."

"Tanner," came Naomi's curt tones from the doorway. "Please let your father rest."

Tanner strode from the room, too angry to

280

speak to his mother who followed after him. Finally she grabbed his arm and stopped him. "Make peace with your father. He has little time left on this earth."

"He could make peace with me. Why should I be the first?"

Naomi's features softened. "Because he has done wrong by you and he knows it. Harlan can't say the words to ask your forgiveness. He is very much like a child who has harmed a parent and wants to say he is sorry but yet doesn't wish to speak for fear that he'll be rejected for his misdeed. Go to him, Tanner. Call him father. That's all he wants."

"He asks too much, Mother."

"Ah, you are hardhearted, my son."

"No just thick-skinned. Otherwise, the night he allowed Kingsley to beat me would have killed me." Breaking from his mother's hold, Tanner ran down the stairs and into the bright sunshine of the afternoon.

He was so aggravated that he threw himself onto a chair beside a window that opened onto the porch, unaware of the meeting taking place inside until he heard Farnsworth speaking to Smythe and McCall.

"Once we take Eutaw Springs," Farnsworth said, "we'll control the Santee. Camden is ours, though we did lose Cowpens, but Eutaw Springs will be the turning point. And we must win there. General Cornwallis is in charge of the troops in the area since Rawdon's return to England. I should like to gain the old fellow's

281

attention and advance in the ranks."

Tanner felt perspiration dripping down his forehead into his collar and onto his chest. He wasn't warm, but excited, so excited that he had to contain himself to stay seated and remain quiet. He feared to move a muscle lest the chair squeak and give him away. This was what he'd been waiting for, this was the very reason he'd left Diana. And now his opportunity presented itself. Only this time the head would belong to Captain Samuel Farnsworth.

Tanner listened until he was certain that the details of the campaign had been thoroughly discussed. When he heard them moving about, their strategy at an end, he quickly disappeared from the porch and went to the room he'd shared with Diana.

He was in the process of rummaging through a drawer when Hattie entered. "What you lookin' for, Mr. Tanner?"

"A ribbon, Hattie. Where does Miss Diana keep her hair ribbons?"

"What you want with a hair ribbon? You ain't got a fancy gal in town now, do you, Mr. Tanner?" Hattie directed a condemning look in his direction, causing Tanner to laugh.

"No, but soon I expect Miss Diana to be home again. So, get me the ribbon."

Hattie dutifully opened a drawer and took out a bright blue ribbon. "Will this do?"

Tanner hugged Hattie and lifted her off her feet and swung her around the room. "It's perfect!" he cried and set the old woman on her feet again amid half protests.

"You sure is actin' strange," Hattie observed, her eyes wide with pleasure.

"You're right, but love does strange things to a man, Hattie, mighty strange things."


Mr. King was feeling better, Mike Candy could tell. He wasn't grumpy as usual, probably because his leg was finally starting to heal. Maybe the warm weather helped. Mike Candy hoped so. He was tired of caring for his surly patient.

"So you took a small walk today," Candy noted, and Mr. King nodded. "Where'd you go?"

"No place in particular," said Mr. King, noncommitally. "But I expect to walk a bit each day, you know, to strengthen my legs. I've been off of them for a long time now."

"Aye, that you have. So what you planning to do when you're well again? You thinking of staying here?"

"Here? In Rawdontown? Candy, you must be crazy." King dusted specks of dust from his threadbare jacket. "I'm going to be living in grand style as soon as I can reclaim my property."

"I see."

King shook his head and smirked. "No, you don't see, but then I wouldn't expect you to understand. However, I would appreciate it if you'd run an errand for me."

Candy gritted his teeth. "I ain't some toady, a menial to do your bidding."

"My dear Candy, I'm aware of that. I need you to get some information for me, if you would."

"What sort of information? If it's illegal . . ."

"No, no, just find out for me if the owner of a certain townhouse is about . . . that's all."

"Nothing else?"

"I assure you that's all you have to do, and I'll reward you handsomely as soon as I recover my property."

"All right," Candy reluctantly agreed.

Mr. King basked in the bright September sunshine. For the first time in well over a year he actually smiled.

# Chapter 15

By the early part of October, word had spread to Oak Island of a decisive American victory at Eutaw Springs. The British had withdrawn from the Santee region and had taken refuge in Charlestown, the only part of South Carolina to be under British rule and the remaining bastion of British power in the war for independence. "It's just a matter of time now," David sagely predicted, "before we can return home. The war is all but won by our forces. God, how I wish I could have been at Eutaw Springs!"

"David, you're not considering joining your regiment again." Anne's brow creased into a worried frown.

David assured her that he wasn't, and Anne believed him, causing a twinge of envy to slice through Diana. David's word was good enough for Anne because David wouldn't deceive her. He always followed through with whatever he said. Diana couldn't say the same for Tanner.

She received a letter from him two weeks before, informing her that a schooner would soon be arriving to take her home to Briarhaven. The messenger, whom Tanner had sent with the letter, had waited patiently for a reply while Diana read it. Her face had turned scarlet with rage at Tanner's nerve. Didn't the impossible, deceitful man think she possessed any pride at all? How could he possibly consider that she'd return home after he had tricked her so? Apparently the information she'd provided about Clay and Colonel Marion had garnered him nothing. The American rebels had won, and the knowledge that the great Mariah had failed filled her with immense satisfaction.

But she penned a hasty note, telling Tanner that she'd be waiting for the schooner, that she couldn't wait to return home to savor the American victory, and that she wanted to see Harlan. Finally, she wrote that she didn't wish ever to lay eyes upon Tanner Sheridan again, and asked him to be gone when she arrived home. If he chose not to obey her wishes, then she'd take up residence someplace else. He had deceived her and she didn't trust him, not after he'd extracted information from her and then hurried to inform Farnsworth. As far as she was concerned, their marriage was over.

Since she hadn't received a reply, Diana wasn't at all certain what situation she'd be walking into at Briarhaven. But on a misty morning, filled with the hint of autumn, the schooner duly arrived. Tanner wasn't on it. Anne and David chose to remain at Oak Island until the British left Charlestown, so Diana boarded the schooner alone.

She arrived at Briarhaven after dark. Her body ached, the early stage of pregnancy sapped her energy and she felt slightly nauseated, having eaten very little that day. In fact, she found it impossible to force even a small amount of food down her throat, so worked up was she over whether or not Tanner had vacated the house.

Diana needn't have worried. Hattie met her at the door and imparted the information that Tanner had packed his bags and left shortly after receiving her note to him. "Did he leave a message for me?" Diana asked, feeling foolish for even inquiring when nothing Tanner could say would change her mind or soften her heart.

"No letter, no nothin'." Hattie sadly shook her head and tears welled in her eyes. "But that boy was in no mood to say or do nothin' when he left here. I guess you don't know, but Mister Harlan done died last week."

Diana's fingers ceased unbuttoning her cape. "Harlan is dead?"

Hattie nodded and wiped her eyes on the edge of her apron. "Got pains in his chest real sudden like and called for Mr. Tanner. Mr. Tanner was with him when he died."

Disbelief and shock shrouded Diana's features, and she barely made it to the sofa in the parlor before she started crying. "I should have been here." Sobbing out her misery and pain, she knew that she'd miss Harlan. The old man had saved her from Kingsley and she owed him her life. She'd anticipated his pleased reaction when she told him about the baby, but now that pleasure would be forever denied her. As much as she tried to block out Tanner's face from her mind, she couldn't. How he must have suffered, she found herself thinking. No matter their differences, Diana had always thought that Harlan and Tanner had loved one another, that it was their pride that had kept them apart. Now they'd never make amends. Sometimes life was like that, Diana thought, very much aware of her own pain.

During the next few days, Diana busied herself around the house. Since the British had withdrawn things were much quieter but the pantry was also emptier. Still, she couldn't complain. Thanks to the British occupation, Briarhaven was better off than its neighbors along the Santee.

One morning Diana rode across the plantation on the last decent horse left. She knew riding was dangerous in her condition, but since Tanner now resided in Charlestown—news that Naomi had been only too pleased to impart—she decided that the business of rice growing would commence in earnest the following spring. However, the fields were in pitiful condition, and with only a few loyal slaves remaining at Briarhaven, the possibility of even a small crop within the next year was remote.

Somehow they'd survive, they always did, but now the responsibility for Briarhaven and its occupants rested on her frail shoulders. They'd need money and slaves, and both were in extremely short supply.

When she returned to the house she couldn't conceal her surprise and delight at finding Marisa and Aunt Frances sitting on the sofa in the parlor. "Whatever are you two doing here?" Diana asked after the three of them had embraced.

"Why, Tanner came to our house," Aunt Frances explained and sipped her tea. "He looked awful, just terrible, didn't he, Marisa?" She didn't wait for Marisa to answer but continued heedlessly, "What happened between you, Diana? The man is beside himself, but he refused to speak about your troubles. He told me he stopped by to tell us that Harlan had died and he wanted to know if Marisa and I could visit since he felt you might be lonely."

"I am lonely," Diana admitted and brightened just a bit. "But now my favorite aunt and cousin are here with me. How long do you plan to stay?"

"As long as you allow us, Diana." Aunt Frances began sobbing into a kerchief. "Those damnable British. Things in Charlestown are more impossible now than before. The entire city is packed with redcoats, and we were forced to give them quarter at our home. I couldn't stand it another minute. Marisa and I had to leave." Aunt Frances sent Marisa a teary-eyed smile and the two women clasped hands.

Diana could tell that something was being left out of the conversation, but when Frances asked if she could rest, Diana didn't hesitate to show her aunt to one of the guest rooms. It was not until Diana was opening the window in another bedroom that she noticed Marisa appeared distracted. Diana sat on the bed and patted a spot for her cousin to sit next to her. "Tell me what happened in Charlestown," Diana said gently.

Marisa surprised Diana by burying her face into the hands and sobbing. "Oh, Diana, it was awful! Just terrible! I feel so dirty."

"What is it?" Diana removed Marisa's hands away from her cousin's face.

Marisa gulped back her tears and wiped her eyes with the kerchief she took from her reticule. "What Mother told you about Tanner coming to see us was the truth. He did ask if we'd come to Briarhaven and he did tell us about Harlan. We were shocked, but he didn't want to leave our home. It wasn't until," and here Marisa faltered, but then went on in a trembling voice, "Captain Farnsworth commandeered our home that we knew we had to leave.

"You see, he tried to take liberties . . . with me. And he would have done more than kiss me and . . . touch me . . . if not for Tanner.

290

Oh, Diana, I'm so grateful to him. He happened by the house just at that moment and saved me. And he gave that nasty Farnsworth a good punch in the nose." Marisa started to giggle. "The man bled terribly, but he deserved it. I can't stop thinking about what might have happened to me if Tanner hadn't been there to intervene and to get us out of Charlestown so quickly."

"You poor dear." Diana hugged Marisa and patted her back, feeling extremely worldly and maternal. If Marisa only knew the horrors a man could inflict upon a woman. . . . But a warmth suffused her face, in fact, her whole being, to know that Tanner had saved her cousin and sent her and Aunt Frances to Briarhaven and safety. "I'm grateful to him despite the fact that our marriage is over."

Marisa crumpled the kerchief and stood up to stand near the window. Her eyes held a question. "Is it really?"

"Yes, but I can't speak about what happened."

"I'm sorry, because I like Tanner, but I think you need to be aware of something. It's better that you hear the news from me than from someone who won't be as kind."

Fear clutched at Diana's stomach and she jumped off the bed. "Is something wrong with Tanner?"

"He's perfectly healthy," Marissa assured her. "Very healthy. Oh, I should just come out and tell you because there's no easy way. Tanner has a mistress living with him at the townhouse."

Diana's stomach flip-flopped. She should have expected this news, but somehow she hadn't thought about Tanner seeking out a woman. "Gabriella Fox, I presume."

"Oh, no. Gabriella is home with her husband now and no threat to you. This woman is quite unlike Gabriella. In fact, from what I've heard of this woman and seen of her, I much prefer Gabriella."

"What have you heard? Who is she?" demanded Diana, despite her resolve not to care about Tanner.

Marisa's earlier distress vanished, and she pulled Diana down on the bed, eager to confide. "I heard Farnsworth talking to one of his men about this woman. Her name is Annabelle Hastings. She's some sort of a spy, at least she was. I don't think she is now. From what I gathered there was unpleasantness connected with her in Philadelphia and she lost her value to the British. One day she came to the house to visit Farnsworth and I thought she was his kept woman, but it seemed that she wanted to know about Tanner. She'd seen him from a distance and needed to know where she could find him. Farnsworth told her, and ever since that time she's been living at the townhouse." Marisa grew suddenly quiet. She squeezed Diana's hand. "I didn't mean to upset you, but I have, haven't I?"

"Heavens no!" Diana rose to her feet, hoping she hid her lie well. It would never do to have anyone think she still had feelings for Tanner, that she could be jealous of him and this Annabelle Hastings. She knew very well who Annabelle Hastings was. Tanner had told her about his affair with the woman in New York. He had even thought he had loved her. "Whomever Tanner wishes to trifle with is none of my concern any longer."

"But Diana, you're having a child."

A beet red blush consumed Diana's face. "I didn't know it showed yet."

"Don't you think you should tell Tanner about the baby?"

"Definitely not! And don't you tell him, Marisa. That deceitful bounder doesn't deserve to know."

"All right, I won't," Marisa promised and sighed. "Still, if I had a husband as handsome and rich and kind as Tanner I'd tell him about the baby. I'd fight for him, too. No conniving woman would steal him away from me."

Diana winced, not wanting to admit that Marisa might just be right.

"Well?" Mr. King asked Mike Candy upon his return from the townhouse. "What did you discover?"

Candy practically snarled at the man who waited like a huge black vulture, ready to pounce and prey upon the unsuspecting just like the vultures who now sat upon the roof of the market. But he hid the smile in his heart. No matter what it was this Mr. King wanted, he was going to be denied it. "The master is at home," Candy proclaimed, "and you should have told me that the townhouse belonged to Mr. Tanner Sheridan. If I'd have known that I wouldn't have been sneaking around like a damned thief. That servant fellow who works for Mr. Sheridan discovered me nosing about."

"Good Lord, man! You didn't open your mouth about me, did you?"

"I ain't stupid, King," Candy shot back. "I told him I wanted something to eat, that I was hungry, and he sent me to the kitchen for some grub. Filled me up real good, too. I was going to ask the cook about the master being there, but I didn't have to. I saw him eating in the dining room. Recognized him as Mr. Sheridan. He was with a lady, so you see, he's home."

"Dammit!" King kicked at a rock out of frustration. "So Sheridan and his wife are both there."

"I said a lady was with him, not that it was his wife."

"What lady? Tell me!" King demanded.

"I don't know who she was. She had pretty, silver-blonde hair, and from the looks of things they knew each other real well."

King got a far-away look in his eyes, then he turned on Mike Candy. "Don't expect any payment from me."

That was the straw that fueled Mike Candy's temper. Grabbing King by the frayed lapels of his coat, Candy hissed into his face. "I don't want payment from you, you spoiled and arrogant lout. I don't want anything to do with you. From now on you do your own legwork, and don't be returning to my house. I don't want to see you ever again." With that, Candy turned and rushed away into the crowd.

King's face had turned a mottled purple, and he was the unwelcome recipient of disapproving stares from the many people who thronged the market. Heading in the direction opposite the one Candy had taken, he soon discovered himself on a side street. There he waited in front of Tanner Sheridan's townhouse. Within seconds a carriage neared the house. King stepped into the shadows of a large hedge and watched it stop only feet away from him.

Tanner disembarked and held out his hand for a woman with silver-gold hair. Evidently this was the same woman whom Candy had seen. She was a stunning creature, dressed in a pale blue silk gown with small rosebuds embroidered into the design. She had a lovely laugh, high but not boisterous. But although she appeared to be the perfect lady, he'd been around enough women to spot her kind in an instant. He knew that the woman who entered the townhouse with Tanner wasn't a lady. More likely a highly paid whore, he decided.

But where was Diana? At Briarhaven? He'd have to discover that later. For now, he had to retrieve his property from the townhouse and he needed help to do it.

A smile clung to his dirty and bearded face. Why, the woman would help him. He knew how to deal with the likes of that one. No woman ever turned down Kingsley Sheridan.


Tanner woke in a cold sweat. He'd been dreaming again, dreaming about the day his father had died.

Would he ever escape the pain of Harlan's death? He didn't think so. For years they'd hated one another, but when he saw his father's pale face, a face that matched the pillow beneath his gray head, a wrenching sensation had squeezed his very heart. Somehow, Tanner had never pictured him as anything but alive. The realization had struck him when he'd found Harlan, gasping for breath and calling his name, that they'd wasted too much time, too many years, hating each other.

He'd never forget the moment Harlan had grabbed for his hand, clutching at it fiercely. For a man who was about to die his grip had been surprisingly strong. Harlan's voice had been a grunt but Tanner understood when he said, "Tanner, you . . . are . . . my son."

In that instant, Tanner's soul nearly ripped from his body with joy, at the same time he experienced such a profound sadness that tears streamed down his face. Finally, finally, Harlan was acknowledging him. "You are my father." Tanner breathed, and Harlan's features relaxed. The old man actually smiled at him, then he was gone.

But even now Tanner knew no peace, something he'd always expected to feel if his father admitted to his paternity. Granted, Tanner experienced a sense of fulfillment, but it seemed that a great emptiness dwelled within him, too.

It was because he'd lost Diana. He knew he had lost her, and he knew that he could very easily claim her again with the truth. However, he wouldn't. She must believe in him, and it was quite apparent to him that she didn't trust him. So why bother going to her and trying to convince her of anything at all? She'd made up her mind about him long ago.

And then there was Annabelle.

Annabelle Hastings, a woman he'd thought never to see again. The conniving wench was now sleeping in the guest room and he didn't know what to do with her. He knew what he would *like* to do with her, should *want* to do to her. But no matter how he tried, he couldn't summon those same old feelings he'd had for her in New York. She'd been such a whore, but at one time he'd foolishly thought that Annabelle would replace Diana in his affections. He'd imagined he loved her until he discovered just how unscrupulous she could be. She'd fancied herself in love with a privateer who paraded as a loyalist, and in order to have the man for herself she'd turned his wife into the authorities as a rebel poetess — which she indeed was. Even so, the beautiful, gentle woman didn't deserve such a fate.

Tanner, however, realized he was no better when he accepted money from a despicable man in exchange for the woman. Sometimes he wondered how that poor lady had fared. He hoped well, but that was the last time he ever accepted money for any dirty job. Shortly after that, Tanner had returned to Charlestown, determined to win back Diana.

He'd wanted to put his spy days behind him, but it seemed destiny wouldn't allow him to lead a normal life. First, Farnsworth wouldn't let him be, and he'd very nearly harmed his own wife, then he'd undertaken a mission for which Diana would never forgive him, and now Annabelle was a daily reminder of what he had been.

Would he ever know a sense of peace?

Sighing, he got out of bed and sat naked before the fireplace. He'd lighted it earlier to dispell the slight chill in the air, a chill he'd never felt before. "I must be getting old," he sneered into the dying flames.

Tanner watched the pirouetting flickers of light, unaware that Annabelle had eased open the door to his room and stood watching him, radiantly beautiful in her own nudity. It was only when she whispered his name that he glanced up to find that her eyes were filled with that lustful gleam that he knew so well.

"I heard you moving around," she said and licked her sensuous lips. "I couldn't sleep."

"Have Cammie bring you up some warm milk," he suggested.

Annabelle laughed uncertainly. "Heavens, Mariah, if I didn't know better I'd swear you didn't want me."

"Don't call me by that name ever again! Mariah is dead. And you're right, Annabelle, I don't want you."

Her soft laugh flowed over him like silk. Annabelle came closer and sat upon his lap, brushing her small breasts against his chest. "I don't believe you. Remember how much you used to like it when I did this? You'd put my breasts in your mouth and feast upon them for hours. Your dessert is ready."

Now Tanner knew why he'd been so besotted with the wench. She was damned good in bed, knowing exactly what would please a man and how to please herself. She also used such filthy words that just the images they conjured up could make a man hard with wanting. He'd never slept with a woman who was as wanton as Annabelle. Even now, he felt his shaft springing to life, nudging her thighs, and she felt it too, the conniving whore. Annabelle wanted to wield her magic over him again, she wanted him so enamored of her that he'd forget everything and everyone. He'd be no better than the man he had been in New York, a man who had accepted money from a lecherous rake in exchange for a sweet, gentle woman.

"Oh, Tanner, you're so hard," Annabelle praised and rotated her delectable bottom against his manhood. "No other man has ever given me as much pleasure as you did. I've always remembered how it was between us, darling. Always. Forever."

Forever. Diana. Love. This woman wasn't Diana, she was nothing like Diana. He didn't love Annabelle, and no matter what his body wanted, he didn't want to make love to the lusty wench.

Tanner's arms grabbed her gyrating hips and stilled her movements. "Stop, Annabelle. I want you to return to your room and leave me alone."

"What?"

"You heard what I said." Tanner stood up, forcing Annabelle to do the same. "I don't want to make love to you."

"Well, whyever not?"

Her pale blue eyes flashed fire, and he noticed that her eyes were a shade or two lighter than Diana's and not as pretty. At one time, Tanner had thought Annabelle was beautiful, but that was because he'd wanted to forget Diana. Well, he couldn't forget her and he never would. Diana was his wife, his love. If he spent the remaining years of his life as celibate as a monk, then so be it. He didn't want any other woman but Diana.

"I don't love you," was Tanner's response, and he pulled on his robe.

Annabelle looked almost disbelieving. "What does love have to do with it? I loved someone once, Tanner, and he broke my heart."

Tanner nodded. "I remember. The man loved his wife."

Placing her hands on her slender hips, Annabelle laughed. "Is that why you're turning me down? You're in love with your wife? Well, where is this woman who has captured your heart? I don't see her. Is she hiding in the wardrobe?" Annabelle made an attempt to pull open the wardrobe doors, smirking at him as she did so, but the smirk disappeared when he grabbed her wrist.

"Go to bed," he said in a low voice, and Annabelle flinched. She stormed out of his room to return her own, slamming the door behind her.

"Bastard!" she whispered angrily as she threw herself onto her bed, burrowing beneath the covers. How dare he turn her down. She remembered nights when he practically begged for her favors. . . .

Were all men so stupid about their wives? She recalled the man she'd loved, and even now humiliation stained her cheeks pink to remember how he'd rebuffed her, mistrusted her. But she'd had her revenge, oh, yes, she loved thinking about the day she'd turned in the man's wife to the British.

She'd avenged herself then and she could do it again. But she'd never met Tanner's wife and didn't have any idea as to what she might be up against. However, Annabelle wouldn't allow Tanner's sentimentality to get the best of her. His wife was absent and she wasn't. And from the looks of Tanner's surroundings, he was quite rich — rich enough to please even her own mercenary little heart.

# Chapter 16

A sense of calm pervaded Briarhaven over the next few weeks. In November, a driving rain had drenched the area and brought with it the first bitter chill of winter. Now, on a cold afternoon, Diana sat with Marisa and Aunt Frances in the parlor. The insistent clacking of three pairs of knitting needles was drowned out by Hattie's gentle humming as she rocked little Jackie, who'd been ill, in the rocker that had quieted generations of Sheridan children. Jackie was one of those children, and though at one time Diana would have begrudged the child his heritage, she now smiled at the sweet picture he made nestled against Hattie's bosom.

Soon she'd rock her own child in that chair, and a keen sense of anticipation filled her. She touched her bulging abdomen when the child, her daughter, suddenly kicked. Diana couldn't think of the baby any other way, and she couldn't think about the child without her thoughts instantly straying to Tanner. At odd times she found herself wondering what he was doing, who he was with, if he was well, before having to drive his image away with some sort of chore. Dwelling on him only caused her pain.

The week before she'd received a letter from him, inquiring after Marisa and Frances. He said he hoped they were well. It wasn't until the end that he even wished her good health, causing Diana to feel a bit slighted that he'd asked after her relatives before herself. Then she was angry for feeling that way. Of course, she didn't reply to him.

"Diana," Frances said, peering over her spectacles at her niece, "what will you do if the baby is a boy? Everything we've knitted has some pink on it and can't be undone."

"Never fear, auntie, I'm carrying a daughter."

"A daughter without a father," Frances reminded her and instantly lowered her eyes to her knitting.

Diana noticed that Marisa appeared uncomfortable but didn't dispute her mother's remark. They wanted, as did Hattie, for her to write to Tanner or go to Charlestown and tell him about the baby. Well, she wouldn't do it! None of them had any idea why she ignored him, and she couldn't bring herself to tell them that Tanner was a spy, a traitor to his own people, that he'd used her for valuable information and betrayed her, too. The only person at Briarhaven who was happy that she didn't claim Tanner was Naomi. Tanner's mother hated her, and for the life of Diana she didn't know why. No matter how kind she tried to be to the woman, Naomi barely acknowledged her. She sent such cold, icy glances her way that Diana had given up any hope of winning her friendship. Since Harlan's death, Naomi had returned to live in the small house near the swamp and no longer had anything to do with Briarhaven's inhabitants.

Diana suspected that the cabin might be unbearably cold this time of year and had already decided to go and speak to Naomi, to try and convince her to live at Briarhaven. They certainly had enough room, and Diana felt that Harlan would have wanted Naomi there.

A loud knock on the front door startled the four women and woke Jackie from his nap. "Who in the world can that be?" Frances looked fearful, immediately clasping Marisa's hand. "Suppose it's one of those outliers I've heard tell about. We're all alone here. Anything can happen to us without a man nearby. Oh, I do wish you'd mend your fences with your husband, Diana."

"Hattie, where's Ezra?" Diana ignored her aunt and put down her knitting. With a calmness she didn't feel, she rose from her chair.

"He's in the barn," Hattie told her, fear in her eyes that someone would be out near dusk in such cold weather.

The knock came again, louder than before. "Oh, dear!" Marisa cried.

"Now, now, don't take on so. Stay in here, all of you, but be prepared to run." Diana's orders were taken seriously. All three women and a wide-eyed Jackie looked ready to flee. Their fear intensified when Diana went to a large bookcase and moved aside a heavy book. Behind the impressive and weighty tome was Harlan's pistol, already loaded.

With the gun clutched in her hand, Diana slowly entered the foyer. "Who is it?" she called to the person on the opposite side of the door.

"Diana, it's Clay, Clay Sinclair."

"Clay!" Instantly she threw open the door, joy consuming her face to see Clay standing there, a sack thrown over his shoulder. Diana literally pulled him into the house and hugged him. "I never thought I'd see you again. I didn't know if you were dead or alive. What are you doing here? Where have you been?"

"Hold on now." Clay laughed and kissed her mouth but suddenly drew back. "You planning to shoot the man who is bringing you a Thanksgiving feast?"

Diana remembered the gun, which was pointing straight at Clay, and quickly lowered it. "Forgive me, Clay. We're alone here and didn't know who you might be."

Moments later Diana had put the gun away and had introduced Clay to Frances and Marisa.

Hattie bustled happily about, Jackie following behind her, after Clay handed over his sack, a sack filled with a wild turkey for a real Thanksgiving dinner. "How did you ever get a turkey?" Marisa asked, much impressed. "I heard that game had been almost entirely wiped out because of the British. You must be quite a huntsman."

Clay actually blushed, something Diana didn't miss, nor did she miss the appraising looks exchanged by Clay and Marisa. Something was brewing here, Diana could tell.

"Oh, I've just lived in the wilderness for a while," Clay told her, shrugging off the compliment.

"How fascinating!" Marisa exclaimed, as did Frances, who began grilling the young man about his family connections. She beamed from ear to ear to learn that Clay Sinclair was one of the Santee River Sinclairs.

"A finer South Carolina family is hard to find," Frances proclaimed, putting her stamp of approval on the young man.

Diana couldn't help grinning. She remembered thinking long ago that Marisa and Clay would be perfect for one another, and now it seemed that she may have been right.

Leaving the two young people and Aunt Frances alone, Diana walked to the kitchen where she found Hattie busily preparing the turkey. "Our Thanksgiving is gonna be a few weeks early, Miss Diana. I ain't never seen so many waterin' mouths before."

"Mine, too, Hattie." Diana noticed Jackie sitting on a kitchen chair, his eyes not about to leave the turkey. "So you're ready to eat that bird, I can see. Leave some for me, all right, Jackie?"

"Oh, I will, Miss Diana," Jackie said in all seriousness. "But, Granny's gonna give me the drumsticks cause I like 'em so much. Is that okay?"

"You can have all the drumsticks you can eat."

Jackie looked puzzled and a bit upset. "A turkey's only got two, ma'am."

Diana laughed and embraced him. "You can have both of them and any other part of it you might want."

The child's eyes lit up, eyes that at one time had reminded her of Kingsley but that now reflected only happiness and relief. "I'm going to speak to Naomi," Diana told Hattie and pulled on her warm cloak. "If I can't talk her into moving back here, maybe she'd like to have dinner with us tomorrow."

"I wish you well, Miss Diana, but that Naomi's a hard woman."

Diana knew that very well. Though she didn't want to see Tanner again, she thought she should develop a relationship with Naomi. Afterall, she was her baby's grandmother. Ezra helped her mount the horse, and soon she found herself before the cabin in which her husband had been born. This is the place where Tanner grew up, she thought, not caring for the image of the deprived child that swirled around her brain.

The cabin was clean, from what she could see in the waning evening light, but it was such a small, fragile looking place that she wondered how a good wind hadn't blown it apart by now. Perhaps this sort of deprivation had left its mark upon Tanner, maybe this was why he felt he had to become a spy and receive lucrative payments for information. Perhaps she'd been too harsh on him, not realizing the extent of his deprivation. *But he betrayed you!* her mind screamed.

"What do you want?" Naomi asked suspiciously when she answered Diana's knock.

"I'd like to speak with you," Diana began. "Could I please come inside? It's cold out here."

Naomi stood aside and grudgingly allowed Diana inside her tiny house. Diana discovered that the sitting room was just as clean as the outside. It contained two chairs, a table on which rested mounds of dried herbs, a small cot near a window, and a fireplace in the corner.

The woman didn't offer her a seat but waited in wooden silence. She wore a warm flannel shirt and a beaded and fringed leather skirt. On her feet were soft moccasins. With her hair pulled back in a braid, Naomi truly resembled an Indian squaw, something that Diana had forgotten when Naomi took care of Harlan. At those times she usually wore a dark-colored gown, simple and unadorned.

"We're having an early Thanksgiving dinner tomorrow. I'd like you to join us."

"Harlan's dead," was Naomi's immediate response, almost as if she'd anticipated Diana's offer. "You don't have to be kind to me. I don't want to set foot in Briarhaven ever again."

"Why is my being kind to you so horrible? You're the grandmother of my child. If I didn't want to invite you, I wouldn't. Please come."

"No."

Diana was getting nowhere with Naomi and knew better than to suggest that she move into the house. Despite the cold outside, the cabin felt quite warm with the small, crackling fireplace, and it smelled wonderful with the scent of burning pine. Naomi appeared to have everything she needed. "If you change your mind, you're very welcome," Diana told her. Naomi made no move to open the door, but Diana turned and blocked her way. "I'd appreciate it if you'd tell me why you hate me so much, Naomi."

"Why do you think I hate you?"

"Because I know you do. I'd like to know why. What have I done?"

The cold, icy quality of Naomi's face dissipated and she didn't bother to hide the contempt and hatred that flushed her cheeks. For a second, Diana thought Naomi was going to strike her, but her voice, low and filled with venom, hurt worse than a physical injury. "I do hate you, Diana Montaigne. You, you who married a Sheridan because of your high birth, shouldn't bear claim to such a noble name. Your husband, Kingsley, should have been the bastard son because he acted like a bastard, while my son, my Mariah, was ignored and beaten.

"Yes, I hated Kingsley and I hate you. You could have stopped the beating, you should have stopped it! My Mariah lay right there," Naomi gestured wildly toward the cot, "and I thought he might die. His back, oh, his poor back was so broken and bleeding, so raw. But he didn't cry out his pain, and your husband wanted him to cry. I saw how he was lashed to the tree, tied like an animal and whipped by Harlan's evil spawn until he couldn't stand. And I hoped my son might die rather than live with the humiliation and the pain of loving a deceitful woman." Naomi grabbed Diana's hands. "Why did you lie to Harlan and Kingsley? Why did you tell them that Mariah tried to rape you when you knew it wasn't true? Because of your hateful lie, Harlan let my son be harmed. Because of you, my son left Briarhaven. Yes, he may have committed evil after he left, but you're to blame for that evil. You, Diana, you and your deceit!"

Naomi dropped Diana's hands, her face was purple with rage and filled with hatred. What was Naomi talking about? Why did she believe she'd lied to Harlan and Kingsley? She'd never

311

said Tanner had tried to rape her. "I never did that," she protested, growing weak as Naomi pushed her out of the door. "I didn't . . ."

"Then look at my son's back for proof! Or didn't you ever notice the scars there? But then again, you see nothing but what you want to see. People like you seldom do." Naomi slammed the door in her face.

Diana could hardly mount the horse. Her mind and stomach churned, causing her to feel unbearably ill. The brisk winter wind only increased her discomfort, and by the time she reached the barn, she was so sick that Ezra had to carry her into the house and into her room.

Hattie and Aunt Frances clucked over her, insisting she drink some hot tea. But Diana couldn't drink or eat. Nothing the two women did for her, from removing her shoes and clothes to covering her with the warm quilt and lighting the fire in the hearth, eased her discomfort.

"She's in shock," was Hattie's assessment, spoken in low tones to Frances.

They both shook their heads in dismay, wondering what could have happened to cause it. "Ladies who are *enciente* shouldn't be riding horses in this sort of weather," Frances avowed. "Her husband should be with her, that's what. Diana wouldn't disobey Tanner."

Tanner. His back. The scars. He'd told her he'd received them years ago, that they were unimportant, but he had gotten them on the

312

night he'd kissed her. Kingsley had done that to him; Harlan had allowed it. No wonder he hated his father and brother. And he had hated her, too.

That was the reason he'd always regarded her with suspicion: he'd believed Kingsley's lie. But hadn't she felt a sense of forgiveness for this in him? She hadn't known what it was he'd silently been accusing her of, yet she'd sensed a change in attitude. But she'd been wrong.

She had wondered why he used the information about her association with Clay, why she had no sooner divulged it than he left Oak Island. The answer was quite simple. Tanner wanted to avenge himself upon her, not because she was a Sheridan but because he'd believed a stupid, idiotic lie!

"Didn't he know I wouldn't do that?" she cried aloud.

Apparently not.


Dinner the next day was a festive occasion. The ladies gathered around the dining table dressed in their best gowns and bestowed upon Clay their undivided attention. This year thanks was offered for saving Briarhaven from the British, but a sadness permeated the room as all eyes were momentarily trained upon Harlan's empty chair.

As usual, Hattie had outdone herself. The wild turkey literally melted in everyone's mouths, the sweet potatoes with sugar oozing out of the jackets were instantly devoured, as was the simple dessert of nuts and raisins. "I'm about to burst," Clay good-naturedly complained, and leaned back in his chair to smile at Marisa when he finished his meal. Marisa poured some of the tea that the British had left into a cup for Clay, agreeing with him. Diana thought that Marisa would agree with Clay if he told her the sky was green instead of blue.

But love was like that, blind and trusting. Diana pushed her plate away, having eaten very little. Frances chastised her. "If Tanner was here you'd eat, I warrant."

Hurriedly, Diana rose from her seat, afraid she might say something she regretted. "I'm fine, Aunt Frances. There's no need to worry about me."

Leaving the dining room, Diana went into the parlor and gazed out at the cold November afternoon. A dark wall of pines in the distance fringed fields that had once been a shimmering gold, but now lay brown and overrun with weeds. Diana sighed. How was she going to have the fields in any condition for spring planting when there was no one to work them? Precious few slaves were left on any of the plantations. And many who had stayed had either perished during fever epidemics or were sickly or old, or both. It seemed that Briarhaven was luckier than most plantations because it was still intact, still offering a roof and warmth from the elements. But without the rice crop and slaves to work the fields, what would happen to all of them a year from now?

A slight noise behind her caused Diana to turn around. She saw Clay smiling at her. "What are you thinking so hard about?" he asked her.

"The future, or rather the lack of one."

His gaze traveled over the fields, instantly comprehending. "The British have made it hard for us, but somehow we'll survive. Briarhaven will survive, you must believe that."

"I shouldn't be feeling sorry for myself or Briarhaven," Diana said, an apology in her voice. "Sinclair House was burned and your family forced to leave. We've been very, very lucky."

Clay nodded and shifted his attention from the fields to Diana's hauntingly beautiful face. "I won't argue with you about that, because you're right, but we both know luck had nothing to do with it."

"What do you mean?"

"Don't act coy with me, Diana. I discovered that Sinclair House was to have been Farnsworth's headquarters but that Briarhaven was chosen instead."

"How do you know that?"

"Tanner told me."

Diana's jaw dropped, her surprise so apparent that Clay grinned and helped her to the sofa. "Sit down before you fall down," he advised.

"Why did Tanner tell you that?" Diana asked when her shock had abated some. "When did you speak to Tanner? No, don't tell me. I think I know. He was waiting for you in the swamp, ready to capture you, but you escaped."

"Yes, and no. Yes, he was waiting for me in the swamp. In fact, I think this is yours." Clay withdrew a blue hair ribbon from the pocket of his shirt. Diana gave a groan of dismay, but he took both of her hands in his, his steady comfort silencing her. "I found it hanging from a tree limb and I assumed you'd placed it there. Imagine my surprise when I returned that night and found not you but your husband."

"Oh, Clay, I'm so sorry . . ."

"Nothing to be sorry about, Diana, because he wasn't there for what you think. He wanted to help the rebel cause by passing on information about the British plan to capture Eutaw Springs. It was because of his advance warning and assessment of what the British planned that we won at all. Your husband is a hero."

"I . . . can't . . . believe . . . it."

Clay's expression became extremely solemn and he sounded concerned and serious. "Tanner loves you; otherwise, he wouldn't have changed sides. He admitted to me that he left you at Oak Island because he felt he needed to make something up to you, that he'd misjudged you and hadn't trusted you about something, and this was the only way he knew to make amends." Clay smiled. "He said he feared you'd be the madder than a hornet, but he hoped you'd somehow trust him when things looked darkest. I can tell you didn't."

Tears of joy and pain mingled in Diana's eyes and ran freely down her cheeks. *Tanner hadn't betrayed her!* He'd left to gain information from Farnsworth, something of value that he could pass onto Clay and Colonel Marion and bring the war to a quicker end. And it looked like he'd accomplished his mission. But then again, Mariah never failed.

But the joy was mitigated by the horrible knifelike wound that suddenly tore at her heart as she remembered the terrible things she'd thought about him, the awful things she'd written in her letter to him. She hadn't trusted him; she had behaved in the same way he'd behaved all those years ago. She had believed a lie, too.

Diana found herself in Clay's comforting embrace, weeping copious tears. "Now, Diana, crying offers only a momentary relief, but it doesn't solve any problems."

"I know that," she agreed and took the kerchief he handed her to compose herself.

"Then what are you going to do about it?"

"It's too late to do anything now, Clay." She disengaged herself from his arms and leaned tiredly against the back of the sofa. "I can't go crawling to Charlestown now and beg Tanner's forgiveness."

"Why not?"

"Because I'm too big and awkward to get on

my hands and knees." She patted her bulging abdomen and smiled weakly.

Clay grinned. "Tanner wouldn't want you to beg anyway, because he isn't the sort of person who expects it. Why don't you just show up and do the simple, decent thing and apologize to him? If he kicks you out on your posterior, then you'll know where things stand, or rather where they don't."

"You make things sound so simple."

"That's what comes with living in the wild, I guess."

"Will you escort me to Charlestown, or as close as you can get? I know you can't enter the city since it's under British occupation and dangerous for you."

"I'll take you as far as I can," Clay readily agreed and chucked her chin in brotherly fashion. "But I expect your husband will escort you home; otherwise, I'll have your Aunt Frances give him a proper scolding."

Diana couldn't help but laugh at the image of Frances, the diminutive woman whose tongue never ceased wagging, berating a man twice her size, one who talked only when he had something to say. "I bet Tanner would take me all the way to the equator to escape a lecture from Frances Delaune."

"Then start packing," Clay advised.

Diana didn't hesitate. She knew Clay was right. She had to apologize to Tanner, and he must still want her. He *had* to want her. But she remembered Annabelle Hastings and regarded her ballooning abdomen with trepidation, not certain that she could compete with Annabelle, or with any woman for that matter. Now that she thought it through, she wasn't certain of anything.

# Chapter 17

Diana's coach halted before Tanner's townhouse. She had parted with Clay barely an hour
before, and now Ezra waited, reins in hand, his
eyes wary and guarded.

"You gonna be safe, Miss Diana?" Ezra
asked. "I don't like bein' around these redcoats
too much."

"I'll be fine," she assured him, but she felt
quite vulnerable herself and started trembling
anew now that she was finally here. "Go around
back to the servants' quarters and tell Cammie
to prepare you a hot meal and find you a place
to sleep."

"How long we gonna be stayin'."

"I don't know, Ezra. I really can't say."

"Should I unload your trunk?"

"Just wait in the kitchen until I send word
either way."

Ezra nodded he understood, and Diana

320

watched while he guided the horses around back to the carriage house.

The urge to call Ezra back and return home gripped her, but she quelled it. She had to speak to Tanner, that was the reason she'd come all of this way. Taking a deep breath and pulling her cloak tightly about her, she grabbed the knocker and gave it a hearty thump.

While she waited for someone to answer she noticed a man across the street watching her with an intensity that sent shivers of apprehension along her spine. He was an ill-kempt looking man, poorly dressed. His beard was in need of a decent trimming, and from what she could see of his shaggy hair, covered by a frayed hat pulled low over his eyes, it could do with a good washing as well. She'd seen sorrier looking men, but there was something about this particular man that unnerved her. Now her hands shook so badly that she didn't know if her condition was from seeing Tanner again or being the object of this person's insulting stare.

"Hurry up," she mumbled under her breath, and knocked once more. The door opened a crack, and Diana grinned to see Cammie.

"Oh, Mrs. Sheridan!" Cammie cried and opened the door wider for Diana to enter. "I'm so pleased to see you. Let me take your cape and hang it up."

"No, no," Diana protested and shot Cammie a thin smile. "I'm not certain how welcome I'll be."

Cammie immediately understood and whispered, "Mr. Sheridan has visitors—and a house guest."

"I know about Annabelle Hastings. Who else is here?"

"Captain Farnsworth and some of his officers."

Diana didn't stifle her groan. "Just exactly what I need. I'll be in my room. Please tell Mr. Sheridan I've arrived."

Diana hurried up the stairs, unaware that Annabelle and Samuel Farnsworth had seen her. Annabelle fluttered her fan. "So that's Tanner's wife, is it?"

"Yes, that's her. I hope her consumption is better," he worried aloud.

"She looks quite healthy to me, Samuel, and stop being such a great baby about illness. You've been with so many women of dubious reputation that it's a wonder you haven't caught the pox."

"Annabelle, please . . ."

She tapped him with her fan. "Is Diana Sheridan a threat to my securing Tanner?"

Samuel blanched and gripped her wrist. "You know I love you, Annabelle! Why do you want Tanner when you can have me? I'd be good to you, treat you like a queen. My grandfather left me a small piece of property in England; we could be happy there."

"Are you wealthy?"

He stiffened. "I'm comfortable."

Annabelle sighed. "You mean you're poor."

"I'm not!"

"I won't mince words with you. If you're not poor then you're certainly not wealthy enough for me. I know how it feels when silk slides across the skin, how satin feels cool and crisp, and how diamonds and rubies warm my flesh. I lost all when I left Philadelphia, and I admit I was quite stupid not to marry Tanner when he wanted me in New York. I could have had all of this right now." Annabelle sent a withering glance up the stairs. "And stop twisting my wrist or I'll scream."

Releasing her, Samuel smirked. "I wager that Tanner will send you packing now that his wife is returned."

"Don't be so certain, Samuel. I do hate it when you try to appear smug."

Standing beside the bed she had shared with Tanner, Diana grasped a handful of sheer red silk. It was a woman's negligee, certainly not her own. Of course, it belonged to Annabelle Hastings, and most certainly she had been sleeping in Tanner's bed—with Tanner. Diana had suspected as much, but the gown was confirmation of Tanner's affair.

Don't cry, she silently ordered as she blinked away the tears. It seemed she cried so easily these days.

"Diana," came Tanner's voice from the open

doorway. She started, not having heard his approach. "Cammie told me you had returned."

A peach-tinted flush consumed her entire body, deepening the color of her cheeks almost to rose. "Yes, as you can see I'm here, but from the looks of things, you've been too occupied to notice my absence." She purposely dropped the gown onto the floor by Tanner's feet. "I do hate cheap clothes littering the room."

Tanner didn't say anything about the gown but kicked it aside. "Do you intend to stay?"

"I don't know. Am I wanted?"

"This is your house, too, Diana. I told you that when I married you."

She fingered the tassel on her cape, feeling horribly ill at ease. "Yes, you did. We'll be married a year next month, do you realize that?" God, she sounded stupid, almost as if she were using their wedding anniversary to make him feel guilty about Annabelle Hastings when Annabelle wasn't the reason they were separated in the first place.

"I can count," he said.

Diana took a step forward, aching to touch him, to beg his forgiveness. "Tanner, I must apolo . . ."

"Oh, there's my gown. I had wondered where it went to." A woman with silver-gold hair appeared at the doorway, and Diana immediately knew she was Annabelle Hastings. She immediately disliked her. Annabelle bent down and picked it up, sending a sly glance in Diana's direction before placing a hand on Tanner's arm and training her pale blue eyes upon him. "Introduce us, Tanner, dear."

Stiffly, Tanner did just that. Diana inclined her head and Annabelle grinned. "How delightful to meet you," she told Diana. "I think I've interrupted a private conversation. Do continue and forgive me." She squeezed Tanner's hand. "Don't be long, darling, we have guests." And then she breezed out of the room.

"It isn't what it looks like," Tanner began to explain.

"You don't have to go into details, Tanner, I don't want to know anyway. What you've done here with that woman is your business."

"I haven't done anything. Her gown was in here because she used the bathing room earlier today."

"Oh, so you allow her personal use of my effects. Does she wear any of the gowns I left behind?"

"Diana, stop." There was a distinct warning tone in his voice, but Diana didn't care. She'd come here to apologize and now she found she couldn't, wouldn't, humble herself to him, not after he'd allowed Annabelle to bathe in her tub, probably scenting her whore's body with her perfumes, and then, no doubt, to sleep in *her* bed. All of his prattle about loving her forever, wanting to make a child, was a lie too. He couldn't ever have loved her to forget her so quickly.

325

"Yes, I will stop," Diana acknowledged with a stiff nod of her head. "I made a mistake in coming here."

"Where in hell do you think you're going?" Tanner growled and gripped her arm when she made a movement toward the door.

"Back to Briarhaven, you silly fool. I'm not wanted here and I won't stay."

"You didn't tell me why you came in the first place."

"It wasn't important."

"Good God, Diana, sometimes I'd like to wring your beautiful neck. You can be the most stubborn and uncommunicative woman I've ever known. Just admit to me that you've had a change of heart and want to apologize to me. Is that so hard to do?"

"Yes!" she snapped. "It's very hard to do when you've got a woman parading around our house in a red negligee and acting as if she owns you."

A delighted grin split Tanner's sensual lips. "Annabelle wasn't wearing her red negligee just now."

"But she has, I bet."

"I guess so," he said with all seriousness, "but I've never noticed. You're the only woman I think about or want, and it's damned distressing to be so in love that pretty women hold no allure for me. If you don't rescue me by apologizing to me, Diana, I might have to enter a monastery."

"You're definitely not cut out for that sort of life," Diana agreed, and noticed a definite leer in his eyes. "So I suppose I will have to apologize to you." Diana's face crumbled suddenly, and she started to cry. "Oh, Tanner, I'm so sorry for not trusting you. Clay told me what you did. I should have believed in you. Forgive me, please for . . . give . . . me."

Barely a second passed before Diana felt the warmth of Tanner's lips pressing against her own. Hungrily, she kissed him back, realizing that he had forgiven her, that with Tanner, words weren't always important. "I've missed you so much," he breathed between kisses. "I've been miserable without you, so grumpy and unpleasant that it's a wonder Cammie and Curtis didn't shoot me."

"I'm glad they didn't," she told him, "otherwise I wouldn't be able to do this." With nimble fingers Diana began unbuttoning the front of his jacket and pulling it off.

"We have guests," Tanner reminded her, but the way he held her told her he'd forgotten them.

"That never stopped us before."

"And it won't now."

Fiery sparks, as brilliant as diamonds, exploded between them when Tanner pulled at her cloak. Diana trembled with raw anticipation; her body ached for his possession and instinctively she pressed closer against him, heedless that her cloak fell about her feet. The warmth of Tanner's hands when he reached into her bodice and temptingly caressed one of her breasts nearly undid her.

"You are a hungry wench," he whispered against her ear.

"Hmm, hmm, but only for your expert touch, Tanner, never anyone else's . . . ever."

His mouth slid sensuously along her neckline, findings its way to her collarbone and coming to rest atop the tempting swell of her breasts. With ease, Tanner pulled her gown past her shoulders at the same time as her camisole gave way, baring her enticing bosom to his lusty gaze. "You're more beautiful now than you've ever been," he praised as he worked the lacings at the front of her gown lose. "Especially now."

"Now?" Diana was so lost in her own passion that she didn't realize that Tanner wasn't blind to her condition.

He smiled and placed his hand upon her abdomen. "Our baby," he reminded her. "I only received Marisa's letter telling me about the baby yesterday. There was a postscript at the bottom from your Aunt Frances, taking me to task for not coming home."

Diana's high color faded some. "Are you angry with me for not writing you that I was having a child?"

"Some."

"I'm sorry, I should have. I wanted to share my joy with you, but I've acted like a fool for weeks. You really shouldn't forgive me at all."

Tanner finished with the last remaining lace and watched while Diana shrugged out of the gown. "With the way you look now, my sweetheart, I'd be foolish to be angry at anything you did."

Diana immediately came into his arms again, wanting, aching for him. Powerful arms lifted her gently from her feet and placed her on the bed. Diana's eyes glazed with desire as she watched Tanner undress, knowing in her heart of hearts that no man could ever be as handsome or strong or forgiving. She was so lucky to have his love, and from now on nothing would mar their happiness.

Smiling at him, Diana was more than ready for his kiss when he joined her on the bed. Almost instantly she felt his mouth move from hers and seek her breasts. Pressing them together, she made them more available for his greedy feast, moaning when he drew a lush mound into his mouth and erotically tugged upon her nipple.

His hands journeyed along her thighs, coming to rest near the soft down that shielded her femininity from his rapacious gaze. With expert fingers he found it, stroking and priming until Diana could stand no more of his torment that was both torture and heaven. "Oh, Tanner, that feels so wonderful," she panted and writhed wantonly upon the bed. "I want . . . you."

"Is it safe?" he asked in concern, but his face was dark with passion. "I don't want to hurt

329

you or the baby. . . ."

"If you don't, you'll hurt me worse," she told him, and kissed him with such fire that her intention was clear.

Rising above her, Tanner straddled her and inch by heart-stopping inch, he slid into her. Her breath caught in her throat and she exhaled on a wave of blinding passion. Her body responded instinctively to the rhythm of his strokes. They moved in unison, their bodies glowing like twin torches in the dark of night, flaring and straining for the ecstasy. Diana sensed that Tanner held his passion back, probably because he didn't want to hurt her or the baby. But Diana wanted all of him, and she pushed her body into his, writhing against him, communicating as no words could how much she wanted him. It was then he lost control and gave her all she craved, pushing them both beyond the earthly bonds to spiral and merge with the universe.

"I think I finally got it right," Diana said later.

Tanner kissed her. "You've got it down to an art."

"I owe you so much, Tanner, much more than I can ever say to you or repay. You've taught me passion. . . ."

"Shh, Diana." He placed his fingers on her mouth. "Whatever I've done for you, I've done out of love. I want you to remember how much I love you."

Diana shifted her weight and moved behind him. Her fingers gently traced the scars on his back. "You suffered the sting of the whip because of Kingsley's lie about me. I'm surprised you forgave me at all, but you did forgive me, even after you thought I had told Kingsley and Harlan that you tried to rape me. You never mentioned the incident to me because you loved me and didn't want to bring me pain. But I wish you had told me. I would have understood so many things." Her lips touched each scar, tenderly kissing every inch.

"Oh, God, Diana!" Tanner pulled her to him, and tears streaked his face. "I never wanted you to know about that. Who told you?"

"Your mother. She hates me, and I can't blame her. You suffered because of me." Diana held onto him tightly, knowing that this man truly loved her. "Don't cry," she crooned to him as if he were a small child. "Everything's all right."

Tanner framed her face in the palms of both his hands. "I'm going to spend the rest of my life making amends to you. There are so many wasted years . . ."

"Time is never wasted where love exists," she whispered. "Our love wasn't destined to happen years ago, but now it is. Think of the time we spent in preparation for this very moment. No matter what we both suffered in the past, we're free to love now, to touch and kiss. We belong to one another, always and forever."

"Forever," he said and kissed her forehead.

"And soon we'll have a daughter. So you see, our love was predestined."

Tanner didn't stifle the grin that rose to his mouth. His hand tenderly massaged her abdomen. "You seem certain we're having a girl. If so, I'd say from the look of things, she's going to be a *big* girl. Maybe she'll be able to lend a hand in the fields when she's older."

"Oh, Tanner, you're impossible!" Diana pretended outrage. "All women look like this when they're expecting. Don't they?"

"No," he said and drew her back down upon the pillows, and fondled the spot between her thighs. "Not all expectant women look like you. If they did, their husbands wouldn't get any work done but would spend all their time in bed making love to their wives."

"That seems like a very pleasant way to pass the time," Diana said, growing breathless and shaking anew with desire.

"Oh, it is," Tanner agreed and kissed her until she could no longer speak.

Annabelle lounged on Marisa's bed in the Delaune home, radiantly flushed after just having made love to Samuel. In fact, if the truth were known, she barely paid any attention to Samuel, who now puffed on a cheroot. He could be anyone as far as Annabelle was concerned. After she'd finished with the man who bedded her and made certain she'd received her own gratification, she wanted only to sleep for a while. But apparently that wasn't to be the case tonight.

"I think we should discuss something," Samuel began, grinding the cheroot on a porcelain try that rested on the bedside table.

"Can't it wait?" she asked testily. "I'm so utterly drained."

Samuel didn't hide his smirk. "You are a lusty piece who requires quite a ride before you tire, and that's what I love about you." He stroked her rounded derriere. Despite her protest of tiredness, Annabelle responded instantly. Samuel, however, got out of bed and pulled on a dressing robe. "I think you should know my plans."

"What plans, Samuel?" Annabelle resolutely sat up and arranged herself against the pillows, pulling the sheet about her. There would be no more play tonight.

"In case you haven't realized it, we've lost this war. Yorktown's fall nearly three weeks ago is more or less the end. I expect that soon we'll be packing it up and sailing for England. God knows I'll be glad to return."

This news was a bit startling to Annabelle, who'd been a spy for a number of years and couldn't imagine what it would be like when the British were permanently gone. But unlike Samuel, she had no real desire to return to England. She'd had an unhappy life there, filled

333

with too many things she'd rather forget. "I fail to see how any of this shall effect me. Certainly I'll miss you, but I have a life here."

Samuel gave a huge guffaw. "With Tanner Sheridan, I presume. Well, think again, old girl. If Sheridan wanted you at all, you would have been in his bed tonight and all those other nights, but instead you come sneaking over here. When are you going to accept what's offered you instead of always reaching for the unattainable? Or is the allure in trying to have something you know you can't?"

Sometimes Samuel amazed her. Of all the men she'd ever known, he was the only one who seemed to know what drove her. And she had to admit that he was a good lover, but he wasn't wealthy. Why was it that all of the men she could have cared about never had money? Why did she constantly make the same mistakes over and over? Either she thought she loved a man she couldn't have or she got rid of one she could have had only to realize too late that she'd erred. Like with Tanner.

"Maybe I enjoy reaching for the moon," Annabelle confessed. "It's so much farther away than a brass ring."

"But Annabelle, the moon is impossible to reach, unless you can sprout wings or somehow wish yourself there." Samuel came and sat beside her and took her hand. "I love you. For the first time in my womanizing existence, I've fallen in love. You haven't a clue what that means, I can tell you don't. Well, I'll tell you that over the years I've been a faithless cad, a man who'd have pulled up the skirts of any woman and had my way with her. I had convinced myself that I was such a handsome piece of work that any woman would fall willingly under my spell with little effort on my part. With you, I've tried harder than I thought possible to make you love me. Annabelle, I want to marry you."

"Oh, Samuel, please, I'm going to cry if you keep this up. I don't want to marry you. You're too poor. Tanner is my last hope at getting what I want out of life. I can make him want me again, I can do it."

Samuel stared at her a long time, and Annabelle began to fidget. Finally he sighed and handed her her dress. "You better leave now. My driver will take you back to the Sheridans."

"But . . . but I'm not ready to go yet."

"I want you to leave."

"Samuel . . ."

"Go, Annabelle."

Stiffening her shoulders, Annabelle got up and started to dress. She'd have cried if she hadn't been so annoyed by Samuel's high-handed treatment of her. What had gotten into him? If he loved her as he said he did, he shouldn't behave so callously toward her. "Will I see you before you leave Charlestown?" she asked, though she wasn't certain why she cared if she did or not.

"I doubt it."

"Good bye then, Samuel."

Annabelle headed for the door without looking back, expecting him to call out to her and forget all of this silliness. They'd spend the night together and everything would be forgotten. However, she didn't hear a word. Departing the house with as much dignity as she could muster, Annabelle stepped in a huff into the carriage that waited outside the house.

The driver started off, the dark night enveloping the interior. No carriage lantern had been lighted. Annabelle found this oversight most baffling since Samuel's driver was quite efficient, but she didn't dwell upon it. Instead, Samuel's marriage proposal and his departure weighed heavily upon her.

Suddenly a creaking noise drew her out of her reverie. The hair on the back of her lovely neck stood on end, for now Annabelle sensed a presence in the carriage. It was a man. She knew it. She smelled him, as one grown long accustomed to the male scent. And as far as scents went, this man needed a good washing. The stench was odious. Yet she also knew he didn't want her body; he wanted something else. She could tell because he didn't grab for her.

"I know there's someone here," she slowly said. "What do you want? Who are you?"

"The question isn't so much what I want but what you want, Annabelle Hastings," came the disembodied voice.

"And just what might that be, sir?"

They passed under a street lamp at that instant and Annabelle saw the bearded man, instantly taking in his ragged attire and the feral gleam shining in his greenish-brown eyes. She shuddered in revulsion, but she'd dealt with worse in her time. "Tanner Sheridan, my dear," he answered. "Do exactly what I say and he'll be yours. All yours."

By the time Annabelle had heard out the man and had returned home to sleep in the room next to Tanner's and Diana's, she didn't find the man in the carriage to be that revolting anymore.

# Chapter 18

Diana thought they made an odd threesome: Tanner, Annabelle, and herself whenever they took their meals. She knew that if she demanded that Annabelle leave, Tanner would send the woman packing, but Diana didn't say a word about the beautiful woman's presence in her home. In fact, Tanner was the one who finally brought up the subject the day after Diana's arrival. "I'll tell her to go," he proclaimed. "I'm certain Annabelle can make other arrangements. Sure of it. Samuel Farnsworth admitted to me that he's in love with her and wants to marry her."

"Poor Captain Farnsworth." Diana woefully shook her head but she was smiling. "Annabelle is welcome here, Tanner, for as long as she wants to stay. There's no need to put her out on my account."

Diana recalled Tanner's stunned silence. She was a bit stunned herself for her liberal attitude.

But now as she swallowed a sip of her wine and sweetly smiled at Annabelle, who was regaling Tanner with gossip about acquaintances they had once shared in common, Diana knew she'd done the right thing by not forcing the hussy to leave. Annabelle was up to something, she just knew it, but what she couldn't discern. The woman had been more than friendly to her, given the odd circumstances. Diana believed Tanner when he told her nothing had happened between them since New York, though Annabelle constantly made sly references to the contrary. Annabelle must realize that Tanner wanted to be rid of her; most of the time he just tolerated her or was indifferent. And she treated Diana so sweetly, always casting a ready smile in her direction, that Diana knew Annabelle was false. But what was she up to? This is what Diana aimed to discover.

When Tanner reached for a cheroot after dinner, Annabelle was at his elbow, ready to light it for him. "My, Annabelle, you are accommodating," Tanner noted. "But I could have done that myself."

"Oh, posh, Tanner, I just wish to be useful. I am a guest here and don't want to wear out my welcome." Annabelle glanced at Diana, who sat at the opposite end of the dining table. "And, may I say, Mrs. Sheridan, that you've made me feel so at home. Thank you so much."

"You're quite welcome, Miss Hastings." A becoming smile fringed Diana's mouth. "May I call you Annabelle? And you can call me

Diana."

Annabelle clapped her hands in glee, almost like a child. "I should like that!"

Confusion, and a touch of suspicion, clouded Tanner's eyes, yet he said nothing. After the meal had ended he went into his study and the ladies retired to the parlor, where Cammie placed a silver tea service and dutifully poured both women a cup of the warm brew before leaving.

"Cammie is a most dutiful servant," Annabelle noted as she sipped her tea.

"Yes, she keeps an eye on everything around here. Nothing escapes her notice."

"Really?"

"Yes, Annabelle, and to prove how nothing gets past her, just this evening she told me that she discovered you in our bedroom after Tanner and I left for church this morning. I'd appreciate knowing what you wanted there."

"I was looking for an earbob I've misplaced, and I thought it might have been in there. I'm sorry if I've overstepped my bounds, Diana."

"Please don't enter our bedroom again, Annabelle," Diana said, her voice dripping with honey. "But if you'd like, I'll have Cammie search the room for you."

"No, that won't be necessary. It wasn't there."

"I doubt it ever was."

Annabelle's eyebrows lifted. "Are you insinuating that I'm lying?"

"Yes."

"I'm quite insulted that you feel that way."

Holding her hands up to her cheeks, Annabelle looked quite hurt and embarrassed. "I'd never do anything to upset you."

"Yes, you would, but I haven't figured out what sort of game you're playing." Diana placed her tea cup on the sofa table and appraised Annabelle with such open scrutiny that Annabelle squirmed. "I'm not a fool, and I'm not as stupid as you think I am. Whatever you're about, I'm on to you, Annabelle. And don't think for a moment that I wish to be your friend. Most certainly you don't want to be mine. You want my husband, but you won't have him, no matter this strange game. I'll make certain of that."

Annabelle's pale blue eyes turned icy. "Quite sure of yourself, aren't you?"

"Not all of the time, but where Tanner's concerned, I am. Don't expect me to step aside and let you become mistress of my home and my husband's heart. I won't. Also, you can't. Tanner loves me. You missed your chance with him a long time ago."

"Ah, he told you about us."

"He did, but your past relationship doesn't bother me. The past is done."

Annabelle licked her lips and smiled. "Sometimes the past is very much alive," she announced cryptically.

"Not in this case," Diana said. "Now, do we understand one another?"

"We do."

"Very good. I believe I'll retire for the night. I

need rest, and I advise you to do the same, and please, no wandering into our room by mistake in search of lost earbobs."

"I wouldn't dream of it," Annabelle retorted, pasting a fake smile on her face. When Diana left the room she cursed under her breath and went to the sideboard where she liberally laced her tea with brandy. She liked the way it slid smoothly down her throat. Only the best for Tanner, she decided, in his liquor *and* his wife. And there was no doubt in Annabelle's mind that Diana Sheridan was of the highest caliber, a lady in the truest sense—something Annabelle would never be. This was why she hated her.

Why did men want to marry ladies? They made such a big to do about women who were good in bed, something she was quite proficient at, but when they wed, they married ladies. And if the lady happened to be a tigress beneath the sheets, so much the better. Apparently Tanner had married the perfect combination of lady and tigress. And it was plain to Annabelle that Diana would bare her claws in defense of Tanner.

"It's not going to be as simple or as easy as I thought," she thought as she sat on the chair by the window. But Annabelle should have expected that. Nothing was ever easy for her. Years of struggle had hardened her to life's misfortunes, but she'd assumed that trapping Tanner would be child's play. It wasn't, and not only because of his wife. Tanner wasn't interested, making the game all the more impossible.

If that wasn't enough, she also had to deal with that despicable Kingsley Sheridan. She heaved a huge sigh and got up to make her way to the dining room, where she took her cloak from the wall peg. Luckily, no one was about. Annabelle went outside, braving the cold wind that streaked past her face. Nearing the outside kitchen, she suddenly halted when Cammie appeared, followed by the large black man named Ezra. Their delighted laughter faded when they spotted her.

"Miss Hastings, you're going for a walk in this freezing weather?" Cammie asked, her face a puzzled mask.

"Er, yes, Cammie, I am. I adore the cold." Annabelle hated it but she grinned as if she loved it. "I won't be long. I need to walk off that delicious meal you prepared."

"Maybe Ezra should follow after you. There's no telling what could happen to a lady out walking after dark."

There was something in the way Cammie said *lady* that caused Annabelle to grimace. The nosy servant obviously didn't think she deserved such a fine title. "I'll be all right; don't either one of you worry."

And with that Annabelle whisked away, leaving the property by the back gate. She waited on the sidewalk behind the carriage house until she was convinced that Cammie and Ezra had entered the townhouse. Then she reentered the yard and gingerly sneaked into the door that led to the vacant upstairs room in the carriage house.

It didn't surprise her that Kingsley was waiting for her. She found him standing near the door, looking as bedraggled as ever. Immediately he grabbed her wrist.

"Well, hand over my jewels. It took you long enough to find them."

"Unhand me, you simpleton," Annabelle insisted. "I don't have your precious jewels."

Kingsley's face fell in disappointment. "Why not? You're not planning to rob me, are you? I won't stand for any duplicity," he blustered. "If so, you'll never have Tanner—"

"Shut up! I never got the chance to search for them. That nosy Cammie appeared and shooed me out of the room. Now Diana's suspicious and she's determined to discover why I was in her bedroom."

"Stupid bitch!" Kingsley began pacing the small, empty, and extremely cold room like a caged tiger. Annabelle wasn't certain who was the bitch—her, Diana, or Cammie, and she didn't ask. Something disturbed her about Kingsley. He wasn't right in the head, but she had to use him as he was using her. Without his help, Tanner would never belong to her. But first she had to find the jewels.

"I did the best I could," she offered by way of a defense.

"Then your best wasn't good enough." Abruptly he ended his pacing and pressed his body quite close to hers. "Maybe you need some inducement to hurry along. It's been a while

344

since I bedded a woman, and it shouldn't take much to please a whore like you, Annabelle, either to get her fanny moving beneath me or to retrieve my property. The choice is yours."

Annabelle sucked in her breath, appalled at the notion of being bedded by Kingsley Sheridan. Granted, she'd pleasured many, many men in her time, but none of them were insane . . . or as mean as this man. And Kingsley was cruel, she could tell that. How had Diana Sheridan lived with this beast for years as his wife? Annabelle wouldn't have suffered his kisses or his touch for a day, and certainly never a raised hand, but then again, Diana had been his wife and a lady, and women in Diana's position weren't free to choose. Annabelle couldn't help thinking that maybe being a lady wasn't all it was cracked up to be.

Kingsley did frighten her. There was a maniacal quality in his eyes, something menacing in his tone of voice, but she refused to show her fear to him. Kingsley Sheridan wouldn't get that satisfaction from her!

"You're a disgusting toad of a man," she found herself saying, drawing herself to her full height, which was rather tall for a woman. "I can't imagine anything more disgusting than bedding you."

"Why, you whore . . ."

"Oh, do be quiet with your name calling. I can think of some rather choice ones for you."

"Really. Well, I can think of some choice ways to make you suffer."

Annabelle was truly scared now. Alone with this demented man, anything could happen to her and no one would hear her screams. She realized that Kingsley was desperate to have his jewels, and she was desperate to find them, but not at the expense of her own safety. "Touch me and you've lost your opportunity of ever getting the jewels," she reminded him. "And you should know that Captain Farnsworth will gladly track you down if I'm harmed. I've written him a letter, which I placed in safekeeping with a friend to give to him if anything should happen to me. And you're the prime suspect."

Her lie plainly worried him. Kingsley backed off and threw himself into a corner, huddling like a small boy. "Just bring them to me soon. I want to be gone from here. I want to go home and take my wife with me."

"I guarantee that you will, but you promised delivery of Tanner to me if I help you. And you promised he wouldn't be harmed."

"Certainly, dear Annabelle." Annabelle didn't like the sound of that, but she hastily retreated from the small room and rushed back inside the house, nearly bumping into Tanner at the door. "Cammie told me you left earlier," he said. "Did you enjoy your walk?"

He looked so warm and comforting, so very handsome as he stood there, that Annabelle did something totally unexpected, even for her. Genuine tears rolled down her cheeks and she threw herself against Tanner's chest.

"What's wrong?" he asked. "You're shaking."

"I'm just cold," she replied, but she knew her trembling was more than a winter's chill.

Kingsley sat huddled against the cold and cursed Annabelle threefold. The stupid wench had failed. He had hoped that he'd be in possession of the jewels he'd stolen from Diana's jewelry box, the same jewels he'd taken when he left Briarhaven—or, to be more accurate, when his father had run him off. But like everything that had happened to him during these last agonizing months, he wasn't surprised by the delay.

Before joining the army, he'd come to the townhouse and hidden the jewels behind the fireplace in the master bedroom. He figured that the war would soon end and that he could retrieve them later and sell them. However, the war dragged interminably on. He had joined David Richmond's regiment in expectation of proving himself a hero, knowing that word of his valor would trickle back to his father and his wife. They'd realize how horribly they'd treated him, and both of them would get on their knees and beg him to return home. He might, and then again he might not, that's what he'd have told them. But Kingsley realized almost immediately that he wasn't cut out to be a hero. Fighting, especially hand-to-hand combat, frightened him. Dreams of being run through by a bayonet filled his nights, and the thought of capture, spending time in an enemy prison camp, caused him to break out in a cold sweat.

But Charlestown fell, and so did Kingsley. He remembered the pain that welled inside him when the fighting began, how he couldn't breathe. He ran, and during his flight he was shot in the leg by a British soldier. Somehow he returned the fire and shot the man, instantly killing him. The man's dead eyes still haunted him, as did the memory of stripping the corpse and exchanging uniforms. Now Kingsley Sheridan was a dead hero, for better or worse, rather than a live coward.

Somehow he made it to the ragged settlement of Rawdon Town and Mike Candy's succor. If not for Candy he'd have died. As it was, he'd been ill for months, sometimes healing, then growing suddenly sick and wishing he'd die. But he wasn't going to die, he was going to live and make it to the townhouse, to reclaim his bounty. But as fate would have it, the British commandeered the property and he'd been too ill to care about the jewels.

Yet when he felt better he was ready to make his move, only to be thwarted by, of all people, his black-sheep half brother. Tanner was in residence. God! It was all too much to bear, especially the knowledge that Tanner had married Diana.

Kingsley still didn't know how that had happened, but their days as a happy couple were numbered — he'd see to that whether Annabelle helped him or not. Diana was his wife, she belonged to him, not his half-breed brother.

And soon, very soon, he was going to claim her again and wipe all traces of Tanner from her mind — and her body.

And as for Tanner, well, Diana would most likely grieve for a few days, and Annabelle would most likely believe she'd been duped, and she'd be right. But what could he do, how could he have had any forewarning of Tanner's sudden and unexpected demise? After all, he wasn't God, was he?

Kingsley laughed, a heinous sound even to his own ears, at the notion. The more he dwelled upon the image of himself as omnipotent, the more he began to believe it.

## Chapter 19

"Must we attend Captain Farnsworth's soiree tonight?" Diana asked as she snuggled closer to Tanner. "He and his friends are such obnoxious bores."

Tanner nuzzled her neck, then kissed her soundly on the lips. "Yes, but this will be the last Tory event we'll have to attend. Farnsworth confided to me that the British are withdrawing from Charlestown soon."

"And going where?"

"Back to England. Your side has won, Diana."

Diana didn't think of it as "her side," and it bothered her that Tanner still thought in terms of divided camps. Now that he'd leaked information about the Eutaw Springs battle to Clay Sinclair, he was no longer a loyalist spy. "Our side has won," she corrected him, and ran a fingernail along his muscular forearm. "For good or ill, you've tossed in your lot with me."

"Definitely for good." Tanner smiled at her and lifted one of her dark curls, wrapping it around his index finger. "We should have finished dressing an hour ago. Curtis is already waiting with the carriage and must wonder what happened to us. Why is it, do you think, that we can't ever be ready on time?"

He was teasing her and she knew it. Tanner didn't give a fig about arriving anywhere late. "That's a difficult question to answer." Diana puckered her forehead into a frown. "I really can't say."

"Cunning vixen," came his seductive whisper as he pulled her hard against him. "I thought you knew the answer very well, but apparently you've forgotten all I taught you."

Diana wriggled wantonly beneath him. "Then you must refresh my memory."

"It will be my pleasure." And it was.

Oh, why were Diana and Tanner dawdling? Annabelle paced her bedroom, her blue negligee flowing around her. She listened for some sound that would assure her that they were leaving. All she heard was a muffled giggle and Tanner's deep groan. "Dammit! So that's what's keeping them. They might never leave at this rate."

Annabelle flounced onto the bed, her kerchief crumpled in the palm of her hand. This business of retrieving Kingsley's jewels was taking its toll upon her. She wished the Sheridans were already gone so she could sneak into their bed-

351

room. Her only problem would be the officious Cammie, but somehow, some way, she'd get the jewels tonight and end this torture of being forced to help Kingsley Sheridan and knowing that at this very moment Tanner was making love to his wife. That thought hurt a great deal.

But Diana really wasn't Tanner's wife, Annabelle realized. For all intents and purposes, Diana was still married to Kingsley, which meant that once Kingsley claimed her Tanner would be free. And then Tanner would take a new wife— her.

"I'm going to be happy, finally and completely happy, and have all I've ever wanted," Annabelle spoke aloud to a porcelain figure of a shepherdess on the bedside table. "Things will work out for me, they must."

However, by the time the clock in her room chimed nine, Annabelle had nearly lost all hope of getting into the Sheridan's bedroom that night. She started suddenly when she recognized Tanner's knock on her door. "Annabelle, are you ready to leave for the soiree?" he called.

Bolting beneath the covers, Annabelle arranged herself against the pillows, and in a weak voice she called to Tanner to enter.

"Are you sick?" he asked. He appeared so handsome as he stood beside her bed that Annabelle trembled with desire. "You're shaking," he noted. "Perhaps I should send for a physician. You might have a fever."

"No, no, Tanner, don't trouble yourself," came her hurried response. "I'm not feeling too well tonight, but not sick enough that I require medical assistance."

"I'll convey your regrets to Samuel."

Annabelle sighed. "I doubt Samuel shall care. We didn't part on amiable terms."

"I'm sorry to hear that. Samuel told me he's in love with you. I hope you didn't break his heart too badly."

"Ah, Tanner, you're to blame for Samuel's pain, and my own. I told him that I love you and could never marry him."

Tanner's face remained a mask of indifference. "You should have accepted Samuel's proposal. *I* don't love *you*."

"But you did; I know you did," Annabelle protested strongly.

"At one time I thought what I felt for you was love, but I know that I was wrong. I never loved you, can never love you. Do the wise thing, Annabelle, and get out of your bed and tell Samuel that you'll marry him."

"I won't!"

Annabelle didn't care for the way Tanner dismissed her heated retort with a shrug. She heard him speak to Diana in the hallway, then he laughed in utter and intimate delight. Clenching her teeth until they hurt, Annabelle threw back the blanket and went to the window. She watched Tanner's carriage disappear into the darkness and envied Diana Tanner's company. But soon Tanner would belong to Annabelle Hastings, and this thought calmed her.

"Now to check on that nosey maid," Annabelle mumbled as she threw on her robe, having decided that she'd plead thirst if she ran into Cammie. All she needed was a few minutes to get into the master bedroom and search the fireplace, but she must know where Cammie was first.

Going downstairs, she walked the length of the house and went outside, braving the cold night air, until she came to the structure that housed the kitchen. Cammie wasn't there and Annabelle was vexed. Where was she, anyway? The woman spent almost as much time preparing food as she did nosing about the townhouse.

It wasn't until she neared the slaves' quarters that Annabelle decided to nose around herself. Perhaps Cammie had retired for the night.

By a strange quirk of fate, Annabelle noticed one of the windows was open enough to allow her to see inside the bedroom she knew belonged to Cammie. Shivering from the cold, Annabelle found herself peeping into the room, lighted by a thin candle. She widened her eyes in utter astonishment and envy as she watched Ezra ride upon Cammie's writhing body. The pleasurable mewls coming out of Cammie's mouth and Ezra's passion-starved visage adequately convinced Annabelle that Cammie wouldn't be wandering around the townhouse that night.

Running back inside the house on swift but silent feet, Annabelle rushed up the stairs and wasted no time in entering the master bedroom.

She closed the door and instantly knelt before the large fireplace, counting eight bricks up from the floor on the left side of the hearth, as Kingsley had told her. Her fingers fastened on the seventh and eighth bricks. She pulled outward and winced at the scratchy sound they made. Laying them on the floor beside her, she then reached into the dark crevice. Immediately her hand clutched the sack.

"At last! I've found it." How easy it had been, she smugly decided and replaced the bricks before returning to her bedroom, where she sat cross-legged on the bed and emptied the sack's contents onto the coverlet.

Annabelle gasped at the glittering flash of garnet earbobs and a matching ring. They were mingled with an emerald and sapphire necklace, a diamond pendant, and gold and silver rings and bracelets. It had been a long time since she'd been able to touch such pretty and expensive jewels. She hurried to the mirror, pinned the diamond on the front of her robe, and hung the garnet earbobs from her ears. My, but she looked so different when she wore fine things! Almost as if she'd been born to them.

"Soon Tanner will buy me furs and jewels," she informed her reflection. "And I'll be a proper lady, just like Diana Sheridan."

She giggled, then sighed and replaced the jewelry in the sack. When she handed it to Kingsley barely five minutes later in the carriage house, he insulted her, as usual. "I hope I don't find any of my property missing."

"It's all there. Check for yourself."

Which is what he did. Apparently satisfied with her honesty, Kingsley rewarded her with a smile. "When are you leaving?" Annabelle asked him. "And when will I finally be able to lay claim to Tanner?"

"Not so fast, my eager whore. You must do something else for me first. I need you to sell these jewels for me. I must have money and clothes before I return to Briarhaven. I'm master there now, and the master can't return in rags. Besides, Diana can't see me like this."

"You do looked wretched," Annabelle agreed, "but where am I going to sell your jewels? Who has such money these days?"

"Many people still have money. They pretend to be bad off so no one will try to take it away from them." Kingsley handed her the small sack. "There's a man named Cyrus Thompkins who lives on Orange Street. His house is in deplorable condition, but within its walls is a veritable treasure house. Take the jewels to him. He'll pay you a good price."

"And then?" Annabelle inquired, wondering how many more errands she'd have to perform.

Kingsley grinned broadly and scratched his head. "Then we put our plan in motion."

Annabelle hoped so. After she was in her room again, she took out the jewels. The garnet earbobs and ring were quite beautiful, and she'd always been partial to garnets. She looked much more fetching in them than some dowager lady would. When she closed the sack and hid it in a drawer, the garnet set rested in Annabelle's jewel box. "Kingsley owes me something for all of my trouble," she insisted aloud, but she knew that Kingsley might wonder what had happened when she didn't hand him the sum of money he thought Cyrus Thompkins would pay him.

To prevent Kingsley from becoming too suspicious, she substituted a copper bracelet and choker Samuel had given to her in exchange for the garnets. Of course, the garnets would have fetched a higher price, but the copper wasn't worthless either. Kingsley would have to take her word that Mr. Thompkins couldn't pay her what the jewels were worth. Bad times and all that sort of rubbish, that's what she'd tell him. He'd never be able to dispute her, not if he didn't want to play his hand too soon.

A shiver of apprehension slid down Diana's spine, and she glanced around the garden, seeing no one. Lately she felt as if she were being watched; it was an extremely unpleasant sensation, but one she couldn't shake. She didn't see anyone standing at the windows in the house, or in the kitchen or the slave quarters. Her gaze suddenly shifted upward to the room above the carriage house and she started.

For a second she imagined she saw someone watching her, but she blinked and saw nothing when she looked again. Evidently it was the sun hitting the window at a certain angle, the light playing tricks on her eyes. But she trembled and wondered if she might be losing her mind. Perhaps she was dreaming and believing herself to be awake.

She could have sworn that the face at the window was Kingsley's.


Cammie bustled around Diana's room, pulling the expensive satin gowns from the wardrobe and repacking them in the trunk that Diana had brought with her from Briarhaven. "I bet I'll like Briarhaven, Mrs. Sheridan. Ezra's told me all about it, and it sounds so pretty. I just know I'm going to be friends with Hattie, but do you think little Jackie will like me? I hope so. I like children."

Diana glanced up from the chair before the fireplace, a letter from Anne rested on her lap. She smiled encouragingly at Cammie. "Jackie is a dear little boy and he needs a mother. He has a great deal of love to give, and so do you, Cammie. I predict that once he sees you, he won't let you out of his sight."

Cammie flushed and returned to her chore. Diana was so happy for her and Ezra. As soon as everyone was at Briarhaven again there would be a wedding between those two. Maybe the wedding would herald a return to normalcy at Briarhaven. Diana hoped that the scars of this ravaging war would heal quickly. Even now, the British were preparing to flee Charlestown and the American force was ready to enter. The evacuation of military personnel could come at any time. The harbor buzzed with activity; British frigates constantly entered and waited.

Anne mentioned in her letter that the Richmond family wanted to return home to Charlestown very much, but that they didn't dare risk entering the city at that time. "We'll wait until we're certain that the British are withdrawing," Anne had written. "So far, all we ever hear are rumors. No one really takes the war too seriously on Oak Island. Sometimes it seems that it was all a bad dream."

"You're thinking too much again."

Diana looked up with a wrinkled brow to see Tanner standing before her, dressed in a white linen shirt with a slight ruffle along the edge and tight-fitting breeches. She held out her hand to him and he took it to plant a warm, caressing kiss upon her palm. "I was thinking about Anne and the war. Do you believe that we can go on from here?"

"Yes, of course. The war is ended, not our lives."

"But Briarhaven is in ruins, Tanner. I doubt we'll ever get the fields into shape in time for planting season."

Tanner drew Diana to her feet and placed a gentle hand upon the swell of her abdomen. "This is all you need to worry about now, Diana."

Imagining their child always caused Diana to smile. "I bet she'll have hair the color of pitch with eyes to match. Just like you."

"Sounds like a little devil you're describing,

but she'll be an angel — just like her mother."

"An angel, is it?" Diana wound her arms around Tanner's neck and kissed him deeply. The sound of Cammie's delighted giggle broke the spell, and Diana found herself flushing, having forgotten Cammie was still in the room.

"Don't forget to close the door when you leave, Cammie," Tanner said, not even glancing her way. All of his attention was centered on Diana.

"Sometimes I hate being an angel," Diana drawled after Cammie had left. "It's so boring."

"Are you bored now?"

"Most definitely." Tanner whisked her from her feet but groaned when he deposited a laughing Diana on the bed. "I'm not so easy to lift any longer," she said.

"And my back isn't what it used to be, either," he told her, and slowly began to untie the laces on the front of her gown.

With a hand on his, she stopped him. "If you'd rather not, if you think I'm not attractive enough . . ."

"Be quiet and let me love the most beautiful woman in the entire universe."

Diana instantly obeyed.

# Chapter 20

Diana dreamed about Kingsley again, feeling the sting of the riding crop and the coolness of the floor beneath her knees when she fell. His face loomed before her, his eyes cruel and cold, his curses hot and filled with hatred. She cried out in her nightmare but woke in a pool of sweat, only to find Tanner was sleeping peacefully beside her.

What a horrible, tormenting nightmare, one she thought she had buried within the dark recesses of her mind. Why did she dream about Kingsley now, especially now that she was so happy and looking forward to the future—a future with Tanner and their child?

She pulled the cover about her, suddenly chilled, and sought Tanner's body in the darkness. Even in sleep, his arm wrapped protectively around her, and finally Kingsley's face and brutality faded, and she fell into a dreamless sleep.

"Remember, Cammie," Tanner instructed the servant, "to close up the house tight, make certain all windows and doors are locked when you and Ezra leave for Briarhaven in a few days. The carriage might be crowded with all of the trunks. Can you both manage on your own?"

"Oh, yes, Mr. Sheridan. Ezra and I will manage just fine. Now you and Mrs. Sheridan have a pleasant journey and leave the rest of the packing to me." Cammie's ready smile faded some and she whispered lowly, out of earshot of Diana, "But what about Miss Hastings? She hasn't left yet."

"Miss Hastings will be leaving tomorrow," Tanner assured Cammie. "We had a nice talk and she agreed to find accommodations elsewhere."

"Yes, sir, Mr. Sheridan." Cammie made a small curtsy to Tanner and Diana and departed for the kitchen.

Hugging Diana when he drew near her, Tanner bestowed a light kiss on her forehead. "Curtis is waiting with the carriage outside. I've instructed Ezra and Cammie about getting things in order before they leave Charlestown. Are you ready to go?"

"Yes . . ."

Tanner, ever alert to Diana's changing moods, frowned. "What's bothering you?"

Diana waved a hand in the air in a dismissive

gesture. "Nothing really, but I have this odd feeling?"

"The baby?"

"No, more like a . . . oh, I'm being silly . . . but I've been wondering if we should leave Charlestown now. The British are still here and Farnsworth might wonder why the great Mariah is willingly heading into American territory."

"Samuel knows I have interests at Briarhaven," Tanner explained, "and he's more than eager to return to England, so I expect no trouble from that quarter. Just what is bothering you, Diana?"

Tanner hugged her tighter and Diana buried her face onto the front of his heavy cloak. "I dreamed about Kingsley last night," she admitted.

"He's dead." Gently, he lifted her chin and smiled down into her eyes. "There's nothing to fear any longer, from Kingsley or the British. You're safe in my arms."

Diana stood on tiptoe and kissed him. Tanner was right, she decided. She was safe, safe, safe. But why was she plagued with this gnawing feeling of dread?


"Everything's in readiness. Attacking Tanner's carriage on the Charlestown road will be very easy. My two accomplices await me." Kingsley couldn't help but smirk at Annabelle's sneer.

"Just where did you get these accomplices?" she asked, her gaze straying to the street where

Curtis waited with the carriage to drive the Sheridans for their trip home to Briarhaven.

"In Rawdontown, and I admit that the two of them pounced on my offer, so eager were they to earn a bit of money—and a bit is all they're getting. You know, there's something to be said for hard times, Annabelle. It brings out the worst in people and they work cheap."

Annabelle knew all about hard times and what one would do for a little money. However, it seemed that Kingsley Sheridan was prospering. Dressed in a decent suit of clothes, his hair combed back in a queue and a new tricorn upon his head, he was almost handsome. Almost. There was something about those eyes that always sent a shiver up Annabelle's spine, and she'd been around men who were less gentlemanly than Kingsley, people who'd slit a person's throat for a bottle of ale. But they had never frightened her like this man, and though she wanted to be free of Diana, she couldn't help but pity the woman who'd soon find herself in Kingsley's clutches. "Just make certain Tanner isn't hurt," was Annabelle's reminder to him after she told him that Tanner and Diana were now entering the carriage.

Kingsley made a mocking bow and left. Seconds later Annabelle was in her room waiting for Tanner's return—to her.

Tanner smiled to himself. He was happy, not only happy but delirious with joy. The woman he loved leaned against him, her gloved hand resting in his. His child grew in her belly, each day becoming stronger. And he was wealthy, rich enough that he'd be able to get Briarhaven on its feet again. There wasn't anything more he wanted in life than what the Creator had already given him. A surge of gratitude overcame his hesitancy at praying—it had been so long—but he offered a silent prayer of thanks and wondered what Diana would think if she knew that while he held her in his arms he was praying. Probably she'd approve, and this brought a secret smile to his lips.

A bright and cool morning, with no threat of rain, promised an easy trip. The horses swiftly thundered down the road, the carriage wheels clicking rhythmically in their wake. More than likely, they'd arrive earlier than they anticipated at Briarhaven; however, no one expected them since they hadn't sent a message on ahead. But it didn't matter when they arrived home. Tanner knew that Hattie would cry with gladness, Aunt Frances would good-naturedly lecture them about something, and from what Diana had told him about Clay and Marisa, those two would gaze rapturously into each other's eyes and probably not realize anyone had arrived. Yes, he was suddenly eager to be home again, thinking of Briarhaven as his home. And it *was* his, finally and completely his.

Diana dozed in his arms, and Tanner nodded off for what he thought was a few seconds but could have been minutes. Suddenly he was jarred awake as the carriage came to an abrupt halt. Diana fell to the floor, her head cracking against the door, though he stayed in his seat. Making a mad reach for her, he cursed aloud, intent upon taking Curtis to task but wondering why they'd stopped. "Diana, are you all right?" he cried and pulled her from the floorboards.

"Oh, God!" he groaned to see blood dripping from a cut on her forehead.

She stared up at him with glazed eyes. "Tanner . . . my head . . . hurts so."

Taking a kerchief from his pocket, he dabbed at the blood. "Lie still. I'm going to see why we've stopped." Gingerly he placed her on the seat and got out of the coach, his face a thunderous black. That damned Curtis! What in the name of God were they doing stopped here . . . ?

But Tanner's rage died when he stepped to the front of the carriage. There he found Curtis, no longer sitting on his perch but lying now in the middle of the road with a gaping knife wound in his stomach. He was dead, and the murderer stood over his victim's body and calmly wiped the knife clean on Curtis's coattail.

For the first time in his life, for the only time in Mariah's experience, Tanner didn't react quickly enough. Being a spy had sharpened his wits, but he wasn't a spy now and he hadn't expected any danger. Contentment had dulled him, lulled him into a false sense of security, something he instantly regretted as he felt the cold blade of a knife rip through his cloak and mercilessly slice through the wall of muscle on his back. He made a move to turn and get to Diana, but another man blocked his path and stabbed at him again, this time in the side.

"Di . . . an . . . a," he moaned, determined to get to her, to protect her somehow, someway. But once again the knife found him and Tanner fell face down in the roadway.

Kingsley came from behind a tree that lined the road and passed a quizzical eye over his brother. "Did you kill him?" he asked the second man.

"Of course I killed him, guv'nor. What you take me for, an amateur?"

Kingsley had no recourse but to believe that the man was proficient with a knife. After all, he'd never hired killers before now. "Then get their bodies off the road, bury them somewhere, anywhere, for all I care. Just get rid of them."

"Whatever you say, guv'nor. But how's about our money? We done did the job for you."

"Aye, we did," the other henchman chorused.

"Here then, you bleeding bandits." Kingsley took a small pouch of gold from his pocket. "I'm giving it to you now because I can't stand here all day arguing with you. Just do as I say."

"Sure, gov, but there's a lady in the carriage who seems to be knocked out. Should I see if there's somethin' she might be wantin'?" the man queried with such a leer on his face that Kingsley was instantly on his guard.

"The lady is my responsibility." Kingsley rose to his full height and looked down his nose at the man. "Do as I told you." Not wishing to waste time checking on Diana, Kingsley quickly climbed up to the perch and took the reins in his hands. He nodded coolly at the two men, keeping his eyes away from Tanner's body and that of the driver. And then he was off.

"What we gonna do with 'em?" the man who'd killed Curtis asked the other man, warily eyeing their victims.

Tanner's killer shrugged. "I dunno. I ain't never killed nobody before. Have you?" The other one shook his head. "We did our job, like we was hired for, but I ain't haulin' 'em off somewhere, takes too much time. The bloody bugger should have paid extra if he wanted 'em buried. Let's put 'em on the side of the road. My palms are itchin' to sample some fine liquor and good women, and I don't mean the church-goin' type."

The other man laughed in agreement, and they dragged the two bodies to the side of the road and ran the distance into Charlestown like Lucifer was behind them.

About two miles down the road Kingsley stopped the carriage to tend to Diana. He found her lying on the seat, blood dripping from a gash on her head. She moaned. A good sign, Kingsley decided, because he wanted her alive. His loins ached for her, and she was the reason he hadn't died. He wanted her with a fierceness that shook him. If he'd dwelled upon his consuming desire for a woman he had tormented during all of their married life, he'd have understood that most of his lust came from the fact that Diana had willingly given herself, body and soul, to Tanner—a man he loathed. But Tanner was dead now, and Diana was his. She'd do whatever he said, whenever he said it, and derive great amusement from knowing he'd taken Tanner's woman from him.

"Diana, look at me. It's your husband."

"Tanner." Making a soft moan, she opened her eyes and focused her gaze on him. If he thought she had hated him in the past, the absolute terror and horror on her face now caused him to crow aloud his utter and complete delight. "No! No!" she cried and pushed weakly at him.

"Yes, yes, my dear. It's me, your beloved husband, your darling Kingsley. I've come to claim you, pet, and bring you home to Briarhaven. Is this any way to behave after I've sprung from the grave?"

"Tan . . . Tan . . . ner."

"Shut up about him and stop moving around so. You're not going anywhere, but I wouldn't put it past you to try to escape me. You always did have a bull head. I'm left with one alternative." Out of his pocket he took a kerchief, which he promptly stuffed into her mouth, then he withdrew a coiled piece of rope and bound her hands behind her back. "That should keep

369

you quiet. Just think about your coming child, my dear, and how delighted it will make some deserving, childless couple. And believe me, there are many people who'll pay a small fortune for a baby. Looks like that bastard brother of mine did me a good turn after all." Kingsley laughed at her terror, the pitiful and weak way she tried to kick out at him.

He climbed upon the front of the carriage with a huge smile on his face. It was wonderful to have her fear him again.


Mike Candy wasn't in the habit of walking the roads, but the day was so pleasant that he felt the need to leave Rawdontown for awhile. Maybe he could find some employment up this way. There were no jobs in Charlestown, and with the British leaving soon he doubted any patriot would hire him even to sweep his chimneys. Maybe he should go back to the sea, but his joints acted up on him sometimes, making him doubt he'd be able to take the damp sea air for long.

He didn't expect to find a job and wasn't quite certain why he had decided to take a walk—especially on this road that was rumored to be frequented by outliers, those notorious men with no allegiance who robbed and killed their victims. Mike shrugged off his fear; he didn't have any money, so no outlier would lay claim to him. As he walked he found himself enjoying nature's beauty and feeling a bit of hope that things would eventually turn out right for him.

From the height of the sun in the sky, he realized it must be past midday, most definitely past midday if the emptiness in his stomach was any indication. For his breakfast he'd eaten a stale piece of bread and was more than used to the hungry rumbling sound, but he'd have turned back to Rawdontown, except he had no meal waiting for him. Not even a crumb. Maybe if he continued on for another mile or so he might come across some wild berries or even some wild game. Mike's mouth watered to imagine feasting on rabbit, pheasant, or squirrel. Hunger propelled him onward.

Minutes later, Mike's ears perked up at the strange moaning sound coming from the bushes along the roadway. For an instant he thought he'd at last found his dinner. But it was an odd sort of noise, reminding him of the gut-wrenching sound a dying animal makes when it's been injured. Tempted to turn back, Mike steeled himself to see what he could do for the poor thing. Maybe if it was a dying deer . . .

Following the trail of fresh blood on the road, he made his way behind the bushes. His hope turned to absolute horror at the scene before him. Two men, one covered in blood and from the look of him a servant, was dead; the other man was lying face down and moaning. Mike Candy didn't believe this one was long for this world. Some men would have run away, worried that outliers might still be sneaking

371

around and would kill him, too. Candy wasn't like most men. His heart filled with pity for a fellow human being, the same pity that had caused him to offer help to Mr. King. He couldn't leave this man here to die. Maybe he could flag down some help if someone passed by.

"Lordy, look at you." Mike gently touched the man's face and turned it toward him, instantly recognizing him. "Mr. Sheridan! Who'd want to do this to you?"

Now Mike knew he had to help this man. On his very back, he wore Tanner Sheridan's hand-me-down coat. He remembered Tanner's kindness and his pretty wife the day they came to Rawdontown. Somehow he'd save Tanner Sheridan himself. He needed help soon or he'd die.

Mike's one alternative was to carry Tanner. Tanner was a big man, and weak from loss of blood, so no doubt he would be limp. Mike was a large man, not as strong as he once was, but sturdy enough to help a friend. When he lifted Tanner into his arms and heard his agonized groans, Mike steeled himself to the sound and hardened his heart. "I'm doing this for your own good, Mr. Sheridan. I don't like hurting people, but one day you'll thank me—if you live."

# Chapter 21

"Is he going to live? Please, tell me Tanner will be all right." Annabelle's impassioned plea to Dr. Ridgely, the army doctor who'd been called in by Samuel Farnsworth to care for Tanner, wasn't lost on Samuel. He waited by the foot of Tanner's bed, his shoulders thrust back in a military stance, and didn't bat an eyelash when Annabelle grabbed at Tanner's hand. He thought Annabelle was making a damn fool of herself over Sheridan, and he wanted to thrash her for acting like such an imbecile when it was obvious that even in his delirium, Tanner didn't want her. He wanted his wife, and hers was the name he mumbled.

"I've done all that can be done, Miss Hastings." Dr. Ridgely smiled kindly at her, but it was a smile meant only to comfort, not to convey hope. "Fortunately, Mr. Sheridan's wounds weren't deep enough to sever any arteries; however, he lost a great deal of blood and is suffering from an infection. If the infection clears, there's a chance he'll pull through. If not . . ."

"He has to get better," Annabelle insisted, clinging tightly to Tanner. "I'll nurse him day and night."

"You're to be commended for your concern; however, please don't overtax yourself. I don't want you to fall ill."

After Doctor Ridgely left, Samuel broke the strained silence by applauding. "A remarkable performance, my dear. It's wasted, however, for your audience is unconscious."

"How dare you patronize me, Samuel! I'm in love with Tanner, otherwise, would I still be here?"

Samuel adored Annabelle when she was aroused, either sexually or in anger, and her eyes turned from a pale blue to sparkling sapphires. Those eyes, combined with her silver-blonde hair, presented such a striking image that Samuel's knees grew weak with longing for her. But while she professed not to love him, he didn't believe that for a moment. He knew very well what Annabelle loved and bluntly told her so. "You'd have been long gone if Tanner had turned out to be poor, dearest. I remember seeing you with him in New York. I knew you were sleeping with him for the exercise. If you'd loved him at all you would have stayed with him for love and not for what you hoped to gain by moving on to greener pastures. You're a whore, Annabelle, but I want you anyway. Tanner doesn't and never will. He wants his wife."

"Diana is gone and isn't coming back!"

"How do you know that? Do you have any idea of what happened to Tanner or where Diana might be? If so, you better tell me now."

"I don't know anything!" was the heated protest that immediately sprang to Annabelle's lips. "That Mr. Candy said he thought Tanner and Diana had been attacked by outliers."

"Mr. Candy didn't mention Diana," Samuel observed.

"No, but she left with Tanner, and the driver was killed. Since there's no sign of the carriage or Diana, then you tell *me* what happened to her. She could be dead now."

Samuel nodded and walked over to her. He lowered his voice. "Yes, she could be dead, and I pray she is if she was captured by those ruffians. She'd be horribly used and death would be a mercy, but I doubt men of that ilk would steal the carriage with the horses. They're traveling back roads and wooded areas, places carriages can't navigate. And if she is dead, you'd be most pleased, wouldn't you?"

"Yes, I would." Annabelle turned defiant eyes upon Samuel.

"What a pity that I should love a heartless woman like you."

"I never asked you to love me." Her voice shook for a second. "I never asked you for anything, Samuel."

"True."

Annabelle stayed near Tanner when Samuel

started to leave the room. "Will you search for Diana?" She asked him.

Grabbing the doorknob, he faced her and shook his head. "She's in enemy territory and my forces are scheduled to leave Charlestown within the next two weeks. I fear the only thing that will save Diana Sheridan is a miracle."

"Good-bye, Samuel."

"Good-bye to you, my love. I wish you well with Tanner, because I fear that once he awakens and learns what has happened to his wife, you'll cease to exist, no matter your diligent bedside vigil."

Annabelle sat in the chair, keeping her hand in Tanner's. He looked so pale, deathly still as he lay there beneath the sheets. His breathing was shallow, and this frightened her more than all the blood she'd seen when Samuel had arrived at the townhouse with Tanner and the man who'd found him on the road. She remembered that her mother had breathed in the same fashion before she died, that no matter what the leech had done for her, she hadn't regained her strength. But Annabelle was glad she had stood up to Doctor Ridgely earlier that day and had protested against bleeding Tanner to cure the infection. He'd already lost blood, so what was the point in taking more? Her mother had been bled, many times, and each time weakened her. Annabelle didn't want the same for Tanner. She wanted him alive and healthy and in love with her.

"Tanner, forgive me," she wept, not relinquishing his hand. "If I'd only known what Kingsley had intended I'd never have helped him. I wanted Diana out of the way, but not at your expense. I . . . hate . . . that man. He's despicable. How can he be your brother? How?! But when you're well, I'll make everything up to you. I promise. You'll forget Diana and . . ."

Annabelle stiffened as Tanner opened his eyes and looked directly at her. Her heart caught in her throat to imagine he might have heard her.

"Di . . . an . . . a," came his tortured groan. "Di . . . an . . ."

And then he shut his eyes, drifting into unconsciousness again. "It's only Annabelle," she told him as she stroked his furrowed brow. She recalled what Samuel had told her earlier, that when Tanner awoke, her efforts would be overlooked in the face of the loss of Diana. A sense of futility filled her, and she got up to walk on the piazza, peering into the star-filled night at the many British ships in the harbor. Soon they'd sail for England, her home. She suddenly realized she'd never see Samuel again, and grew unaccountably melancholy at the thought.

It was well past midnight when Kingsley halted the carriage at the Sheridan cemetery and opened the creaking door to enter the tunnel. With the service of some flint and a tinderbox that stood on the ground just inside the opening, he soon lit the wall torch in order to survey his surroundings.

Nothing had changed. Kingsley smiled to see that the tunnel he'd played in as a child was still intact. He did notice that the water markings on the walls, the dirty yellow lines that indicated the depth of the water whenever the Santee overflowed, were faint. Evidently Briarhaven had enjoyed a flood-free period since his departure, quite unlike the disastrous floodings the plantation had suffered when Kingsley was a child. There seemed to be no warning when these flash floods would occur, but now the tunnel was dry and not too cold, considering the chilly temperatures.

Retracing his steps, he opened the carriage door and heard Diana moaning. "What's the matter?" he cruelly taunted her as he hauled her to her feet, bringing her to rest outside. "Can't you take suffering or adversity? Tsk, tsk, my loyal wife, I've grown quite used to pain and the cold, to going hungry. When I was in Rawdontown, the gnawing of my belly was welcome relief, because I knew I was still alive. Sometimes that was the only indication I had. But you were always sheltered and protected." His cold green eyes raked over her in distaste and he pushed aside her cloak. "From the look of your figure, I presume Tanner took good care of you. I should have known you'd sell yourself to the highest bidder, but I didn't think it would be that half-breed."

Lifting Diana into his arms, he carried her into the tunnel. For an instant, she fidgeted and made as if to kick at the narrow wall and throw him off balance, but for some reason she seemed to think better of it. "That's a good wife," Kingsley icily commended her. "Better start learning now who's master of Briarhaven, Diana. You'd do well not to cross me."

They reached the end and he set her on her feet, keeping a firm grasp on her waist while he pushed open the sliding panel that led into the wine cellar.

"Ah, home, sweet home, my dear. This is where you shall spend many happy hours until I decide what to do with you. I can't bring you into the house; it would arouse suspicion. Too many questions about me which I don't want to answer. And then of course Hattie would want to know about you and Tanner." Diana made a strangling sound behind the balled kerchief, and Kingsley seemed to realize that she was still gagged. "Sorry," he apologized as he removed it, and Diana took a deep, shuddering breath.

"Coward!" she ranted through parched lips. "I hate you. What did you do to Tanner?"

"Watch your tongue, Diana. I always hated it, you know."

"I don't care what you hated," she retorted spitefully, but Kingsley noted her complexion was quite white and that she trembled, though she didn't seem about to back down. This was a very different Diana than the one he remembered, the one who cowered every time he raised his voice or touched her. He wasn't certain he cared for her open defiance, but then again, a bit of spirit could be amusing if one knew how to take proper advantage of it.

"Ah, Diana, you should care about my hates and my likes, but let's discuss my hates for a moment, shall we? I hated my father, and to a lesser degree, I sometimes hated you, too. Not always." He leered at her, and his hand brushed against her breasts. "There were some times I was quite undone by your beauty and particularly enjoyed some of the special tricks I taught you, things I learned from my Charlestown ladies."

"Your whores, you mean!"

Kingsley colored, but he threw back his head and laughed. "How entertaining is your sharp little tongue, but I'll put it to better use than to insult me." Narrowing his eyes, he impaled her with his green-slivered gaze. "What I felt for my father and for you is nothing compared to the hatred I felt for Tanner, that half-breed who dared to usurp my position here, who dared to take you from me. A loathsome bastard, that's what he was, a contemptible, disgusting son of an Indian whore. But he got what he deserved. I didn't desert that hellish war to be called a coward. I knew I had to find a way to recover what one has lost. I took my vengeance out upon that bastard who was my brother." Kingsley chuckled. "And I didn't have to lift a hand to do it."

"What . . . what do you mean, *was* your brother?" Diana asked and swayed against Kingsley.

"I thought I mentioned he was dead."

Kingsley caught her when she fainted.

Kingsley hadn't anticipated Diana's family being at Briarhaven. Granted, it was her aunt and Marisa, but now he not only had to lie to them about where he'd been the last two years—letting it be believed he had been in British prison camp—but he also had to contend with Clay Sinclair, someone he remembered as a lad but who was now a grown man. He didn't like it, didn't care for any of it at all. And Hattie, well he didn't expect too much to be made over him from the others, but Hattie had been his nurse.

He also had to pretend he didn't know that Diana had married Tanner and had gone to live in Charlestown. This news was divulged with just a hint of sadness in Aunt Frances's voice. He heard a touch of vengefulness, too, because the old biddy hadn't encouraged his wooing of Diana years ago. She'd been the only family member to speak against him.

Still, he felt he'd acted distraught enough to be believed. He'd shaken his head with just enough astonishment, and his eyes had filled with tears, a trick he learned when he was little and his mother had admonished him. The tears always broke her down, as they did the hypocritical Frances. "You poor man," she'd said, patting his back. "Just home from the war, having been falsely listed as dead, and to find your wife is married. Such a tragedy."

Kingsley hid his disdain for the woman. No doubt whenever she returned to Charlestown she'd crow the news from the rooftops.

"It's just that I love Diana so much!" he blurted out. He laid his head on his arms and cried on the dining room table.

"Oh, Clay, my heart is fluttering." Frances moaned. She reached for Clay, who took her hand. Instantly Marisa was there to offer her a glass of water, and Kingsley, too.

Kingsley had refused it, of course. How could he drink or eat when his beloved wife was married to another?

"Perhaps a glass of wine," Marisa suggested to Kingsley. "I can go to the cellar and see if there are any bottles left —"

"No!" came Kingsley's harsh and sudden shout. He reddened, realizing that everyone was looking oddly at him. "I don't want any wine," he said and made tears well anew in his eyes. "Don't trouble yourself by going in the cellar, Marisa. I intend to familiarize myself with Briarhaven again on my own, to see what needs to be repaired. Since Diana is gone, I need something to keep myself occupied until I can get into Charlestown and speak to her." It sounded like a feeble excuse, even to Kingsley, but it was the best he could come up with at that moment.

After a few minutes, in which he gave the impression he'd finally composed himself, he turned his attention to Clay. "Are you going to rebuild on your property?"

"Eventually. But Marisa and I are going to be married soon."

"The best of luck to you both, but don't wait too long to start rebuilding. Your bride needs a home." And the sooner he got rid of them, the better off he'd be.


Diana tried the knob on the cellar door again, found it locked, and knew no amount of jiggling would open it. She had ceased to count the number of times over the last two days that she'd gone to the door to pound on it, to cry out until she was hoarse. Nobody heard her, nobody came, except for Kingsley. Twice a day he brought her some food, somehow managing to elude Hattie, whose kitchen was her domain and whose eyes never failed to miss anything. Apparently she'd missed the extra helpings Kingsley took, or her eyesight was poor.

Kingsley had even thought to lock the door that led into the tunnel. Diana couldn't budge it. She cursed herself for her lack of strength, the sudden weakness that periodically assailed her. The cut on her head didn't hurt, but her head had pounded ever since the accident and the headache wasn't made any better by Kingsley's cruel joke about Tanner's death. He wasn't dead; he couldn't be dead. She'd know it, would feel a part of herself missing if he'd been killed. She still wasn't certain what had happened that day on the road. All she knew was that Tanner wasn't with her now, that some-

383

how Kingsley was involved in whatever happened, and she was trapped in the cellar with little hope of freedom unless someone heard her cries.

And she was pregnant, tired, crabby, and frightened. Feeling miserable, she made her way to the pallet Kingsley had made for her and pulled the blanket about her. What did he intend to do with her? He couldn't keep her here forever, and since he was feeding her and tending to her wants, he evidently didn't want her dead. Did Kingsley even know what he wanted? Probably not, and this thought caused her more than a few moments of uneasiness. Kingsley was a volatile person, more than a bit unhinged in his thinking, and capable of almost anything.

"Dear God, let me out of this mess," Diana prayed aloud to break the tomblike silence of the cellar. "And please protect Tanner. I love him so much, and I don't believe Kingsley's lie. You wouldn't separate us now, not when we've been so happy. Please . . . please . . ." Tears fell onto Diana's cheeks and she couldn't go on, but she finished the prayer in her heart.

# Chapter 22

Ten days later, the winter's chill that had besieged South Carolina had weakened, and now a balminess hung over the area. The doors and windows of Charlestown had been thrown open in the hope of catching a cooling breeze off of the Ashley River, and more than one person who had complained about the cold spell now bemoaned the heat.

"Goodness, but it's warm in here," Annabelle commented as she dabbed at her forehead with her kerchief. "A cooling breeze is just what we need."

Tanner looked at her from his place on the bed, disinterest on his face both for her and for the book she'd been reading to him. "I need to find my wife," he said.

Annabelle bit her lower lip and shook her head. "Please accept the fact that Diana is most probably dead. If she isn't, and you do find her after what those men may have . . . done to her

. . . would you still want her? She'd be so . . ."

"Certainly I'd want her!" he groaned. "I love her and I want her back, no matter what may have been done to her. If I wasn't so damned weak, I'd leave this bed and find her."

"Remember you tried that the other day." Annabelle's eyes reproached him. "You made it no further than the door before you collapsed. You're lucky to have any strength at all, considering what happened to you."

Tanner leaned toward her, determination shining in his eyes. "Every day I grow stronger, but soon, very soon, I'm going to search for Diana and find her. I'm also going to find the people responsible for all this. And when I do, they'll beg me for mercy."

Annabelle recognized that look and shivered with dread. She'd seen it many times in New York when he was on someone's trail, dogging the person until he seemed almost relieved to be caught. She wondered what he'd do if he knew that Kingsley was behind everything and that she had helped him. She didn't want to think about it. . . .

"Sometimes, Tanner, I don't think you're grateful that I'm caring for you. I helped you when even Dr. Ridgely had given up hope. I stayed by your bedside and nursed you. I've had very little time alone and less sleep. And you don't . . . appreciate . . . my efforts." Annabelle gave a tiny sob, quite pleased at the way her voice broke in the appropriate place. Tanner couldn't help but be convinced at her sincerity, and if her playacting would divert his attention from finding Diana's kidnapper and make him feel awful for how he was treating her, then so be it. Annabelle glanced at him from under lowered lashes, congratulating herself on the tiny teardrop that mingled there. A nice touch.

"Don't cry, Annabelle. Please. I hate seeing women cry." Tanner took her hand and clumsily patted it. "I'm very appreciative of your efforts. They won't go unrewarded."

Annabelle gritted her teeth. That sounded almost as if Tanner intended to pay her in cash, rather than in what she truly wanted—matrimony. Yet she knew it was too soon to think in those terms. Everything hinged upon Kingsley, but the hateful cur must believe Tanner was dead. In that case anyone could ride into Charlestown from Briarhaven and discover that Tanner was still alive and inform him that Diana was alive. Annabelle knew she was alive, and this was a threat to her. Somehow she had to convince Tanner to leave South Carolina entirely, not only for his protection but hers, too. She didn't want to bear the brunt of Tanner's vengeance.

Clasping his hand, Annabelle moved from her chair to sit beside him on the bed. She gazed up at him with tear-filled eyes. "My reward shall be your good health."

"Annabelle?"

"What, Tanner?"

"What in blazes are you up to?"

"I don't understand what you mean. Why

should I be up to anything? I assure you that I'm not."

He assessed her with a half sneer and grabbed her wrist, pulling her very close to his face. "Don't lie to me. You're an expert at working your wiles on unsuspecting men and getting away with it. In Philadelphia you had half the town eating out of your hand, believing you to be a sweet and untouched waif—and all the while you were turning in patriots who posed as loyalists. They never suspected it was you. When we were together in New York, when we were lovers, you weren't honest enough with me to admit you weren't in love with me. You used me for sex, but I didn't mind, because I thought I loved you. Even then you kept secrets from me, and I think you're being secretive now. This tearful act doesn't move me at all. Out with it! What is it that you're up to?"

Her mouth fell open in exasperation. All she had to do was make a whimpering sound and Samuel gave her anything she wanted, believed anything she told him. It wasn't fair that the very man she wanted so desperately didn't believe her. She was thankful that he couldn't read her mind, otherwise, he'd have known about Kingsley. Maybe if she turned the tables on Tanner, he'd be put off the trail and she could lure him away from South Carolina.

"You're a cruel, suspicious man. You make it difficult for a woman to be honest with you. And yes, I do admit I'm up to something, but nothing devious, I can assure you. However, I

388

doubt you'll be interested or approve of what I want." She had his attention now, she could tell.

"Well, I'm waiting for an explanation, Annabelle."

She got off of the bed and purposely didn't look at him, knowing the effect would be more theatrical and tragic. Before she was finished, Tanner would believe the sun was an orange if she told him so.

Her gown made a swishing sound when she turned away. "I fear that you'll hate me for what I'm about to say, but I will tell you anyway. I love you, Tanner, and when your grief over Diana has passed, I want to marry you. Oh, I know I hurt you in New York and I've come to regret it. And I'm perfectly aware that you can't love me now, maybe you can never love me, but I'll take whatever you're willing to give. I've done some terrible things in my life and I've hurt so many people, but I want another chance with you." Annabelle sighed raggedly, loudly enough that Tanner heard, and with just enough emotion that her shoulders quivered with the effort. "When you're better, I'm aware that you'll go in search of your wife, but I'd be dishonest if I wished her well. I don't. I hope Diana is dead so you can forget her and come to want me."

Annabelle faced him in a swirl of lavender and blue satin skirts. "I also believe you'd do well to leave South Carolina forever, to put the past and the pain firmly behind you. Whatever you decide is fine with me, but know that I love you and want you."

On that poignant note, Annabelle left the room.

Tanner stared at the door long after she'd gone, then he whistled lowly. "God, she's a damned good actress!" And that was saying quite a bit. Not for a blasted minute did he trust Annabelle Hastings. Somehow, some way, he was going to discover what it was she was hiding. But first he must regain enough strength so that he could search for Diana on his own. Unbeknownst to Annabelle, he'd summoned Mike Candy to his bedside the previous day while she napped.

Tanner thanked Mike for saving his life. To show his gratitude, he'd offered him money, but Mike had refused it. "I'd have done it for anybody," Mike had told him shyly. Tanner appreciated Mike's attitude, but from the looks of the man, Tanner knew he was hungry and needed a decent place to sleep. In short, Mike needed employment, which is exactly what Tanner offered. Mike readily agreed to becoming Tanner's driver, taking poor Curtis's place.

"I'd appreciate it, too, Mr. Candy, if you could nose around some and try to get some information about my wife and who did this to me. Especially about my wife. I need to know where she is and who has her."

"I'll do my best, sir," Candy promised. Twisting his hat between his fingers, he hung his head in shame. "Maybe this can be my way of making up for helping that nasty bloke I nursed back to health. He was quite interested in you, sir."

"Who are you talking about?"

Candy shrugged his shoulders in a helpless little gesture. "A hateful man named Mr. King. He was a British soldier who'd been injured, was real sick for a long time, too, but I felt sorry for him and took care of him. Well, when he was better he asked me to come by here and find out if the master of the house was home. I did as he asked me to do, 'cause that's all I was supposed to discover. Your man Curtis found me, and I pretended to be hungry, and I guess I didn't have to pretend too much there. Cammie fixed me up real good with some food and I saw you in the dining room with your lady friend, Miss Hastings. And then I left and told this King fellow that you were home."

Tanner's eyes glinted like black marble. "That was all there was to it? He wanted to know if I was home. Why?"

"I don't know. He did say something about retrieving his property though, but I never did understand that."

"Where can I find this Mr. King?"

"I can't tell you that. I haven't seen him since we had a less-than-friendly parting of the ways right after I left here that day."

Tanner thanked Mike Candy for his candor, and now as Tanner considered what Candy had told him, he didn't understand any of it. Who was this Mr. King? Tanner didn't know anyone by that name. He said that the man had been a

British soldier. Perhaps he met him years ago and didn't remember him, but if so, what property could this stranger have hoped to obtain from the townhouse? Had King intended to rob him? Was there some sort of a conspiracy afoot involving this person? Had Tanner not been a random victim of outliers but the target of a premeditated attack?

The thought had crossed Tanner's mind that Diana could be a hostage for ransom, but no one had asked for money. Besides, whoever was behind the attack on the road wanted him dead. The only reason he wasn't dead now was because the would-be assassins were bunglers.

Nothing made any sense but one thing. Tanner wanted Diana back—alive.


Jackie watched Kingsley with more than a childhood curiosity. The man fascinated the little boy, and he hung onto each word and remembered every one of Kingsley's gestures, sitting in the shadowy corners like a cornhusk doll so Kingsley wouldn't sense his presence. So far, Kingsley hadn't seen him, and this pleased Jackie very much. His early memories of Kingsley weren't all that pleasant. He'd never liked him then, and he didn't particularly like him now. But Kingsley Sheridan was his father and this was the man's appeal to Jackie.

His granny had said Kingsley was his father, but she hadn't known he'd been listening. Granny Hattie had been speaking to Ezra, the man he loved and thought of as his papa, something different in Jackie's estimation than a father, shortly after his mother's death. They'd been speaking about Kingsley being Jackie's father and how, now that Kingsley was gone, no one at Briarhaven need fear him any longer. But Mr. Kingsley had returned, and Jackie needed to examine this strange phenomenon known as his father.

He secretly trailed after him when he went into the barn or up the stairs to his room, or whenever he went into the door that led to the cellar. Jackie didn't dare venture down those stairs. It was dark and scary, and Mr. Kingsley always locked the door after himself. Jackie noticed he went down there a lot.

There was one time when Jackie worked up sufficient courage to put his ear to the door. He'd been shaking with fear that his father would discover him, but he tiptoed forward and listened. "Eat, Diana," he'd heard his father order gruffly. And then, "But I feel sick. I can't eat."

That voice sounded like Miss Diana's. Was Miss Diana back home? A sense of joy exploded within Jackie. He liked Miss Diana so much, and she was always nice to him, letting him eat whatever he wanted. But when he heard his father's footsteps coming up the stairs, Jackie ran and hid behind some drapes in the hallway and watched while Kingsley locked the door and pocketed the key. Afterward, Jackie went into the kitchen where Granny Hattie was

393

cooking stew.

"What's in the cellar, Granny?" Jackie asked as he sampled the gravy right out of the pot.

"Oh, just empty wine bottles now. Those redcoats drank up all our stock."

"Mr. Kingsley goes in the cellar a lot."

"How you know that, boy?"

A sliver of fear coursed through Jackie. He was somehow frightened to hear his gentle grandmother raise her voice or to see her eyes grow wide with something he couldn't name. "I . . . I . . . saw him," Jackie stuttered.

"You been spyin' on Mr. Kingsley?"

Jackie, ever honest, nodded guiltily.

"What else you been doin' that I should know about?"

"Nothin', Granny Hattie. I just been followin' after him. He ain't seen me."

"Jackie, promise your old Granny you won't be doin' that no more. Mr. Kingsley keeps to himself and don't want no little tadpole trailin' after him. Hear now?"

Her face and voice had softened and Jackie eagerly nodded his understanding. He wouldn't follow after his father any more. Realizing Hattie had forgiven his transgression, he grew brave. "When can I see Miss Diana?"

Hattied stirred the stew. "You know Miss Diana's in Charlestown with Mr. Tanner . . . at least for now." Hattie's forehead puckered with lines.

"Naw, Granny, she's in the cellar. I done heard her talkin' to Mr. Kingsley."

"Jackie! I'm gonna take this here spoon to your bottom for tellin' tales."

"I ain't, Granny, I heard . . ."

"Go on outside and start choppin' that wood out back for the stove. Maybe doin' chores will keep you from thinkin' up stories."

"Yes'm," was Jackie's response. He went behind the woodshed and found his little ax. Tears gathered in his eyes. He disliked being eight years old. No one ever believed him or took him seriously, everyone was always telling him what to do. And now Granny Hattie had accused him of making up stories, but he knew what he had heard.

Wiping his nose on the cuff of his jacket, he managed not to cry. "One day I'm gonna be big and nobody gonna tell me what to do. And people will believe what I say." With that, he industriously commenced chopping the pine into kindling for the stove.

## Chapter 23

"Stop acting so petulant, Diana, and eat up. See, Hattie made her special sweet potatoe pie because she knows how much I like it. Go on, be a good girl and eat." Kingsley pushed the plate toward her, a coaxing grin on his face.

Diana barely looked at it. "I'm not hungry and I'm not your child bride any longer. You can't force me to do what I don't want to do."

"Hmm, Tanner must be responsible for such rebellious talk, and for your sudden spunkiness. I don't think I care for this new you."

Diana's eyes glittered dangerously and Kingsley backed off. "I don't care what you like! I want to get out of here. For God's sake I'm having a child and I feel awful. Haven't you any compassion, if not for me then for my baby? I could lose my baby."

"I know," was Kingsley's quick retort, but Diana didn't hear one iota of sympathy or guilt in his tone.

From where she stood, her back against the cellar wall, fearful to sit or recline in Kingsley's presence thereby to give him the advantage of height, Diana felt a great wave of nausea rush over her. Kingsley didn't care about her or her child. She suddenly realized that he'd kidnapped her to assuage his own perverted sense of vengeance. Tanner had taken her away from him, and now he had done the same. Whether Tanner was dead or alive didn't matter to Kingsley, because it was the deed that counted. Though she felt horribly sick, she had to get away. She'd considered trying to knock him down and run, but she couldn't summon the strength. Her head hurt, her very bones ached. Perhaps she could appeal to Kingsley's logic.

"Keeping me down here isn't accomplishing anything," she told him. "Please allow me to go upstairs."

He shook his head, and incredible pleasure shone in his eyes. "You're wrong, my dear wife. The longer I keep you here in the cellar, the more your soul is purged of the wrongs you committed against me with that half-breed."

"I never did anything against you, Kingsley."

"Ah, but you did. Kindly remember the night of our engagement ball, when I found you writhing beneath the bastard like a bitch in heat. And then after we were married you were pining away for him, I know you were. Sometimes you'd get a dreamy look in your eyes, and

I knew you were thinking about him. After I was declared dead, you wasted little time in marrying him. Tell me you never wronged me, Diana. Lie to me now."

Kingsley grabbed her and pulled her against him, startling her with the suddenness of the action and frightening her immeasurably with the potential violence that hovered below the surface. "Yes, you should look afraid, you should tremble from fear. At this very moment I could lay you down and have my way with you and no one would hear your pitiful cries for help. This time my father can't come to your rescue, and that's another wrong you've committed against me. He loved you more than me. He put your welfare over mine, and I was his son." He smiled wickedly and whispered into her ear. "Now you might have a son—Tanner's child. I'd say it would be poetic justice that I take the child as my own, and as for you, dear Diana, you belong to me already. I'm your husband still, not Tanner."

"Don't . . . don't," Diana begged. She knew she was begging but her pride deserted her. She recognized the lust in his eyes, felt the heat of his hands upon her arms, tightening around her like freshly forged steel. Kingsley was insane and strong enough to rape her. He could harm her, force her to miscarry, and if she lost her child, she'd lose her mind. She had to think of something, anything, to prevent the inevitable and unendurable pain that would follow. Suddenly she knew what it was that aroused Kingsley to act like this. It was her fear of him that gave him power. If she didn't act afraid . . .

Diana yawned in his face, somehow able to control her shivering, her voice, and her facial features. "Heavens, you're a tiresome fellow with all of this silliness. And I'm quite exhausted playing along with you."

"What do you mean, playing along with me? I'm the one who has the upper hand here, Diana."

Suspicion crossed his face, and Diana realized what a weakling Kingsley truly was. "I'm a different woman than I was when we were married. To be honest with you, Tanner has taught me a number of things about passion that you overlooked, Kingsley. Perhaps instead of your having your way with me, I should give you a few pointers about how to please a woman, because either your Charlestown whores were inept in their tutorship or else you were a poor pupil. So take your hands off me. I'm not the cowering wife you remember."

Diana was more than stunned when he let her go and backed away from her. "No, you're the same," he remarked. "Maybe you're not as frightened of me as you used to be, but you still hate me. You think that I'll let you out of here if you're no longer afraid of me, but I won't. You'd go blabbing to everybody about me, and I can't have that. But I wouldn't turn you out into the cold with a child growing in your belly. Your defiance leads me to believe that I want your little bastard more than I originally thought. You know how much I wanted an heir, and now, my dear, you're going to give me one."

The breath caught in her throat, nearly choking her. "What . . . what are you going to do with me, with my baby?"

"Well, I'll tell you," he said and rubbed his hands together. "There are two choices, and I trust you'll think on both of them well. You will have the child and I'll claim it, and maybe I'll allow you to stay on at Briarhaven and be my wife, servicing me with the new tricks Tanner taught you. A fit punishment since you detest me so much. Or, if you don't behave by keeping your mouth shut about me, and that includes never back talking or insinuating by word or deed your unhappiness, you'll find yourself in one of the fanciest whorehouses in Charlestown. And I know the high regard you hold for those ladies. Maybe, if you get very good at your trade and aren't too used by the the gentlemen who frequent you, I might even take a turn with you myself."

"I'll run away and take the baby with me." From where did the courage come to say that? Her body quivered with disgust and fear, but she wasn't going to give in like a docile dog.

"You may, but I'll find you, and I guarantee you'll never make it home alive."

"Kill me now, then. I'd rather be dead and

take my child with me than ever give in to you!"

"Think it over, Diana," he commented with more calm than she expected.

Kingsley left the cellar, locking her inside. For once she was too overcome with hatred and despair to try the knob or beat upon the door.

Annabelle was unprepared for the sound of voices coming from downstairs so late at night. She looked at the clock on the mantle and noticed the time was quarter past twelve. Curious, she got out of bed and pulled on her robe, but she grew even more curious when she noticed that Tanner's door was ajar and that he wasn't in his room. Just then Cammie came bustling up the stairs, followed by two little girls and a boy.

"These are Mrs. Sheridan's sister's children," Cammie explained when she saw Annabelle's puzzled look. I'm taking them up to the attic bedroom to settle them in for the night. Their folks are downstairs in the parlor with Mr. Tanner, but I wouldn't go down right now."

"Why ever not!" Annabelle was affronted that this servant woman, who was little better than a slave, should tell her what not to do.

Cammie's eyes flashed. "Because he's telling Mrs. Richmond about her sister and I don't think he wants you down there at a sad time like this."

Annabelle's hands clutched at her white throat. "Have . . . have they found Diana yet?"

"No, Miss Hastings." Without further word, Cammie ushered the three sleepy children forward but waited for an old black woman to catch up with them. The woman wept into a kerchief and Cammie put her arm around the woman's shoulders. "Don't cry, Ruthie. Mr. Tanner's doing all he can to find Mrs. Sheridan."

"I know," Ruthie said brokenly. "But I held that child in my arms before her own mama. Miss Diana is like my baby girl. Oh, poor Miss Anne. What she gonna do without her sister? They loved each other so much." Cammie comforted Ruthie again and they disappeared up the attic stairway.

Annabelle couldn't help but groan. Now she had to contend with a houseful of Diana's relatives, who'd be constantly there to remind Tanner of her. She clenched her fists, rushed into her room, and slammed the door behind her.

In the parlor, Anne wept softly against David's shoulder.

"We didn't have any idea we'd be coming home to such tragic news," David explained to Tanner, who sat across from them as still as a brooding, morose statue. "And we wouldn't have returned now, with the British still being here. As it was, we had to sneak into town. But

402

Anne," he looked at his wife and kissed the top of her head, "Anne wanted to see Diana. God, I can't believe any of this!"

"I *don't* believe any of it!" Tanner exploded and jumped up from his chair and paced the room restlessly. "People tell me to stop hoping that she'll turn up alive, but I can't. I don't feel that she's gone—in here." He roughly tapped the spot by his heart.

Anne lifted her head and wiped her eyes with the back of her hands. "Is anyone searching for her?"

"I have people scouting the area, under the direction of a man named Mike Candy. But so far no one knows anything."

"She isn't dead, Tanner." Anne's face brightened with hope.

"Anne, now don't start imagining . . ." David began.

"David," Anne's tone was frosty, "I'm not imagining anything. Tanner's hopeful and so am I. Diana isn't dead, I know she's alive somewhere. And we're going to find her, we will, but until that time, we'll stay here with Tanner. He needs looking after, and I know Diana would want me to see to him while she's gone."

Tanner couldn't help smiling. Anne made Diana's absence sound almost as if she'd gone on a short sojourn from which she would soon return. Yet Tanner didn't dispute Anne. Evidently that was her way of dealing with the tragedy, and he approved. At least Anne had hopes of finding her sister, unlike Annabelle, who hoped Diana was dead. He shivered to recall Annabelle's heartless remarks.

Tanner sat beside Anne and kissed her cheek. "Thank you, Anne. I very much appreciate your care, and you're all very welcome to stay here for as long as you like."

David acknowledged Tanner's invitation, but he shook his head regretfully. "We're returning to our home on the morrow."

"No, you aren't," Tanner told them. "Brace yourselves, but some British soldiers are quartered there. The city is overrun with them, now that they'll soon be leaving our shores."

"Oh, no!" came Anne's strangled cry.

"It will be over soon." Tanner comforted her. "Within the next few days, they'll all be gone."

"I hope so," Anne said, and that sentiment was silently echoed by Tanner and David as well.


"Looks like we're going to be in for a spell of bad weather," David commented two days later as he and Tanner sat on the piazza.

Tanner had noticed the dark clouds that malevolently pushed aside the blue ones. He felt about as black inside. No word of Diana yet, but he wouldn't give up hope, even though with each day the possibility that she was alive faded. Clenching his hands into tight fists, he braced himself from moaning aloud his torment. "We need the rain," he said instead. "This sudden heat wave's been oppressive."

Tanner felt David watching him. "Diana will be found," David told him and smiled.

"If I were able to search for her . . ."

"You'll be able to soon. Remember what the doctor said, any vigorous activity might start you bleeding again. You need time to heal, but I'll admit that you're healthier looking today than when we arrived. Your color is better and your face is fuller, probably because of all that tonic Anne is force-feeding you."

Despite his preoccupation with Diana's plight, Tanner laughed. "That has to be the most awful tasting brew this side of the Atlantic, but Anne means well and I appreciate the fact that she cares about me."

"She does. We all do, Tanner. In case I never adequately expressed my gratitude to you for what you've done for my family, for me, let me do it now." David extended his hand and Tanner shook it.

Tanner smiled, finally feeling as if he were part of a family, as if he truly belonged. If only Diana was found, then his life would be perfect.

After a few moments more in conversation, Tanner excused himself from David and walked around the grounds. He decided that David was right about his looking better. He felt stronger. Soon, soon, he'd search for Diana himself.

"Tanner, darling," came Annabelle's well-modulated tones as she came up behind him as he neared the carriage house. Dressed in a mauve-colored gown, Annabelle presented a very pretty picture, with her long curls swept atop her head. When she took his arm in hers, her eyes glowed brighter than the garnet earbobs and ring she wore, but she made a mock pout. "I'm so peeved with you. Ever since the Richmonds' arrival, you've ignored me."

"Sorry, Annabelle, but don't you think it's time you left here?"

"Oh, no, darling, don't be absurd. I'm your nurse, you know. You need looking after, a great deal of looking after." Annabelle wrinkled her nose. "And I'm just the person for the job."

"I appreciate your efforts," Tanner remarked, weary of Annabelle's constant hovering over him and her proprietary attitude. Why didn't he just throw her out? he asked himself but he couldn't do it. For all her brazenness, Annabelle had nowhere to go, and Tanner knew how it felt not to have a home to call one's own.

"I'm so glad to hear that. 'That woman' told me I was being too bold and should restrict myself only to periodic visits."

"What woman do you mean?"

"Anne Richmond, that's who!" Annabelle placed her hand on her hip and sneered. "She had the nerve to tell me that I shouldn't be caring for you, a married man, that it isn't the proper thing to do. For heaven's sake, Tanner, why don't you tell her that we were lovers once, that we may be again if—"

"Enough!" Tanner pushed her away from him. "Diana will come home—soon. And Anne is right. You really shouldn't be looking after me."

Annabelle started to mouth a retort, but Mike Candy appeared and hailed Tanner. He grinned broadly. "Got some news for you, Mr. Sheridan. Two blokes from Rawdontown been arrested by Captain Farnsworth for cutting you up and killing your driver."

Tanner's face brightened at the news. "I've got to speak with them. They can lead me to Diana."

"Hmm, not too sure," was Candy's assumption. "But I'll drive you to see Captain Farnsworth."

Without another word to Annabelle, Tanner immediately joined Mike Candy and left. Worry was deeply etched into Annabelle's face. She didn't care for Candy's news. Those two men, if they were the same ones hired by Kingsley Sheridan, could implicate her in Diana's disappearance—not that she'd had a direct hand in it—but just the same, Annabelle's mood was very glum indeed when she joined Anne for tea in the parlor some minutes later.

"I notice that you aren't your usual chattering self," Anne mentioned as she stirred her tea. "Is something wrong?"

"No, Mrs. Richmond, everything is fine, I find that I have nothing to talk about this afternoon that would interest you."

"On the contrary, Miss Hastings, I find you

most interesting."

"You do?" Annabelle was on her guard. She didn't like Anne Richmond or her polite assessment of Annabelle's person.

"Oh, yes, why shouldn't I think you're interesting? You're quite pretty and wear such lovely things. Those earbobs and that ring, for instance. Tell me, where may I get a duplicate set? I've always been partial to garnets."

Annabelle touched the garnets at her ears for merely an instant. I bet she believes Tanner gave these to me, she thought and ached to viciously wipe that smug smile from Anne's lips. "Thank you, but these can't be duplicated. You see, they belonged to my grandmother and have been passed down to me."

"Ah, a family heirloom. I understand exactly, my dear." Anne inspected them more closely. "And you're right, they can't be duplicated."

"Don't be downhearted, sir. We'll find your lady. Those two buggers just don't know nothing about where she's at, but they'll be swinging for their crimes on the morrow. Captain Farnsworth promised you that."

Tanner barely heard Candy's speech, a speech meant to comfort him, he was certain. However, Tanner didn't feel any sense of comfort. He identified the two men as the ones who'd attacked him and killed Curtis, but the man who was behind the plot to kill him, the man who had kidnapped Diana, was gone. Neither of the men knew his identity, and their description of him was general at best. Candy said the clean-shaven and well-dressed man who had kidnapped Diana didn't seem to be the same one he knew as Mr. King. So Tanner still didn't have a clue as to where to go or who to go after.

But the hope had strengthened inside him that Diana was still alive.

He'd no sooner arrived inside the house than Anne and David pulled him into the parlor and securely shut the door. "Tanner, I want you to do something about that Annabelle Hastings," Anne pronounced, and David nodded solemnly in agreement. "She's wearing stolen property. Those garnet earbobs and the matching ring she wore today belonged to Diana."

"But Diana didn't leave any of her jewels behind when we packed to leave for Briarhaven. Anne, calm yourself, you look ready to burst." Tanner calmly folded his arms as Anne's face crumbled.

"Those . . . jewels . . . are Diana's. Believe me, they are. I'd know them anywhere because they belonged to our mother. Mother gave them to Diana in her will. I remember that I was rather jealous, but I couldn't begrudge Diana the jewels because I knew how she always asked Mother if one day they'd be hers, and Mother had assured her they would be." Anne gained her composure and looked directly in Tanner's eyes. "The setting is one of a kind, garnet with gold filigree. And on the back of the earbobs and inside the ring is an engraved letter M for Montaigne. Diana was quite distressed when her jewels were stolen."

Tanner raised an eyebrow. "Stolen by whom?"

"By Kingsley Sheridan, on the day he was thrown out of Briarhaven by Harlan."

# Chapter 24

Tanner knocked on Annabelle's door with a mixture of anger and sadness. Not for a moment did he doubt Anne's word about Diana's jewelry, but he felt like a fool for trusting Annabelle. Oh, he thought she might be up to something, but it never crossed his mind that she knew about Diana's disappearance or that she was involved in it. He still wasn't certain about that, but he couldn't help but wonder where she got the jewels. Could Kingsley still be alive and holding Diana?

"Darling, come in," Annabelle offered and practically dragged Tanner into the room after she'd found him standing on the threshold. "I was watching the lightning outside on the piazza. Come join me."

Dutifully, Tanner followed Annabelle through her room and out the french doors to the covered piazza. The ebony night's calm was disturbed by periodic flashes of jagged silver streaks in the Atlantic, but with each ear-shattering roll of thunder it became more and more apparent that the storm was fast approaching. "Can you smell the rain in the air? I can," Annabelle told him and tucked her arm through his. At that moment he noticed the garnet ring on her finger. Just then lightning sparked, and when she turned to look up at him, the matching earbobs gleamed like two scarlet teardrops.

"I've always enjoyed watching the rain," she explained. "When I was a little girl my mother worked for a wealthy family who had glass on their windows. We didn't, of course, because we were poor. But whenever the thunder started, I'd stop my chores at home and go running to the big house and creep into the dining room to watch the raindrops skate down the glass. Believe it or not, I spent many happy and contented hours doing that."

"Were you ever caught?"

Annabelle laughed. "Never! I've always been careful, Tanner. That's what made me so valuable as a spy."

She seemed so vulnerable as she stood there with her hand on his arm. Annabelle was the epitome of beauty and innocence, but Tanner knew Annabelle better than most people, and he knew how her mind worked. For months she'd kept the whole city of Philadelphia in her thrall, no one suspecting that the woman they thought of as a poor orphan, a patriotic heroine of the fight for independence, was a calculating imposter. But he'd known, and he suddenly knew that somehow Annabelle thought he might be on to her. Any sympathy or doubt he had felt for her now fled on feet swifter than the approaching storm.

Tanner smiled malevolently and quickly wrenched an earbob from her pretty lobe, causing Annabelle to squeal in what sounded like pain but that was probably more indignation than anything else. "Just what are you doing?" she shrieked, and made a move to grab the garnet object from his hand.

"Tsk, tsk, Annabelle, I'm examining your precious family heirloom, that's all." Tanner turned it over in his hand. Holding the earbob up to the lighted torch on the piazza wall, he saw the letter M clearly engraved on the gold backside. "Ah, you've been keeping secrets again, my dear."

"God, I hate it when you sound like that!"

"Sound like what?" he asked, but Tanner already knew what she meant, purposely changing from Tanner Sheridan to his alter ego.

"Like Mariah, damn you. Your face gets a frozen look, like you might be smiling, but you're not really pleased. And your eyes, well, a person can't see anything in them but blackness. And your voice becomes hard edged but monotone and . . . and I hate it!"

Tanner bent close to her, his mouth skimmed the bare spot on her earlobe. "In New York you didn't seem to mind. Remember, Annabelle, how it was between us."

"But we were different then. We forgot who and what we were." Annabelle's lower lip trembled.

"That was wrong of us, because it only makes it harder now." He straightened and took the other garnet from her ear and grabbed her hand to slide the ring from her finger. "Now, for old times' sake, tell me where you got these jewels."

"They were my grandmother's . . ."

"You're lying, love."

Annabelle shook her head defiantly. "They're mine! I told Anne Richmond they are heirlooms. That's it, isn't it? Anne told you a lie about me. Don't believe her, Tanner." She pushed close against him, rubbing suggestively against the lower half of him. "Anne Richmond hates me because she knows I love you, that you might love me, too."

"Stop it!" he barked, and savagely threw her from him. "I don't love you and never will, and you don't love me either. You want my wealth, as you've always wanted money, and would do anything to have it. And merciful God, I admit I've been no better! But for once, Annabelle, be honest and tell me about these jewels. I know they belong to Diana and that they were stolen. Admit the truth. Otherwise, my lovely Annabelle," and here his voice lowered and seemed to chill the very air, "your life will be as nothing, if I even let you live. . . ."

414

Tanner loomed over her, seeming larger and more menacing than the storm whose whipping wind stirred up the trees. The palmettos beat raggedly against the house, sounding like Annabelle's own heartbeat. For the first time in her life, she tasted genuine fear, unable to force a bravado exterior. She knew what Mariah was capable of doing, had seen his handiwork with her own eyes, but he'd been doing jobs for money then. Now his wife's life and safety were at stake. Annabelle doubted he'd be as gentle with her as he had been with some of the men he'd turned in to the British. There were times she still shuddered to remember what Mariah had done to force the truth from them.

Tanner and his wealth would never belong to her now, even if Diana didn't return. She was so horribly tired of lying, of assuming other identities, and with the ending of the war, she didn't have to any longer. She was free now, free only if she appeased Mariah, and the man who watched her with hooded lids *was* Mariah — there was no doubt about that.

Annabelle licked her lips. "I . . . want to know what you'll do with me if I tell . . . you the truth."

"Wonder what I'll do if you don't," was his intimidating reply.

"I have, and I don't relish the thought, but I still have to think of myself, you know. I want your assurance that I'll leave here with no fear of reprisals from you."

"You have my word, but when you leave here, I want your promise never to return and upset my life. Otherwise, you'll have no life of your own left to worry about."

She could tell he meant what he said, and she nodded in agreement, her face extremely pale. "Kingsley Sheridan enlisted me to get the jewels for him. He'd stored them in the bricks behind the fireplace, and I found them for him. I did it to have you. He promised me that you wouldn't be harmed, but I know now Kingsley meant to have you killed. And Diana, well, I admit that I didn't think too much about her fate."

Annabelle gasped as he gripped her wrist and hauled her to him. *"Kingsley is alive?!"*

"Y . . . es."

"Where did he take Diana? Tell me where he took her."

"How in the name of God do I know where he took her? Briarhaven, I'd assume, because he seemed obsessed with claiming Diana and his rightful place as master. Now what is to become of me?"

Tanner stared at her with piercing black eyes, eyes that suddenly shot flames. "Get your things together. I'm going to make certain you're taken care of, and in a kinder fashion than you imagine. Just say I'm being generous for what we shared in New York."

Annabelle didn't even ask what he had in mind, but as she hurriedly packed her belongings, she knew better than to try to escape from Tanner's clutches. In fact, she was more than a bit curious about how he intended to deal with her. An hour later Annabelle had her answer. After a furious ride through the city, Tanner pulled her from the carriage and she found herself on the docks before a large British frigate. He dragged her unceremoniously up the gangplank and thrust into a room where Samuel sat at a table, going over paperwork.

"Sheridan, what's the meaning of this?" Samuel rose and immediately grabbed for Annabelle. Never in her life had she been so glad to see anyone.

"This wench belongs to you, Farnsworth. I suggest you take her back to England with you when your regiment departs, and if I ever find her on my doorstep again, playing havoc with my life . . ."

"I understand," was Farnsworth's instant acknowledgement of the situation.

"I hope you do. And you, too, Annabelle. Remember what can happen even to such a pretty thing as yourself if you ever cross me again."

Annabelle nodded, too frightened to say or do anything else, but a great sense of relief seized her. Tanner was turning her over to Samuel!

Like a great, black wind, Mariah departed and Annabelle found herself staring into Samuel's narrowed eyes.

"Whatever have you done?" he asked her.

"Let's just say I displeased Mariah . . . Tanner," she corrected. "Samuel, do you still want to marry me?"

"Yes, my dear."

Annabelle's eyes glowed with happiness and relief. She knew marriage to Samuel was her only answer now. "I agree to your proposal."

For a second, he examined his fingernails and then he lifted his head in a smile. "Life with me will be quite hard, my dear. I'm not a wealthy man, but I hope to advance myself."

"That's fine, my darling," she said and kissed him. "Anything you want." And for the moment that *was* fine with Annabelle. All of her promises made to herself only minutes ago when she thought she'd face a fate worse than Samuel slipped away. She'd marry Samuel Farnsworth and once again be on English soil. Once she'd tired of him, she'd find someone else who'd want her. Someone wealthy.

"I'm going with you to Briarhaven," David informed Tanner after Tanner's return home. "I can't have you going by yourself. You're still not well enough, and heaven only knows what Kingsley is capable of. And . . . and I feel some responsibility for this atrocious situation since I gave my permission for Diana to marry the bounder in the first place."

"Don't blame yourself," Tanner said. "No one

418

had any idea things would turn out this way."

"I shouldn't have encouraged Diana to marry him," Anne said, clutching her kerchief in her hand. "I knew how much she didn't want to marry Kingsley. And I thought you were wrong for her, but she was so happy with you, Tanner. And now Kingsley is alive. What has happened to my sister? I can't bear for Diana to be harmed by that monster!"

"I'll find her," Tanner assured Anne and kissed her cheek. "I promise you that Kingsley Sheridan shall rue the day he took her from me."

As Tanner and David rode hard away from Charlestown, the heavens broke and pelted them with rain. Rivulets of water ran down their faces, their cloaks offering little protection against the deluge. Tanner had no time to think about his physical well-being. Perhaps it was because he at last knew where to look for Diana that he no longer felt weak. Heaven help Kingsley, he vowed, because he was determined to show no more mercy than Kingsley had shown him.

None.


Marisa glanced worriedly at Clay early the next morning. They stood at the window on the upper floor and watched the rain deluge the fields, clearly seeing the swirling yellow waters of the Santee push over the banks. Clay frowned. "The rain started so fast that there was no time to start sandbagging, but no matter, we don't have adequate hands to help. The river's rising higher every hour and soon we're going to be flooded. Tell your mother we have to start moving furniture out of the way. I'll pull up the carpets. Before this day's over, we're going to be soaked."

"But Kingsley may object," Marisa worried.

Clay grunted. "Kingsley's dead drunk. He must have found a bottle of brandy or something in the cellar. I doubt he cares about what's done with the house. He isn't much of a master, and besides, the house doesn't belong to him but to Tanner."

Marisa placed her hand on Clay's arm. "Something isn't right about all of this. I mean, it's so odd that Kingsley is suddenly alive, yet he hasn't made the effort to go into Charlestown and claim Diana or to talk to Tanner about what is to be done. Mother's in a frenzy about how people will gossip. Diana's a bigamist and doesn't know it."

"It will work out," Clay assured her with a smile. "But right now, we've got a more immediate worry with the Santee."


"Tanner, Tanner," Diana moaned and moved restlessly in her sleep. She dreamed he stood outside the cellar door and called her name, but she couldn't move toward the sound. Her body ached, her legs were unable to move. In her dream she cried out that she was going to die, their baby was going to die, but she suddenly woke to find her face was wet with tears.

Diana came alert to the pounding of rain outside, but what truly roused her was the dampness on her back and legs. She adjusted her eyes to the dim light of the cellar and realized with a start that water was coming in from beneath the tunnel door. Evidently, the tunnel was flooding, and now the water seeped slowly in the cellar. What was worse than the flooding was the horrible, achy way she felt. She knew she burned with a fever. Getting up, she dragged her damp blanket with her, wrapping herself inside of it. Making her way laboriously up the cellar steps, she found she couldn't go any further than half the distance before she was forced to sit down from exhaustion. She took deep, aching breaths but was unable to summon even the strength to move and bang upon the door in the hope that someone would hear her. Somehow she knew no one would.

"Oh, Tanner," she sobbed. "You can't be dead. I don't believe it. But if you aren't, then why haven't you come for me? Why? Why?"

Despair sliced away at her heart like a sharp-edged sword. She had no idea if what Kingsley told her about Tanner was true; she wondered if Kingsley even knew the truth sometimes. He seemed to speak in riddles and he frightened her with his threats. If only she could make it into the tunnel, somehow force the door open—but in her present, weak condition she could barely hold up her head. Her fate was crystal clear to her; she would die in the cellar.

"Miss Diana, Miss Diana, is you down there?"

For more than a few seconds, Diana thought she might be dreaming. But it came again, and she recognized Jackie's childish tones. "Jackie, I'm . . . here," she managed to cry feebly, but Jackie heard her.

"You need help?" he called through the door.

"Yes, yes. Get Hattie . . . or Clay." God, she was losing her breath and could barely speak.

"I will, Miss Diana, never you worry."

Jackie knew she was down here. He was going to get help for her. "We're going to be all right," she whispered to the baby that kicked in her abdomen. "Jackie's going to help us." A sense of peace washed over her as she waited on the stairs for Hattie or someone to free her.

When Kingsley awakened the house was in an uproar. Voices filtered up to his room and he heard the thumping sound of something being dragged up the stairs. Getting out of bed, he went into the hallway to complain about all the noise. Clay Sinclair pushed a heavy chair with Marisa's help, and Diana's Aunt Frances fluttered busily about the landing amid a group of chairs and small end tables.

"The bottom floor is flooding," Frances told him, not hiding her contempt. "The water's coming into the house and we're trying to save whatever we can, unlike *some* people I could name."

"I'd appreciate a hand with this, Kingsley, if you can tear yourself away from your bottle," was Clay's less-than-subtle comment. "Marisa isn't strong enough to help with moving the heavier pieces of furniture."

"Let the slaves do it," Kingsley retorted, his head throbbing from his hangover.

"Cousin Kingsley, I should remind you that there are no slaves here now who might conceivably be able to lend a hand but Hattie, and she's down with a dreadful fever. The slaves who are left are too old or too young to help. So that leaves you!" That was Marisa's scornful retort. Her face expressed her utter disdain for him.

Kingsley sighed his exasperation. Oh, why didn't these people just leave him alone so he could think what to do about Diana?

"Give me a chance to dress," he snapped and headed into his room to pull on his boots. Catching sight of himself in the mirror, he realized he looked awful, but then he'd probably looked worse than this months back. Yet the face that stared back at him didn't seem to belong to him. Gone were the handsome features that all the ladies had adored. All except Diana that is, and the thought of how much she truly hated him ate away at his pride. He'd tended to the ungrateful bitch for weeks now, but not once had she thanked him for the food he brought her. Didn't Diana realize that he could have kept her hidden in the swamps? But Kingsley didn't care for the watery swamps himself, never having learned to swim, or did he like the abundant animal population.

As it was, he needed to fill his own stomach and get breakfast for Diana, but first he'd been volunteered to help with the furniture.

Before leaving his room, he leaned against the window frame and gazed out at the torrential downpour. The rain fell in steady sheets, and from where he stood he saw that the fields were already overrun with water. The water extended outward in all directions, even now lapping at the porch to enter the house. "Good grief, what next?" he mumbled under his breath.

But he nearly strangled on his own breath when he suddenly saw the answer to his question. There in the rain rode Tanner, resembling a sodden black eagle in his dark cape. David Richmond was beside him, looking equally wet. Kingsley felt hot then cold, then both sensations mingled within him at once and he thought he might die from the pain of it. And there was a damned good chance he would, if the determination he noticed in Tanner's bearing was any indication.

"The bastard's alive!" he shouted and grabbed for his coat. He ran into the hallway, oblivious

424

to the three people who stared and called after him. By all accounts, Kingsley had less than five minutes, the amount of time it would take Tanner to make his way through the mire and get into the house, to move Diana from the cellar. He couldn't take her with him into the swamps, but he'd place her in the tunnel, where she'd be safe until he could escape with her. And he *would* take Diana away. Never would he allow Tanner to have her.

Rushing headlong down the back staircase, he arrived at the cellar door and took the key from his pocket. Clicking open the lock, he nearly stumbled upon Diana, who sat on the stairs leaning against the wall. Without looking up she asked, "Jackie, is that you?"

He didn't answer her. Instead, he scooped her up into his arms and hurriedly retraced his steps, leaving by way of the back door. With Diana in his arms, he ran the distance to the barn and pulled Diana up with him onto one of the horses he'd taken from Tanner's carriage. She leaned like a rag doll against him, and Kingsley doubted she even knew where she was or who held her. Just as well, he decided. He didn't need a screaming female now. If only he hadn't locked the door from the cellar into the tunnel as a precaution against Diana's escape, this mad dash could have been avoided.

Spurring the horse along, he was more than surprised to discover that the animal didn't balk at the flood water. The trip to the cemetery was made in less time than Kingsley had anticipated. His only problem was the rain that beat mercilessly down upon him and Diana. Within minutes he had entered through the tomb and found a spot for her to sit in the tunnel. The ground was wet, but he had no other alternative. Tanner would never find her in here. Kingsley would rather Diana died than be claimed by his half-breed brother, but Kingsley vowed that Diana wouldn't die and neither would he. Before this day is over he told himself, Tanner would be dead once and for all.

# Chapter 25

Tanner rushed into the house and David ran behind him, only to discover that the main floor was no drier than outside. "Where is everybody?" Tanner yelled, oblivious to his soaking wet state.

"Goodness gracious, Tanner, you gave us a start," came Frances's voice as she waddled down the stairs. "And David, too. Marisa, Clay," she called up to the landing, "Tanner is here with David. What a surprise."

Tanner didn't think Frances was pleased by his abrupt appearance. She stood on the stairs, one side of her gown bunched in her hand to keep it from becoming wet and the other pressed against her pale face. When Clay and Marisa started down the steps, Frances clutched at her daughter's hand. "Do you think there will be unpleasantness?"

"Mother, please," Marisa mouthed lowly.

Before Clay could say anything, Tanner had bounded up the stairs to face him. "Where's Diana? Where's Kingsley? I swear I'm going to kill the bastard."

"Tanner, I don't know what you're talking about," Clay admitted with a baffled demeanor.

"Tanner, you're dripping all over the carpet," Frances wailed at him.

Tanner ignored Frances, keeping his attention on Clay. "Kingsley kidnapped Diana," he briskly explained. "I've reason to believe that he's brought her here."

"To Briarhaven? No, he hasn't. Kingsley has been here for a few weeks, but Diana isn't with him. Why do you think he kidnapped her? What is going on?" Clay asked.

Backed up by David, Tanner quickly explained what had happened to him and Diana. He finished by saying, "Diana must be here. I've got to find her!"

"Kingsley was upstairs," Marisa piped in.

Bounding up the stairs, Tanner stalked from room to room, but Kingsley wasn't to be found. "The bastard probably saw me coming and took off," he growled at David and Clay.

"I'll help you find him," Clay volunteered, his face hardening. "If he's hurt her, he'll answer to me."

"No, my friend," Tanner interjected coldly. "He's going to answer to me alone."

When Tanner and the two men rushed out onto the porch, little Jackie came running toward them. "Mr. Tanner! Mr. Tanner! I've got to tell you somethin'."

"Not now, Jackie," Clay warned. "Go check on your Granny Hattie like a good boy."

Jackie stopped in his tracks, tears welling up in his eyes. "I was just talkin' to Granny Hattie and she ain't feelin' too good today yet. She told me to stop spinnin' tales, but I ain't lyin'. I swear I ain't. Nobody ever listens to me."

Something in the urgency and pain behind Jackie's statement caused Tanner to bend down to him. "What have you got to say to me, Jackie?"

Jackie wiped his eyes with tiny fists. "I got to get help for Miss Diana. Mr. Kingsley done locked her in the cellar and she needs to get out."

Patting Jackie on the back in gratitude, Tanner and the others practically flew into the house. They were down the cellar steps in seconds. Though her wet pallet and a plate of uneaten food sat on the floor, Diana wasn't there.

"He must have taken her away somewhere," was David's assessment.

"But where?" Clay asked.

Tanner didn't say anything to either of them. His stormy black eyes were enough to convince anyone that he was so angry and disappointed he probably couldn't speak. Tanner suddenly stalled in his steps, remembering the tunnel.

On the night he'd warned Clay, he went into the swamps by way of the tunnel. He knew how to open the hidden doorway, and this he now did while Clay and David looked on. But the spring that released the door panel wouldn't budge, and when Tanner leaned against the door to force it open, he found it impossible to move.

"The panel's locked from the other side," he said aloud with a grunt. "I believe I was the last one to open it, and I didn't lock it, unless Diana has. Or Kingsley." Somehow Tanner knew that Kingsley had placed Diana inside the tunnel. A cold shiver of fear slid over him as he looked down at the six inches of water that covered his boots. The water had risen rapidly since they'd been down here, and this part of the house, with the tunnel behind it, was the lowest point. Tanner remembered as a boy how the Santee had flooded out the cellar, though he hadn't known about the tunnel then. Four feet of water appeared almost overnight, but the flooding had been low because they'd had slaves to reinforce the river's banks. Now, there was no one to help, and if the water kept rising as steadily and as swiftly as Tanner feared, then if Diana was in the tunnel with no way out, she just might not survive.

Tanner gave up pushing at the heavy door panel. Instead, he left the cellar with instructions to Clay and David to fan out in search of Kingsley. He was going to the cemetery to rescue Diana. David flashed him an odd look but Clay understood, and the two men moved in opposite directions, sloshing through the rising water.

Because the water was rising so quickly, Tanner's horse was skittish and easily spooked. He took a longer time than normal to traverse the distance. Tanner couldn't help but curse under his breath. With every minute that passed, Diana's life was in greater and greater danger. He couldn't believe that Kingsley had harmed her, but if he'd placed her in a tunnel that gave every indication of already being flooded, then she might fall ill. Their baby, too, might suffer from Kingsley's vengeance.

"Diana, please be all right," Tanner mumbled. "Please, God, let her be safe."

So intent was Tanner on saving Diana that he failed to notice Kingsley standing behind a nearby tree with musket aimed, until the ball whined past his head, missing him by scant inches. Tanner threw himself from his horse and landed in a watery ditch. He heard Kingsley's diabolical laugh.

"The great overseer doesn't look so high and mighty now!" Kingsley crowed.

"I want Diana!" Tanner shot back and pulled his pistol from his waistband.

"Diana's buried to you, half-breed! You'll never have her. She belongs to me."

Tanner now knew for certain that Kingsley had placed her in the tunnel. The only way to enter it now was through the tomb. "If you cared anything about her, Kingsley, you'd never have put her in the tunnel."

There was a long pause before Kingsley shouted, "She's still my wife. Diana was never

431

yours."

For a brief instant, Tanner lifted his head. Once more, Kingsley took a shot at him. "Bastard," Tanner lowly hissed, and would have returned the fire but Kingsley ran the short distance to a clump of bushes that shielded the river from view.

Crawling on his hands and knees through the water, Tanner managed to remain low in the ditch. He remembered that the ditch ran the circumference of the fields, ending near the bluff on which Kingsley had taken refuge. It might take him a few minutes longer this way, but he reasoned that Kingsley wanted him to come out in the open so he could shoot him in the fields. But the ditch led directly behind where Kingsley now squatted, thus Tanner could take him by surprise.

Tanner hadn't realized how slow and laborious the whole process would be. The soft, sodden earth sucked at his knees and he was tempted to crouch low and run on his feet, but he feared Kingsley would see the top of his head. By the time he was halfway, his knees felt numb and his hands were bleeding from constantly pushing and falling upon them. More than once he'd gotten a mouthful of dirty water.

When he did reach the end of the ditch, he saw Kingsley with his back to him. God! it was too good an opportunity to miss. He'd fire his pistol at his target and Kingsley would be dead. How simple it was. Tanner felt that he'd been handed a gift by the fates or whoever decreed such moments in life. But though he stood up and aimed the gun at Kingsley's back, Tanner couldn't kill him.

No matter how despicable Kingsley was, and there was no doubt in Tanner's mind that he'd be doing the world a favor by killing him, Kingsley was his half brother. They shared the same father, a father who had been unjust by favoring one son over the other, but a man who had loved both of them in his own way. Tanner had no idea what he was going to do with Kingsley, but he wasn't going to kill him.

Tanner made a slight noise, and Kingsley turned, his eyes wide with fear, but he held the musket away at an angle. When Tanner didn't make a move to pull the trigger of his pistol, Kingsley smirked.

"So, Harlan Sheridan's bastard is a coward. I should have known you didn't have the guts to shoot me. But then, you can't shoot the master of Briarhaven, can you?"

"You're my brother."

"Yes, but don't let that stop you. You never thought anything about taking Diana from me, so you shouldn't feel guilty about killing me."

"I don't want to kill you." A muscle twitched in Tanner's face. Rain dripped down his cheeks, but he didn't take his gaze from Kingsley, not even when a piece of the bluff crumbled and fell into the Santee. "Come back to the house and we'll discuss this, find some sort of a solution."

"Do you mean that, Tanner?"

Tanner nodded and Kingsley mumbled that he agreed. As Tanner started to lift himself from the ditch, he was prepared for Kingsley's assault. The musket roared deafeningly near his ear, but Tanner had already decided that Kingsley had given in too easily and couldn't be trusted. Tanner's shot found its mark in Kingsley's shoulder.

Despite the fact that he was bleeding, Kingsley lunged at his brother and pushed Tanner to the ground with the butt of his musket. For a second, Tanner felt the wind rush from him, but he knew now that Kingsley intended to kill him. Still weak from his ordeal, Tanner wrestled with him but dropped his gun. He realized Kingsley was stronger, though the blood flowed freely from his wound.

"Arrogant half-breed. I'm going to kill you know."

Kingsley withdrew a knife from a scabbard on his waist, but Tanner kicked out at him before he did any damage and Kingsley lost his own wind and the knife. But Kingsley was wild and crazed and wouldn't admit defeat. The two men wrestled until they were near the edge of the bluff. It was only Tanner's will that fueled his strength. The river rushed and swirled like a yellow pinwheel beneath them, clumps of bluff falling away in the onslaught.

Somehow Kingsley was on top and Tanner was pinned beneath him, but he feigned defeat. "Diana is mine, half-breed," Kingsley reminded him in a ragged whisper. Tanner watched

Kingsley through hodded lids as he got up to make a move for the knife. But in that moment Tanner stretched out a long leg and Kingsley instantly faltered, losing his balance on the bluff.

"Why, you bastard . . ." Kingsley shouted, and would have tackled Tanner again, but suddenly the bluff gave way beneath his feet and Kingsley fell into the river.

Tanner swiftly rose at Kingsley's screams. "Tan . . . ner, save . . . me. I can't swim." He held out his hand, imploring Tanner to take it. Fear swam in Kingsley's eyes. He went under once only to surface again, sputtering and choking.

Holding out his hand, Tanner leaned forward as far as he could while bracing himself against a pine tree. "Grab on!" he shouted.

Kingsley strained to catch Tanner's fingers but was unable to reach them as he was swept out of Tanner's reach. Tanner watched as his brother flailed helplessly about, gulping water as he was carried down the river. Finally Tanner lost sight of him. The Santee had claimed Kingsley as her victim.

Unable to waste any more time, Tanner traversed the distance from the river to the cemetery. The water was now up to his knees and he feared that Diana might already be dead. Approaching the tomb, he saw that the opening had crumbled and water freely poured inside.

The door gave way under his weight. Upon entering, he discovered that the torch was wet, so he meandered along the tunnel without light. He found himself thrust into a hellish black pit as he felt his way along by touching the walls, wading through the flood waters. "Diana!" he yelled her name until he was hoarse. "Answer me, dammit! Where are you?"

By the time he was halfway through the tunnel, Tanner felt tears on his cheeks. Dark despair surrounded him, for he feared that Diana was dead. He'd lost his precious, beautiful Diana—the scarlet temptress on the river bluff. Without her, his life had little meaning. He knew that he'd be unable to live without her. He thought he was making the tiny, sobbing sounds he heard, but suddenly he realized that the sounds weren't coming from him but from five or ten feet away.

"Diana, are you here?"

"Tanner."

Her voice sounded so pitifully weak that Tanner had to strain to hear it. It was her! And she was alive! Pushing through the water, he found her by touch. Somehow she was sitting on a sort of ledge, not out of the water but at least not inundated by it. Tanner picked her up in his arms, immediately feeling the heat of her body and knowing she ran a high fever.

"Is that you, Tanner?" she asked and coughed.

"Yes, sweetheart, it's me."

She leaned her head against the broadness of his chest just as Clay and David called out. Within seconds, light appeared as they came forward with torches in their hands, and it was this light which led them out of the tunnel.

Tanner stayed constantly near Diana's bedside, refusing to budge despite Frances's constant clucking. "You need looking after, too," she gently scolded him. "We're doing all we can for Diana."

"Don't bother with me. I'm not the one with the raging fever, the delirium, the one who may lose her child. There must be something else that can be done!" Tanner's words were uttered with a sense of hopelessness. Ever since he'd taken Diana from the tunnel she'd been so horribly ill that he feared she would die. And the doctor from Camden couldn't seem to do much for her except to pour a nasty-smelling brew down her throat four times a day.

As Tanner sat beside her bed with his hand on her abdomen, he felt the baby kick. It seemed the child was all right for now, but Diana might die. Once again cold fear clutched at his heart. So this was retribution. At that moment he knew he was paying for all of the wrongs he'd committed while he was a spy, yet perhaps his retribution would not be complete until he paid in full by taking Diana and their child. If that happened, he'd suffer such torment of soul that only his own death would assuage the pain.

"Diana," he pleaded with her, "get well. Please try and get better. I love you so much, more than you can possibly know. Without you I'm a shell of a man. I'm nothing. You're my obsession, my love. Always and forever. Please, please . . ."

Diana didn't respond. Her face was ashen, more pale than he'd ever seen it, and she had such trouble breathing that he doubted she could hold on for much longer.

He buried his head upon the covers, slowly coming to the realization that his mother was touching his shoulder.

"I heard the woman is ill," Naomi said.

"Her name is Diana, Mother, and yes, she's ill." Glancing up at his mother, fresh tears filled his eyes. "I'm going to lose her and the baby."

"Mariah, my son, have you forgotten the Indian ways, the ways of your ancestors, which I taught you at my knee? The white man has little knowledge of natural cures, but if you let me help her, I think your Diana will live."

"Can you help her, Mother?" Tanner grasped her hand hard and looked like a little boy again.

Naomi nodded. "But only if you keep that busybody out of the room for a few days."

Tanner knew she meant Frances, and for the first time he smiled with hope. "Anything you want, my mother."

"Humph, I don't know what that woman's doing in there, Marisa, but I think we should barge in and see. Why, Diana's very life may be in jeopardy." Frances stood in the parlor doorway, her face expressing horror and disapproval. "All of that chanting and those smelly herbs Naomi brings into the house is heathenish. Tanner's no better than his mother to allow it."

"Mother, don't interfere. I know you have Diana's best interests at heart, but without Naomi's help, Diana might die. Tanner told me this morning that over the last few days Diana has improved a great deal."

"Then I want to see my niece."

"No," Marisa said, and she meant it.

Frances gave up, realizing she wasn't going to win. "What will the neighbors say about this? If the truth ever reaches Charlestown about Diana having two husbands we'll never be able to live down the gossip."

"Oh, posh. I don't care what those old biddies think."

"Marisa! I'm shocked at your attitude. The sooner I get you back home to Charlestown and away from these disturbing influences, the better off you'll be."

A delighted grin turned up the edges of Marisa's mouth as she beckoned her mother to sit down and have tea. "By disturbing influences, do you mean Clay?"

Frances lowered her voice to a whisper. "Yes. Really, it's not proper for a young unmarried lady and young man to inhabit the same house, even under these trying circumstances. I know Clay wants to marry you, dear, but you need a proper courtship. Anything could happen, you know, if you two are constantly together."

"It's already happened. I'm having a baby."

"My God, my heart!" Frances leaned against the sofa, her hand on her chest.

"Now, Mother, don't take on so. Your heart is perfectly healthy and you know it. Besides, Clay and I have been legally married for over a month. We went to Camden one day and were married."

That news caused Frances to recover immediately.

"I'm so pleased!" Frances gushed.

"So am I," Marisa admitted, accepting her mother's kiss on her cheek. "Now if only Tanner and Diana can know such happiness again."


After a week of Naomi's remedies Diana's fever broke, she didn't cough as often, and her cheeks began to bloom with a pinkish tinge. "I think you're healing," Naomi advised her. It was a lovely December morning. A chill was in the air, but the glow from the fireplace warmed the room. "I'll find Tanner for you."

"Naomi," came Diana's strengthened voice from the bed. "I want to thank you for saving my life. I know how hard this must have been for you, because I understand the way you feel about me."

"Tanner explained all to me," Naomi admitted.

"Then you don't hate me?"

"No, Diana, I do not hate you."

440

"Can we be friends?" Diana held out her hand.

Naomi took it, and for the first time that Diana could remember, she saw Naomi's face light up with a lovely smile. Diana realized then why Harlan had fallen in love with her. "Yes, we are friends."

When Tanner entered the room seconds later, he kissed Diana's lips. "Mother told me that you're doing better and that you're going to be fine."

"Yes, and we've made peace with each other, thanks to you."

"All I did was explain about the lie Kingsley told me, a lie I foolishly believed."

Tanner sat on the bed and held her against his chest. He stroked her hair then held her hand. "Everything's all right now, Diana. We're going to have our baby and be a family. You're mine, my love, forever."

"Not quite, Tanner. You're forgetting one very important point."

"What?" he asked, troubled.

"We're not legally married."

Tanner nodded. "Our first wedding anniversary was last week, but you were too sick to celebrate it."

"Aren't you going to marry me again?"

"Hmm, that's an interesting question. I seem to remember that the first time I asked you, you refused me."

"I didn't, and anyway you forced me into it, Tanner. Don't you want to marry me?"

441

Tanner shot her an assessing look before squeezing her arm like a garden tomato. "You're rather scrawny."

"And you're impossible! So, I suppose I shall have to bury my pride and do the asking, and I shall ask you but one time. Tanner Sheridan, will you marry me?"

"Yes."

"Good. And don't ever tell me you were tricked into doing the right thing by me!" Diana retorted with a mischievous gleam in her eyes, until Tanner seductively silenced her with his kiss.

# Chapter 26

"I feel so sinful to be doing this," Diana complained to Tanner with a naughty twinkle in her eyes. "What if Jenny wakens and needs me?"

"Then Hattie will tend to her," Tanner said and took her hand to guide her away from the house and toward the river. "Jenny is three years old now and has slept through the night for the last two years. So you have no excuse not to indulge your husband in a midnight tryst."

"I'm always indulging you, Tanner Sheridan." Diana laughed up at Tanner, his face made more handsome by the brilliant light of the full moon. What she said was true. No matter what Tanner wanted Diana indulged him, for she realized early on that his needs were hers and vice versa. He seemed contented looking after her, Jenny, and Briarhaven. Under his hand, Briarhaven was now a thriving rice plantation again. Jenny was the most adorable child, a minature of her father, and Diana was the happiest she'd ever been in her life. There was nothing left for her to want except many more years of the same. "But what about prickly pine needles and gnats? I don't want my backside to be permanently engraved or to serve as a feast for hungry insects."

"We have a blanket," he reminded her, and when they reached the bluff, he laid it upon the ground and gently lowered her onto it.

"Sometimes I think you're depraved."

He joined her on the blanket, took her in his arms, and nuzzled her neck. "And aren't you glad for it?"

Diana laughed and wrapped her arms around his shoulders. "Yes," she admitted. "And speaking of depraved, I forgot to tell you that I ran into Gabriella Fox last week when I visited Anne."

Tanner reigned tiny kisses on her neck and parted the bodice of her gown, totally absorbed in his task and not paying any attention to what she said until Diana repeated herself. "What about Gabriella?" he asked.

"Dear Gabriella is having a child again."

"How many will that make?"

"Four. It seems that old Mr. Fox wasn't quite as old as Gabriella originally thought. He's not about to leave this life without making Gabriella earn her keep as his wife and the mother of his children."

"Good for old man Fox," Tanner mumbled as

he pulled the bodice away form Diana's shoulders.

"But the tart had the audacity to insinuate that something was wrong with either you or me because we have only one child."

"So?"

"Doesn't that bother you, Tanner? Don't you wonder if there may be something amiss with us. After all, Jenny is three years old and I haven't conceived again and . . ."

"Diana."

"What?"

"If you don't be quiet and let me kiss you, then we may never be able to match the Fox brood."

Diana's smile dazzled and bewitched Tanner as she arched against him, inviting him to take what had belonged to him from the very first moment they met. Her voice was a breathy whisper in his ear. "Whatever you say, my love. We have a great deal of catching up to do."

# FIERY ROMANCE

**CALIFORNIA CARESS** (2771, $3.75)
by Rebecca Sinclair

Hope Bennett was determined to save her brother's life. And if that meant paying notorious gunslinger Drake Frazier to take his place in a fight, she'd barter her last gold nugget. But Hope soon discovered she'd have to give the handsome rattlesnake more than riches if she wanted his help. His improper demands infuriated her; even as she luxuriated in the tantalizing heat of his embrace, she refused to yield to her desires.

**ARIZONA CAPTIVE** (2718, $3.75)
by Laree Bryant

Logan Powers had always taken his role as a lady-killer very seriously and no woman was going to change that. Not even the breathtakingly beautiful Callie Nolan with her luxuriant black hair and startling blue eyes. Logan might have considered a lusty romp with her but it was apparent she was a lady, through and through. Hard as he tried, Logan couldn't resist wanting to take her warm slender body in his arms and hold her close to his heart forever.

**DECEPTION'S EMBRACE** (2720, $3.75)
by Jeanne Hansen

Terrified heiress Katrina Montgomery fled Memphis with what little she could carry and headed west, hiding in a freight car. By the time she reached Kansas City, she was feeling almost safe . . . until the handsomest man she'd ever seen entered the car and swept her into his embrace. She didn't know who he was or why he refused to let her go, but when she gazed into his eyes, she somehow knew she could trust him with her life . . . and her heart.

*Available wherever paperbacks are sold, or order direct from the Publisher. Send cover price plus 50¢ per copy for mailing and handling to Zebra Books, Dept. 2854, 475 Park Avenue South, New York, N.Y. 10016. Residents of New York, New Jersey and Pennsylvania must include sales tax. DO NOT SEND CASH.*

## HISTORICAL ROMANCES BY VICTORIA THOMPSON